The Hellish Vortex

To order additional copies, please contact us.
BookSurge, LLC
www.booksurge.com
1-866-308-6235
orders@booksurge.com

The Hellish Vortex

Between Breakfast and Dinner

Richard M Baughn
Brigadier General USAF (ret)

2006

The Hellish Vortex

PREFACE

A few years ago, I read a "Best Seller" about a World War II P-51 pilot flying combat with the British based 8th U.S. Army Air Force. It was an easy and enjoyable read, but didn't tell the story.

Since I had flown P-51's in combat with the 8th AAF during WWII, I decided to try my hand. I wanted to present a historically accurate accounting of the air war and a realistic story about how the young airmen lived, fought and died. It took several years to finish a carefully researched historical novel that tells what a 19-year-old fighter pilot saw and felt while flying in the fiercest aerial combat the world has ever seen.

But the story goes beyond what the young fighter pilot experienced. He learned how the U.S. Army ground forces and Navy had for years battled to stifle the development of Army airpower. It was a rivalry that started with the Army's reluctant purchase of its first aircraft in 1909 and continued until WWI. After WWI, the battle intensified and delayed the USAAF's preparedness for WWII. Following WWII the Army and Navy fought even harder to prevent the US Air Force from becoming a separate and equal service. The young fighter pilot also learned how American/British politics sometimes diverted the air effort from vital targets. Essential elements of these factors have been woven into the story to give it greater depth.

Most Americans rightfully believe the D-Day invasion of France to be the centerpiece of the battle to end the Nazi occupation of Europe. Almost forgotten are 60,000 American/British airmen who were shot down or killed during the two years preceding D-Day--battling the *Luftwaffe* and reducing Germany's military might to make the invasion possible. Although heavy air losses continued during the larger and more devastating air attacks that followed D-Day, much of that story has also been overlooked or downplayed.

While flying combat, it was obvious the US Army Air Forces in Europe suffered high losses. But I never realized how high they were and was surprised to learn that 41,802 American airmen were killed from the force of approximately 100,000 pilots, navigators, bombardiers and aerial gunners who fought in Europe. By comparison, the US Navy, with a force of 3.3 million, lost 36,950 during WWII and 19,733 Marines were killed from a total force of 475,604

Despite the airpowers enormous contribution during WWII, its detractors have de-emphasized it in the war against Germany. But the *Wehrmacht* generals and their men, who were on the receiving end of American/British air attacks, knew the true effectiveness of their air attacks. They said that the superior American and British airpower had been a major factor in Germany's defeat. In addition, General Omar N. Bradley, who commanded American ground forces in the D-Day invasion of France and the capture of Germany, said after the war, "From the high command to the soldier in the field, German opinion has been agreed that airpower was the most striking aspect of the Allied superiority."

My book is dedicated to the airmen of the U.S. Army Air Force who served in WWI and WWII and to the millions of past, present, and future airmen of the United States Air Force.

Many people encouraged and helped me while I worked to finish my book. But two are worthy of special mention. My wife, Mary Pat, never wavered in her support and encouragement. Secondly, Colonel Henry Zeybel USAF (ret), who is an outstanding writer, provided immeasurable assistance at a time in need. I thank them very much.

Last but not least, I want to mention the "Four B's" who have enjoyed 64 years of camaraderie. We came from Iowa, California and Michigan and the U.S. Army Air Forces' alphabetic roster brought us together. We became fighter pilots, served our country and went our separate way. Today, the "Four B's" and wives share many memories and laughs when we rendezvous. To maintain the roster's alphabetic integrity, the other three "B's" are George Becker, Donald Bloodgood and Robert Boydston.

A Touch of Terror Before Breakfast

Low black clouds raced across RAF Station Goxhill--like soot from hell. Inside the Nissen hut, Second Lieutenant Robb Baines listened to the howling North Sea wind and the drumbeat of rain on the tin roof. Their discordance grated on him more than a Spike Jones rendition of the *"Anvil Chorus."* Back in the States, November 13, 1943, would've been a down day, a day to play cards or Ping-Pong. A day to do anything—but fly.

Robb had been elated when assigned to Great Britain, since flying P-51's in Europe had been his first choice. His second choice had been a P-51 assignment in the Pacific. He had no third choice. Rather than the fulfillment of a dream, the thought of his first P-51 flight today seemed like the beginning of a nightmare.

He and his group of replacement pilots had been warned about RAF Station Goxhill. Goxhill, better known as Goatshill, was said to be the asshole of creation. In addition to being a full day's train ride from the pleasures of London, it had bad food, lousy living facilities and some of the coldest weather in frigid Britain.

Nothing about Goatshill seemed right. Everyone wondered why the flight instructors, who had completed their combat tours, had been exiled to Goatshill rather than returning to the States with their peers to bask in glory. Even the 12 war-weary P-51's, on loan from the RAF, were candidates for the aircraft boneyard.

Robb tapped his fingers on the folding table, then checked his watch again and wondered when his instructor would arrive. More than 30 minutes had passed since the other six replacement pilots and their instructors had gone to the individual briefing rooms to review the P-51's *Flight Handbook* for this morning's flight.

Robb's anxiety finally turned to anger. He stood and shoved the chair back from the table with his foot. "If I'm gonna lay my ass on the line the least that son-of-a-bitch can do is show up on time," he said to himself.

WHAAM! The front door flew open and banged a chair. Robb spun around. A captain, wearing a dirty garrison hat with a sixty-mission crush, stepped inside. His rumpled trench coat looked more like a sleeping bag. He reached for the door and kicked it shut, spread his feet like a drunken sailor on a rolling ship, jutted his unshaven chin and surveyed Robb through bloodshot eyes. "You Baines?" he slurred, exhaling a cloud of stale booze from his lipstick-smeared mouth.

"Yes...sir, " Robb growled, making no attempt to conceal his anger.

"Hang slack, sonny." The captain swaggered out of the room and returned with a P-51 *Flight Handbook*. He tossed it on the table in front of Robb. "Read that, sonny. I'll be back in a little while."

For the next hour-and-a-half, Robb struggled to control his anger and tried to concentrate on the *P-51 Flight Handbook*.

When the captain returned, he had a clean face and fresh shave. He poured himself a cup of coffee and lit a cigarette. "Gonna ask ya a few questions while I drink my breakfast. How many engines this machine have?"

Robb stared in disbelief.

"God damn it, don't ya want'a fly?"

"Yes...sir!" Robb snapped.

"Well, answer the frickin' question."

"One engine...sir."

"That's better. How many seats does it have?"

"One...sir."

"Get your helmet and goggles, and grab a chute, sonny. You're gonna take a little joy ride in the Mustang."

The captain swung the jeep into the aircraft-parking revetment. Neither dark clouds nor rain could hide the P-51's sleek lines. They portrayed beauty and speed. *Perpetual Paula* was painted across the P-51's nose and there were two swastikas below her canopy.

As they got closer, Robb saw several aluminum patches covering battle scars on the fuselage and a new landing gear indicated at least one crash landing. Fast living and neglect had given *Perpetual Paula* a premature grizzled look. He wondered if combat aged everything before its time.

"Get strapped in, sonny. Give ya a preflight check when it ain't rainin'."

Climbing onto the wing, Robb noticed a new left aileron. He hoped it had been installed properly and wouldn't come off in a tight turn or fast roll. Inside the cockpit, switch decals were missing and a layer of grime covered everything.

"Dirty...beat-up," Robb mumbled, as he climbed into the cockpit.

"Ain't no beauty queen. This's a combat machine, sonny. Hurry up and get familiar with the location of the cockpit controls and switches. I'm gettin' wet."

In flight school, Robb had been taught to always make certain the ignition switch was off when entering the cockpit. He located it on the center console and saw that it was off. He released the flight control lock at the base of the control stick and moved the stick, elevator and rudder. He glanced at the left side of the cockpit. The flight handbook showed 27 controls and switches in this area. He spotted the trim tab controls and set the rudder trim at 6 degrees right and the elevator trim at 3 degrees nose-heavy. He recalled how a classmate had accidentally set the rudder trim to the left instead of the right and couldn't control the P-40's engine torque on takeoff and crashed. Robb then made certain the throttle and mixture control were off. Behind the throttle, he saw the oil radiator and coolant radiator switches. He might have to open the coolant doors manually to increase the airflow and keep the coolant from overheating while on the ground.

The center console and instrument panel contained a maze of 41 flight and engine instruments, switches and controls. The right side of the cockpit had another 23 dissimilar switches, levers and a long row of circuit breakers.

Other than the stick, throttle and the grouping of the airspeed indicator, directional gyro, attitude indicator, altimeter, needle and ball and rate of climb indicator, the cockpit layout was completely different than the P-40. *Shit...hope I can find what I need when I need it in flight.*

He glanced back to the left side of the cockpit and worked his way around to the right. This time he concentrated mainly on the controls and switches he needed to start the engine.

"Close your eyes," the captain barked before Robb could complete his third swing around the cockpit. "Gonna give ya a blindfold check. Touch the switches and controls, when I call 'em out."

"What's the hurry...sir? Could use more cockpit time."

"Time's a wastin' and besides it's rainin' harder. Now close your eyes!"

Robb closed his eyes and the captain called out several switches and controls and Robb eventually found them.

"Crank her up, sonny."

"Sir! I need more cockpit time!"

The captain's bloodshot eyes bulged like two Ping-Pong balls. "Anybody with an ounce of fighter pilot's blood can hack it. You got an ounce, sonny?"

Robb's jaw tightened. He grabbed his leather helmet, pulled it on, plugged in the radio cord and connected the hose to his oxygen mask.

"You can look around some more, while yur taxiin' out," the captain grunted, before signaling the crew chief to plug in the battery cart.

Although he had memorized the engine start procedure while studying the *Flight Handbook*, he worried that he might do something wrong like over priming the engine and flooding it. He moved the throttle forward about an inch, made certain the mixture control was in idle cutoff, then checked that the battery switch was off, found the starter switch, raised the red cover, took a deep breath and shouted, "Clear!"

"Clear!" the crew chief, shouted back.

Robb flicked the spring-loaded starter switch and the huge propeller rotated. He turned the ignition switch from off to both magnetos, turned on the fuel booster pump and pumped the fuel primer three times. The engine coughed; the propeller jumped and blue flames exploded from the exhausts. Robb released the starter switch, pushed the mixture control to normal. The engine cracked like gunfire, as the big propeller blades slapped the cold air and rain. The oil pressure gauge showed 50psi. *Thank God...I got it right.*

The crew chief held his hands together then pulled them apart, signaling that he was ready to disconnect the external battery cart. Robb gave him a thumb up and flicked the battery switch to on. The captain leaned inside the cockpit, turned on the radio, checked that the trim tabs were set for takeoff, then gave an okay signal and jumped off the trailing edge of the wing.

Robb lowered the canopy, slid the side window back a few inches, pressed on the brake pedals, placed the icy oxygen mask over his face and snapped it to his helmet. He kept thinking they would call off flying, before he had to take-off.

Finally, he signaled the crewchief to pull the chocks, took a deep breath and pressed the mike button on the throttle, "Tower, Cricket 24, taxi and takeoff."

"Cricket 24, runway zero-nine-zero, altimeter is 29.87, wind zero-six-zero at 20, with gusts to 30. Cleared to taxi."

"Cricket 24 taxiing," Robb transmitted as he released the brakes. *Perpetual Paula* rolled forward and he turned her onto the taxiway. Wind gusts banged the rudder and ailerons, while the rain pounded the canopy. *Surely they'll cancel flying before I get to the runway.*

Near the end of the runway, he stopped and turned *Perpetual Paula's* nose into the wind to complete the engine checks. But first, he wanted to see if he could find the landing gear handle without looking. His hand went right to it.

Hope I can do that on takeoff. In this bad weather, he knew that looking for the gear handle could be a deadly distraction.

He closed the side window, searched for the instrument panel's light switch, turned it on and wondered what else he'd forgotten.

Easing the throttle forward, *Perpetual Paula* started to move. He pressed harder on the brakes to hold her. At 2300 RPM, he cycled the prop pitch, checked the mags, then reduced power and double-checked that the trim tabs were set for takeoff. Something, he didn't know what, reminded him to lock the canopy. *Shit... what else have I missed? First hop in the world's hottest fighter...first flight in real weather...damned little preparation...this is triple jeopardy.*

The thing that worried him most was flying in real weather for the first time. As an aviation cadet, his instrument flight training had been limited to 40 hours of simulated weather time, half in the back seat of a training plane under a canvas hood, referred to as the "bag." The other half had been in the abominable Link trainer. Flying the Link had been similar to wrestling a greasy pig. It provided damned little training and instilled absolutely no confidence in his instrument flying ability. After graduation, instrument flying in the P-40 had been prohibited. Due to a shortage of artificial horizons, the number one instrument for flying in bad weather, all artificial horizons had been sent overseas to combat units.

"Cricket 24, ceiling's 300 feet, visibility's one mile in rain. You're cleared, on and off," the tower snapped.

"Cricket 24, roger," Robb replied. *Bastards are in a hurry...lookin' for excitement... probably washed-out cadets.* His mouth felt like it was filled with sand and drops of sweat ran into his eyes. He blinked to clear the sweat, took a deep breath and swallowed, trying to remove some of the sand and taxied onto the macadam runway. Something reminded him to reset the directional gyro to the runway heading. He hurriedly scanned the cockpit, looking for other things he may have missed. He noticed the pitot heat switch and turned it on. *Shit...what else have I forgotten?*

Beyond *Perpetual Paula*'s nose, the low black clouds and rain hid the horizon--like an inky curtain of death. For the first time in his life, dying became a reality, not something that happened to others. He remembered what his P-40 instructor, who'd flown combat in the Pacific, said, "Fear can tighten your pucker string. If it gets tight enough, it can cause a bad case of anusitis. That really can become a giant pain in the ass."

"Cricket 24, you're cleared to roll," the tower repeated.

Robb pressed hard on the brake pedals and slowly eased the throttle forward. Blue flashes thundered from the twelve exhaust stacks and lit the rain around *Perpetual Paula*'s nose—like hellfire.

At takeoff power, Robb had to stand on the brake pedals to keep *Perpetual Paula* from leaping forward. Beyond the hellfire, he saw the curtain of death. He felt like the tormented character in a horror movie with a cocked pistol jammed to his head.

"Cricket 24, are you having a problem? You're cleared to roll."

I'll show those bastards...I've got more than an ounce. He blinked the sweat from his eyes. Robb prayed that he hadn't forgotten something that could kill him and released the brakes.

Perpetual Paula leaped forward through the blinding rain. Engine torque jerked her nose to the left.

Robb's pucker string tightened another notch. He jammed in the right rudder pedal and overcorrected to the right. He stomped on the left rudder pedal and overcorrected to the left. Two more quick corrections got *Perpetual Paula* going straight down the runway.

Runway lights streaked past on both sides; her tail rose and she skipped on her landing gear. Robb glanced at the airspeed indicator; it showed 120 mph, 20 mph above takeoff speed. He eased the stick back; she leaped into the air.

Without looking, he found the gear handle and pulled it up to retract the landing gear. It thumped into place.

Heavy rain reduced the forward visibility to zero. To see the ground, Robb had to look out the side window. The blur of trees, roads, small fields and hedgerows shot past.

He held *Perpetual Paula* at 200 feet to keep her from entering the black clouds. Her speed increased and her nose pulled to the right. Robb pushed hard on the left rudder to center the ball to keep her going straight.

He glanced at the airspeed indicator. It showed 190 mph. *Rudder trim...dummy.* He rolled in left rudder trim and she flew better than a souped-up P-40.

At 240 mph, she bounced and wallowed through the rough air like a speedboat racing across choppy water. Robb reduced power and skimmed the bottoms of the clouds, wondering if he would ever catch up.

The Humber River streaked past below the right wing. *You gotta climb before you slam into something.*

WHOOSH! *Perpetual Paula* hit a downdraft. It felt like a car hitting a giant pothole. Robb's butt left the seat; his feet flew off the rudder pedals; the safety belt dug into his gut.

WHOOMP! A powerful updraft slammed into *Perpetual Paula's* belly and flung her upward. The footrests banged Robb's heels; the seat flattened the cheeks of his butt.

He reached for the safety belt to tighten it, but couldn't find it. He looked down, spotted it and yanked it tighter, but inadvertently pulled back on the stick.

Black clouds swallowed *Perpetual Paula*; death seemed certain. Robb's body turned to rock and his mind tried to spin out of control. He recalled something else his P-40 instructor had said, "There'll be times when you think the grim reaper's scythe is about to slice you in half. That can flip your think-switch, which'll cause your mind to disengage from your brain, give ya mental whiplash and make an instant seem forever."

Robb took a deep breath and glanced at the flight instruments. They showed that he was in level flight. He eased the stick back, pushed the throttle forward and *Perpetual Paula* began to climb. At 700 feet he felt safe for the first time since takeoff. He relaxed his grip on the stick and throttle and suddenly realized that flying in real weather was easier than flying under the canvas hood. *It's amazing...I don't I have vertigo. I wonder why?*

Every time he'd been under the bag, in the back seat of a trainer, insidious vertigo had hoodwinked his senses and convinced him that his airplane was twisting or turning, doing something other than what the flight instruments indicated. He wondered if fear had overpowered vertigo.

"Cricket 45, you're cleared on and off," the tower transmission broke the silence.

"Cricket 45, rog. On the roll."

Oh shit. . .I forgot to change the radio frequency. Go fighter common, dummy. His left hand searched for the VHF radio control box, but he couldn't find it. He looked down and pushed the fighter common button.

As his head came up—vertigo knocked his senses cockeyed like a bowling ball crashing into tenpins.

Certain that *Perpetual Paula* was rolling upside down, his body turned to rock. He fought off the urge to follow his instincts to stop the roll and instead checked the flight instruments. They showed her in a straightaway climb; yet he couldn't shake the rolling sensation. He took a deep breath to steady himself, then depressed the mike button, "Cinderella, Cricket 24's on fighter common."

"Cricket 24, Cinderella copies," the Goxhill controller replied.

Still fighting vertigo, Robb recalled how his hard-nosed instrument instructor had growled, again and again, "If I teach you only one thing, I hope it'll be to trust your flight instruments. Never believe your senses in the soup!"

His instructor had earned the nickname of Iron Ass, because of his toughness and high washout rate. Most instrument instructors waited until they'd lined up on the runway, or were airborne before having their students close the canvas hood. But before Iron Ass started the engine, he would yell, "Get under the bag, mister!"

Robb made a blind takeoff on every flight. Once they reached their flight altitude, Robb had to close his eyes and look over his shoulder, while Iron Ass took control and maneuvered the BT-13 through rolls, dives and tight turns, to induce vertigo. With the BT-13 in a steep climb, dive or turn, Iron Ass had Robb open his eyes and take control.

Regardless of what the flight instruments indicated, Robb's mind and body always told him something else. Gradually, he learned to ignore the sensations that had guided him all his life and rely on the unnatural instruments. But the struggle between the natural and unnatural never ended.

Racing blindly through the dark clouds, Robb rechecked the P-51's flight instruments. *Everything looks good...just keep climbing or you'll play tag with a cloud full of rocks.*

Perpetual Paula popped out of the overcast at 7000 feet. White cumulus clouds, resembling giant snowmen, towered above the undercast. Ribbons of stratus linked some of the puffy giants; others stood alone, beneath rakish cumulus caps.

Above, Robb saw blue sky for the first time since he had arrived in Britain two weeks ago and it made him feel good. But he knew the moment of bliss was a fragile, because eventually he'd have to penetrate the thick blanket of clouds to get back to Goatshill. *Like being trapped aloft...I can't believe I'm making my first P-51 flight in such lousy weather.* But he'd been warned that combat would be a different ball game, with no time to coddle. *Better do some stalls and acrobatics...get the feel of this little baby.*

Robb swung *Perpetual Paula* around a giant snowman's fat belly, into a clear area. He brought the throttle back to idle and pulled up her nose, until she shuddered and stalled. He dumped her nose, added power and regained flying speed. Then he stalled her in turns to the right and left. He repeated the stall series with her gear and flaps extended.

After retracting the gear and flaps, he added power and let her accelerate to 300 mph, rolled her to the right and the left, then racked her into tight turns and pulled until she shuddered. He lowered her nose and added more power. Her speed increased to 350 mph did a series of 4-G loops. Going over the top of the third loop, a giant snowman appeared to smile.

Coming down the backside of the loop, Robb held the dive until her speed reached 400 mph. He pulled back on the stick and she zoomed straight up. When her airspeed dropped through 100 mph, he did a vertical recovery by rolling her to the left using the rudder. Her nose sliced down toward the horizon. The jaunty white giant's smile broadened and Robb smiled back.

Enjoying the freedom of the sky, in the best fighter in the world, was a heavenly union.   For a year he had dreamed about flying the P-51 and *Perpetual Paula* flew better than he had imagined.

Another P-51 pilot checked in with Cinderella and Robb remembered that he and Hugh Pitford had agreed to join over the field 30 minutes after takeoff to practice formation flying. He glanced at the aircraft clock. *Been airborne for 27 minutes. . .time to rendezvous. . .call for a steer.*

"Cinderella, Cricket 24, for a steer to home plate," Robb transmitted.

"Cinderella here, give me a short count Cricket 24," the controller replied.

"Cricket 24, one, two, three, four, five; five, four, three, two, one. Cricket 24, out."

" Cinderella here. Cricket 24, steer 150."

"Cricket 24 is turning to 150."

Robb extended his turn to avoid a snowman's fat belly. Three miles ahead, he saw a P-51 in a left turn. "Cricket 36, this is Cricket 24. If you read, rock your wings." The P-51's wings rocked. "Cricket 24 is approaching from your seven o'clock."

"Cricket 36 here, I have a tally. Take the lead, 24," Hugh replied.

For the next ten minutes they practiced formation turns, climbs and descents, then Hugh took the lead. After ten minutes, he called, "Want'a nip into the clouds, 24?"

"Cricket 24 here. Okay."

They descended into a snowman's huge belly. Its bumpy-gray innards bounced and rocked the two 51's and the thick clouds made it difficult to see one another. Robb eased *Perpetual Paula* in closer to keep Hugh in sight. He wondered if they should've saved their first weather formation for another time.

WHOOMP! A giant pothole jolted him and dense gray clouds swallowed Hugh's 51—except for the green wing tip light.

Seeing nothing but the green light blindsided Robb's senses and gave him an overdose of dizziness. *Oooh. . .shit!*

He wanted to sneak a peek at his flight instruments to break vertigo's insidious stranglehold on his senses. But he was afraid to, because he might slam into Hugh's 51.

Suddenly, the green light started moving up and away, through the gray nothingness, adding a new dimension to the insidious vertigo. Fear ricocheted through Robb's body like a bolt of lightening. *Iron Ass never mentioned flying formation in the weather.*

Before he could react, the clouds thinned and Hugh's P-51 reappeared. Robb exhaled, blinked the sweat from his eyes and felt his heart pounding in his chest. His 51 had dropped less than ten feet below Hugh's, but in the soup it had seemed more like 100.

Shit. . .worst case of vertigo I ever had. Robb tried to steady his breathing. *I wonder if my vision's really bad. Maybe I shouldn't be a pilot.*

He recalled the problem he had during his first eye exam, when his dream of becoming an Army Air Force pilot got shattered. While taking a pre-college physical, he had difficulty reading a cardboard eye chart in the poorly lit room. The premed student conducting the exam said he needed glasses.

For the next six months, while he waited for his eighteenth birthday so he could apply for the Army's Aviation Cadet program, he reconciled himself to becoming a navigator or bombardier. But when he took the Aviation Cadet physical, he passed the eye exam and qualified as a Pilot Trainee.

In Primary Flight School, he soloed first in his class and never had a problem after that. But during every checkout in a new aircraft, or at the beginning of a new phase of flight training, the uncertainty about his eyes returned. Finally during a routine physical examination two weeks before graduation, he decided he had come too far not to graduate. He knew the slightest indication of an eye problem would be reason for the Army to open the floodgates and wash him out. While waiting in line to read the eye chart, he listened to cadets ahead of him and memorized the 20/20 and 20/10 lines.

Robb eased *Perpetual Paula* back into position on Hugh's right wing. Hugh looked over and gave a thumbs-up signal, just like John Wayne had in the movie *Flying Tigers*. Suddenly Hugh's hand dropped from sight; his head snapped around; his P-51 wobbled and started a right turn.

Perpetual Paula's flight controls got stiff and her nose pulled to the right. Robb rolled in left rudder trim, hurriedly glanced at the flight instruments. They showed a descending turn, with an angle of bank of 40 degrees and a speed of 300 mph.

"Cricket 36, you're too steep and losing altitude." Robb waited, but Hugh didn't answer. "Cricket 36, you need to recover." But Hugh didn't reply.

Knowing they'd worked their way north of the field, where some of the hills were around 3000 feet high, Robb glanced at the flight instruments. The airspeed showed 320 mph and the altimeter's needle swung through the 5000-foot mark—on the way down. With altimeter lag, he knew they were several hundred feet lower.

"Cricket 36, recover, or I'm breakin' off!" But Hugh maintained his frozen silence.

Another shot of fear bolted through Robb's body, as he tried to think of how to break away, while on the inside of a steep descending turn, without slamming into Hugh—or over controlling and crashing into the hills. *Do something before you splatter your ass on a hill! Throttle back...slide behind and recover."*

He pulled back the throttle. Hugh's 51 disappeared in the soup. Robb hurriedly leveled *Perpetual Paula's* wings. The altimeter needle swung past the 3600-foot mark and was heading down. *OOOOh shit!*

Robb's heart pounded and blood thundered in his ears; he yanked back on the stick. Seven-G's shackled his 189-pound body, making it feel like 1400 pounds of lead. His oxygen mask pulled down across his nose and stretched tightly over his upper lip; blood drained from his head; his vision shot through darkening shades of gray—then went black.

In the blackness, Robb continued to pull and pray. Several instants passed, a seemingly eternal wait. He couldn't believe that he hadn't crashed. Or maybe he had. But surely he'd know if he had died. Or would he?

Perpetual Paula shuddered like a spirited mustang that had its fill of a greenhorn's touch.

Thank God! He released some stick pressure to keep her from snapping out of control. Any other time, a shudder while flying in the soup, blacked-out, would've scared the hell out of him. But not today. It told him that he was still alive.

Perpetual Paula shuddered several more times and each time he released a little more stick pressure. Gradually, the blood returned to his head; his vision passed from black through lighter shades of gray. Finally he could see.

What he saw triggered an overdose of terror. The most useful flight instrument of all, the artificial horizon had tumbled. Losing it made everything else that had happened to him today seem like kid's stuff.

Fear coiled tightly inside him then recoiled like a high-tension spring suddenly expanding in his chest. Blood thundered in his ears; his mind spun out-of-control and twisted into a bottomless whirlpool with no past, no present, no future. Death seemed inevitable and he felt too tired and weak to resist.

Since he had started flying, Robb had wondered how he'd react the first time death seemed certain. As a pilot, he had expected the end to come lightning fast before the roar of the thunderclap. He never dreamed there would be time to agonize over it.

Suddenly, something jolted him, got his mind back in gear with his brain, and triggered his will to live. *If I'm gonna die it'll be in combat.*

When Robb had practiced unusual positions without the artificial horizon, Iron Ass always told him, " Center the needle and ball, then work on the airspeed and altitude."

He moved the stick right to center the turn needle and leveled *Perpetual Paula's* wings, then quickly stomped on the right rudder pedal and centered the ball. He checked the rate of climb indicator. Its needle was pegged on the climb side like *Perpetual Paula* was heading for outer space.

The airspeed indicator passed through 110 mph, on the way to zero. *Add power before you fall outta the sky!* He jammed the throttle to full power. The airspeed dropped to 50 mph, held momentarily, then started to increase. The rate-of-climb needle dropped past zero then showed a dive.

You're upside down...on top of a loop...starting down the backside. His pucker string tightened. But he fought off the jitters, while he kept the needle and ball centered and reduced the backpressure on the stick.

Perpetual Paula's speed jumped to 140 mph and her rate of descent increased to 4000 feet per minute. *You're going straight down.*

He let the airspeed build to 180 mph, then pulled a little harder on the stick. *Perpetual Paula* shuddered. He released a slight amount of stick pressure to keep her from stalling. *Don't get ham-handed now. . .keep the needle and ball centered...watch altimeter...rate-of-descent...airspeed.*

His eyes circled the flight instruments as he continued to hold backpressure on the stick and reduced the power. *Perpetual Paula's* rate-of-descent decreased; her altimeter stopped unwinding. He released all of the stick pressure, retarded the throttle to cruise power and her airspeed stabilized at 250 mph. *Level flight... you made it!*

His eyes flicked from the needle and ball, altimeter, rate-of-descent and airspeed indicator as he held *Perpetual Paula* in level flight. But without the artificial horizon, he felt like a blind man on a tightrope. More than anything he wanted to get out of this gray netherworld—the devil's aboveground retreat—and see the earth or sky.

Gotta turn to the east, get away from the hills. . .get over the North Sea. . .then let down below this crap. Even the most experienced pilots admitted to difficulty making turns without the artificial horizon, so Robb climbed 500 feet higher. He eased *Per-*

petual Paula through a shallow turn and rolled her out on a heading of 90 degrees. To be certain he was over water, he flew for ten minutes before starting down. At 800 feet, *Perpetual Paula*'s nose popped out of the black clouds.

The North Sea's icy water, which could kill you with hypothermia within a couple of minutes, looked as welcome as a beautiful spring dawn after a nightmare. Robb leveled *Perpetual Paula* at 500 feet, turned her back to the west. He wanted to call Hugh but was afraid he might not answer. *Wait until you get over land then call.* Ahead, foaming breakers marked the coastline. A few miles inland, the ceiling had risen to 1500 feet and the visibility had increased to three miles. Robb released his death grip on the stick and throttle, opened and closed his aching hands. Then he rotated his head to relax his neck muscles and noticed how much his butt ached from the hard dinghy. He never realized fear could mask so much discomfort.

Robb recalled classmates in flight school and P-40 training who had been killed during simple emergencies. He wondered how he had survived his roller coaster struggle with death. *I flirted with it three times and ended doing a loop in the soup on partial instruments. Even a Hollywood writer on a hemp-high would have difficulty creating this checkout flight. Combat can't be any worse.*

He suddenly remembered Hugh. Robb took a deep breath and transmitted, "Cricket 36...Cricket 24 here...you read?"

"Cricket 36. Read you five square." The sound of Hugh's voice was as uplifting as a Glenn Miller rendition of the *Wild Blue Yonder*.

Robb and Hugh called for steers to the field and joined in formation. While waiting for their landing time, they remained close to Goatshill and avoided the clouds, not wanting to tempt fate again. That night, over several beers, they shared their stories.

"When I gave you the thumbs up, vertigo jumped all over me, knocked my senses for a loop and scared the hell outta me." Hugh paused and took a sip of beer. "Heard your call. Can't remember what you said. I was too shook."

"Yeah, know what you mean."

"Finally got it through my thick skull that having vertigo in the soup's no different than having it under the bag in the back seat of the Baker Tango-13. This breakthrough didn't happen, until you'd gone bye-bye...and I'd nearly played tagged with old terra firma." Hugh took another sip and stared at the floor. "Those few seconds seemed a lifetime."

"Yeah," Robb sighed.

"Anyway," Hugh continued. "I finally got my head screwed back on. Grabbed a handful of G's, got my bird squared away and inhaled a hundred percent oxygen for a while. Straight oxygen's good for more than hangovers," he smiled. "After I got my O-two pumped up, gave you several calls."

"Didn't hear a thing. Guess my pucker string short circuited my hearing," Robb replied with a smile.

"Robb, when you didn't answer I had the sickening feeling that I'd just killed a friend. I yelled and banged on the canopy with my fist. Begged God to go back and skip that part of the flight...start over. Words can't describe it. Don't want'a go through anything like it again." His voice trailed off. He stared into space as if he was searching beyond the horizon, trying to see the future. "Do you think fighter pilots, facing death in isolation are affected more by fear than bomber crews who face it together?"

"Don't have a clue. All I know is that I'm happy we're both sitting here drinking a beer." Robb smiled and took a big swig.

Robb never saw his instructor again and wondered what happened to instructors who couldn't hack it at Goatshill. For the remainder of his stay at Goxhill, the weather behaved itself, holding to overcast skies with a few miles of visibility. He knew his next flight in really bad weather would come on a combat mission.

All of the replacement pilots received only four of their six scheduled flights. The last two flights got scrubbed, due to the lack of flyable aircraft. With six hours flying time in P-51's, they were stamped Combat Ready and cleared for the Big Leagues where the score would be tallied by killed in action (KIA) or missing in action (MIA).

Hugh received orders for a P-51 group in the 9th Air Force and Robb got assigned to the 345th Fighter Group in the 8th Air Force. As they shook hands before departing Goxhill, they wondered if they'd ever see one another again.

CHAPTER I

A Dance of Death

BAM! The Nissen hut's door slammed against a steel bunk and the duty sergeant hurried inside. He grabbed the door and forced it shut against the blowing rain, then pulled the wake-up roster from his coat pocket, shined the flashlight on it and took a step.

THUMP! He stumbled over a footlocker. CLUNK! A GI helmet hit the floor. Its steel dome grated on the coarse concrete as the helmet rocked back and forth.

Robb opened his eyes, peaked from beneath the blankets and heard the rain pounding on the tin roof. "Oh shit!" he whispered. The thing he had been dreading most was about to happen—going on his first combat mission in weather unfit for flying.

"Mission briefing in an hour-and-a-half, sir," the sergeant said.

"Okay, Sarge," Robb replied. He rolled onto his back, stretched and inhaled deeply. When he exhaled, his warm breath condensed in the cold air and the icy mist settled on his face. He felt tired and his eyes burned from the lack of sleep. Although he'd gone to bed at 9:30, Ned Rathman and Rocko Fazzio had awakened him when they stumbled into the hut around midnight, after their drinking bout at the club.

Robb threw back the rough British blankets. *Damned things are like sleeping in a bed of Texas cactus.* He sat up and snatched his green uniform shirt from the top of his footlocker and put it on, then reached for a pair of socks and slipped them on over the pair he had slept in. He stuck his feet into the legs of his pinkish-gray gabardine trousers, arched his back and pulled up the trousers and buttoned them. Sitting up, he swung his feet around, held them above the icy concrete and pulled on his GI shoes, then dropped his feet to the floor.

"Okay, okay, Sarge," Rocko grunted after the sergeant shook the bunk a third time. "Sumbitch...short frickin' night."

Robb grabbed his winter flight jacket from the foot of the bunk and slipped it on. He jerked the white nylon scarf from the jacket's epaulet and wrapped it around his neck. When issued the scarf, he had been told that in addition to its warmth, it would keep his neck from being rubbed raw while scanning the sky for enemy aircraft.

With his towel, toothbrush, tube of Ipana toothpaste and gooseneck flash-light, he headed for the door. Before opening the door, he turned on the flashlight and once again wondered why all GI flashlights shined at right angles. *Damned thing's not made to be used in the cockpit of a fighter at night.*

Outside, the icy rain stung his face. He hunched behind the jacket's fur collar, pulled the zipper higher and hurried along the macadam lane leading to the latrine. A British Lancaster, returning from Germany, rumbled overhead. Its four in-line engines sounded like a flight of four Spitfires.

WHOOMP! Another Lancaster roared past at about 300 feet. Solid blue fire shot from the exhausts of two of its engines. The third engine sputtered ragged-orange flames and the fourth engine was dead.

The stormy blackness quickly swallowed the Lancaster. Robb listened to its uneven roar and waited for the crash. But the crippled giant limped on toward the west. He recalled the RAF combat intelligence reports he had read and wondered what could be more frightening than eight to ten hours of night combat over Germany. RAF aircrews reported that flying through the pitch-blackness magnified the muzzle flashes from antiaircraft cannons. The orange flashes from the exploding shells looked bigger and deadlier. Each time a bomber took a hit and blew up, the huge fireball burned a hole in the pitch-black sky for other bomber crews to see.

In between flak attacks, radar equipped night fighters lurked in the blackness. Without warning, they too would blow a bomber to bits, while other bomber crews watched and waited, wondering who would be next.

Those who survived the living hell returned through the darkness to fog banks or blinding storms. Before the war, flying in such bad weather at night had been unthinkable. But for over two years, RAF bomber crews had faced more than the unthinkable.

A strip of light marked the bottom of the latrine door. The unheated Nissen hut had been divided into three sections with washbasins lining the walls in the center. On the left were eight rusty showers and on the right, two rows of eight closely spaced commodes faced one another. At this moment, seven fighter pilots faced eight on the line of scrimmage.

GI latrines reminded Robb of the ancient Rome's public baths that he had read about. But latrines had more functions. They also served as a bus stop, reading room and meeting hall, where the latest scuttlebutt was exchanged. The only thing private was a person's innermost thoughts.

Robb splashed cold water on his face, brushed his teeth, then wiped the damp towel back across his crew cut.

BAAM! The door flung open and banged the wall. Rocko Fazzio stormed in and slammed the door shut. His shaggy black hair, heavy black beard, bushy brows and bloodshot eyes made him look more like a hung over poet than a fighter pilot. He went to the unoccupied commode—now eight faced eight. Robb wondered how long Rocko would've lasted in ancient Rome.

£££

Outside the latrine, the line of fighter pilots hunched behind the fur collars of their flight jackets waiting to board the GI truck that would take them to operations. Silhouetted by the red glow from the truck's taillights, they appeared as faceless gnomes rather than guardians of the skies.

Robb recalled the Army Air Force's recruiting poster in the Austin, Texas post office. It featured a tall aviation cadet wearing a flight suit, helmet and goggles, standing next to a Stearman and gazing at the blue yonder. He wondered how many cadets could be recruited with this morning's scene.

The last pilot climbed onto the canvas covered truck bed. Someone pounded the cab's metal roof. The truck's engine roared; its gears growled and the truck jerked forward through the darkness. Speeding along the twisting country lane, the crack of the truck's exhaust mixed with the howling wind and slapping canvas. Huddled behind their fur collars, the 21 apprentice warriors stared into the noisy blackness and wondered which of them might die before dinner.

The driver double-clutched and downshifted, the engine growled, the exhaust rumbled and cracked as the brakes squealed. The truck jerked to a stop in front of the clump of black Nissen huts that housed the three fighter squadrons, intelligence, operations and the group commander's office. The apprentice warriors leaped from the truck and raced to the warmth of their squadrons.

Robb's flight commander, First Lieutenant Ted Tyler, was standing at the snack bar drinking coffee when Robb entered the pilot's lounge.

Ted was a six-foot version of the movie star Alan Ladd. He had lived in California before entering West Point and although he never mentioned it, everyone knew his Rhodes Scholarship had been delayed until after the war. He had been awarded the Distinguished Flying Cross and featured as The Hero of the Week on national radio when he guided his burning P-40 away from Los Angeles, before bailing out. When the 345th Fighter Group arrived overseas three weeks ago, Ted and three other flight commanders flew five combat missions with a P-47 group as part of a combat indoctrination program. Ted shot down a ME-109 on his fourth mission.

"Robb, have you seen Ned and Rocko?" Ted asked.

"Saw Rocko in the latrine, haven't seen Ned."

"Probably be on the next bus. Let's have something to eat."

Behind the snack bar, Private John Branham grilled Spam sandwiches on the kerosene grill while Corporal Clyde Perkins served them.

"Good morning Lieutenant Baines," Corporal Perkins said. He wiped his hands on his soiled apron and refilled Ted's coffee cup. "What can I get you gentlemen?"

"Two battery acids, a couple of Spams," Ted replied.

Corporal Perkins was a frail five foot-five. Three jagged pieces of toilet paper covered the razor cuts on his whisky-red face. The collar and cuffs of his wool, olive drab shirt were blackened with kitchen grease.

"Perkie needs an oil change," Ted whispered, while Corporal Perkins turned and poured the grapefruit juice from the large olive drab can into the tin cups.

Robb nodded and smiled.

"I got the Spams," Private Branham barked, before Corporal Perkins could reach for the sandwiches. "Mornin' Lieutenant Tyler, sir."

"Good morning, Big John."

The muscular six-foot-four private had a ruddy complexion and graying hair. His spotless uniform shirt had a dark area on the sleeves, where the chevrons of a master sergeant had been sewn. In 1920, after Big John's second assault and battery charge, the juvenile court gave him a choice—the Army or reform school. Britain was his third overseas assignment and the third time he'd been knocked back to a buck private. His first bust came in the Philippines when he'd battered two Marines in a Manila bar. In the Panama Canal Zone he'd been busted from staff sergeant when he got in to a fight with two sailors in a brothel.

Two days ago Robb heard him telling about his third bust. "Ended up in a London pub called Dirty Dick's. Had a snoot full. Doin' some dance called the hokey cokey, when this here broad says, 'Let's 'ave a bloody knee trembler out back.' I asks, 'What the hell's a knee trembler?' She says, 'Step outside Yank and ah'll show ye.'

"We went outside. She leans against the wall. Just as I moved closer, a bolt of lightnin' hit me. I came to, sprawled in the alley, with my wallet missin.' But I learned years ago to keep my ID card and most of my loot in my socks.

"Went back inside, had a belt of gin with a beer chase. A few minutes later this same broad comes in the back door with some big limey son-of-a-bitch. I grabbed her and the big limey takes a poke at me. So I tore into 'em.

"Someone called a cop. The bloke cop gave me a shove; I shoved 'em back. Bloke cop's piss pot went sailin' off his head. When he let go of me to get his piss pot, I started after the big limey again. But the pub keeper clobbered me over the head with a spittoon. Woke up on the way to the pokey.

"Lieutenant Tyler got me outta the clink or I'd still be there. If it hadn't been for that big fat broad, I'd still be a first shirt. First time I ever got busted without gettin' laid. *C'est la guerre.*"

"Perkie, get Lieutenant Tyler more coffee," Big John snapped.

Corporal Perkins refilled Ted's coffee and slid the olive drab can of Carnation milk closer. "Anything else, Lieutenant Tyler, sir?" he squeaked.

"No thank you, Corporal Perkins." Ted turned to Robb, "Nervous?"

"Yes. Lousy weather, hope I don't screw up, get separated."

"We probably will see the ground twice today. Once on takeoff and again on landing. But you can hack it. Just fly tight formation like you normally do."

"Wonder if the Krauts'll be up?"

"Count on it. Keep your eyes peeled and your head on a swivel." Ted surveyed the room and frowned. "I'll be back in a minute. Gonna send a jeep for our two delinquents."

In a few minutes, Ted motioned for Robb to join him. "Let's go to the group briefing room, check the game plan."

A big sign above the guarded door to the group briefing room read, **Strictly Out of Bounds–Except Authorized Personnel**. The guard found Ted and Robb's names on the mission roster, checked their identity cards and motioned them inside.

Black models of German fighters and bombers dangled from the ceiling in a cloud of blue cigarette smoke. Three floodlights shined on the ten-by-twenty-foot acetate-covered map of Europe mounted on the front wall. Red, green and yellow strings of yarn marked the bombers' route of flight. Extending from East Anglia, the strings converged over the North Sea and ran across Northern Holland into Germany.

"Looks like Bremen," Ted said.

Red and black circles had been drawn along the colored strings. The red circles contained the sizes and numbers of flak guns at that location, while the black circles gave the number and types of fighters within striking range along that portion of the route. Inside Germany the circles became more numerous and a clump of red circles surrounded the target.

There was a foot high platform in front of the map, with a lectern on the right side. A shiny cue stick leaned against the lectern.

To the left of the map, the three fighter squadrons had their pilots names listed. Each squadron's numerical designation, 13th, 14th and 15th and their respective radio call signs Snapper, Bug Eye and Hot Rod headed the lists.

Eight columns followed the pilots' names. Each column had a title: DNIF (an acronym for Drunk, Not Interested In Flying, but meaning sick); PASS (indicating a few days off); R&R (meaning Rest and Recuperation, a week at an English estate, referred to as the Flak House); NUMBER OF MISSIONS; CONFIRMED KILLS; PROBABLE KILLS; DAMAGED and OTHER.

To the right of the map was a four-by-twelve-foot plywood board titled MISSION SCHEDULE. It was divided into thirds, one for each squadron. Each squadron's square was divided into fourths, one for each flight. The flight squares were painted red, yellow, white, and green. Four metal silhouettes of P-51's, with a pilot's name, were placed on each colored square.

5

Below the mission schedule was a sequential list of key times, beginning with START ENGINE TIME, followed by TAXI TIME and TAKEOFF TIME. Then came the RENDEZVOUS TIME, COAST IN TIME (crossing the coast of the Continent), IP TIME (meaning Initial Point for the beginning of the bomb run), TOT (Time Over Target) and the ETE to HOME PLATE (estimated time en route from the target to Boxted). The last item on the list was the SAFE HEADING HOME, a heading that would keep the pilots from missing the British Isles in case of bad weather and radio failure.

Below the list of times were the mission call signs. They started with the bomber commander and his deputy; plus call signs for each of the three bomber division commanders, followed by the call signs for each of P-47, P-51 and P-38 groups. Then came the call signs for the British radar controllers, Air Sea Rescue, Royal Navy and RAF Station Manston (a large emergency field on the coast). Last were the MISSION CANCEL--RECALL code words.

The call signs made no sense: Dirty Bird, Stinky, Dickory Dock, Bo Peep, Hot Dog, Four Eyes, Rough House, Crumb-Bum, Honky-Tonk, Hot Tamale, Irish Stew, Betty Boop, Goofus, Bad Breath, Shotgun, Ringo, Hot Pants, Broken Spoke, Mickey Mouse, Rusty Spike, Big Bear, Bent Spear, Purple Stick, Country Club, Rough House, and Sticky Wicket.

The briefing room chairs were divided into thirds, one section for each fighter squadron, with Snapper on the left, Bug Eye in the center and Hot Rod on the right. To match the Mission Schedule board, the first four rows of folding chairs were painted red yellow, white and green. The remaining chairs were blue.

Bug Eye squadron had an additional chair in the front row. It had red, yellow, white and green stripes with COLONEL printed in bold purple letters across the back. Below COLONEL was his personal call sign, SHOTGUN ONE.

Ted and Robb sat in the first two white chairs in the third row of Snapper squadron. Ted wrote the recall code words, safe heading and flying time from the target area to Britain, on the back of his hand then passed his pen to Robb. He wrote the info on the back of his hand and passed the pen back to Ted.

Robb stared at the striped chair. While in flying school he had read a story in *Time* magazine about the Colonel leading his squadron on a dangerous mission over France. Ted said he had first heard about the Colonel from his father while he was in high school in California. He said the Colonel worked his way through two years of college at the University of Nebraska during the depression so he could apply for pilot training with the Army Air Corps. He graduated in 1936 and had little hope of remaining on active duty so he flew combat for 14 months in the Spanish Civil War. While there he shot down three German and two Italian aircraft.

THE HELLISH VORTEX

Ted said that following the war in Spain, General Henry H. "Hap" Arnold, who was then the Assistant Chief of the Army Air Corps, offered the Colonel a regular commission. In May 1941, General Arnold sent him to Britain to observe RAF fighter operations. RAF friends he had met in Spain got sub-rosa approval for him to fly combat with a Spitfire squadron. He shot down three more Germans, but never claimed them. After the Japanese sneak attack at Pearl Harbor he got official permission to fly combat with the RAF.

When the first American fighter group arrived in the summer of 1942, General Carl A. "Tooey" Spaatz, the 8th Air Force Commander, promoted him to major and gave him command of one of the fighter squadrons. Ted said the Colonel had more combat time then anyone in the Army Air Force.

A strong gust of wind howled and rain pounded the tin building. Robb glanced from the striped chair to the big map and the mission information. *This room's like a carnival House of Horrors.* His mind entered a sea of anxiety and doubt. *How can I remember all of this crap or know when to use it?*

The Colonel leaned back in the steel Army-green swivel chair, with his feet resting on the matching green metal desk. He sipped his coffee, listened to the wind and rain and thought about his eight years of service. Like many pre-war officers during the explosive growth of the Army Air Force at the beginning of World War II, he had gone from first lieutenant to full colonel in two years. He enjoyed the rank and responsibility but felt the loneliness of command.

Back in the early days of his career the Army Air Corps had been a sleepy little flying club and nothing moved very fast, especially the wood and fabric airplanes. But in 1939 things started to change. A few all-metal, high-performance fighters replaced some of the slow flyers.

He would never forget his first P-40 flight. The P-40 had been big, powerful and noisy. Its speed had been nearly twice as fast as anything he had flown. However, his first P-51 flight in 1940 had been more impressive than anything he had flown, even the P-38 and P-47. At the time he wondered why only the RAF had ordered them. He tried hard to get the Army Air Corps to buy some P-51's, but the headquarters staff weren't interested.

Several B-17's suddenly roared through the dark stormy sky struggling to join-up. The Colonel thought about his young pilots, most of whom had just graduated from flight school and averaged only 300 hours of flying time, with less than 15 hours in the P-51. Many were teenagers fresh from high school or a couple of years of college. A year ago, most of them had never been close to an airplane.

He recalled how nervous he'd been the morning of his first combat mission in Spain when they launched 30 slow flyers into the clear Spanish sky. His challenge had been nothing compared to the one his young pilots faced. Today 490 fighters and 546 bombers would join-up in lousy weather and face the heaviest fighter and flak defenses the world had ever seen.

He knew the London and Washington moguls would be watching this first P-51 mission like no other. Many of them believed the P-51 would be the key to the survival of the United State's daylight precision bombing program—maybe the survival of the Army Air Forces. The 8th AF eggheads had estimated a slightly reduced loss rate for today, but after four years of fighting the Colonel knew the chaotic variables of aerial combat could screw up any egghead projection.

He looked at his wristwatch, downed his coffee, swung his feet off the desk, and pushed himself out of the chair. As he walked toward the office door he whispered, "This's gonna be a no-shit ballgame and my belly button'll be talkin' to my asshole all day. But you gotta a job to do. Now get with it!" He grasped the knob, sucked in his gut, opened the door and strode briskly down the hall toward the group briefing room.

£££

The cigarette smoke had thickened and most of the nervous chatter had ended, in the carnival-like room. All the colored chairs were filled, except for Ned's, Rocko's and the Colonel's.

Standing next to the lectern, the adjutant fiddled with the cue, checked his watch then the wall clock. He leaned the cue stick against the lectern, stepped off the platform and walked toward the guarded door. A stone silence spread across the room.

SKAA-RUNCH! Ned and Rocko skidded to a stop next to Ted. They eased past Ted and sat down in their two white chairs and looked straight ahead to avoid Ted's fierce glare.

Another wave of silence spread across the room. Robb strained not to be the one to break it. He noticed how the spotlights seemed to brighten the Colonel's empty red, yellow, white and green striped chair. *Like waiting for The Second Coming.*

"HOFFICERS, TEN–SHUN!" the adjutant roared. The apprentice warriors sprang to their feet.

"Please take your seats, gentlemen." The Colonel hopped onto the platform, picked up the cue stick and faced the pilots. Nearly three years of looking into the sun for Nazi aircraft had tanned the area around his eyes not covered by his helmet and oxygen mask. The tanned area resembled a leather eye mask with steely blue eyes.

"Gents, today with our long-range P-51's we're gonna skip lunch, write a little history, six miles high, deep inside krautland. We're gonna start a new phase in the air war by protecting the bombers all of way to the target. Bomber guys have waited a year-and-a-half for this day, while takin' the highest losses of the war, higher than the infantry, Navy or Marines. So we're gonna do our damnedest to protect 'em. Stormy, give us your sad tale."

The weather officer, Captain Frank "Stormy" Knight, a former All Big Ten center at the University of Minnesota, gave a detailed run-down on why the weather was bad and would remain that way all day.

Major Geoffrey Watson, the group intelligence officer, was from Virginia. He was a tall blonde with narrow shoulders, big hips, squeaky voice and a funny walk. He'd been a Department of State employee before the war and mentioned it at every opportunity.

The Colonel shifted uneasily in his striped chair, as Major Watson strutted back and forth like a pompous actor enjoying center stage. He outlined the importance of the target and told them about German defenses. He casually mentioned that in addition to the hundreds of German fighters along the route there were more than 300 within striking distance of the target.

Robb couldn't believe what he had just heard and looked at Ted. But Ted appeared unfazed. *Shit. . .gonna be completely outnumbered and Ted doesn't seem the least bit concerned. Why in hell are we still so short on P-51's two years after the Japs bombed Pearl Harbor?*

Major Watson finished and handed the cue stick Major Bob Hunt, the group operations officer. He was a tall lean, no-nonsense Iowan, who had flown combat with the Colonel for more than a year. He gave the taxi, takeoff, en route procedures and turned to the Colonel, "Sir."

The Colonel took the pool cue and held it with both hands in front of him while he scanned the pilots. "Gents, nothing about this mission's gonna be easy. Navigation and timing's critical. Late rendezvous and we'll leave the bombers exposed to kraut fighters on the way in. Early rendezvous and we'll leave 'em exposed on the way out.

We'd all love to rip around the sky shootin' down kraut fighters, but we're gonna stick with the bombers like jealous lovers. We'll engage the krauts long enough to screw up their attacks. If we zonk a few Nazi in the process, that'll be peachy keen. Gonna be damned difficult to get on the tail of one of those bastards and not finish 'em off. When we get more 51's over here that's exactly what we'll do. We'll take 'em to the deck if we have to and nail their asses. But today, the fastest way to get on my shit list is to leave the bombers and go lollygagin' after kraut fighters.

"It looks like we're facin' a stacked deck. Weather's lousy and the krauts got us out numbered. They also have radar to guide their fighters around the sky and we're stuck with our Mark VII eyeballs. In addition, they're workin' in their backyard and don't have to sweat fuel or ammunition. We've got to save enough gas and ammo to fight our way home. So we're gonna have to fly smart.

"Many of you are probably wonderin' about the ME-109's and FW-190's. Both are damned good. But our 51's are better. Just keep your speed up, because we can turn with the best of 'em at high speed. Don't get suckered into a low, slow fight and you'll be okay."

"Remember, from a distance, we look like ME-109's. So don't let one of those new, double-breasted 38 drivers stooge in behind ya and shoot your ass down. You guys with the anti-G suits, be sure to debrief with Captain Maison after the mission. Gotta get the poop back to the Air Proving Grounds at Eglin Field so they can go final on those G-suits. Need 'em over here right away.

"We can't waste a lot of fuel on the ground. So when the red flare's fired from the tower, don't dillydally. Start your engines and get with it. Any questions?"

Robb looked to the left and right hoping some one would ask why we have so few P-51's, but no one did. *Shit...they're just like me...afraid to ask.*

The Colonel leaned the cue stick against the lectern. "Okay guys, let's get strapped up and head for Germany with blood in our eyes, ready to fight. Keep yur heads on a swivel and stay off the God-damned radio unless you got somethin' important to say."

Everyone jumped up and stood at attention as the Colonel hopped off the platform and walked briskly down the aisle.

"CARRY ON!" the adjutant shouted as the Colonel passed through the guarded door.

£££

Corporal Perkins finished drying the tin plates and cups while Big John sat in one of the folding chairs, drinking coffee and reading the *STARS and STRIPES*. His foot kept time with Glenn Miller's recording of *In the Mood* that blared from the radio behind the snack bar.

"Perkie, after you mop the floor today, pick up the raisins and prunes from the mess hall. Get more sugar, too. Gotta get a new batch'a kick-a-poo joy juice started. Gettin' low."

"I will, Big John."

"Jocks are comin'! Can that radio!" Big John hurried behind the counter and placed slices of Spam and bread on the kerosene grill.

Ned and Rocko raced to the snack bar; each grabbed a cup of grapefruit juice and gulped it down. They quickly refilled their cups and each of them snatched a Spam sandwich and took big bites.

"Come with me. I wanna talk to you guys," Ted said without his usual smile.

Ned and Rocko followed Ted to the far corner of the room. Unable to choke down their big bites, they nodded with bulging cheeks while Ted spoke. When he left, Ned and Rocko slumped into chairs, stared at the floor and started to chew.

"Gentlemen, Major Brown," Captain Draper, the squadron operations officer, announced. Major Brown, the squadron commander, had flown combat in Spitfires and P-47's with the Colonel for the past 16 months.

"Guys, I'd like to add my two cents to what the Colonel said. We're gonna be on center stage with our P-51's. Gotta keep our heads out and fly smart. Fly the airplane to the hilt, be aggressive, but don't get drawn away from the bombers. They're the reason we'll be over Germany and we can't forget it. You heard the boss man. He means what he says. You're either on his team, or you'll become a bean-counting grunt. Enough said. You all know what's what, so let's heard for the locker room, get strapped up and have at 'em."

Robb watched Ted take the experimental G-suit from his locker. The G-suit had a rubber bladder for the stomach, one on each thigh and calf. In a tight turn or a sharp pullout from a dive, the bladders inflated to slow the loss of blood from the pilot's upper body and delay his blackout. *Wish I had a G-suit...gonna need all the help I can get. Need it a lot more than Ted. It really pisses me off that we don't have enough P-51's...don't have G-suits. People back home are being told their fighting men have everything they need. What a bunch of crap.*

"Robb, I moved you back to number four on Ned's wing," Ted said, zipping the G-suit leg. "You can help Ned more than Rocko, today."

Ted's words echoed in Robb's ears like a bass drum. He tried to think of a reason for not flying with Ned, but his mind failed him.

"You okay, Robb?"

"Uh...yeah...I guess," he muttered. *Shit...flying on a sop-head's wing in bad weather on my first combat mission and being outnumbered six to one in the target area is like being handed a one-way ticket to Germany. What the hell did I do to deserve this?*

£££

One minute before the start engine time, Major Hunt moved outside the control tower onto its walkway. He held the flare pistol in his left hand, shined the flashlight on his wristwatch, trying to shield its face from the rain. At five seconds to go, he raised the flare pistol and counted, "Five...four...three...two...one," and fired.

The red flare disappeared into the black clouds. He dropped the flashlight, fumbled for another flare, reloaded and fired horizontally. The flare struck the ground halfway across the field and shattered. The burning pieces ricocheted above the P-51's parking revetments.

Seeing the flare Robb flipped the starter switch, counted six blades, turned the ignition to both mags and pumped the fuel primer twice. Blue flames exploded from the exhaust stacks; the prop spun. The 1490 horsepower Merlin engine cracked like gunfire as he pushed the mixture control to normal.

Robb quickly adjusted the cockpit lighting, flipped the wing tip lights switch to on and punched the VHF radio button. Just as the radio came on, he heard the Colonel call Bugeye squadron to start their radio checks.

Robb looked out through the windshield. The engine exhaust flashes lit the blowing raindrops as they exploded across the windshield like blue meteorites.

In the parking revetments along the taxiway, clusters of red and green wing tip lights, white taillights and blue exhaust flashes sparkled in the rain. Any other time the bright colors would've been a joyful reminder that Christmas was only five days away.

"Shotgun One, let's taxi." The Colonel's crisp transmission shattered the pseudo-Christmas scene and set the ground crews in motion.

They darted back and forth, snatching fire extinguishers and wheel chocks from in front of the P-51's. Their shadowy forms, scurrying through the rainy darkness, renewed Robb's doubts about his eyes at the very moment he needed all the confidence he could muster.

"Snapper Red, check," Major Brown called.

"Red Two."

"Three."

"Four."

"Snapper Yellow, check."

"Yellow Two."

"Three."

"Four."

By now the Colonel and Bugeye were taxiing through Snapper's area.

"Snapper White, check," Ted transmitted.

After several seconds Ned called, "White Three here. Two can't get his engine started."

"White Four," Robb answered, wishing Ted would hurry and call for a spare to take Rocko's place.

"Snapper Green, check."

"Green Two."

"Three."

"Four."

An armament truck pulled into Robb's parking revetment. The truck's dim headlights shined on three ravens that were facing the rain and clinging to the top wire of the revetment fence. Their ugly black heads seemed to be cocked in disbelief that anything would try to fly in such weather. Robb shared the ill-omened blackbirds' disbelief.

"Snapper Red's taxiing." Major Brown pulled in behind the last P-51 in Bugeye squadron.

"Snapper White One, White Two here," Rocko transmitted. "Had a flood-ed engine. Crew chief said he had a problem with the engine fuel primer during run-up this morning. But said engine's okay once it's running. Running good now, so I'm gonna take it. But I'll write it up when I get back."

"Shotgun One here. Can the crap and taxi!" the Colonel barked, as he led Bugeye squadron onto the pierced-steel planking (PSP) runway. Bugeye pilots cocked their 51's at 45-degree angles with their tails pointed off the runway, to avoid blasting one another with prop wash during the engine checks.

A thunderous roar blanketed the field, as the 16 Bugeye pilots checked their 51's engine magnetos, cycled the propeller pitch and flicked their super-chargers on and off. Engine checks complete, the pilots throttled back and the thunder faded. All 16 P-51's pointed their noses down the runway for takeoff.

The Colonel and his wingman went to takeoff power. Their engines roared and white vapor circles formed around the tips of the speeding props.

"Shotgun One's on the roll." The two 51's raced forward. Their vapor circles stretched back along their fuselages and formed foamy cylinders—whose misty sides turned blue from the light of the exhaust flames.

Two more 51's roared and rolled, wrapped in their ghostly cylinders.

"What the hell's that?" Robb muttered to himself. *Ted never told me about this.* Robb barely heard the Colonel's call to retract the landing gear.

Two more 51's roared and rolled, as Bugeye Red Three called for their gear retraction.

Major Brown led Snapper Red and Yellow onto the runway, parked at an angle behind the Bugeye's last ten 51's.

Two more 51's roared and rolled.

From the end of the runway, Robb saw the red and green wingtip lights bracketing the steamy blue cylinders as the two 51's raced down the runway. They resembled noisy Christmas ornaments fashioned in hell.

Two more 51's roared and rolled. The closer to takeoff Robb got, the more the pace appeared to quicken and the shorter the three-second spacing between takeoffs seemed.

Ted led White flight in behind Yellow and cocked his 51's tail.

Two more 51's roared and rolled.

Robb's world suddenly jumped into fast motion as he swung his 51's tail around for the engine checks. He tried to hurry, but felt like he was moving through a sea of molasses.

Two more 51's roared and rolled.

Snapper Red's engines growled and howled.

Robb's pucker string tightened another notch. The thought of taking off in this weather to join with nearly 1000 aircraft made his first flight at Goatshill seems like a piece of cake.

Two more 51's roared and rolled.

One by one, Snapper Yellow's engines growled and howled.

Two more 51's roared and rolled.

Ted's and Rocko's 51's growled and howled as they started their engine checks.

Major Brown and his wingman roared and rolled.

Robb yanked the stick back into his lap and tried to hurry as he stomped on the brakes and jammed the throttle forward to 2300 rpm.

Snapper Red Three and Four roared and rolled.

Behind, Robb heard Snapper Green's engines growl and howl.

The molasses thickened. *Gotta hurry. . .just check the mags...skip the rest.* He flicked the mag switch to the left and right, then back to both, without waiting for a drop.

Ted and Rocko turned their 51's down the runway.

Snapper Yellow One and Two roared and rolled.

Ned turned his 51's for takeoff; Robb followed.

Snapper Yellow Three and Four roared and rolled.

Ted and Rocko's engines roared to takeoff power; their prop wash blasted Robb's 51. It shook violently while the rudder pedals banged the soles of his GI shoes and the stick tried to jump out of his hand.

Ted and Rocko roared and rolled. White vapor cylinders shrouded the fuselages of their 51's; their prop wash blasted the water puddles on the PSP runway and turned them into muddy plumes.

Robb blinked the sweat from his eyes, yanked the stick back into his gut, stood on the brakes, jammed the throttle to takeoff power and started counting. "One thousand...one. One thousand...two. One thousand...three," he whispered, waiting for Ned to roll. *Let's go you sopheaded bastard before they get to Germany.*

Ned finally nodded his head and released his brakes; Robb released his brakes. Their 51's charged down the runway.

Sweat trickled into Robb's eyes; he blinked the left eye, then the right one, trying to clear them. The misty cylinder stretched back past his canopy but he could see the green wingtip light and the dim outline of Ned's 51.

A gust of wind flung Robb's 51 to the left, toward Ned. Robb's body turned to rock. He stomped on the right rudder pedal; his 51 jerked to the right.

Ned's 51 lifted off the ground; Robb pulled back the stick and followed.

"White Three, gear up...now," Ned called.

Robb raised the landing gear handle; the gear thumped into place. He blinked more sweat from his eyes. The misty cylinders had disappeared. He wondered when.

WHOOMP! A downdraft sent their 51's plunging. Robb's safety belt dug into his gut. His feet flew off the rudder pedals, but his eyes remained riveted to Ned's 51.

WHOOSH! The updraft flung them into the dark clouds.

The foot rests banged Robb's heels; the rock-hard dinghy flattened the cheeks of his butt. He scrambled to get his feet back on the rudder pedals while struggling to hold formation.

For the next two minutes, they bounced and rocked through the dark clouds, climbing to the west. At 3000 feet the air got smooth. They started a climbing turn to the left and rolled out on a heading of due east.

"Shotgun One is level angels nine with 16 chicks in between layers. Gonna skin it back, hold airspeed at 190 for join-up."

Ned and Robb broke out of the clouds at 8500 feet, leveled off at 9000 and let their 51's accelerate. Although the thick clouds blocked the first rays of the morning sun, there was enough light to see. A quarter of a mile ahead, Ted and Rocko were pulling in behind Snapper Yellow and Red. Beyond Snapper, Robb saw the Colonel with Bugeye squadron.

Robb eased his 51out a few feet away from Ned's, so he could relax and look around. "Thank God we made it," he whispered thinking about the takeoff in the horrible weather. *Old Ned did okay but I wonder how he'll do in combat?*

Ned raised his right hand and made a backward motion to signal a power reduction. They eased their throttles back, slowed to 190 mph and moved in next to Ted and Rocko.

"Green's in, Snapper Lead," the last flight commander called a few seconds later.

"Rog, Green. Snapper's chicks are tucked in, Shotgun," Major Brown called.

"Shotgun copies."

Within a minute the third squadron commander called, "Hot Rod's chicks slidin' in, Shotgun."

"Shotgun's pushin' it up." *So far so good.*

Climbing over the North Sea, German radar started humming in Robb's headset. *Bastards got us on radar...feel like Lady Godiva but with peekers bent on killing.*

Ted turned a few degrees to the right and puffs of smoke came from his four 50 caliber machine guns. Rocko, Ned and Robb took the cue and test fired their guns.

The Colonel leveled at 27,000 feet and had Bugeye squadron spread out in combat formation. Major Brown took Snapper squadron to the right of Bugeye, leveled at 29,000 feet, then fishtailed his P-51, signaling the squadron to spread out. Hot Rod squadron climbed to the left of the Bugeye and leveled at 31,000 feet and spread out.

"Shotgun has Big Friends eleven o'clock low," the Colonel called approaching the Dutch-German border. Robb saw the formations of B-17's and B-24's. Their formations stretched 50 miles to the east. The Colonel raced past the bombers, close enough for the crews to get their first look at the new fighter that could escort them all the way to the target. Half-frozen waist gunners waved from the open fuselage windows. They faced death in 50-below-zero air supercooled by the 200-mph slipstream.

Robb recalled the 8th AF's summary covering its first twelve months of combat, a period when it was a struggle to get 200 bombers on a mission. Yet 1600 airmen had to be taken out of action just due to severe frostbite.

But facing frostbite was a minor concern for the ten young airmen in each bomber. Many were too young to vote but all were old enough to die. Some would die outright when the bomber took a direct hit and exploded. Others unable to bailout would burn to death in flaming bombers. Many more became trapped inside when their damaged bombers spun out of control. They died a thousand deaths during their five-mile fall from the sky. Those lucky enough to bail out became prisoners of war, provided they weren't hung from telephone poles or mounted on pitchforks by angry German civilians.

Droning toward Bremen, the bomber crews prayed for just one more dinner—because 14 months of aerial combat had taught them not to ask for more.

"Shotgun has bandits, two o'clock high, headin' west," the Colonel's transmission shattered the silence.

Robb shielded his eyes from the sun with his left hand. Above a patch of canopy frost, he saw the contrails five miles south. Eight of the Germans peeled off and dived toward Snapper squadron.

"Snapper White One has eight bandits headed our way," Ted transmitted, before Robb could call.

"Take 'em Snapper White," Major Brown replied.

"It may be a feint, Snapper. Don't let 'em draw you away. Shotgun here."

"Snapper White copied. White, let's go 2700 rpm, full power. Goin' up and right."

Instead of yanking and banking to stay with Ted and Rocko, Ned made a loose turn and swung wide. Robb looked back; two ME-109's were closing on him fast.

"Snapper White Four has two 109's drivin' up my ass! Suck it in, Three!" Robb called. *Dumb shit Ned's gonna get me shot down with this candy-assed turn.*

Ned didn't answer nor tighten the turn.

Robb looked back. Orange bursts exploded from the first ME-109's 20-millimeter nose cannon, then the 7.92-millimeter machine guns spit fire.

"WHITE FOUR'S BREAKING LEFT!" Robb yanked back the control stick, stood on the left rudder and jammed the throttle and prop pitch to full. His body took on the density of lead; his oxygen mask pulled down across the bridge of his nose and he blacked-out.

In the blackness, ME-109's shells slammed into the tail of Robb's 51. The stick jumped in his hands; the rudder pedals banged the soles of his GI shoes. His feet did the dance of death.

Robb yanked harder on the stick; his 51 shuddered and the dance of death stopped. But he continued to pull, because he knew the German would tail him like a predator who had tasted blood.

In the tight climbing turn, Robb's 51 lost airspeed and tried to snap out of control. He had to ease off on the stick pressure to keep it flying. Gradually, the blood returned to his head and his vision passed through decreasing shades of gray until he saw the sky through the windshield.

He was going straight up. The needle on the airspeed indicator swung past 100 mph on its way to zero. He released all stick pressure and with zero G's, he rudder rolled his 51 to the left. It shuddered to the horizon and ended up on its back.

Glancing down through the top of his canopy, Robb did a double take and his body turned to rock. The ME-109 was only 20 feet below. He and the German were canopy to canopy, eyeball to eyeball.

Robb's heart pounded and blood thundered in his ears as the 109 started sliding back.

Robb jammed the stick forward, raised his 51's nose; the 51 shuddered and tried to stall. He reduced the stick pressure and the 109 kept inching back.

Hanging from the safety belt, Robb racked his mind trying to think of something he could do to keep from being shot down. From his *Principles of Flight* classes during flight training, he knew that making steep turns or flying upside down reduced the efficiency of his 51's wings and his aircraft would stall at higher speeds. *Why couldn't I be the one who's right side up instead of that damned kraut?* Robb's mind started spinning.

"COME ON DUMMY...SNAP OUT OF IT!" he shouted to himself. *But Shit...with my 51 on the edge of a stall and that kraut directly below I can't roll or try to break away or I'll slam into the bastard.* "DAMN IT...THINK OF SOMETHING! LOWER SOME FLAPS...DUMMY!"

He flipped the flap handle to the second detent, dropped 20 degrees of flaps, rolled in forward nose trim and pushed hard on the stick to hold his 51 in level flight. Each instant seemed eternal, as the safety belt dug deeper into his gut and he struggled to keep his feet on the rudder pedals.

He looked down through the top of the canopy. The German's cold blue eyes were looking up through the ME-109's rectangular shaped canopy. In his black leather helmet and jacket, the *Luftwaffe* pilot resembled an executioner measuring Robb for the kill.

OOOH SHIT! The cliché that fighter pilots dreaded most echoed in Robb s ears like a death knell. *Out of airspeed, altitude and ideas.*

CHAPTER 2

A Batch of Hell

Robb pushed hard on the control stick to keep his inverted P-51 in level flight, while he looked down through the top of his canopy at the ME-109. The tips of the 109's speeding propeller were ten feet behind and 15 feet below Robb's head. He could see the barrel opening on the its 20-milimeter nose cannon and the black smudge it had left on the propeller's yellow spinner.

As the 109 continued to inch back, Robb had to turn his head all of the way to the right and tip it fully back to keep the German in sight. Suddenly a neck muscle knotted. He gritted his teeth and tried not to flinch—but did.

His 51 dropped a few feet; he jammed the stick forward. His 51 shuddered and its right wing dropped. He kicked the left rudder to stop it. His arms and legs began to shake, as he struggled to hold his feet on the rudder pedals and push harder on the control stick. He looked back over his shoulder.

SHIT! I CAN'T SEE THE SON OF A BITCH…HIS PROP IS PROBABLY JUST BELOW MY TAIL. THIS IS IT!

Before Robb could take another breath, the nose of the 109 appeared 30 feet below. It kept moving forward and Robb saw 50-caliber armor piercing incendiary shells sparkling behind 109's cockpit.

Robb and the German pilot were once again eyeball to eyeball. But this time, the German's cold blue eyes were filled with terror.

WHAAP! WHAAP! More API's hit the 109 and sparkled; the German pilot quickly leaned forward and lowered his head. The 109's canopy flew off.

WHAAP! WHAAP! Another cluster of API's ripped into the 109's fuselage.

WHOOM! The fuselage fuel tank exploded. The orange fireball lit Robb's cockpit and chunks of metal blew past.

Just as the German pilot started out of the cockpit, the 109's nose flipped down. The pilot's upper body and head slammed back against the fuselage, while his legs remained stuck inside the cockpit.

The 109 snapped into a spin and the German's limp arms flailed the fuselage like rubber hoses. His brownish-yellow parachute streamed and wrapped itself around the fuselage and tail. Trailing smoke, the 109 twisted earthward—like a flag-draped coffin.

Robb rolled his 51 right side up and lowered its nose. As his 51 gained speed, he retracted the flaps, adjusted the trim and throttled back. It seemed like he'd been upside down forever, but it had been less than a minute.

He recalled the terror in the German's blue eyes and looked back to the left, trying to spot the 109. But it had dropped too far behind.

Robb noticed a thin streak of black engine oil sliding across the lower edge of his windshield. SHIT! *Must've taken a hit. . .hope it's not serious. Dear God. . .please let me make it back to Britain.*

Ted and Rocko pulled up on the left side. Robb pressed the mike button to tell Ted about the oil leak and thank him for shooting down the 109 and saving his life, but the radio had no side tone.

Damn it...my radio's been knocked out. Then it dawned on him that he hadn't heard a radio transmission since his feet had done the dance of death.

Ted pointed a finger at Robb, then gave the okay signal, asking Robb if he had been wounded. Robb shook his head no and gave the okay signal. Ted and Rocko moved to the right side to check for damage. A few seconds later, Ned pulled up on the left. Ted and Rocko turned back toward the bombers.

Ned and Robb set course for Britain. *Damnit...why isn't Ted taking me home instead of old shit face.*

By the time they reached the German-Dutch border, black oil covered most of Robb's windshield and canopy and the oil pressure had dropped from 75 to 60 pounds. To keep Ned in sight, he had to peek through a small clear streak on the side of the canopy. *A peek hole and a drunk...my only link with the outside world. Shit. . .this's 300 mile an hour solitary confinement.*

Over the coast of Holland, Robb saw the icy waters of the North Sea through a break in the clouds. He knew that if he bailed out in the near freezing water he would die from hypothermia in a couple of minutes. He double-checked the oil gauge. The pressure had dropped to 40 pounds. *Lost 35 pounds of pressure in 29 minutes...losing more than a pound of pressure per minute.* He estimated that it would take 22 minutes to reach Britain. At that rate, he could make it with 13 to 14 pounds of pressure.

But then he wondered if there was a true correlation between the oil pressure and the amount of oil remaining. *Maybe the damned gauge's inaccurate. I could have oil starvation and engine failure before the pressure gauge drops to zero. Maybe I should bail out over Holland rather than risking a bail out over the North Sea. Forget it...don't wanta spend the war in a kraut prison camp. Dredge up an ounce and press on.*

Twenty miles west of Holland they entered thick clouds, forcing Robb to overlap the wings of his 51 with Ned's. *Get any closer and I'll smell old shit-face's whiskey breath.*

Thin ribbons of black oil started spreading across his peek hole. His body turned to rock and his heart pounded. *SHIT...peek hole's about to snap shut...gotta hurry. . .find a new one before I lose sight of old shit-face.*

Robb's eyes flicked up and down, back and forth, frantically searching for another clear streak. He spotted one near the bottom of the canopy. *Gonna have to fly with my head in my lap to see out. Won't be able to check the oil pressure...can't do anything about the oil anyway...just hang on to old shit-face and pray.*

Robb leaned forward until the right side of his chest rested his right leg. He had to slide his right hand halfway down the control stick to hold it. He turned his head 90 degrees to the left and peeked out at Ned.

Having his chest in his lap and his head turned to the left short-circuited his senses and gave him a double-dose of vertigo—the worst he'd ever had. It felt like the two 51's were doing a tight barrel roll through the thick clouds.

Being rolled into a ball while vertigo hoodwinked his senses made seconds seem like minutes. After ten minutes, he thought about breaking away from Ned, so he could sit up to relieve the pain in his back and neck, look at the flight instruments and ease his vertigo. But he needed Ned's radio to call Air-Sea Rescue in case his 51's engine quit. If he made it back to Britain, he also needed a radio to get a steer to an airfield. *Gotta stick with old shit-face...he's my soggy ticket home.*

Suddenly he remembered that he hadn't changed fuel tanks in over an hour. *How'n the hell am I gonna switch tanks with my body tied in a knot? Crap just keeps piling higher.*

Another thing Robb's P-40 instructor had told him, "Being by yourself in a fighter where you're also the copilot, navigator, bombardier, gunner and flight engineer can sometimes change simple tasks into life threatening events that'll test your will to live."

Gotta think of some way to change tanks without slamming into old shit-face or losin' sight of 'em and gotta do it fast. THINK DUMMY. . .stabilize your bird with his bird then let go of the throttle and raise up...hold the stick with your left hand...change tank with your right hand.

But I'm workin' the hell outta the throttle just to hold formation. Let go of throttle lose sight of old shit-face.

Your tank runs dry you'll lose 'em for sure. So get with it.

Robb held the throttle with his thumb and forefinger to avoid overcontrolling. Gradually, fewer throttle adjustments were necessary to hold his 51 steady with Ned's. Eventually, a second or two passed before he had to make a throttle adjustment.

Feel like a blind man about to take my first step on a tightrope. Just dredge up an ounce and make your move.

Robb gently worked the throttle, until he got his 51 stabilized with Ned's.

GO NOW! His head and shoulders came up; he let go of the throttle and snatched the stick with his left hand. His right hand plunged like a piston to the fuel tank selector; he twisted it with all his might.

"Got it," he exhaled.

His left hand shot back to the throttle; his chest slammed back against his right leg; his right hand grabbed the stick half way down. He snapped his head to the left and peeked through the hole. Ned's 51 was gone.

RICHARD M BAUGHN

Fear ricocheted through Robb's body. His heart pounded, blood thundered in his ears and vertigo gave his senses another double tweak. *Come on dumb-dumb... look around for old shit-face.*

He strained to see ahead, but saw nothing. He twisted his head full swivel and peeked to the rear. What he saw made his gut wrench and he tasted bile.

"OOOH SHIT! " he grunted. Just behind his 51's tail loomed the eleven-foot propeller of Ned's 51. The prop's speeding yellow tips formed a circle that resembled a huge yellow lariat. A saw-toothed lariat—one rotation away from chewing him up.

In Georgia, Robb had watched a P-40 taxi into another P-40. Even at idle power, the smaller P-40 propeller slashed through the other fighter's aluminum fuselage as if it had been crepe paper. The P-51's prop at cruise speed would grind him into mincemeat.

Robb's eyes remained frozen to the saw-toothed lariat and he waited to die. But after an eternal instant something, he didn't know what, broke his death-wait.

He choked down some bile, gave his head another twist for a better look at the deadly prop. A neck muscle knotted; pain knifed through his neck and exited his ear. His jaws tightened until the roots of his teeth felt like they were being driven deeper into the bone. Racked with pain, he didn't care whether he lived or died.

"Gotta get with it," he finally moaned.

He blinked his eyes to clear the tears. Even that hurt. He held his breath, eased in the right rudder pedal, retarded the throttle slightly and his 51 inched back until it was in formation where he could see Ned without a full twist in his neck.

Robb inhaled and exhaled deeply to regain his breath. He moved his head slightly to ease the neck pain. Then he opened and closed his mouth to relax his jaw muscles and take the pressure off his aching teeth. *Dear God thank you.*

Ned looked straight ahead at his flight instruments, never once looking over at Robb. *That drunken bastard didn't see any of this. If the son of bitch had just glanced out to check on me, he could've easily moved forward and joined on me. My bird could blow up and old shit face Ned would take off his oxygen mask and pick his damned nose.*

A few minutes later, Robb had to make a slight turn to the right to stay with Ned, indicating that Ned had gotten a steer from a ground controller. Robb rotated his left wrist, looked at his watch. They were about eight minutes from Britain. *Oil pressure has to be low...engine don't fail me now...we're gettin' close.*

Without facing Robb, Ned raised his forearm, held it vertically and made a backward motion with his hand, signaling a power reduction. The two 51's started down through the dark clouds.

THE HELLISH VORTEX

At 500 feet, Robb got a fleeting glance at the North Sea through a small break in the clouds. Within seconds he and Ned popped out of the clouds and leveled at 300 feet. Robb moved his 51 away from Ned's where he could peek at the oil pressure gauge. It showed 15 pounds of pressure. *Hold baby just a little longer.*

Robb looked out at Ned to make sure they had separation. Then he straightened up, moved his head and stretched his back to ease the pain. As some of the pain eased, he became aware of the free-for-all that was raging in his bladder. The two cups of coffee and cup of grapefruit juice were battling for space.

Shit...forgot to take pre-mission leak after I got teamed up with old shit-face. Can't take a leak now while I'm rolled up like a ball.

The battle for space intensified. He fought back the urge until a stabbing pain shot through his bladder like a knife being thrust from the inside out. He lost control and tried to stop but couldn't.

"Might as well relax and let it rip," he whispered as he peed with reckless abandon. Warm urine flowed around the cheeks of his butt, raced along the inside of his thighs, ran down his calves, into his socks and GI shoes.

After what seemed the longest pee of his life, it stopped. In seconds, his urine-soaked clothes turned icy cold. His teeth chattered; he knew how the proverbial brass monkey felt.

Stop feelin' sorry for yourself and check your oil pressure. The gauge read 10 pounds. He glanced down at the North Sea. Strong winds blasted the foaming white caps, sending steamy sprays across the dirty-green water to the next foaming crest. *Bail out now winds'll drag me under and I'll drown...won't have time to freeze to death. Ain't that nice.* "Keep runnin' baby," he prayed.

Although it was early afternoon, the dark clouds and angry North Sea had already started to blend. But most winter days in Britain had no dusk nor dawn. Only shades of gray separated the long black nights. Since arriving in Britain, Robb felt a little closer to hell. *Today I gotta front-row seat in the devil's hangout.*

Ned signaled another power reduction. Their airspeed dropped below 200 mph. Robb pulled down his goggles and slid back the canopy's side panel. The open panel allowed him to sit up and look out.

With the straight jacket removed, he rotated his head to ease the neck pain, then stretched his back. After more than three hours of sitting on the cold, rock-hard dinghy, his butt not only ached, but the cold wet clothes made it feel like he was sitting on a block of ice. He shifted from cheek to cheek trying to ease the pain.

One-mile ahead, foaming breakers pounded the coast. He checked the oil pressure gauge; it indicated seven pounds. "Hold baby hold," he prayed.

Their airspeed slowed to 170 mph. Ned held up a closed fist with his thumb pointing down, then nodded his head. They lowered their landing gears.

As Robb's gear thumped down, he checked the indicator light and hydraulic pressure gauge to make sure it was down and locked. He pushed the mixture control to full rich, increased the prop pitch to 2700 rpm and checked that the fuel boost pump was on normal. He switched to the left wing tank, recalled how changing tanks had nearly cost him his life a few minutes earlier.

At 150 mph Ned signaled for full flaps. A quarter of mile ahead runway lights glistened in the rain. He and Ned were about 30 degrees off the runway's heading. *Huge runway...must be RAF Station Manston.*

Manston was an emergency field located about sixty miles east of London near Margate. Its two-mile-long and 300-foot-wide surface would allow them to land, even coming from this direction.

Ned reduced power; Robb moved in closer for the touchdown. But at 30 feet, Ned suddenly jammed on power and started a steep turn to the left. Unable to see ahead, Robb had to follow Ned because there might be something on the runway. He slammed the throttle forward to hold formation.

Riding high in the turn, Robb watched the first third of the huge macadam runway pass below their wing tips. He didn't see anything that would have kept them from landing. *Dumb son-of-a-bitch...there was no reason not to land. Engine quits now I've had the schnitzel...too low and slow to bailout...have to make a blind crash landing.* Robb's pucker string snapped tight.

They zoomed across small green fields with thick hedgerows, passed over a row of red brick houses—just missed a church steeple. Cyclists, pumping down the country roads, raised their red, wind-chilled faces and watched the 51's roar past.

Robb felt engine vibrations. *Gettin' rough...keep runnin' baby.* His pucker string crunched a peach seed.

Ned rolled out of the turn, throttled back. White lights, marking the end of the runway, passed beneath them. Ned rotated his 51 for landing; Robb followed. Both fighters made a three-point landing. Robb pulled back the throttle, then the stick and pushed hard on the brakes.

Ned added power, took off and headed for Boxted. The group needed every serviceable aircraft for tomorrow's mission. *At least old shit face got me back in one piece.*

After slowing, Robb opened the canopy, so he could see to taxi. *Runway's wide enough to launch a squadron line abreast.* He glanced at the oil gauge; it read zero. *Gotta shut her down.*

He taxied his 51 to the right side of the runway and cut the engine. After taking off his oxygen mask, he unbuckled his safety belt, removed his shoulder harness and unsnapped the dinghy from his chute harness. Placing his hands on the sides of the cockpit, he raised his butt off the hard dinghy. The cheeks of his butt felt like they had been impaled by the very bones they were supposed to cushion.

"Damned dinghy'll never win the *Good Housekeeping* Award for comfort," he grunted.

He rotated his head to loosen his neck muscles. Then he tilted his head back and faced the rain. The same rain that'd just threatened his life now flushed the salt from his eyes, rinsed the sour crust off his lips and moistened the sand in his mouth. But the rain had an odd taste. It reminded him of the burned sulfur matches he'd once stuck in his mouth as a child.

B-A-N-G! Robb jumped and looked down. An old snub-nosed truck raced directly at him. He tried to scramble out of the cockpit but the oxygen hose held him.

B-A-N-G! B-A-N-G! Two orange explosions shot from the truck's exhaust as the driver downshifted. The brakes squealed, the right front wheel locked; the truck skidded sideways. Two GI's in the rear clung to the wooden cab. The ancient truck stopped—a few feet in front of Robb's 51.

"Crazy bastard," Robb growled, easing his butt down onto the dinghy. "Don't need that kind'a crap after what I've been through."

The driver, a middle-aged RAF corporal, turned off the ignition. A big puff of black smoke chugged from the truck's exhaust; the engine clanked to a stop.

"It's back to bikes for you, Alf," one of the GI's growled.

"Up yur bloody arse, yank," the corporal yelled, then jumped out of the cab. "Looks like ye've lost a bit of oil, guv," he said walking toward Robb. "Hmm, ye've got some 'oles in 'er, too. Ye've 'ad a bloody go, yank."

"Yeah, had a little tussle. Happy as hell to be here. This's Manston, isn't it?"

"That's right, guv," the corporal grinned, displaying blackened rims of teeth, interspersed with yellow stumps. His bloodshot eyes sat in wrinkled nests below scraggly-brown eyebrows and above his cheeks that were reddened by a maze of tiny veins. He snuffed and swallowed, then wiped his bulbous red nose on the sleeve of his blue uniform jacket. "Ye looks all clapped-out, mate."

"You'll never be a stand-in for Cary Grant either, you bloke son-of-a-bitch," Robb mumbled to himself.

"Sir, climb down. We'll take this sick little doll to the barn, see what's ailin' her," said the American staff sergeant who'd been riding in the cab with the RAF corporal.

Robb unsnapped the leg straps of his chute, disconnected the oxygen hose from his mask and stood up in the cockpit. The breeze chilled his urine-soaked clothes. He stepped over the side, onto the wing and straightened up, but had to grab the windshield to steady himself.

"Let me give you hand, sir."

"Been flyin' with my chest in my lap. Guess my gyro's tilted."

"Understand, sir. Let me have your chute and helmet. I'll put 'em in the truck, keep 'em dry."

"We're ready Sarge," one of the GI's yelled.

"Okay. Alf, back around, we'll hook up the tow rig."

"In due course, mate." The RAF corporal unbuttoned his fly and releaved himself. He finished, buttoned his fly, then climbed inside the cab, turned on the ignition and pressed the starter. The engine groaned. He released the starter and tried again. On the fourth attempt, the engine clanked and coughed, backfired twice and started.

After the GI's hooked the tow rig to the truck, Robb and the sergeant climbed inside the cab and sat on the wooden seat with the corporal.

"You can roll!" One GI shouted, as he jumped onto the truck bed.

The RAF corporal pushed the accelerator; the engine's uneven clanking and popping changed to an unsteady roar. He pushed in the clutch, jammed the gearshift into low and the gears growled. He released the clutch and the old truck jumped forward.

"Take it easy, Alf!" one of the GI's yelled.

"Ye bloody bugger, if ye can do any better, get ye arse up 'ere!"

Bumping along the side of the runway, Robb shifted from cheek to cheek on the wooden seat, trying to ease the pain in his butt. This time the shifting reminded him of the song *Cheek to Cheek* that Fred Astaire and Ginger Rogers had danced to in the movie *Top Hat*. *Like to be cheek to cheek with Ginger now.* He smiled—his first of the day.

Black Nissen huts broke the greenness of the grassy area that sloped down from the side of the runway. The huts reminded Robb of oil drums that had been cut in half and laid on their flat sides. Nissen huts seemed to be strewn everywhere in Britain. Their ugliness clashed with the beautiful countryside and brought back memories of Goatshill. But today they were a welcome sight.

Robb thought about the ME-109's attack. *A few more rounds from that 109 I'd be marchin' to some goose-steppin' Nazi's bayonet. Or worse...I could be fish bait in Davy Jones' locker.*

While bouncing along the runway, a fine mist replaced the rain and the wind stopped blowing.

They turned into a taxiway leading to a large dark hangar covered with giant blotches of camouflage paint. The RAF corporal double-clutched and downshifted; the engine backfired twice; the old truck slowed. In front of the hangar, the corporal jammed on the brakes. They squealed; the right front wheel locked and skidded. The truck tried to pull to the right before it stopped.

Robb jumped to the ground, bent over and touched his toes. He straightened up, rubbed the cheeks of his butt and pulled at his cold, sticky long johns.

THE HELLISH VORTEX

The sergeant and two GI's pushed the hangar doors open; the dull-orange light shined on his 51. The sleek little fighter looked like a battered bird that'd been dipped in oil and dumped at the gates to hell.

A tall dark figure emerged from a puff of fog near the corner of the hangar and moved slowly toward them. The dull-orange light highlighted the gaunt face of a rawboned man in a black uniform.

"Suh, Ord, Salvation Army," he said, extending his huge hand. "May I be of assistance?"

"Robb Baines. Gotta check my aircraft, then call my squadron. Could use somethin' to eat. Haven't had anything since early this morning," Robb said, pulling his hand free of Mr. Ord's steel grip.

"We can sort that out, Lieutenant. You can call from the canteen after we get a spot of tea and a bite to eat."

"That'll be great. I'll check back with you, Sergeant."

"Never mind, sir. I'll come over to the canteen when I've finished."

"Been in England long, Lieutenant?" Mr. Ord asked as they walked along the macadam path next to the hangar.

"'Bout five weeks. Flew my first combat mission today."

"Heard over the wireless that you Americans had a big show today. It appears you took a bit of a bashing."

"Yeah, we ran into a bunch of 'em. Had an ME-109 work me over."

"This way," Mr. Ord said, turning onto a wooden walkway that led to an old unpainted building with the red and white Salvation Army shield above the door.

"Loo's out back Lieutenant, if you're so inclined."

"Too late, sir."

A smile softened Mr. Ord's gaunt face as he opened the door.

The thick stench of cooked cabbage hit Robb head-on. He stopped short of the door, took a deep breath like a swimmer coming up for air.

Behind the counter a chubby woman stirred the steamy contents in the large black frying pan that sat on top of a pot-bellied coal stove. She stopped, turned and wiped her hands on the soiled blue wrap-around covering her dark dress.

"Mrs. Walker, can you fix Lieutenant Baines something to eat? He hasn't had a morsel since early this morning."

"Ah've got some 'ot bubble-and-squeak. Ah'll brew-up a fresh pot of tea," Mrs. Walker's broad smile revealed two missing front teeth.

Robb wondered what besides cabbage was in bubble-and-squeak, but wasn't sure he really wanted to know. He had heard the British had a taste for hog brains.

Mr. Ord went to a small table with a telephone on top. He reached inside his vest pocket, pulled out a tiny key, unlocked the table drawer and took out a small medicine bottle and a glass. He pulled out the cork, poured some of the brownish fluid from the bottle into the glass and handed the glass to Robb. "Hope you like Scotch," he beamed.

In high school Robb had a drink of Scotch expecting it to have a butterscotch flavor. He recalled how the bitter-woody taste had made his stomach surge. But today his nerve endings felt exposed. For the first time in his life, he wanted a drink.

Knowing how scarce Scotch was for the British, he downed it, trying not to make a face. Its bitterness lingered while it warmed and soothed his nerve endings.

As he ate, Robb wondered why they called the overcooked cabbage and mushy potatoes, bubble-and-squeak. *One thing's certain it'll never ever win a gastronomic award.*

"Sir, we've finished our quick look at your bird," the American staff sergeant said closing the door. He took the cup of tea that Mrs. Walker had waiting for him and sat down with Robb. "Sir, the engine was completely out of oil and we found metal filings in the filter. It'll have to be changed. Also need some sheet metal work. You were really lucky, sir. Another few seconds, engine would've quit."

"You can say that again." Robb downed his tea. "I'll call the squadron, let 'em know."

After three tries, Robb got through to Captain Draper, the squadron operations officer, who told him to catch a train back to the field the next day.

"Think I'll go to London tonight, because it's on the way to my field," Robb told the sergeant.

"Good idea, sir. Quarters and food here are not the best."

WHAM! The front door slammed open.

"Gorblimey! Colder than a bum-boy's bumie in an outdoor bog!" The RAF corporal roared as he kicked the door shut with his hobnailed boot. "'Ow about some 'ot tea, dearie?" he said to Mrs Walker.

She glared then turned to help Mr. Ord install a blackout blind. Afterward she poured a cup of tea. "'Ere ye go, Alf," she said without smiling.

The corporal filled his red cheeks with air, blew into the cup of tea, then slurped a gulp. "Bloody 'ot," he croaked, walking to the table and flopping onto the chair next to Robb. He snuffed deeply, swallowed, smacked his lips and grinned.

Robb's nostrils flared. *RAF must be outta soap...raunchy bastard's 21 goat-power.* The bubble-and-squeak started to churn; Robb took a sip of tea.

"Alf, when you finish, we'll take Lieutenant Baines to Margate. He's gonna catch the 5:30 train to London," the sergeant said.

THE HELLISH VORTEX

"Ye goin' to London, eh guv? Blimey! You Yankee Doodle dandies know 'ow to fight a bloody war. A little fightin,' then bugger off to London for a lotta luvin.'"

Yank my doodle...it's dandy. . .you bloke bastard, Robb had wanted to say.

CHAPTER 3

A Touch of Heaven

Robb's ride from RAF Station Manston to the Margate train station in the open cab of the ancient truck seemed like a trip through the ice age. Inside the unheated station, he paced the floor and swung his arms, trying to raise his chill index.

The elderly stationmaster put on his uniform cap, twisted the ends of his white mustache and marched out of his tiny office like a regimental sergeant major and posted 5:24 in the arrival column on the lined blackboard.

Robb's watch read 5:17. He had seven minutes to go before he could begin to thaw out. Trains and beds seemed to be the only warm places in Britain. He wondered if the blokes would ever discover central heat.

At precisely 5:24 the trained pulled into the station. Robb hurried to his first class compartment the stationmaster had sold him without asking. Double-checking that the blackout blinds were secure, he huddled next to the compartment's heater. For the first time that day the nagging chill began to leave his bones.

Six minutes later the trained pulled from the station and Robb felt warm enough to take off his winter jacket and flight suit. He stuffed them under the straps of his backpack parachute, along with his leather helmet, goggles, oxygen mask, fur-lined boots and his holstered 45.

He peered into the compartment's mirror. The depressions left by his oxygen mask still lined the bridge of his nose and cheeks. He brushed his crew cut with the palm of his hand, tightened his white scarf and stuffed the ends inside the open collar of his green shirt. He tugged at his silver-pink gabardine pants, trying to smooth the wrinkles. In the warm compartment, he smelled the urine. He hoped it wouldn't be as strong once the pants and long johns had dried.

He sat down and opened the *Daily Mail* he had bought at the station. The date, December 20, 1943, jumped out at him. Tomorrow would be his twentieth birthday. He still had a year to go before he could vote or buy a drink in a stateside bar.

A year ago he had only three flights remaining before graduating from the Chickasha, Oklahoma Primary Flying School. He'd all but cleared the second of four major hurdles on the way to becoming an Army Air Force pilot. His ten weeks at Chickasha had seemed like heaven after the 119 days of pure hell at the San Antonio Aviation Cadet Center undergoing Classification and Preflight Training.

Due to the thousands of prospective cadets it had taken 21 days at the Classification center to complete the two-day physical and three days of psychological examinations, aptitude tests and psychomotor evaluations. The remaining 16 days were spent marching, running, doing calisthenics and pulling KP. Each day many aspiring cadets failed some part of the examinations and were washed-out. A few more got fed up and quit. Those who made it were stamped pilot, navigator, or bombardier. In the steamy Texas heat, Robb and his fellow pilot selectees marched across the road to Preflight School to receive their first round of intense academics, physical training, hazing and all-out culling.

At Preflight, everything had to be done in unison and by the numbers. Within days, robots could have performed no better. Cadets spent six hours a day, six days a week in sweltering classrooms, studying math, physics, meteorology, hydraulics, theory of electricity, electrical systems and the workings of internal combustion engines. They also learned how to use aeronautical maps and charts, practiced recognition of German and Japanese aircraft and were taught how to send and receive Morse code. They fired the 45-caliber pistol, carbine, Garand rifles and the Thompson machine gun. Many more hours were spent on military customs of the service and the West Point honor system. The remainder of their twelve-hour days included a two-mile run, an hour of calisthenics, barracks inspections, parades or just plain marching—all conducted beneath the boiling Texas sun.

Five-minute breaks became known as furloughs and many more aspiring cadets fell by the wayside. But Preflight had been designed to determine not only who had the ability, but also who had the desire to continue on to flight training. Robb breathed a sigh of relief when his name appeared on a roster for the Chickasha, Oklahoma Primary Flight School.

Chickasha, like most primary flight schools, had been a sleepy pre-war civilian airfield where a single aircraft taking off or landing could attract a crowd. Overnight the airfield became a beehive of activity. Cadets sang as they marched to classes and the flight line, while bright yellow and blue Army Air Force PT-19's swarmed overhead.

Civilian instructors conducted the ground school and flight training with a small cadre of military providing oversight. The hazing eased slightly and classroom instruction dropped to four hours a day. Cozy open bay barracks and innerspring mattresses replaced stark military barracks and Army bunks. A civilian restaurant with good food and operated by local women, supplanted a GI mess hall. For the first time since entering the Aviation Cadet program, Robb got every weekend off and could even leave the airfield to go into town. Everything had been done to make it easier for the 200 aviation cadets to concentrate on flying.

THE HELLISH VORTEX

Robb's first flight in a military aircraft had been a dream come true and would remain locked in his memory—forever. It was a cool autumn morning with a clear sky and a gentle breeze, a perfect day for flying. Dressed in his newly issued gabardine flight suit and leather A-2 jacket, Robb and his instructor walked toward the two rows of PT-19's with seat pack chutes slung over their shoulders. The low-wing monoplanes were parked wingtip to wingtip in front of four white hangars and their yellow wings, blue fuselages, red and white striped tails glistened with morning dew.

After completing the preflight checks, they climbed into the open cockpits, fastened their chutes and safety belts. Robb slid the gosport's rubber hoses over the metal tubes in the earflaps of his leather flight helmet that permitted one-way communications from the instructor to the student pilot.

Eddie Anderson, a fellow cadet from San Antonio, stood next to the nose of the PT-19 ready to crank the inertia starter. Robb had cranked for Eddie the day before.

"Ready!" the instructor yelled.

Eddie turned the crank with both hands. The deep growl of the flywheel changed to a high-pitched whine as it gained speed. The starter moaned when the instructor engaged the flywheel. The wooden propeller jumped; the 175 horse power engine belched blue smoke and cracked a steady beat. Eddie stowed the crank, pulled the chocks, jumped clear and gave a thumbs-up.

The instructor nodded and pushed the throttle forward. The exhaust cracked; the wooden prop slapped the cool morning air and the morning dew rolled off the windshield as they pulled out of the parking spot. They taxied onto the grass field and pointed the PT-19's nose into the gentle north breeze and stopped. The stick came back; the engine roared. The instructor checked mags then shouted into the gosport, "Ready mister."

Robb nodded.

The throttle went full forward; the engine gave a thunderous roar. The PT-19 rocked on its landing gear; its fuselage canvas buzzed against the wooden stringers. Robb pulled hard to tighten his safety belt remembering the story about a cadet who had fallen out when the instructor flipped the PT-19 up side down on the first flight. Most cadets didn't believe the story, but all of them took off with a tight safety belt.

The PT-19 lurched forward and bounced across the field gaining speed. At 70 mph, the tail rose and the PT-19 skipped from bump to bump then leaped off the ground and climbed through the cool morning air toward Oklahoma City. A patchwork of red and green rectangular fields lay below. A few were divided by angling creeks. Clumps of trees marked the red waters of the Canadian and Washita Rivers.

Soon, Oklahoma City's buildings broke the flatness of the plains. At 5000 feet, the instructor rolled the PT-19 upside down and jammed the stick forward to hold it level. Robb's butt left the seat, his feet fell off the foot rests and the safety belt dug into his gut. He grabbed the armrests.

"HANDS OUT!" the instructor roared into the gosport.

Robb raised one hand above his head, then the other. His head dropped below the windshield. His arms whipped and he had to lock his jaws and press his lips tight to keep the air from rushing down his throat. It was like hanging from a trapeze 5000 feet above the ground in an 80-mph wind.

The instructor looked back and smiled. Seconds later, the engine sputtered from fuel starvation. The instructor rolled the PT-19 right side up. Robb's butt slammed onto the seat. Gravity returned fuel to the engine and it regained its steady beat.

The instructor looked back again. "You okay, Mister?"

Robb nodded and forced a smile.

They performed stalls, turns, and chandelles until the instructor said, "Good flying, Mister. You've had stick time."

Robb nodded yes.

"We'll try some rolls and loops."

Robb nodded.

The instructor demonstrated a roll to the left and right, then shook the stick, "You got it, Mister"

Robb rolled the PT-19 to the right twice, then to the left. After four rolls the instructor demonstrated a loop and gave control back to Robb. As the inverted PT-19 started across the top of the third loop, Robb felt the stick shake.

"I got it, Mister," the instructor shouted into the gosport. He snapped the throttle to idle, pulled back the stick until the PT-19 went straight down toward one of the auxiliary fields.

"We'll shoot some landings," he shouted with the PT-19 standing on its nose.

Robb watched the ground leap at them. *When the hell's he gonna pull out?*

The instructor finally yanked back on the stick. Robb's butt jammed against the parachute's cushion. His arms and legs suddenly felt like lead and his head pulled forward. His vision got fuzzy and gray before he blacked out. He had learned about centrifugal forces, called "G" forces that pilots experienced during tight turns and recoveries from steep dives. The forces caused the blood to drain from a pilot's head and he blacked out.

Robb's vision slowly returned after the instructor had leveled the PT-19 at 1000 feet and entered the downwind leg of the traffic pattern. The instructor demonstrated a landing and gave Robb control of the aircraft. On the eighth landing the instructor turned and smiled. "Nice job, mister. Take us home."

Speeding through the clear blue sky, Robb wanted the feeling to last forever. His dream had finally come true.

A week later, the instructor mistakenly soloed Robb with seven-and-a-half hours instead of the required ten. For three days, Robb had been the only underclassman wearing solo wings on his flight cap. For the first time in his life he had made center stage.

Robb's time at Chickasha was the best ten weeks of his life. The airfield might change or even vanish, but he knew that he would never forget looping, rolling and spinning his PT-19 in Oklahoma's blue sky.

£££

"Suh, Charing Cross, five minutes," the conductor said. "Charing Cross, five minutes, suh," the conductor repeated while gently nudging Robb's shoulder.

"Okay, okay." Robb wondered how long the conductor had been trying to wake him.

"Charing Cross in five minutes, suh."

"I copy." Robb smiled.

"Over and out." The old conductor smiled back and saluted before closing the door.

Outside the station, cold drizzle settled through the blackness. Taxis and buses darted back and forth on the street. Their tiny blackout lights resembled fireflies on a hot summer night. All other signs of life were hidden from Nazi bombers. Robb walked toward the row of waiting taxis thinking about his dream. Charing Cross and Chickasha were a world apart and he wondered if he would ever see Chickasha again.

"Where to, guv?" the driver asked opening the rear door.

"American Red Cross Junior Officer's Club off Piccadilly, please." Robb placed his chute and flight gear on the floor. The soft leather seat felt good on the tender cheeks of his butt.

Passing through Trafalgar Square, the faint glow of cigarettes and blackout lights helped silhouette Nelson's Column. Crossing Piccadilly Street, the driver threaded his way through the stream of people, buses and taxis like a nocturnal predator. Three Piccadilly Commandos, bottled blondes wearing rabbit furs, hawked their wares on the corner.

Two blocks down, the taxi turned right and stopped on the left side of the street. "'Ere ye go, guv," the driver said opening the door.

Robb paid him and walked up the steps. As he opened the door, he saw a woman standing behind the counter. Beside her was a tall slender vase with a single yellow rose.

She looked up. Raven hair draped her ivory face and dazzling blue, cat-like eyes. The closer he got, the more beautiful she became. Her smile revealed even white teeth, something very rare in Britain. "May I help you, sir," she purred huskily, looking into his eyes and slowly twisting the slender vase.

His face felt hot and he started to sweat. "I'm...ah...Lieutenant Baines," he paused and cleared his throat. "I called from Manston for reservations." He wondered why such a beautiful woman with an upper crust, la-di-da English accent would be working at an American club.

"Oh yes, Lieutenant Baines." Her purr deepened. She swallowed as she stroked the long slender vase between her thumb and forefinger, keeping her cat-like eyes fixed on his. "Please fill out this card, Lieutenant."

His hand shook as he completed the registration card and slid it back to her.

"Only spending one night?" she asked, glancing at the card.

"Ah...I gotta get back...to my squadron." He never imagined a beautiful woman's come-on would make him feel intimidated.

"How long have you been in Britain?"

"Just a little over a month." A whiff of urine caused him to step back from the counter. He brushed sweat from his upper lip. "Need a bath. Must be 22 goat power." Beads of sweat trickled across his ribs.

"I'll put you in room 315. Nice and quiet and the bath is close by. By the way, my name is Joyce Freemantle."

"Ah...my pleasure ma'am."

"Would you care for a drink after your bath?"

"Yes ma'am." *Stop calling her ma'am, dummy!*

"I'll have one sent up. Now may I have my pen, please?" she said with a smile.

"Uh, yeah." He smiled sheepishly and handed it to her. More sweat trickled down his ribs.

Robb got off the elevator at the third floor and walked up the narrow staircase leading to his room. Inside, a dimly lit light bulb hung from the ceiling and a blackout blind covered the window opposite the door. Steel bunks lined three walls with a small wash basin and a mirror on the fourth. In the center of the room, two wooden folding chairs sat back to back.

After undressing, Robb slipped on his flight suit, wrapped his 45 in the white towel and tucked them under his arm. With two fingers, he picked up the lower half of his two-piece long johns, locked the door and went down to the bathroom.

A few minutes after returning, he heard a tap on the door. Before he could open it, Joyce walked in. She was carrying a bottle of Scotch and a bottle of seltzer and placed them on one of the chairs. Her perfectly tapered legs and rounded hips swayed with feline grace.

"Darling, close the door." She took two glasses from the shelf above the basin and sat down on the bunk. "Soda?" she asked, pouring two fingers of Scotch into each glass.

"Yes, please."

"Come and sit." She gave each glass a long squirt of soda and handed him his. "Cheers, darling," she purred.

"Cheers," he replied, wishing he'd said it first. He took a swig. The Scotch burned all the way down and he struggled not to make a face. After the second swig, he felt its warmth spreading through his body and he started to relax. "How long have you worked here?"

"I started shortly after the club opened. Wanted to do my bit. My husband has been in North Africa for the past 14 months. He is in the Fourth Indian Division." She took a sip and moved her leg next to his. "Now tell me about yourself."

Robb took another swig. "Not much to tell. As I said, I've been in Britain about a month and flew my first combat mission today. Got shot up, landed at Manston."

"But tell me about yourself, before this ghastly war."

Ever since his father's tragic death 15 years ago, discussing his past had been difficult. "Until the war, I had a dull life. Rather hear about you." He chugalugged the rest of his drink, poured more Scotch into his glass and gave it a long squirt from the seltzer bottle.

"Darling, would you freshen my drink?"

'Oh...uh...sorry." He fixed her drink, handed it to her, and leaned back against the wall, letting his left hand rest against her leg.

She let her right hand drop and gently gripped his. He pulled it free and put his arm around her. She lifted her head. Her cat-like eyes glowed and her lips parted ever so slightly.

When their lips met, her warm soft tongue searched his mouth. After several seconds, she pulled her head back, took a breath and whispered, "Darling... lock the door."

By the time he had locked the door, Joyce had taken off everything but her panties and bra and was sitting on the bunk. Robb placed his drink on the chair and stood in front of her as she unzipped his flight suit.

"Umm nice...darling. Take it off," she whispered huskily.

He peeled it off and she slipped out of her panties and bra and lay back on the bunk.

He knelt on the floor next to her and kissed her as his hands moved slowly around her body. Her skin was like velvet; the smoothest he had ever felt. He wished that he had another set of hands.

"Darling, just a moment." She removed the chain from around his neck that held his dog tags and dropped them. They clinked on the floor. "You don't need them, darling. I won't harm you."

She pulled him close and they became one.

Through the night they remained locked in one another's arms while the world around them vanished again, again and again. Finally, their tangled and exhausted bodies lay motionless on the tiny bunk.

£££

Robb opened his eyes to a dim gray light peeking through the crack around the blackout blind. He heard buses and taxis rumbling on the street below and squinted at his watch; it was 8:30.

"Shit, overslept!" Naked, he struggled to his feet and stumbled across the cold floor to the light switch. He bent over the washbasin and splashed water on his face and rinsed his mouth. *Mouth tastes like a garbage pit. . .wish I had a toothbrush and some paste.*

He grabbed the towel, wiped his face and looked in the mirror. A pair of smiling lips had been drawn with lipstick on the mirror and a red arrow pointed down toward the chair where he saw a toothbrush and a tube of Ipana toothpaste. He smiled and wondered if his breath had been bad last night.

His uniform had been pressed and a yellow rose had been placed in the buttonhole of his long johns rearflap. Robb felt them, expecting them to be damp. But they were dry. *She must have pressed them too.*

He removed the rose and tucked it in his chute, recalling how Joyce had cleansed his mind of yesterday's anxieties, death-waits and anger at Ned. She was the most beautiful woman he had ever seen. But more than that, she had made him feel wanted and needed.

£££

Robb opened the elevator door. Across the lobby he saw Joyce at the desk looking up a tall captain. Her blue eyes sparkled, as she smiled and took his registration card. The captain smiled back and said something. She nodded and stroked the slender vase that contained a fresh yellow rose. The captain looked at his watch and said something else. She smiled and nodded again before he departed. Her eyes followed him across the lobby and out the door.

Robb felt like he'd taken a blow to his gut. *What'd ya expect dumb-dumb? You ain't that charming. And besides she's married and outta your league. Just take what she offers and be thankful for that.* He took a deep breath and walked across the lobby toward her.

"Good morning, Lieutenant Baines," she purred.

"Hi." She was even more beautiful in the daylight. Last night in bed, he had felt her equal, but not this morning. Facing her up close in the crowded lobby with everyone watching made it worse and he started to sweat. He forced a smile, handed her his room key and gave her a dollar in American military scrip to pay for his room.

"Darling, you must be famished," she said, sensing his uneasiness. "I'll join you in the cafeteria."

"Yeah...I'm starved...gotta eat." He turned and started to go the wrong way, turned around, smiled sheepishly and walked toward the cafeteria. The long narrow room had a serving line on one side and a row of empty tables and chairs on the other. Robb carried his flight gear to the last table and returned to the head of the serving line. A young plump woman, in a white uniform, dumped a glob of greenish-yellow powdered eggs onto his plate. She picked up two slices of soggy toast from the steam table, dropped them next to the eggs and flipped a spoonful of orange marmalade on top of the toast. "Milk with ye tea, suh?"

"No thank you." He picked up a STARS and STRIPES and paid her thirty cents in scrip for the breakfast and paper, then walked back to his table.

Looking at the greenish-yellow glob of eggs made him smile. Swoose eggs, he thought. Half swan, half goose. He recalled playing "Kiss the Flying Swoose's Ass" back in Waycross, Georgia with his buddies after they'd finished P-40 training. One person called out the swoose's flight path while the kisser pretended to fly close formation behind it and tried to ease in and gently kiss its ass. The winner was the undefeated swoose-kissing champion from Bird City, Kansas, the birthplace of the swoose and sweese kissing.

Robb took a bite of greenish eggs and soggy toast. Better than bubble-and-squeak, he thought. He picked up the STARS and STRIPES and glanced at the headline:

NEW LONG-RANGE P-51's
ESCORT BOMBERS
DEEP INSIDE GERMANY

Yesterday, 48 of the new long-range P-51's, along with P-38's and P-47's, escorted 470 heavy bombers to Bremen, Germany. American fighters battled more than 200 ME-109's, FW-190's, ME-410's and rocket firing ME-110's. Fighter protection has been credited with holding the bombers' losses to 27.

Pilots of the new high performance P-51 shot down three German fighters and possibly a fourth, while losing three of their own. A damaged P-51 made an emergency landing in England. The P-47's shot down one and lost two, while the P-38's went zero for zero.

Senior 8th Air Force officials are jubilant about the P-51's superior range and performance. Major General William E. Kepner, Commanding General of 8th Fighter Command, said, "The P-51 is distinctly the best fighter that we can get over here...."

It has been reported that General "Hap" Arnold has given the 8th AF top priority for P-51 shipments....

Robb was struck by the inadequacy of the story. A few cold statistics laced with high command gloss and journalistic fluff. It didn't come close to reflecting the hell and fury of aerial combat, or the anxiety of flying through a crowded sky in some of the world's worst weather.

"Darling," Joyce purred, sliding her chair next to his. She sat down, placed her hand on the inside of his leg and looked into his eyes. "Darling, I've been thinking about you all morning. Wanted to come to your room, but I couldn't get away," she purred.

"I...ah...thought about you too." Her fine-tuned fingers tippy-toed along the inside his leg.

"Darling, last night was marvelous," she said huskily, obviously enjoying the power of her touch.

"Uh huh," he grunted, feeling like a puppet on a string—but wanting more.

WHAAAM! A pan banged against the steel steam table. Robb looked up. The woman behind the serving line smiled before she looked down and started to wipe the counter.

Robb's face felt hot; he pushed Joyce's hand away.

"Darling, don't worry about Ann."

"Gotta go." He said, sliding his chair away from the table.

"Darling, when do you think you might return to London?"

"I'm scheduled for a combat pass in a couple weeks."

"Here's my London address and phone number, darling." She handed him a slip of folded paper. "May I have your address?"

"RAF Station Boxted, north of Colchester. Don't know the civilian address. Mailbox number's 383." He glanced back at the woman behind the counter. She was still smiling. "Gotta go."

"Please write, darling."

"I will."

He grabbed his parachute, tried to think of something else to say. "See ya."

Before she could answer, he turned and walked away.

£££

"Liverpool Street Station," he told the cabby, still thinking about his abrupt departure. *What a stupid thing to do. That's the last time you'll see her.*

Leaving the Red Cross hotel the driver turned onto Bond Street, then onto Piccadilly. He worked his way through the mass of American GI's in Piccadilly

Circus. Even at this hour, deals were being struck with the Piccadilly Commandos, leftovers from the night shift--the ones with low customer counts. They had high mileage and no amount of face paint or hair dye could hide it. He wondered what their morning rates were.

On payday, some of the high-grade commandos got five pounds or more. Toward the end of the month, the rate dropped fast. A few days before last month's payday, someone supposedly set a group record when he scored with a run-of-the-mill commando for ten shillings.

The taxi stopped in front of the Liverpool Street station as a group of elderly English gentlemen hurried out of the entrance. Even in the gray light, their dark suits shone with wear. Walking ramrod straight, they headed for their London offices, with Laurel and Hardy bowlers sitting squarely on their white heads. Each carried neatly furled umbrellas and neatly folded newspapers. They resembled a flock of penguins scurrying for their daily catch. GI's, racing to board their trains, slowed and gave way to the venerable Englishmen.

The London-to-Colchester train accelerated through the outskirts of the city and into the countryside. Robb leaned back in the seat and closed his eyes. Yesterday his emotions had gone full swivel and banged their stops. He had a taste of hell and a touch of heaven. His night with Joyce had been like a dream, something out of a Hollywood movie.

He had thought about how much his life had changed in the past 18 months. Before joining the Army Air Force, he'd never been out of the state of Texas and his main modes of transportation in Austin had been a bicycle and a streetcar. Now he was in Britain, flying combat in the world's greatest fighter and last night he had made love with the most beautiful and sophisticated woman he had ever seen.

WHOOMP! From the compartment window, Robb caught a glimpse of four P-47's speeding north. They were flying at about 100 feet and quickly disappeared behind a hill. His thoughts shifted from Joyce to the war. Twenty-four hours ago he'd been eyeball to eyeball with that kraut pilot and nearly got his ass shot down on his first combat mission. Then he recalled how shocked he had been when Major Watson told them during the mission briefing they would be outnumbered in the target area. He knew they were losing hundreds of young men on almost every mission because there weren't enough P-51's to escort the bombers all of the way to the target. Being short of P-51's made no damned sense. It was an American fighter and the RAF had it for more than two years. Why didn't the USAAF have it?

We don't have G-suits either. How in the hell can the Army Air Force be short of so many things two years after the Japs' made their sneak attack on Pearl Harbor? One day if I make it through this damned war, I'm gonna find out why we were so poorly prepared.

CHAPTER 4

The Armed Forces Staff College
Norfolk, Virginia
February 21, 1955

The Army Air Forces and 8thAir Force during World War II

By
Major Robb Baines, USAF
Class 55A

Part I (of III parts).

Student comments: Since World War II, I have wanted to find out why the Army Air Force and the 8th Air Force had been so poorly prepared two years after our nation had declared war. My research revealed that the problem started with the birth of Army air power and continued through the First World War to the beginning of World War II.

£££

Introduction

£££

During World War II, the Army Air Force (AAF) snatched hundreds of thousands of "able-bodied" teenagers from the hangover of the Great Depression, swept them away on a wave of patriotic fervor, taught them how to fly and fight and altered their lives forever. As children, they had listened to radio shows, watched movies, read about the aerial pioneers and stared longingly at the occasional airplane. But until the war, becoming an Army pilot had seemed the impossible dream.

With a cause and innocence as their guidon, they became eager teenage tyros, flying and fighting in strange-sounding places. Combat quickly stripped away the shrouds of their staid pasts, taught them that death had been for all—at an age when they should have been enjoying the last carefree days of teenage bliss.

In the beginning, the tyros viewed the AAF as their patriarch. However, 35 years of neglect had left their patriarch struggling to find its place. When the war started, the AAF had only a small cadre of aviators and enlisted men, armed with a handful of obsolete aircraft. As a consequence, they were forced to fight all around the world while building an air force of nearly 3,000,000 people and 100,000 aircraft.

Everything had to be done yesterday or the day before. Glitches were aplenty and the acronym SNAFU (situation normal, all f---ed up) started its trek toward legitimacy. The Army Air Force's task could be compared to David collecting pebbles from a bed of hot coals while trying to slay a dozen charging Goliaths.

£££

A.   An Unwanted Bastard is Born

In the early days of flying, a pioneer Army aviator said, "If it won't eat hay, whinny and crap on a foot path, ground pounders'll never see a need for it as an instrument of war."

1. History is filled with examples of new and novel weapons being rejected out of hand by the military. Nearly 250 years passed before the English used the longbow to defeat a superior French force in the 1346 battle of Crecy.
2. Never known for its distant vision, the US Army delayed the use of repeating rifles during the Civil War. They were also slow to exploit the machine gun's firepower. Several years before World War I, they ignored a National Guard officer's proposal to develop tanks (the Americans had to use French and English tanks during the war).
3. It's not surprising that a radical new dimension in warfare wouldn't stir the Army's boots on the ground and body count mentality. Their view of military strength remained locked to horse and foot soldiers. No less than a directive from President Theodore "Teddy" Roosevelt was required to get the myopic Army to buy an airplane in 1908. That was five years after the Wright brothers' first flight and several years after European armies had recognized the airplane's potential. Teddy Roosevelt had insisted, because he couldn't stand the thought of Europeans getting ahead in powered flight--when it had been an American invention.
4. Hoping for a stillbirth, the Army gave the unwanted bastard a priority just below elephant saddles. When the bastard could be made flyable, airmen were permitted to circle the parade ground, but only after close order drill and the morning canter.

£££

B. Starve the Bastard—Maybe It'll Go Away.
    1. A comparison of several countries' 1913 military aviation expenditures reflects the United States' myopia.
        France $7,400,000
        Germany $5,000,000
        Russia $5,000,000
        England $3,000,000
        Italy $2,100,000
        Mexico $400,000
        U.S.$125,000 (US funding for 1908-1913, totaled $250,000).
    2. In December 1914, four months after World War I had started and Europeans had been employing airplanes in battle, the Chief of the

Signal Corps, who also was in charge the Army's aviation, told the House Military Affairs Committee, "As a fighting machine the airplane has not justified its existence...."

3. By the summer of 1915, European combatants had about 5000 first-rate military aircraft and 100 dirigibles. Back in the States, the Army's tiny air force of antiquated aircraft shared space behind the barn with heaps of horse manure.

4. The Army's neglect of air power was only a part of their pattern of flawed thinking. While Europeans battled in World War I with machine guns, tanks and airplanes, the US Army service schools continued devoting a lot of study time to Civil War strategy and tactics.

£££

C. The Bastard Gets An Emergency Transfusion

1. When the US declared war on April 6, 1917, the Army Air Service had "mushroomed" to 52 officers, 1300 enlisted men and 55 aircraft (all of which were too flimsy and underpowered for combat). General John J. Pershing, who commanded US forces in Europe, said when commenting on the Army's aircraft, "fifty-one were obsolete, and the other four obsolescent."

2. Major "Billy" Mitchell, the famed air proponent, managed to get to France shortly before the US declared war against Germany. Knowing it would take a giant prod to get an American air effort started, Mitchell helped the French military staff prepare a message for their Premier to President Wilson. Among other things, the message recommended the US produce 4,500 aircraft, train 5,000 pilots and 50,000 mechanics for the 1918 campaign in France.

3. Amazingly, Congress appropriated $640 million to cover the French request for air power. Unfortunately, America's aircraft production program failed miserably due to inept management, labor problems and corruption. A year after the US entered the war the Americans had built only one British designed DH-4. Wartime security masked the scandal from the public until a news story from Europe revealed that air units of the American Army were arriving at the front without aircraft. As a result, more than 5000 French, British and Italian aircraft had to be purchased for combat and training of American pilots in Europe.

4. Probably due to Mitchell's influence, General Pershing took the rapidly growing Air Service out from under the Signal Corps and made aviation a separate branch under his command. Pershing's action rattled the Army's general staff, but about a year later the enlightened general staff followed suit at home.

5.   The Army aviators quickly adopted the lessons of the Europeans and trained their squadrons. The first pure American squadron, flying French Nieuports, started patrolling the front lines in March 1918. By May, the Americans were flying and fighting with pursuit, observation and bombing squadrons equipped mostly with French aircraft.

£££

D.   The Bastard's Two Wars
  1.   Flying air-to-air and air-to-ground combat, in the highly combustible and unreliable wood and fabric airplanes, without parachutes, reduced a World War I aviator's life expectancy to about three weeks.
  2.   The more glamorous air-to-air combat pitted man against man in deadly duels reminiscent of jousting feudal knights. The aerial duels were made to order for reporters vying for a spot on the front page. Aviators like Germany's Baron von Richthofen with 80 victories; France's Lieutenant Fonck, 75 victories; Canadian Billie Bishop, 72 victories; Americans Eddie Rickenbacker, 26 victories; Frank Luke, 18 victories and Raoul Lufbery with 17 victories, became better known than many of the war's leading generals.
  3.   The air-to-ground mission lacked glamour. Diving through walls of lead to "hump" bombs, strafe or take pictures was just plain dangerous and no amount of pilot skill or experience could counter its deadliness. The results of air-to-ground attacks normally got lost in the maze of the ground war and very few of the "air-to-mud" aviators made the front pages except as an asterisk in the loss column.

£££

E.   The Bastard's Wings Spread
  1.   General Pershing promoted the talented "Billy" Mitchell to Colonel and put him in charge of American combat air forces in France. During the first American controlled offensive at Saint Mihiel, 12-15 September 1918, Mitchell's growing force of 609 aircraft was augmented with more than 700 aircraft from the French, British, Italian and Portuguese Air Forces. It would be the largest concentration of air power of the war and gave Mitchell an opportunity to demonstrate the airplane's potential and flexibility.
    a.   Mitchell's aircraft fought to keep the skies clear of German aircraft, bombed and strafed German soldiers in their trenches, attacked their troop concentrations and supply dumps behind the front lines (day and night), while bombing and strafing everything that moved on the roads leading to the Germans' front lines.

b. At the same time, reconnaissance aircraft took hundreds of pictures of German troop movements and other targets. Ground commanders were provided photographs, sometimes in less than an hour after the picture had been taken. Very few, if any, German units moved undetected.

c. Despite bad weather, which at times forced the aircraft down to the treetops, the air forces flew more than 4000 combat hours in three days. Mitchell's skillful orchestration of the multinational air force, which had been hurriedly put together, impressed General Pershing and he promoted Mitchell to brigadier general.

2. General "Billy" Mitchell got his second opportunity to demonstrate air power capabilities during the Meuse-Argonne offensive, 26 September through 11 November 1918. Mitchell's 740 American and 200 British aircraft faced a large concentration of German aircraft. Fierce air battles had to be fought for control of the sky to ensure freedom of movement in the air and on the ground. Losses were high, but replacement pilots and aircraft kept pace.

a. The American ground offensive advanced, then stalled when the Germans' defenses stiffened. At the same time, the German air force started attacking in "battle squadrons" (formations of ten-to-fifteen aircraft). Mitchell quickly countered with low-flying pursuit aircraft. His pilots used friendly antiaircraft fire to locate and neutralize the German battle squadrons.

b. US reconnaissance aircraft found a large concentration of German troops behind the lines being readied for a counterattack. Mitchell attacked them with 200 American bombers and 160 escort fighters, then quickly followed up with a second attack using British bombers. A total of 79 tons of bombs were dropped on the German troops—more than half of the total bombs dropped by the US Air Service during the war. The bombing and strafing blunted the German counterattack and contributed to the American victory that helped end the war on November 11, 1918.

3. General Mitchell's adept and imaginative employment of air power won him recognition and high praise at home and in Europe. In addition to his Distinguished Service Cross and Distinguished Service Medal, he received numerous decorations, awards and honors from the British, French and Italian governments.

£££

F. The Bastard Gains Legitimacy–In Europe

    I. Even in its embryonic state, the airplane proved to most industrial nations that a major part of future conflicts would be fought in the air. The British were the first to give air power equal footing with land and sea forces by establishing the Royal Air Force on April 1, 1918. Other Europeans followed suit after the war. Although Hitler and Goering didn't unveil the *Luftwaffe* until 1935, its development had started secretly in 1920. Closer to home, the Royal Canadian Air Force had its birth in 1920.

£££

G. Once A Bastard–Always A Bastard

    I. World War I did little to change the myopia in the US Army regarding air power. General John J. Pershing's voluminous *After War Report* all but ignored air combat. Pershing's detailed review of American operations allotted the Air Service one small, politically correct paragraph. The paragraph's size and fluffy content was a precursor to what airmen could expect from the postwar Army.

    2. General "Billy" Mitchell and others like Frank "Andy" Andrews, Henry "Hap" Arnold and Carl "Tooey" Spaatz knew that only the tip of aviation's technological iceberg had surfaced during World War I. They believed the airplane, if allowed to develop, would become a decisive weapon system.

    3. Mitchell and "his boys" helped spur enough public pressure for the Administration to evaluate air power's wartime contributions. After studying air operations in Europe, the team of Army, Navy and aviation industrialists led by the Assistant Secretary of War, recommended that a Department of Aeronautics be established. But in a blink the Secretary of War and Army's general staff rejected the team's proposal.

        a. It's interesting to note that the Navy representatives refused to participate in the final proceedings–probably because the Navy saw air power's potential as a fighting machine and wanted to develop air power on their own.

    4. By the end of 1919, the Army Air Service's strength plummeted from 200,000 people to less than 10,000. Their aircraft strength fell from 10,472 to 1364 beat-up aircraft, which defied good maintenance.

        a. Engine failures occurred on about half of the flights. Flying the beat-up aircraft could be compared to an infantryman using a rifle that was guaranteed to misfire half of the time–with a high probability that each misfire would explode in the infantryman's face.

b. In 1920, 69 airmen were killed in the "flying coffins." During
the next four years another 620 airmen died. The Army "ground
pounders" conveniently blamed most of the deaths on "fly-boy"
carelessness.

£££

H The Bastard Sinks the Navy
I. In 1921 Mitchell told Congress that air power should be America's
first line of defense because high-speed aircraft could patrol the coastal
waters faster and cheaper than the Navy. He maintained that aircraft
could destroy or sink **any** naval vessel and requested permission to
prove it by bombing surplus war ships. Due to Mitchell's popularity,
Congress and the Administration reluctantly approved the request.
    a. A few weeks before Mitchell's antiquated aircraft sunk a battle-
    ship, cruiser and destroyer, another Roosevelt—Assistant Secre-
    tary of the Navy, Franklin Delano Roosevelt—said, "It is highly
    unlikely that an airplane or a fleet of them could ever success-
    fully attack a fleet of Navy vessels under battle conditions."
2. Mitchell's success against naval vessels captured the attention of the
world and heightened talk of an independent Air Force, which sent
shock waves through the halls of the turf-conscious Army and Navy.
While the Army tightened their stranglehold on the Air Service, the
Navy quietly developed Naval air and applied their masterful political
skills to help stifle Army air.

£££

I. Keep the Bastard Hungry and Disorganized
I. In 1926, despite the Army and Navy's strong opposition, public pressure forced the Congress and War Department to increase the size of
the Air Service to an Air Corps. Although Congress authorized 2320
Army aircraft in 1930, they never funded the program. As late as
1938, the Air Corps had less than 1700 aircraft, most of which were
obsolete or obsolescent.
2. The Army also continued their heavy-handed tactics against the airmen. In 1933, only two of the Army's seven branches were under-
manned in officer strength. The Signal Corps needed 18 officers—
while the Air Corps had been shorted 368 officers—about 25 percent
of their authorized strength.
3. The Army's subjugation didn't stop there. Instead of establishing a
central authority for the Air Corps like all other homogeneous Army
functions, air units were parceled out willy-nilly to nine "territorial"

Corps Commands. Corps Commands, probably a carryover from the Indian wars, had commanders who knew nothing about air power. But like warlords, each had strong opinions how his air units should function.

£££

J.   If All Else Fails, Bastardize the Bastard

1.   The willy-nilly division of air units continued until 1935 when a presidential review board recommended some form of central authority for the Air Corps. After a great deal of study, the Army came up with what had to be one of the most bastardized schemes in military history.

2.   They split the Air Corps in half, separated the flying units from their support agencies and assigned general officers to command each function. One general had the title "Chief of Air Corps" and controlled procurement, logistics and training. The other general headed something called the General Headquarters Air Force (GHQAF) and he had control of all combat flying units.

   a.   Both job titles sounded like the man in charge, but neither was. They were coequals with the Army Chief of Staff as their boss. To help ensure a higher degree of divisiveness, the nine Corps commanders retained some administrative and court martial jurisdiction over the Air Corps units located in their territories.

   b.   Minor disagreements between the two Air Corps generals, or between the Air Corps generals and the unemployed Indian fighters, had to go to the Army's General Staff for resolution. Simple problems would be studied to death or trampled into oblivion by horse soldiers, cannoneers and footsloggers. Some of the Army's organizational geniuses referred to this staff process as "...salutary control by a beneficent general staff."

3.   Working within the "Rube Goldberg" organization had to be like residing in a house with the kitchen and bathroom located two miles east of the living and sleeping area. Then making the keeper of the house keys a disgruntled neighbor who spoke a different language and lived ten miles south.

£££

K.   The Bastard Gets A Big Bomber

1.   Some believe 1935 to be the year the Army Air Corps took off because that's when Boeing introduced the B-17. Over the objections of many

in Congress and stiff opposition from the Army and Navy tradition-
alists, the Air Corps received 13 B-17's that year.

    a.   The isolationists in Congress rightfully saw the long-range B-17 as an offensive weapon and they wanted only a few small short-range, defensive aircraft.

    b.   A need for long-range bombers, to strike an enemy's war-making industry has always been anathema to the near-sighted Army. Back then, as today, they wanted to keep the Air Corps on a tight leash with short-range aircraft and limit them to close air support for the ground forces.

    c.   Not wanting the Air Corps upstarts to invade their seven fiefdoms with a highly capable long-range bomber, the admirals also fought like hell to kill the B-17 program. During WWII, many of the same admirals reversed themselves and fought even harder to get the AAF's long-range bombers for their use in the Pacific.

2.   Undeterred, Army airmen sought every opportunity to prove their aircraft could fly and fight equally well over land or sea. One notable demonstration occurred in May 1938 when the Air Corps held air maneuvers along the East Coast. Part of the exercise included an air interception of an attacking naval force. But the Navy, fearing unfavorable publicity, declined an invitation to participate in the joint operation.

    a.   Not to be denied, the Army airmen decided to use the Italian passenger liner *Rex*, en route to the U.S., as a simulated enemy naval force. A young pilot named Curtis E. LeMay was the lead navigator for three B-17's that flew through bad weather and intercepted the *Rex* more than 600 miles from the east coast. On board the three B-17's were national newsmen and a well-known radio announcer who gave a live radio broadcast of the interception.

3.   The Army Air Corps' feat hit the front pages around the world. The Navy's powerful lobby immediately went to work to put the locks on their seven fiefdoms. The next day Army Air Corps planes were ordered to remain within a hundred miles of the U.S. coasts, and the War Department announced that no more B-17's would be purchased the next year.

£££

L.   Feed the Bastard (We May Need 'Em)

I. Italy's invasion of Ethiopia in 1935 awakened a few Americans to the possibility of war. Spain's Civil War in 1936 further defined Europe's fascist–nonfascist camps and in 1937 Japan invaded China. A year later, Hitler's saber rattling took on real meaning when he took Czechoslovakia by **coercion**.

    a. American Ambassadors Hugh Wilson in Berlin and William Bullitt in Paris advised President Franklin Delano Roosevelt that one of the main reasons the British and French backed away from Czechoslovakia was Germany's threat to unleash its superior air power.

2. Germany, Italy and Japan's aggressive acts proved to the American public that war could be imminent. A 1938 public opinion poll showed the majority of Americans favored a military build-up, especially air power. As a result, President Franklin D. Roosevelt became a born-again air enthusiast.

3. In November 1938, Roosevelt suggested that the U.S. start producing 10-20,000 aircraft a year. He later reduced it to 6000 because even that would take 300 million of the Army's proposed 500 million dollar budget. In January 1939, Congress and Roosevelt settled on a buy of 3251 aircraft. At the same time, they doubled the Army Air Corps manpower, authorizing 3203 officers and 45,000 enlisted men. But as late as April 3, 1940, Congress' political posturing slowed the Army Air Corps' growth by under funding the approved program.

4. After the Nazi's blitzkrieg of France in May-June 1940, *Life* magazine said the fall of France to the Nazis created a "chilling fear that the national existence of the United States might soon be threatened."

    a. Congress finally got in step with reality and public opinion. Republican Senator Lodge told General "Hap" Arnold, chief of the Army Air Corps, that congress would "provide all the money necessary for the National Defense, and so all you have to do is ask for it." Arnold stated, "In forty-five minutes I was given one-and-a-half billion dollars and told to get an air force."

£££

M. Run Bastard Run!

I. Presidential and Congressional proposals to build up Army Air leaped from one program to the next. In July 1940, the President asked for a total defense budget of four billion dollars, about half of which was for 18,000 aircraft. In December 1940, a 30,000 aircraft buy program was agreed to, but it quickly changed to 50,000 aircraft. Aircraft production continued growing and finally caught up with wartime needs in late 1943. The annual production rate peaked at 96,318 in 1944.

a. From July 1940 through August 1945, the US produced a total of 299,293 military aircraft. Of that total, 99,950 were fighters, 97,810 bombers, 57,623 trainers, 23,929 transport and 20,000 reconnaissance and special purpose aircraft.

2. Congress first authorized 24 air groups, but before the ink dried, they increased it to 54, then to 84 and eventually authorized 273 groups. In 1944, Army Air's manpower strength leveled at 2,400,000 military and 400,000 civil service employees.

£££

N. George C. Marshall Legitimizes The Bastard

1. In 1939, a year after President Roosevelt became an overnight air enthusiast, he appointed the brilliant and even-handed General George C. Marshall as the Army's Chief of Staff. Marshall immediately broke Army orthodoxy by appointing one of the Air Corps best and brightest, Major General Frank M. Andrews, as Chief of Operations and Training for the Army's General Staff. The job was considered a plum and was normally reserved for ground officers believed to have exceptional growth potential.

a. This would be the first of four key jobs General Marshall would give General Andrews over the heads of ground officers. In 1943, when General Andrews was killed in a plane crash in Iceland, he was Commander of the European Theater of Operations, the same job General Eisenhower had held before going to North Africa. People close to Marshall believed that he would have made Andrews a five-star general along with Eisenhower, Arnold and Bradley.

2. In September 1939, General Marshall advised President Roosevelt and Secretary of War Woodring that conventional Navy and Army coastal defenses could no longer guarantee the security of the US. Marshall believed the US had to secure its hemispheric flanks and ocean coasts in greater depth. He suggested long-range aircraft as the most economical means of extending the defenses.

a. As the US beefed up its coastal defenses, Marshall promoted Andrews to lieutenant general and made him the Caribbean Defense Commander. His prime responsibility was the defense of the Panama Canal. At the time, there was no more important command than the defense of America's lifeline between the Atlantic and Pacific.

3. Recognizing the clumsiness of the Army's organization, especially in relation to the Air Corps, Marshall sent a team to Britain to review the British military organization. In June 1941, the Army Air Corps became the Army Air Force (AAF), an equal partner with the Army Ground Forces and Army Service Forces. In November 1941, the airmen got approval for their own staff and all AAF units were placed under General Henry "Hap" Arnold. This move eliminated the thorny yoke of the Army's "beneficial" general staff and gave the Army Air Forces quasi independence.

£££

O. Adolescent Patriarch and Its Tyros
1. The nation became outraged after the "contemptible Japs" made their sneak attack at Pearl Harbor on December 7, 1941. Thousands and thousands of teenage tyros volunteered to fight for the AAF and small cadres of Army airmen stampeded to accept the rush of volunteers. Construction started on hastily established Aviation Cadet Centers and Technical Training Centers. Aspiring airmen had to be housed in tent cities while the construction crews played catch-up.
2. Since it took approximately 15 months to complete the basic pilot and tactical training programs, pilot production became one of the major limiting factors in the Army Air Forces mammoth build-up. The Army Air Force had warned Congress in the early 1930's, that pilot production would be a pacing factor in any wartime expansion. But congress continued to hold the Air Corps to 200 pilot trainees per year.
   a. From July 1939 to August 1945, 193,440 Army pilots were trained. In the process, more than 400,000 aspiring Aviation Cadets were rejected or washed out before flight training and another 124,000 washed out during flight training (numerous pilot eliminees became navigators, bombardiers or gunners).
3. In the beginning, combat requirements forced many Army Air Force pilots, navigators, bombardiers and gunners to go into battle before their tactical training could be completed. But the young tyros put their faith in their adolescent patriarch and made the impossible possible.
   a. They paid dearly, as they learned how to drop bombs and shoot, while flying and fighting from jungle airfields in the Pacific, crude landing strips in Asia, icy Alaskan runways and the battle-filled skies of Europe and North Africa. Their sacrifices and Herculean efforts contributed greatly to the Allied victory during World

War II and provided a solid foundation for the post-war United States Air Force.

£££

Student Comments: Aviation technology exploded during World War II. The teenage tyros flew higher and faster than most airmen had dreamed possible a few years earlier. The unsuspecting tyros helped usher in the greatest compression of time and space in the history of mankind, setting the stage for radical social change and unrestricted mobility.

If I appear to be harping on the US Army, Navy and Congress, it's only because I found so many instances where they tried to undermine Army air power. I've only included a few.

CHAPTER 5

A Tale of Two Songs

WHEEeeeEE! WHEEeeeEE! The shrill whistle of the London to Colchester train awakened Robb. He rubbed his eyes, stretched and felt the stiffness in his back and thought about Joyce. *After your dumb departure this morning you may never see her again.*

WHOOMP! Two Spitfires shot past, speeding east toward the North Sea. Their engine roar raised the curtain on the sights and sounds of war. As the train slowed down on the outskirts of Colchester, Joyce and London suddenly seemed a world away.

To the north, RAF student pilots in yellow Tiger Moths flitted above the grass field shooting touch-and-go landings. To the south, a convoy of Army trucks rolled along the highway that ran parallel to the railroad. Beyond the trucks, there was an ancient Roman wall, a relic from another unsettled period in Britain. Behind the wall, six anti-aircraft cannons pointed skyward like giant spears.

Gray barrage balloons were tethered over Colchester. They floated in the leaden sky like bloated whales.

A huge white billboard stood near the train station. The billboard's only display was one of Britain's main battle symbols—a large red "V" for victory with its Morse code equivalent, three blue dots with a dash below.

The train eased to a stop at the station. On the next track, Salvation Army workers passed out tea and biscuits to a British troop train. A group of junior officers stood outside their compartment sipping tea from large tin cups and smoking Player cigarettes.

In the next compartment, two colonels in immaculate mustard brown uniforms with red lapels and polished Sam Brownes, sat rigidly and sipped tea from white porcelain cups. With their swagger sticks at the ready and their bored eyes at half-mast, they exchanged a few clipped words from lips that hardly moved. They appeared as animated mannequins, a sign of their cultivated stiffness.

Outside the colonels' compartment a dour-faced batman stood at parade rest. The faithful orderly wondered when his turn would come.

In the winter afternoon's half-light Robb waited at the bus stop. Black coal smoke curled from thousands of red clay chimneys and helped to darken the gray overcast. A bomber rumbled east above the clouds and Robb wondered if his group had flown a mission today.

Four British soldiers walked briskly past. Their hobnailed boots clacked in perfect unison, as though they were marching to the cadence of a drill sergeant.

An ancient, white-haired Air Raid Warden hurried by with his white steel helmet cocked over one eye and his gas mask slung over his shoulder. He nimbly threaded his way along the crowded sidewalk.

An old woman came out of the greengrocer. Her netted vegetable bag contained an unwrapped loaf of bread, a few Brussels sprouts and a potato--her dinner and supper.

Down the street a Jeep backed out of an alleyway next to a pub. It turned and sped toward Robb. He recognized Big John and Corporal Perkins and he hurriedly stepped off the curb and waved.

Big John swung the Jeep toward the curb and stomped on the brakes. He had on a pilot's leather A-2 jacket, a white scarf and a garrison cap with a 50-mission crush. With the addition of a corncob pipe, he could've passed for a younger, larger and more handsome version of General Douglas MacArthur.

No other enlisted man could've made it out the front gate of the airfield in the unauthorized garb. But like the "old soldier" MacArthur, Big John had also carved out some special privileges.

"Perkie, put those boxes on the floor. Help 'em with his flight gear. Then get your ass in the back seat," Big John growled. While waiting, he tapped his foot impatiently and filled his lungs with smoke from the half-finished Lucky Strike.

"Thanks, Corporal Perkins," Robb said, handing his flight gear to him. Sitting down in the front seat, he wondered how many drinks they had at the pub. "Have a mission today?"

"Got scrubbed, bad weather," Big John barked before Corporal Perkins could answer. Big John floorboarded the Jeep and sped away.

As usual, Big John's brusque manner annoyed Robb. But he felt relieved that he hadn't missed a mission.

"Were ya scared Lieutenant, when you got shot up yesterday?" Corporal Perkins asked above the roar of the Jeep's engine. Big John eased off on the accelerator to slow down at an intersection. He took a long drag from his Lucky Strike, exhaled and leaned to the right, so he could hear the answer.

Robb couldn't believe his eyes. *First time the big bastard ever paid any attention to what I might have to say.* "Lots of things better than getting shot at. Scares the hell outta ya."

"Tell us what happened?" Corporal Perkins squeaked.

Big John continued to hold his foot off the accelerator and filled his lungs with more smoke.

"Ran into eight ME-I09's. Two of 'em came in on me with their guns blazing. I cobbed my Stang and pulled hard on the stick. My body felt like a I400 pound chunk of lead and I blacked—out."

Big John exhaled and flicked the cigarette butt into the street and snatched the pack of Lucky Strikes from his jacket pocket. He shook the pack, pulled out a cigarette with his lips, then stuffed the pack back into his pocket and pulled out his Zippo lighter. He flipped open his Zippo's lid and lit his cigarette. After filling his lungs with smoke, he snapped the Zippo shut, and stuffed it back into his jacket pocket. Smoke shot from his nostrils, as he exhaled without removing the cigarette from his mouth.

"Just before I blacked out, I saw my face in the rearview mirror." Until this moment Robb had forgotten about glancing at the mirror. He wondered why it surfaced now. "G's had pulled my oxygen mask down. Flesh under my eyes drooped and my cheeks sagged. Before I blacked out, I looked old. At least 40," he added, taking a dig at Big John.

Big John sucked hard on the cigarette and filled his lungs then exhaled through his nostrils.

"Just as I blacked out the kraut's cannon fire ripped into my 5I's tail. Rudder pedals banged the bottom of my shoes, stick tried to jump outta my hand. Thought I was goner."

Big John sucked hard on his cigarette and exhaled without removing it. A long ash dropped onto his lap.

"Still blacked out, I continued to pull on the stick. Rudder pedals and stick suddenly stopped shaking. I knew that I'd gotten outta the kraut's line of fire. But just as I did, my bird shuddered and tried to stall and flip out of control. I had to ease off on the stick pressure to keep from going into a spin. Blood gradually made its way back to my head and my vision slowly returned.

"The first thing I saw was that my 5I was standing on its tail and the airspeed indicator was heading for zero. So I quickly rudder rolled my 5I to get its nose down and ended up on my back. I looked down through the top of the canopy. The kraut and I were canopy to canopy, eyeball to eyeball. Kraut had the coldest blue eyes I've ever seen. Almost immediately, he started inching back where he could take a shot."   Big John eased the Jeep to the curb and sucked hard. A long ash dropped onto his lap.

"Because I was on my back and the kraut was right side up, he could fly slower and slid further back. Suddenly API's ripped into the I09. Lieutenant Tyler clobbered *der Fuhrer's* hired killer before the son of bitch could say *Sieg Heil.*"

"But how'd the German get on ya so fast, Lieutenant?" Corporal Perkins asked.

They know all about it. They're just trying to get some firsthand scuttlebutt. "Gonna have to sort that out later. It all happened so fast." Robb turned to Corporal Perkins. "What do you have in the boxes?"

"GI strawberries, for the mess hall," Big John snapped, as he slammed the gear shift into low and floorboarded the accelerator. He quickly shifted into second gear, and flipped the butt into the street.

"What are GI strawberries?"

"Prunes!" Big John growled and slammed the gear handle into high. "God damned recruits don't know shit," he mumbled to himself.

Robb smiled. *Had his attention for a while.*

xxx

Back at the squadron, Robb stored his flight gear in his locker and returned to the pilot's lounge.

"Cup of coffee, Lieutenant Baines?" Corporal Perkins asked.

"Sounds good." Through the window, Robb saw Big John lock the door on the storage shed behind operations. He crushed the boxes that had contained the GI strawberries and stuffed them into the 50-gallon trash barrel.

"Hey, Robb, welcome back," Captain Draper said, standing in the doorway. "Got a minute? Bring your coffee."

"Yes sir," Robb replied and followed Captain Draper.

"Cigarette?" Captain Draper asked as they entered the office.

"No thanks, sir."

"Have a seat Robb. You had a helluva indoctrination to combat."

"Yes sir."

"Ted did some good shooting."

"Yes sir. Saved my tail."

"We're putting him in for his third DFC. Lucky to have him in the squadron."

"Yes sir. I've learned a lot from him."

"Any Idea how that 109 got on you so fast."

Robb's face felt hot and sweat oozed from his forehead. He tried to think of what he should say. "Ah...a...I think Ned's attention may have been diverted." *What a bunch of crap. I should have said that Ned had his head so far up his ass...that he could've been a seeing eye dog for a proctologist.*

"Robb, you'd probably like to have a shower," Captain Draper said. "If you hurry, there may still be some warm water. I'll have Corporal Perkins drive you back to your hut. Don't have you on the mission tomorrow. Maybe you'd like to have a local flight, to wring out the kinks from yesterday's mission. Let Ted know. I'll set up a bird in case you do."

"I'll talk to Ted about the flight, sir." Robb stood, saluted, did an about-face and walked out, forgetting his cup of coffee.

After the icy shower, Robb hurried to the officer's club to get warm. He went to the lounge where a roaring fire was maintained in the fireplace every day from 5:00 to 10:00 pm. It was one of the few warm places on the airfield.

Ted was sitting near the fireplace reading the *STARS and STRIPES*. "Hey Robb! Heard you were back."

"I owe you for saving my butt yesterday."

"All in a day's work as our British friends say. Have you heard about Ned?"

"Haven't heard a thing."

"We've sent him to Standbridge Earls, the flak house. Doctor Herny went with him."

"Any idea what's wrong with him?"

"Yeah, but we'll let the Doc give us his opinion. How about a beer before dinner?"

"Sounds good. I'm buying," Robb said, entering the barroom. A half circle bar had been fashioned from wooden shipping crates and painted black. A hidden light shined on the iridescent nude woman painted on the front of the bar. Packing crates also provided the lumber for the ten white tables and their chairs, which surrounded the bar.

"Hey Robb!" Rocko yelled from the opposite side of the bar. "Glad to see ya, *amigo*." Rocko had a glass of beer in his hand and a second glass on the bar.

"Hi, Rocko. How are you doing?" Robb asked before ordering two beers.

"Doin' all reat, man. Thought that frickin' kraut was gonna cream your ass, yesterday," Rocko said as he walked around the bar to join Robb and Ted.

"Yeah. I thought I had the *schnitzel*." Robb handed Ted a beer. The three of them touched their glasses.

"Here's lookin' up your old inner tube, *amigo*." Rocko downed what was left in the first glass. He grabbed the full glass and moved closer. "Robb, ya hear Ned's at the flak house? Got that sumbitchin' Herny with 'em. Shit for brains hon-yocker's gonna hold Ned's hand for a week. Big frickin' deal."

Rocko took a gulp of beer. "Old Ned's got his ass in a sling. Gonna be countin' beans soon. Don't know what good that pussy-struck flight surgeon'll do. Like to buy the sumbitch for what he's worth and sell 'em for what he thinks he's worth." Rocko downed the rest of his beer. The bartender replaced the empty glass with a full one.

"Doc Herny doesn't suffer from an inferiority complex," Ted said with a smile.

"Yeah, there's hair around the sumbitch's halo," Rocko snorted. "He'd screw a snake if somebody'd hold its head. Bastard gets horny from bad breath...even his own." Rocko took a swig from his third glass of beer. "Sumbitchin' Herny's gonna come back with a story to please the moguls. Ned's had the *schnitzel*."

"Rocko, none of us want to lose Ned, if we can avoid it," Ted said. "But we can't let him jeopardize lives. Shall we eat?"

"Not me," Rocko snorted. "I'm havin' another blabber-mouth, then goin' to town for fish and chips...get laid."

RICHARD M BAUGHN

Robb recalled the afternoon he had reported in to the 345th Fighter Group. Ned and Rocko had been at the bar. Ned was a tall, handsome and well-groomed second lieutenant. He could've been a model for a recruiting poster.

Rocko's rumpled uniform hung loose on his short stocky body. His thick, tangled black hair needed grooming and the black stubble on his square chin needed shaving. He could've been a stand in for one of the Dead End Kids. He wore the rank of a flight officer, a blue bar trimmed with gold. Pilots who were not considered qualified to be second lieutenants normally graduated as flight officers.

Robb learned later that Rocko was the son of a New York City surgeon and Ned's father was self-styled preacher and junk dealer in East Texas. Ned and Rocko had been friends and drinking buddies since Primary Flying School.

Robb and Ted went through the serving line and helped themselves to the canned ham, dehydrated potatoes, mushy Brussels sprouts and bread and sat down at a table.

"Ted, I don't understand why Ned did what he did yesterday," Robb said after chasing a mushy brussels sprout with a bite of bread. "Flew damned good instruments, in that lousy weather. But when the krauts bounced us, he seemed to freeze. Doesn't add up."

"My dad says aerial combat causes four general reactions. Some people start aerial combat like tigers and finish like lambs if they don't kill themselves first. Others start as pussycats and become tigers then kill themselves. A third type'll maintain an even keel and get better with time. But some guys never get started due to intense fear.

"Previous achievements are not always good indicators of how well people will react to combat. Height, weight, education, or athletic prowess are not always good indicators. Some of the best fighter pilots are the underachievers who are hungry for recognition.

"But the overriding determinant is desire. Desire is the exponent in the fighter pilot equation."

"Your dad's a pilot, huh?" Robb asked.

"He started flying as an Army pilot in World War I."

"Has he been in the service all that time?"

"Stayed in for a while, but he got out when I was eleven."

"Where's your dad now?"

"He's a colonel, assigned to 8th Air Force Headquarters, at High Wycombe."

"Did your dad fly combat during World War I?"

"Yeah. He was General Carl 'Tooey' Spaatz's adjutant in France during World War I. Before the war ended, he flew 51 combat missions and shot down four Germans."

THE HELLISH VORTEX

"Wow! Why did he get out of the Army Air Corps?"

"He'd remained on active duty until 1931 when he got tired of the Army's meager wages. He had a degree in chemical engineering from Cornell and went to work as an aviation specialist for Standard Oil. But he continued to fly with the Army Air Corps reserve."

"When did he come back in?"

"In September 1940. He saw the war coming, requested active duty and came back as a major. When General 'Hap' Arnold sent General Ira Eaker to Britain in February 1942 to learn bomber operations from the RAF and prepare for the arrival of the 8th Air Force, General Eaker immediately asked to have my dad assigned to the 8th Air Force staff."

"Have you met many of our Army Air Force generals?"

"I know Generals Spaatz, Eaker and Doolittle. Met them while dad was in the service. He maintained contact with them after we got out. They were house-guests several times while we lived in California. Met General Arnold too. He came to the house with "Tooey" Spaatz several times while they were stationed at March Field."

"Robb, I'm not advertising this. You're the first I've told. The Colonel knows, but he's never said anything to me about it. If I ever amount to anything in the service, I don't want people to think it's because of my dad and his friends."

"I won't say a thing."

"Did you read the story about the big command shake up that'll take place on January first?" Ted asked, handing his STARS and STRIPES to Robb.

"No I haven't."

"Read this," Ted said, pointing to the story.

£££

NEW AIR FORCE
COMMAND FORMED

Washington announced the activation of Headquarters United States Strategic Air Forces in Europe (USSTAF), effective January 1, 1944, which will be located in Britain. USSTAF's commander will be General Carl "Tooey" Spaatz. He will command the 8th and 15th Strategic Air Forces and as the senior Army Air Force general in Europe, he will also have administrative responsibility for the 9th Tactical Air Force...

General Ira Eaker, present commander of the 8th Air Force will assume command of all Allied Air Forces in the Mediterranean. General James H. "Jimmy" Doolittle will replace Eaker as commander of the 8th Air Force...

£££

"Why so many changes?" Robb asked.

"Dad says General Arnold wants an overall commander of our strategic air forces in Europe to keep our B-17's and B-24's from being wasted on tactical targets that can be attacked by medium bombers, fighterbombers or artillery."

"Really a problem, huh?"

"Yeah. Most ground commanders don't know a damned thing about air-power's capabilities or limitations and don't want'a learn. They've never been hammered by an enemy air force and think our strategic air effort to destroy the Luftwaffe and Germany's war making industry is wasted. All they want us to do is kill enemy soldiers in the front lines. A few years ago one ground commander even suggested that airplanes be assigned to the Motor Pool so they could be dispatched like jeeps and trucks."

"What a dumb thing to say," Robb replied.

"Robb, there's another reason for this reorganization. Although our air forces in Europe will soon outnumber the RAF almost two to one, the Brit's have finagled all the key air command slots. As the senior American airman General Spaatz's will have a stronger voice in how our Army Air Force are employed."

"Sounds like a tough job."

"Yeah, it is. But "Tooey" Spaatz'll get the job done. Let's see what the movie is tonight," Ted said, sliding his chair away from the table. "Robb, I think you should get a local flight tomorrow. It's important to get back in the air as soon as possible after a close call."

"Captain Draper suggested that, too. I really hadn't thought about it. I just figured my next flight would be a combat mission."

"Robb, you had a triple whammy. You had to fly your first combat mission in crummy weather and almost got shot down. Then you damned near lost your engine before you made it back to Britain. An easy flight tomorrow should help limit the aftershock," Ted said with a smile. "It helped me when I almost got fried in that P-40 over Los Angeles. And my close call pales by comparison to yours."

"Guess I'd better take it."

"I'll tell Captain Draper after dinner."

Before going to sleep, Robb thought about his flight in the morning. The more he thought about it, the more he wondered how he would react.

£££

The next morning the roar of engines awakened Robb as the group took off for Germany. In two hours he would take off on his local flight and once again he wondered how he would feel after he got airborne.

"Sunhat, this Snapper 36, taxi and takeoff, please," Robb transmitted.

THE HELLISH VORTEX

"Snapper 36, altimeter 30.01, wind from 280 degrees, at ten, ceiling 1500 feet, visibility three miles. Cleared to taxi to runway 32," the tower operator replied.

"Snapper 36, taxiing." The Merlin engine cracked as Robb taxied his P-51 out of the revetment at 9:24 am, for a 9:30 am take off.

Approaching the end of the runway, Robb looked across the field at the green countryside. He recalled the weather two days before when he faced low black clouds, blowing rain, eerie white vapor cylinders and muddy plumes from the prop wash. It had been a different sky and a different world—a netherworld on the edge of hell.

"Cleared on and off," the tower operator transmitted.

"Snapper 36, copy."

Robb completed the engine checks, pulled onto the runway and stopped. He pushed the throttle forward to takeoff power and stood on the brakes to keep his 51 from moving. He checked the engine instruments. They were in the green and at 9:30 am; he released the brakes.

His 51 leaped forward, quickly gained speed and jumped off the ground. Robb raised the landing gear, held his 51 level at 25 feet, let the speed build and aimed the nose at the guard shack off the end of the runway. All the young guards had a standing request for buzz jobs whenever possible.

Streaking through the smooth clear air, it was difficult to believe that he was flying through the same piece of sky that he'd flown through 50 hours ago. *Weather has to be the Jekyll and Hyde of flying.*

Robb noticed a jeep parked next to the guard shack and eased his 51 a few feet lower. At 200 mph, the Jeep and guard shack rushed at him, then shot beneath his 51's nose. He horsed back the stick and climbed steeply. Just below the clouds, he rolled his 51 upside down, lowered its nose, then rolled right side up and dived. At 50 feet, he pulled up in a steep climb and zoomed into the thick gray overcast.

At 6000 feet he shot out of the gray clouds into the clear blue sky. After the gray half-light, the sun's powerful rays exploded in his eyes like a million flashbulbs.

As always, the sun's rays turned the gray clouds to snowy white. He squinted until his eyes adjusted. Racing through the brilliant blue sky above the white undercast was like a double-guzzle from Doctor Jekyll's renewal portion.

He let his 51 skim the clouds puffy tops. After a few seconds, he pulled up and turned, then looked back. Dancing white twirls lined each side of the wake created by the prop wash. The twirling slowed and settled into the snowy whiteness.

Robb dived and leveled at 50 feet above the clouds and flipped his 51 up side down. He rolled in forward trim to hold his 51 level. Negative G's forced him against the safety belt. Dirt, a piece of safety wire, a cigarette butt and a pencil fell from the cockpit floor and rattled along the top of the Plexiglas canopy.

White clouds cascaded a few feet below Robb's head, giving him the greatest sensation of speed he had ever experienced.

Suddenly on his right he noticed his 51's shadow leaping across the uneven clouds like a playful pup chasing its master.

Robb rolled his 51 right side up; the debris dropped in front of him. He grabbed the wire and pencil and stuffed them into a flight suit pocket. Easing his 51 up to 200 feet above the clouds, he slammed the stick to the right, stomped on the right rudder and rolled his 51. It twisted like a high-speed corkscrew. The blue sky and white clouds swapped places again, again, and again.

Each time his 51 was on its back, Robb got a glimpse of its winged shadow a few feet below in perfect formation. He rolled right side up and added power, then did a series of steep climbs and dives, fast rolls and tight turns, trying to lose the shadow. But the shadow hung in there—matched him trick for trick, G for G.

Robb recalled the song *Me and My Shadow*, first made popular by vaudeville star Ted Lewis during the 1930's. In the movie he made, Ted wore a top hat, tails and carried a cane, while he sang and danced back and forth across the stage. A black man in a top hat, tails and cane, mimicked Ted's every move.

Shortly before the war, "The Ink Spots" recorded *Me and My Shadow*. It became a hit and one of Robb's favorites.

While watching his 51's shadow frolic across the white clouds, Robb whispered the words that Lewis and the Ink Spots had sung. *"Me and my shadow. . .strolling down the avenue. Me and my shadow. . .not a soul to tell our troubles to. And when its twelve o'clock. . .we climb the stair. . .we never knock. . .for nobody's there. Just me and my shadow. . .all alone and feeling blue. . .."*

Robb continued to rack his 51 around the sky until he felt like he was part of his 51. Wanting to hone his fighting skills, he scanned the sky for other fighters but found none. So he continued to rat race with the shadow until it was time to land.

He called for a steer to the field and descended toward the white undercast. In the descent, the shadow moved in closer and closer. Robb leveled ten feet above the clouds. Several times the 51 skimmed a fuffly bubble in the clouds and the shadow leaped higher like a pup begging for the play not to end.

Robb saluted the shadowy playmate then eased the stick forward. His 51's pointed nose speared the white fluffiness and the shadow disappeared.

In seconds he was below the clouds, in the gray half-light. He turned southeast to fly around Colchester and get lined up with the runway. In the turn, he hummed *"Me and My Shadow"* again.

THE HELLISH VORTEX

Three miles from the airfield, Robb put his 51 into a dive and leveled off at 50 feet. Over the end of the runway he pulled up into a steep climbing turn, chopped the throttle to idle, increased the prop pitch to full, lowered the landing gear, then the flaps, and turned to the final approach. His 51 glided over the airfield fence and touched down near the end of the runway.

Rolling down the runway, he hummed another chorus of *"Me and My Shadow."* The ominous kinks had gone into remission to await the next deadly encounter.

£££

Big John sat in the passenger's seat of the Jeep parked next to the guard shack. Inside the shack Corporal Perkins waited as the MP copied the information off the trip ticket. Behind the guard the large wall clock read 9:30 am.

Across the field a P-51 roared down the runway. Its Merlin engine growled louder and louder as it got closer.

WHOOOMP! The 51 shot past, 20 feet above the ground. Prop wash blasted the guard shack; its plywood walls rattled and one of the Plexiglas windows blew out.

Corporal Perkins and the MP scrambled outside to watch. The 51 climbed, rolled, dived, then shot up into the clouds.

Sprawled on the ground, next to the Jeep, lay Big John.

"Lose something, Big John," the young MP said with a smile.

"Just take care of that frickin' trip ticket, junior," Big John growled, getting to his feet. He straightened his sunglasses, fluffed the 50-mission crush in his garrison hat, adjusted his white scarf, flicked mud off his leather A-2 flight jacket and got back into the Jeep

"Wasn't that exciting?" Corporal Perkins squeaked, climbing in behind the steering wheel.

"That second balloon Baines is got shit for brains. Gonna kill somebody."

"I liked it," Perkins said.

"Who in the hell asked ya?"

Five miles down the narrow country road, Big John spied a brick house. Behind the house were six long buildings, each with adjoining pens. The pens were filled with chickens.

"Turn in here," Big John yelled. "Biggest egg orchard ever seen."

Corporal Perkins downshifted, jammed on the brake and turned. He followed the gravel drive to the back of the house and stopped.

"Wait here." Big John grabbed the brown paper bag from under the seat, walked to the back door and knocked.

A tall woman with broad shoulders and breasts that strained the bib of her overalls opened the door. Her green eyes moved slowly from Big John's eyes to his feet and back again. She smiled, revealing a missing front tooth and blood oozing from a crack in her chapped lips. She licked away the blood, fluffed her scraggly brown hair with her big weather-beatened red hand.

"May ah 'elp ye, suh?"

The stench of chicken dung filled his nostrils. "M'am, sorry to bother ya. I'm from..."

"No bother, me good man," she interrupted.

"Well m'am, ya see, I'm from Boxted airfield lookin' for fresh eggs for my fighter pilots. Saw your chicken ranch and thought we could work somethin' out."

"What's ye name, Yank?"

"John Burnham, m'am. But most call me Big John."

Her green eyes danced; she smiled and licked away more blood. "Me name is Veronica Strawson."

"Pleased to meet ya, m'am."

"Ye wants to discuss business, eh?"

"I was hopin' to, m'am."

"Wanta bring your driver in out of the cold?"

"Naw, he's okay."

She stepped back, "Parlour's on the right. Could ah offer ye a spot of tea?"

"Not much for tea, m'am."

"Ah see. And what are you for, mate?" she smiled and licked.

"Maybe a swig of Scotch." He held up the brown bag and smiled.

"Ye 'ave spirits, eh Yank?" She fluffed her hair.

"Yeah," he said pulling the 16-ounce Heinz vinegar bottle from the paper bag.

"Blimey, that would be nice," she said seeing the bottle filled with Scotch. "Ah'll fetch some glasses."

Big John filled both glasses halfway and handed one to her. "Here's to ya," he said, raising his glass.

"Ta. Cheers, chum." She clutched the glass in her big meaty hand and downed the Scotch in one gulp.

He stared in disbelief. "Want another?"

She nodded.

He refilled her glass.

She grabbed the glass and downed half of it in one gulp, then smacked her lips and wiped her mouth on the back of her hand. "Cawn't recalll 'ow long it's been since ah 'ad meself some Scotch," she said, then downed the rest and placed the empty glass on the table. "Ah've done little else then work for the past two years. Me 'usband's in the King's service. 'E's a lance corporal in North Africa. Ah never goes to me local any more. Nothin' but layabouts there tryin' to pinch a few bob off ye and what ever else they can pinch," she said with a smile. "Runnin' this farm by meself 'as been bloody awful. Well, now. What's this about ieggs?"

"Need fresh eggs to feed my fighter pilots before a combat mission."

"Ye know the bloody ieggs are rationed. Ye think it wise to deal in the black-market, mate?"

"Other units are gettin' eggs and I'm not."

"Pity ye're not getting any." She smiled and licked more blood. "Since ye want them for combat pilots, we might sort it out. 'Ow much are ye willin' to pay?"

"Make me an offer."

"Six bob a dozen to make it worth me while."

"Man! That's a bunch. Nearly a buck-fifty American. That's way too much."

"That's a lotta cock, mate. Unlikely ye can get 'em for less. Being a spive is risky business. Me toffee-nosed neighbors. . .scupper me in a blink if they found out ah was dealing in the black-market."

"How many dozen a week can you sell?"

"Can let ye have all ye want." She smiled and licked.

"Need 36 dozen a week," Big John smiled. "You cover that?"

"Of course. Bring a Jeep with a top and sides so me toffee-nosed neighbors cawn't see the bloody crates."

"Fair enough. Well mam, got just enough Scotch for another blast to close the deal."

"Bloody good. But please call me Veronica. Let me put a record on the gramophone." She pulled the thick record from the cabinet, placed it on the turntable then wound the old phonograph's crank until it was tight. She flicked the mechanical lock and the turntable squeaked as it started to rotate and slowly built up speed. She moved the arm and lowered the needle onto the record.

Big John recognized the scratchy rendition of George Gershwin's 1926 *Do-Do-Do*. It reminded him of his favorite bar in the Philippines. He handed Veronica her glass.

"Cheers, dearie." She fluffed her hair, raised the glass with her little finger extended and gulped down the Scotch.

Then she placed the empty glass on the table. "Ah feels so tiddly," she said putting her hand on Big John's leg. "'Aven't felt this way since me 'usband shipped. Ah've been so wretchedly lonely," she sighed as she squeezed his leg.

"I'll bet ya have," Big John said, as he pulled on her hand, trying to remove her vice-like grip from his leg.

She yanked her hand loose, swung her arms around him, pulled him close and planted her lips on his. Her big tongue searched his mouth as she squeezed him hard.

"Uuuuh," he groaned. He pulled his head back, wiped the blood off his lips with the back of his hand. "Ease off, Veronica. Don't be so damned rough."

"Blimey, ah don't know what's gotten into me. Take off your clothes, Jonny.

They scrambled to get undressed and stretched out on the couch. The voice from the scratchy record sang, *"Do, do, do what you've done, done before. . .baby. Do, do, do what I adore. . .baby. Let's try again. . .sigh again. . .Di-de, di-de, di-di-di. . .."*

"Ooooh, dearie," she moaned, as the song's second chorus began.

"So do, do, do. . .what you've done, done, done before. . ."

"No wonder they calls ye Big John," she purred.

CHAPTER 6

Christmas

Robb's flight with his *shadow* was followed by two days of freezing rain, which covered East Anglia with a layer of ice and grounded the 8th AF. The cold dreary days passed slowly and several times he thought about his Goxhill flight and first combat mission. Each time he wondered if he might be one of the so-called "hard-luck pilots" who had one close call after another before being killed.

On the evening of December 23rd, Robb, Ted and Rocko went to the club to watch the movie *Casablanca*. Shortly after it started, the loud speaker system roared, "All maintenance, communications, armament and supply officers report for duty, immediately."

The word soon spread that the freezing rain had stopped and a big mission had been scheduled for the next morning. Within an hour, Merlin engines growled from the run-up stands and 50-caliber machine guns cracked at the boresight target as ground crews readied their aircraft. Robb had trouble concentrating on the movie, wondering what his next combat mission would bring.

Before going to sleep, he prayed that he would make it back to Boxted for dinner the next night.

£££

"Briefing in an hour and a half," the duty sergeant said, turning on the dim ceiling light bulb.

Robb rolled onto his back, peeked out from under the scratchy blankets and exhaled. He saw his breath in the dim light. Then felt it settle onto his face. Remaining under the blankets, he grabbed his pants, shirt and second pair of socks and put them on, then kicked the blankets back. He slipped on his winter flying jacked and put on his shoes.

"Sumbitch, it's cold. Freeze the frickin' balls off a brass monkey." Rocko's gruff voice was always raspier in the morning.

"Yeah. Tin hut's like an ice house." Robb looked for Ted, but he was gone and his bunk was made.

"Had a frickin' dream about last night's movie. I cut old Humphrey Go-cart outta the traffic pattern and teamed up with Ingrid," Rocko grinned as he approached Robb's bunk.

RICHARD M BAUGHN

"Uh huh. We'd better get going so we don't have to stand in line at the latrine," Robb said, picking up his toothbrush and Ipana toothpaste.

After their trip through the cold black morning to the latrine, Robb and Rocko scrambled aboard the waiting GI truck and hunched behind the fur collars of their jackets. The last pilot climbed in and someone in the front of the truck bed pounded on the cab's steel roof. As the truck raced down the country lane Robb wondered if his luck would run out today.

Approaching operations, the driver double clutched and downshifted. The gears growled and the engine backfired. The pilots grabbed the wooden bench and braced themselves. The brakes squealed and the truck jerked to a stop in front of the large black Nissen huts. The pilots jumped out and scrambled to the warmth of their squadron lounges.

"Hurry up, guys," Ted called from the end of the snack bar. "We have fresh eggs...two bits a piece. Covers the special handling charges," he said with a wink and smile.

"Sumbitch. At that frickin' price, they must've come from the King's royal hen house. *C'est la guerre*," Rocko grunted. "I'll have four over easy. Only costs 200 percent more to go first class," he said with a grin. "Haven't had a fresh egg since I shacked up with a farmer's daughter in Arkansas while at primary flight school."

Big John scooped four eggs, two slices of Spam and a thick slice of bread from the kerosene grill, dropped them onto the tin plate and banged the plate on the counter. Corporal Perkins shoved the plate and a cup of grapefruit juice toward Rocko.

"I'll have two over easy." Robb said, trying to remember when he had his last fresh eggs.

Big John scooped two more eggs, Spam and bread onto a plate, handed the plate to Corporal Perkins and refilled the grill with eggs, Spam and bread. Then he made two entries in his notebook.

"Here you go, Lieutenant Baines," Corporal Perkins squeaked, sliding the plate and cup of juice in front of Robb.

"Thank you, Corporal Perkins." Robb took his breakfast to the end of the bar next to Ted and Rocko.

"Colonel's leading our squadron today," Ted said. "Since our flight's short-handed, the three of us are flying with him. And Robb, I scheduled you to fly his wing."

"Hey, *amigo*, you made the first team," Rocko grinned.

"How come I'm so lucky. Rather be Green 16."

"Just relax, Robb. He's as smooth as silk until he gets into a fight," Ted said with a smile.

74

THE HELLISH VORTEX

The MP found their names on the mission roster, checked their ID cards and motioned them inside the group briefing room. Once again, the carnival-like room with its seemingly endless array of colors and information planted more seeds of doubt in Robb's mind.

"Sumbitch. Moguls must've run outta colored string," Rocko grunted. The colored yarn, marking the bomber's route of flight on the big map of Europe, only went as far as Calais. "That can't be the frickin' target."

"That's it," Ted replied.

"Sumbitch, Calais. Old Santa must've laid on this frickin' mission. Can fly it with one foot on the cliffs of Dover. My kind'a combat."

"Wonder what the krauts have at Calais that's so important?" Robb asked, feeling relieved they weren't going deep inside Germany.

"Don't know, but I'm certain Major Watson will give us all the melodramatic details," Ted replied.

Robb sat next to the Colonel's striped chair and watched the adjutant twiddle the tip end of the cue stick between his thumb and forefinger. But in the corner of his eye he could see the striped chair. He wanted to touch it, but didn't.

At 6:59 am, the adjutant glanced at his watch, then the wall clock. He carefully leaned the cue stick against the lectern and walked briskly down the aisle to the door. Silence spread across the room and the lights seemed to shine brighter on the Colonel's striped chair.

"HOFFICERS, TEN–SHUN!" the adjutant roared.

"Please be seated, gents," the Colonel said as he entered. He stopped next to his chair, turned and faced the pilots. "I have some bad news. In the past three days, 15 people in the group have come down with the flu. Last night two pilots got it. They have been isolated to keep it from spreading. So if you start to feel bad, get to the dispensary right away. I'm cancelin' all combat passes for pilots until we get through this mess.

"Now for the business at hand. Our mission today looks like a real milk run. But don't drop your guard; I've tangled with a lotta krauts around Calais. Stormy, give us a break on the weather," the Colonel smiled. He sat down, leaned to his left and said in a hushed voice, "Mornin', Robb."

"Uh, ah, " Robb cleared his throat. "Good morning, sir," he finally whispered.

"Sir, we have good weather today." Captain Knight smiled and took the cue stick. "You'll have 1000 feet ceiling and two miles visibility for take off and should have 1200 and three for landing. There'll be very few clouds in the target area, so the bombers should have no problem seeing their aiming points. But tonight more bad weather will move in from the Atlantic...." Captain Knight finished and held the cue stick for Major Watson.

Major Watson took the cue stick and strutted to center stage. "We've been requested by the British to strike some construction sites near Calais. Although we haven't been told the nature of the construction sites, British sources from my days at State tell me that they are to be German missile launching sites. British intelligence has known about them for months, but for some unknown reason they just told the 8th Air Force about them a few days ago," he said.

"Aerial photos show several large concrete buildings and a series of concrete launching ramps that are under construction. Ramps resemble small ski jumps whose axes all point at Britain. The reinforced concrete buildings are probably missile storage and maintenance facilities...." Watson finished and handed the cue stick to Major Hunt.

"Today the 8th Air Force will launch the largest mission it has ever flown. Nearly 700 bombers will attack these construction sites. Our group has been tasked to conduct a combat air patrol around Calais," Major Hunt said. "We'll split up by squadrons. Snapper will patrol on the east side of Calais, Bugeye will cover the south and Hot Rod will take the west side. Keep your eyes open because the Krauts have been known to fly during the Yuletide season. Sir," he held the cue stick for the Colonel.

"I don't need it, Bob. Not much to say. Gents, just keep your guard up, your eyes peeled and fly smart so you don't get caught with your pants at half-mast and not make it back for Christmas Eve. Okay, let's get strapped up and have at the bastards."

Everyone jumped to their feet and stood at attention as the Colonel walked briskly down the aisle and out the door.

£££

"Shotgun gang, let's split," the Colonel transmitted as they approached Calais from the north. He turned east while Bugeye continued south and Hot Rod turned west. Once in position, the Colonel flew a north-south racetrack pattern, keeping Snapper's 16 P-51's within three to seven miles of Calais.

For the next 40 minutes, Robb watched the bomber formations drop their bombs. Each formation had 21 bombers and each bomber carried eight 500-pound bombs. All 21 bombers released at the same time and 168 bombs streaked toward the target area. Before the smoke and debris cleared, another 168 bombs hit. Each string of bombs resembled a 200-mph pyroclastic lava flow exploding across the ground.

When the last bomber formation departed, the Colonel made a wide turn around Calais. Much of the smoke and debris had cleared and the target area looked like the backside of the moon.

"Shotgun's reducin' power, startin' down and headin' north. I'll steer slightly east of the field, let down through the undercast over the water and turn to a long initial approach with Snapper. Hot Rod and Bugeye start takin' spacin' now," the Colonel transmitted.

"Hot Rod wilco."

"Bugeye copies."

Except for the southeastern coast, a blanket of clouds covered all of Britain. Near the edge of the undercast, Robb saw the white cliffs of Dover. To the northwest he saw a yellowish-brown area where London's coal smoke mixed with the clouds. He thought about Joyce. She seemed so close yet so far away.

Further west Robb saw the bad weather that Captain Knight had mentioned. Its towering wall of clouds stretched north and south as far as he could see.

"Sunshine, Shotgun here. State your oranges, please," the Colonel transmitted.

"Shotgun, oranges sweet. Sunhat has 1200 and three," the Boxted tower replied.

"Shotgun copies. Snapper, let's close it up and we'll duck through the undercast," the Colonel said approaching the clouds.

Ted and Rocko pulled up close to the Colonel's left side and Robb moved in on the right while Snapper Yellow, White and Green moved in close behind. The 16 P-51's roared through the thick gray clouds at 300 mph. In less than two minutes, they popped out of the clouds at 1200 feet. Robb saw the Thames Estuary off to the left.

"Sunshine, this is Shotgun. Need a steer."

"Sunshine roger. Give us a short count Shotgun."

"Shotgun, one, two, three, four, five – five, four, three, two, one. Over to you Sunshine."

"Sunshine here. Shotgun, steer 300."

"Shotgun's steerin' 300. Snapper Yellow, White and Green, take spacin'."

"Yellow, wilco," the flight leader replied.

"White."

"Green."

Within minutes, all 16 of the P-51's had landed and taxied to their dispersed parking revetments. Robb felt relieved that he had completed another combat mission. But it had been so easy, he wondered how he would feel on the next really tough one.

Robb, Ted and Rocko put their flight gear in their lockers and went to the squadron snack bar for a Spam sandwich and cup of coffee before the intelligence and weather debriefs.

"This frickin' mission was the granddaddy of all milk runs. Short and sweet, just right for my tender dago ass." Rocko grinned as he took his cup of coffee and Spam sandwich.

"I only counted about 30 bursts of flak and didn't see a single bomber go down," Robb said before taking a bite of his sandwich.

"Frickin' krauts ain't very proud of those missile sites. They'd put up a better fight to protect a French whorehouse."

"Yeah. Had a similar thought," Ted smiled. "If I were a kraut, I'd be happy as hell to have 700 bombers attack targets near Calais instead of a target in Germany. Looked like a waste of bombs."

Robb took another bite. *This damned mission didn't prove a thing. I could still be a "hard luck" pilot.*

The intelligence debriefing took only a few minutes and Major Watson confirmed that there were no reported combat losses. Then Captain Stormy Knight made note of their weather observations and said that the front coming in off the Atlantic would hold them on the ground for at least 48 hours. "My Christmas present to everyone," he added with a smile.

Instead of taking the operations truck back to the hut, Robb walked to the Exchange to buy two cartons of Lucky Strikes and two boxes of Hershey bars, Christmas presents for his crew chief and the assistant. By the time he dropped the presents off at the barracks and walked back to his hut, everyone had gone to the club.

The light from the fire in the potbellied stove helped Robb find the switch for the overhead light bulb. Chilled to the bone, he added a scoop of coal to the fire and opened the draft with the small shovel. The additional air made the flames dance higher. He turned on the radio to the American Armed Forces Network. Glenn Miller's recording of *"Elmer's Tune"* was playing. It reminded him of home. *Hate being alone in this damned hut...gotta hurry and get the hell out of here.*

He took off his shirt and the top half of his long johns and put on his winter flight jacket. He grabbed his towel and soap, then headed for the latrine.

Except for having three dim lights, the empty and unheated latrine was as depressing as the hut. *Too damned cold to take a shower in icy water. I'll take a whore's bath like Rocko.* He lathered his hands, washed his face, chest and armpits. After rinsing and wiping dry, he slipped into his flight jacket and hurried back to the hut.

The flames were leaping high in the potbellied stove. He unzipped his jacket and moved closer to the heat as he patted some Mennen's on his face and armpits. Bing Crosby's recording of *"White Christmas"* started to play. The full impact of being alone on Christmas Eve hit him. His mind shot back to the worst day of his life.

Fifteen years ago on Christmas Eve, a stabbing pain raced through Robb's five-year-old body when he opened the side door to the family garage. In the dim light, two feet away, lay his father's body, sprawled across the fender of their 1927 Chevrolet. Thickened blood glistened like strawberry jelly on the side of his father's head. A stream of blood had flowed down the fender, off the side of the running board and onto the floor. His father's right arm rested on the fender with his hand above the red pool of blood where the pistol lay.

Robb stood frozen, unable to speak or cry. His mind and body stopped, like a movie projector stuck on a single frame of a film. Ever since that evening, the indelible image loomed before him at least once every Christmas Eve.

A prodigy of the work ethic, Robert W. Baines believed any aspiring person could succeed. But the Great Depression caused his Temple, Texas bank to fail and he blamed himself. He knew that many of his hardworking depositors who had lost their life savings would soon be standing in line for a handout, just like the beggars who had been on the dole for years.

The night before his father shot himself, Robb watched his parents through the partially opened kitchen door. His mother sat in a chair while his father kneeled with his head on her lap.

"I've failed you and Robb," his father said. "I've lost the trust of so many. Everything I've stood for...is gone. We've no friends. Delicate roots of friendship...can not be sustained...when money's involved. How can success be so arduous...yet so fleeting. And failure...so easy...so final. I'll never stand in line for a handout...never!"

A month after his father's death, Robb's mother sold their home and car to help pay off some of their debts. He and his mother then moved to a boarding house where she cleaned and prepared meals in return for their room, board and five dollars a month. All the boarders were men who had a keen eye for his attractive mother, especially an unemployed roughneck from the East Texas oil fields.

On the streets, former friends avoided Robb and his mother. At school, teachers whispered behind his back, students heckled and taunted him in the classroom and on the playground. Robb started feigning sickness to avoid going to school or outside to play.

After only a month following Robb's father's death, his mother called her husband's spinster sister in Austin who worked as a legal secretary for the Attorney General. The aunt agreed to let Robb live with her.

Six months later, his mother married the roughneck and they moved to the East Texas oil fields. But within two months, she died of pneumonia.

During the train ride home after the funeral, Robb sat next to his aunt and looked through the small tin box of pictures and trinkets—his bequest from his mother and father.

£££

Bing Crosby's recording of *"I'll Be Home For Christmas"* was playing on the jukebox when Robb entered the club. He headed for the bar, hoping someone from the squadron would be there.

79

"Hey, *Amigo*. Fall in for a little Yuletide blabbermouth." Rocko had four glasses of green beer sitting on the table. Next to each beer was a shot glass filled with gin. "*Amigo*, you look like you just saw a ghost."

"Yeah, somethin' like that. Where'd you get the green beer?"

"Mixed some Crème de Menthe in the beer." Rocko picked up one of the shot glasses, dropped the glass bottom first into one of the green beers. The shot glass clunked to the bottom. "Little gin depth charge," he grinned and handed the green beer to Robb. Then he dropped a depth charge into the second glass and held it up. "Merry X-mas, *amigo*."

They touched glasses and Robb took a sip of the Yuletide blabbermouth. "Gag a maggot! How in the hell can you drink this crap?"

"Finish that baby and you won't give a shit about the taste. Get'cha in the Christmas spirit, fast."

Nat 'King' Cole's recording of "The *Christmas Song*" flowed from the juke-box. Robb took another sip, put the glass down, stared at the floor and listened. He thought about his mother and father, then his aunt who lost her battle with cancer two weeks before he started attending the University of Texas. She had lovingly filled the gap in his life for 13 years and the scar left by her loss still hadn't healed.

"Sumbitch, that King Cole's the greatest. But that frickin' song makes this happy Italian homesick." Rocko took a big gulp of blabbermouth.

The record finished and clicked back into the stack. Both Robb and Rocko downed big gulps. As Rocko lowered his glass, he looked across the room; his jaws tightened and he glared. Ted and Doc Herny were walking toward the table.

"Guys, Doctor Herny has completed his observation of Ned a few days early. He's consulted with the psychiatrists at Fifth General Hospital, in Salisbury and they say Ned shouldn't fly until he can be evaluated." Ted hoped to blunt some of Rocko's hostility before Doc Herny spoke. "Ned will pick up his things tomorrow morning. But he doesn't want to see any of us."

"What'a ya mean? Ya mean I can't see 'em?"

"That's right, Rocko. Ned wants it that way and Doc thinks it's best. Doc, tell 'em what you told me."

Rocko raised his glass. As he tilted it to take a drink, the shot glass clinked to one side. He downed a big gulp, lowered the glass, clenched it in his thick hairy fist and glared at Doc Herny.

"Gentleman, I've just spent the last three days with Lieutenant Rathman. He has psychoneurosis or what is now termed as war neurosis. In aviation medicine, it is euphemistically referred to as secondary flying fatigue. But it's really an errant fear of combat. "

"How'n the hell would you know? You don't know shit about shrinkology," Rocko snarled. "Yur nothin' but a junior grade chancre-mechanic. Haven't even finished yur God damned residency."

"Rocko, I'm not here to defend my credentials, nor my prognosis concerning Lieutenant Rathman. I came as a favor to Lieutenant Tyler. For your information," he added haughtily, "Lieutenant Rathman admitted that just getting strapped in his airplane for a combat mission made him nauseous."

"Rocko, Ned needs help," Ted added softly.

"Ned's always been a good pilot," Rocko said, staring at his glass. "Near the top of the class in flyin' school. No problems in gunnery...or bombin'. Had his share of close calls in trainin' and it never bothered him. Still can fly with the best of 'em. Who knows what'll happen when those shit-for-brains headshrinkers get hold of 'em. Most of those bastards need shrinks."

"I have nothing more to say," Doc Herny said turning toward Ted. "Would you please excuse me?"

"Sure Doc. Thanks for your time," Ted said before Doc Herny turned and left. "Rocko, none of us knows what's wrong with Ned. We can only guess. Gotta let the experts unravel it and hope like hell he'll be able to continue flying combat."

"I know, Ted. Sorry I got so pissed. That pecker-head Herny just chaps my dago ass. Apprentice pill pusher's got the arrogance level of a big-time sawbones. Wouldn't make a pimple on a real doctor's ass. He thinks his shit stinks like Chanel Number Five, but his bad breath gives him away."

"Understood Rocko. Guys, Bill Spencer will be joining our flight, taking Ned's place. He'll move his stuff into the hut tomorrow afternoon. Lucky we got him. Gotta go. Have a bridge game. I'll see you guys later.

Bill Spencer had been flying fighters nearly as long as Ted and Robb was happy to have him in the flight. At 24, Bill was one of the older pilots in the squadron. He had a degree in mechanical engineering from Purdue and his father owned a large construction company in Springfield, Illinois. After graduating from flight school, Bill married the girl he had dated since high school and they were expecting a baby in five months. He was one of the few pilots who had a job to go to after the war. Everyone liked him, even Rocko.

Robb and Rocko ordered another round of green beer and shots of gin. While they drank their third Yuletide blabbermouth, Glenn Miller's recording of "*Sunrise Serenade*" started to play.

"More frickin' red ass music. Think I'll get shit-faced tonight." Rocko raised his glass. "Here's lookin' up your old inner tube, *amigo*."

They continued drinking until the bar closed, then staggered back to their hut.

The next morning Robb awakened with a throbbing headache and a horrible taste in his mouth. He rolled onto his back, pulled the blankets off his face. The gray light of day peeked though the cracks around the blackout blinds and he could see his fetid breath, steaming into the icy air. He glanced at his watch.

It read 9:30 am. Outside, the wind howled and sleet pinged against the tin roof and windows.

Two bunks down, Rocko was snoring. Each time he snorted in air, he grunted loudly. When he exhaled he smacked his lips like he tasted something good.

Robb raised his head to see if Ted was still in bed, but he was gone and his bunk was made. Then Robb noticed that the blankets had been stripped from Ned's bunk and his clothes and footlocker had been removed.

The movement made Robb's head throbbed harder. *Damned Yuletide blabbermouth.* He opened his footlocker, grabbed the bottle of APC's and dumped two onto his hand. His head pounded harder.

He flipped the APC's into his mouth, screwed the cap off his metal canteen, tried to take a swig of water, but nothing came out. He grabbed the pencil from his flight jacket, jammed it inside the canteen and broke the thin layer of ice, then washed down the two APC's and went back to sleep.

At 4:00 pm Robb opened his eyes. He'd been dreaming about turkey, dressing, mashed potatoes, thick brown gravy, creamed peas, cranberries and spicy pumpkin pie, heaped with whipped cream. His stomach growled for food as he dressed under the blankets. He slipped into his jacket, grabbed his toothbrush, Ipana and razor, then walked to Rocko's bunk and shook him.

"What's the problem, *amigo?*"

"I'm starved. Let's eat."

"Mouth tastes like half the kraut army marched through it barefoot," Rocko grunted, holding his hand in front of his mouth to check his breath. "Wow! Stinks like a sumbitchin' skunk did his thing in my mouth."

After Rocko dressed, they stepped outside and hunched behind the fur collars of their flight jackets. Without speaking, they hurried along the macadam lane toward the latrine, while blowing sleet crunched under their GI shoes.

Inside the cold latrine, they brushed their teeth and shaved with the icy water. Then they splashed Mennen's after-shave lotion on their faces, raised the tops of their long johns and quickly patted some Mennen's on their chests, stomachs and armpits.

"*Amigo*, there's nothin' like a whore's bath on Christmas day. *C'est la guerre*," Rocko grinned as he put on his flight jacket.

"I've been meaning to ask you. Since you're Italian, where did this *amigo* thing come from?"

"My best buddy in high school was Puerto Rican."

Bing Crosby's recording of *"Jingle Bells"* was playing on the jukebox when they entered the club. "More red ass music," Rocko grunted. "Let's have some suds."

"Yeah, let's."

After downing two beers, they hurried to the dining room before it closed. They passed along the service line and loaded their plates with canned ham, canned cranberries, watery dehydrated potatoes, overcooked Brussels sprouts and a piece of mushy, yellow pumpkin pie.

They sat at a table in the empty dining room and began to eat. When Robb finished his meat, potatoes and Brussels sprouts, he took one bite of the spiceless pie and left the rest. Following dinner they watched the movie *"A Guy Named Joe"* starring Spencer Tracy, Irene Dunne and Van Johnson.

Blowing sleet pelted their faces and crunched under their feet on the way back to the hut. Inside they undressed, turned off the dim light and shivered into their cold bunks.

"Merry frickin' Christmas, *amigo*," Rocko snorted.

CHAPTER 7

Ushering in 1944

The day after Christmas, Colonel Tyler called Ted at 7:00 am. "In about an hour I'm gonna motor up to RAF Station Lavenham in a P-47. Can you meet me for lunch about noon, in the saloon bar at the Swan?"

"I'll be there, dad."

Ted took the bus into town and caught the train to Lavenham. He hurried from the train station to the Swan Hotel and saw his father sitting at a corner table in the crowded saloon bar.

Colonel Tyler stood and gave Ted a hug. "It's great seein' you son."

"Nice seeing you, dad. Been waiting long?" Ted asked as they sat down.

"Just long enough to order a pot of tea for two. Rather have Scotch and soda, but gotta fly up to RAF Station Horsham Saint Faith, near Norwich after lunch."

"Dad, the weather's really lousy. You better be careful."

"I'm always careful, son."

"What brings you up here?"

"I had to check on the construction status of the Lavenham fuel storage tanks. The 487th Bomb Group, a new B-24 group, is scheduled to arrive from the States, the first week in April. The British contractor has fallen behind schedule and I had to find out what we can do to help him get back on track."

"Are they having construction problems at Horsham too?"

"Yeah. We're havin' a few construction problems at most of the airfields that are scheduled for new bomber groups. The British work force has been spread very thin. We're doin' some jugglin' so they can meet our deployment schedule."

"The 8th Air Force buildup is really taking shape, isn't it?"

"Yeah. Gotta bomber group arrivin' about every other week along with a few more P-38 groups. Hundreds of P-51's scheduled to arrive by ship. We'll replace the P-47's with 51's first, then replace the P-38's. General Spaatz is sending the P-47's to the 9th Air Force."

"Dad, the P-51's performance is so damned good. It seems like we should have bought more of 'em sooner."

"You're right, son. We should've paid closer attention when North American Aviation designed and built the Mustang for the RAF. The air force guys monitorin' the program thought the Mustang's performance reports sounded too good to be true. Instead of getting out from behind their desks and flyin' it, they sat on both hands and they hung their hats on the P-47's and P-38's. We could've had the 51 in service months ago and could've already been bombin' deep inside krautland."

"Dad, I was surprised to read about General Eaker's move to the Med as part of the big Army Air Force command shuffle in Europe."

"No one was more surprised than Ira Eaker. Ira hadn't heard a word about the move until Hap Arnold officially announced the activation of the USSTAF command."

"Wonder why General Eaker wasn't told before?"

"Ira's notification was probably handled by one of Arnold's headquarters pets. The same guy who's written most of Arnold's hate notes, pressurin' Ira for more and larger missions. Neither Arnold nor his pet has been in combat and they don't understand the problems. Pet had a combat command over here for a while but couldn't find the time to fly any missions.

"If Ira had tried to move as fast as Arnold had wanted without a long-range escort fighter, we would've wiped out the heavy bomber force in short order. We saw what happened when the bombers went deep inside Germany without fighter cover. We lost our hats, asses and jockstraps."

"Dad, since General Eaker inherited this problem, why should he be blamed for it?"

"That's a helluva good question, son. It's a typical Washington hatchet job to pass the blame and take the heat off. Although the 8th Air Force has been picked apart, under supported and over criticized, Eaker put together the greatest combat air command in the world. No one—and I mean no one—could've done a better job. I'm certain the organization developed by the 8th Air Force under Eaker will serve as a pattern for much of the Air Force in the future. Now that he's finally gettin' the forces to do the job, he's bein' moved."

"How does General Eaker feel about this no-notice move? He must be upset."

"Ira feels shafted. He and Arnold have been close for over twenty years. Ira's first set of stars were Arnold's. Arnold even helped pin 'em on. But Arnold didn't handle Eaker's move like a friend. Ira'll march like a good soldier and never bad-mouth Arnold. Never! Ira Eaker'll go to his grave without sayin' a word. Because that's the way he's built."

"What about General Eaker's new job? Sounds big...sounds like a promotion."

"Being the Commander of Allied Air forces in the Mediterranean is a big job. Damned important and technically it is a job promotion. But the war priority has shifted from the Med to Europe as we get ready for the invasion of the Continent. Ike, Bradley, Patton, Spaatz and many of the bloke's first teamers are either in Britain or about to arrive." Colonel Tyler paused and looked at his watch. "Ted, we better order. I need to spend a few hours at Horsham before quittin' time."

"Yes. If I miss the two o'clock train, I'll have to wait until 5:30. Need to get back to the field early. There's a slight chance the weather may break for a mission tomorrow and I'm on the schedule."

"Ted, how's your mother?"

"She's okay. Get a letter every week. She's dating someone now. Said he was a VP from North American Aviation."

"That's good. Our divorce has been final for nearly two years. She's too young and attractive to be sittin' at home."

The weather finally permitted a mission to be flown on the 30th of December and the 345th sent 41 P-51's along with 463 P-47's and 79 P-38's to escort 658 heavy bombers that attacked an oil plant at Ludwigshafen. Bad weather in the target area degraded the bombing accuracy and 23 bombers were lost to flak and fighters. The P-47's shot down seven and lost eleven. Neither the P-51's nor P-38's scored aerial victories and two P-51's from Hot Rod squadron were lost.

When Ted, Bill, Robb and Rocko entered the pilots' lounge to get a Spam sandwich before debriefing, they saw the five new pilots that had arrived that morning. "Sumbitch, fresh meat!" Rocko roared. "Now I can see my London ho."

That night Robb wrote a note to Joyce to tell her he'd be coming to London on the 11th of January. The thought of seeing her rekindled his pent-up desire and built a fire in his gut.

The next day 572 bombers attacked targets in France and 25 bombers were lost. The P-38's shot down three and lost one while the P-47's shot down four and lost two and the P-51's shot down two and lost one from Bug Eye squadron. During the debriefing Captain Knight said another front would move in that night and bad weather would hold them on the ground for two days, setting the stage for the New Year's Eve party.

More than 100 British women responded to the 'New Year's Eve' invitation sent out by the Officer's Club. GI trucks would bring them to the Club and the band was scheduled to play until 2:00 am. Breakfast would then be served and all of the women were to depart by 3:30 am in the GI trucks.

Ted and Bill Spencer were playing bridge, so Robb and Rocko went to the club by themselves. Robb listened to the music and thought about Joyce while

Rocko danced almost every dance with Matilda, a large, rotund woman who towered over him. At midnight, Robb, Rocko and Matilda toasted the arrival of 1944. When the dancing started again, Robb returned to the empty hut and went to bed. A few hours later he was awakened by voices.

"Skinny on down Matilda baby," Rocko grunted.

"Shush dearie, Robby may 'ear ye," she giggled. "Gorblimey, ye are a cack 'anded bugger. Easy mate, ye'll tear me knickers. Don't be so pushy! What the bloody 'el do ye think ah am?"

"Matilda baby, how many times do I have to tell ya? I think you're a damned nice brawdy."

"Bloody well not actin' like it, chum. Relax. We'll have a bash, but no bloody knee trembler. Ye yanks, all the same, always in a big 'urry."

"Yeah, yeah. Wastin' time with all this yack."

The next morning, in addition to Rocko's usual snorts, grunts and lip smacking, Robb heard a harsh quacking sound that resembled a duck caller. He opened his eyes and pulled the blankets off his head. Gray light peeked through the cracks around the blackout blinds. He raised his head. Rocko and Matilda were in the spare bunk next to the door.

After dressing, Robb walked toward the door. He could see the back of Matilda's head. Her long black hair hung off the edge of the bunk. Her hips formed a huge mound in the blanket. The lower cheek of her butt and her pudgy leg were exposed. As he got closer, he saw that her leg needed a shave and noticed a big bunion on the side of her foot. It had turned purple in the cold.

What Robb saw next made him stop, stare, and smile. Sitting on a foot-locker next to the bunk was a set of false teeth. The teeth were big and yellow and the gums were orange. They appeared to be guarding Matilda's pink bloomers that lay next to them.

Rocko looked childlike nestled in the fetal position in front of Matilda. He clutched the blanket under his stubbled chin with both hands while her huge left breast rested on the back of his head like a water-filled balloon. A strand of her black hair stretched across her left eye, down her cheek and entered the corner of her mouth. Her toothless gums were jammed together and her lips, smeared with lipstick, jutted below her nose.

Somehow their breathing had synchronized. Each time Rocko grunted and snorted in a breath, Matilda inhaled deeply and her cheeks bulged with air. When he exhaled and smacked his lips, she exhaled through her mouth and her lips flapped the duck call.

The grunting, snorting, lip smacking, and quacking produced a loud discordant oompah beat, which reminded Robb of Bob Burns, the 1930's radio star known as "The Arkansas Traveler." Burns played the bazooka, a crude instrument whose main parts were a steel pipe and funnel. His constant gab was laced with apocryphal stories that he told between bazooka renditions.

THE HELLISH VORTEX

After showering and shaving, Robb walked to the Officer's Club. There were two GI trucks parked in front. Female voices came from beneath the canvas-covered bed of the first truck. *Looks like some of the ladies are missing in action.*

Inside the club four couples were in the serving line and more couples were seated at tables in the dining room. At one table four unescorted women had mess-trays heaped with powdered eggs, Spam and stacks of toast covered with big gobs of orange marmalade.

In the far corner, Doc Herny sat at a table with a bottled blonde. Her large blue eyes were ringed in mascara. She had rouged cheeks, bright red lips and oversized breasts that tried to spill out of her low-cut, red satin dress. Her shrill voice echoed off the tin walls as she cackled for attention.

Robb sat at a table by himself. The yellowish-green swoose eggs, Spam, soggy toast and orange marmalade reminded him of the Red Cross Hotel and Joyce. *Ten more days to go.*

WHOOMP! A P-51 roared overhead. Robb washed down a bite of eggs with grapefruit juice. *Wonder who's flying today?*

£££

Streaking over the end of the runway at 100 feet, the Colonel snapped the throttle back to idle, racked his P-51 around in a tight turn and skimmed the bottoms of the clouds at 400 feet. He dropped the landing gear and lowered the flaps as he passed over the club. He kept turning until his 51 was lined up with the pierced steel plank runway, then rolled the wings level and the 51 settled onto the runway.

After slowing down, the Colonel checked the aircraft clock. His flight from Northolt had taken only 14 minutes. He pulled into the parking revetment, cut the engine and his crew chief chocked the wheels. The Colonel wished his crew chief a Happy New Year and got into his staff car. While he drove slowly around the airfield's perimeter road toward his quarters, he thought about his conversation with General Spaatz the night before.

£££

When the Colonel's phone rang yesterday morning, General Spaatz's aide, Captain Sally Bagby, said, "The general is having a New Year's Eve dinner, with some poker later. He's also having his assumption of command ceremony tomorrow morning. It will be a very simple ceremony with only a few close friends. Please come early. The General would like to have a drink and chat before the other guests arrive."

The Colonel folded his best uniform, then placed it and his shaving kit behind the seat in his P-51. He flew below the clouds at 400 feet to Northolt. A waiting staff car took him to General Spaatz's headquarters. During the ride, he kept wondering why Spaatz had requested the one-on-one chat. He recalled their first private meeting in 1938 when Spaatz wanted to hear about the ME-109 and the German tactics used during the war in Spain. Since arriving in Britain they had had another chat. Spaatz had wanted to hear about his combat flying against the Luftwaffe. He couldn't help wondering what Spaatz had in mind this time.

Captain Bagby opened General Spaatz's office door and followed the Colonel inside. She poured two Scotch and sodas while they shook hands and exchanged greetings. "Anything else, sir?" she asked, handing them their drinks.

"Nothing, Sally. Thank you," Spaatz replied. They touched glasses and took a sip. "Been a long time since we've had a chat."

"Yes sir. Congratulations on your new job, general. Being the commander of strategic air forces in Europe with administrative control over the 9th Tactical Air Force has to be a big job with many headaches."

"Yeah. Wish I only had to worry about the *Luftwaffe*," Spaatz said with a smile. "Gonna have to battle the RAF. As you know they wanta run everything. It's just their imperial nature. We let 'em get by with it in North Africa while we were learning. From now on, when we have a disagreement, I'll try to persuade them first. But if that doesn't work, I'll let 'em think they're in charge and work around 'em and get the job done the way I know that it should be done."

"Tryin' to please the ground commanders will continue to be a difficult job too," the Colonel added.

Spaatz took another sip of his drink and lit a cigarette. "I anticipate the usual problems from our ground commanders. They figure any bomb that their troops can't see is wasted. They don't realize that the ten German tanks facing them in battle could've been 20 or 30 without a strategic and tactical bombing program. But I can reason with General Eisenhower when it comes to the employment of my forces. Ike's evenhanded and I couldn't have a better boss."

"Workin' those two problems will require a delicate balancing act while you run the air war," the Colonel said before taking another sip of his drink.

"My biggest problem will be the lousy European weather."

"The weather should improve in a few months and we can start bombin' the hell outta the krauts," the Colonel said.

General Spaatz looked squarely at the Colonel. "I can't afford to wait a few months before hammering the krauts. The D-Day invasion of France is getting mighty close. It'll be the most dangerous operation in the history of warfare. Before it has a chance to succeed, we've got to destroy the *Luftwaffe* and reduce Germany's industrial might. Gaining control of the skies and whittling Germany down to size won't be easy. We've got to attack critical German military and industrial targets anytime there's the slightest chance of making it through the weather. When the weather won't permit visual bombing, we now have about a dozen bombers that are equipped with air-to-ground radar that can lead the main force to some targets. Radar is not very accurate, but it's better than dumping our bombs in the North Sea or bombing some secondary target.

"Most critical targets are deep inside Germany and the bombers need continuous fighter protection. The only fighter that can do that job is the P-51. Unfortunately, I can't wait until we get more P-51's to get started. I'm going to depend on your group to protect the bombers in the target area and use P-47's and P-38's to cover the rest of the route. You'll be greatly outnumbered, but you'll have to shoulder the load for a few months until more 51 units become combat ready. I know that I'm asking a lot, but that's the reason I have you commanding the first P-51 group."

"Sir, I appreciate your confidence. And I'll do my damnedest not to let you down."

"I know you will." General Spaatz took a sip of Scotch, then a long drag from his cigarette and exhaled. "The battle for air superiority's gonna be tough. The RAF's night bombing will help, but we've got to strike targets during the day to get the German fighter force up to fight. Consequently, the battle for air superiority is gonna be an American show, with the largest, most fierce air battles the world'll ever see."

General Spaatz sloshed the Scotch in his glass and took a sip. "Winning air superiority through air-to-air combat will be a slow, agonizing battle of attrition. Too damned slow by itself. Gotta speedup the process. So I'm gonna request that our fighters go down and strafe *Luftwaffe* airfields whenever possible after they escort the bombers. This way we can knock out kraut fighters by the dozens. I know that strafing highly defended airfields will more than double our fighter losses, but we've gotta pay the price. As an added inducement for our fighter pilots, I got approval from General Arnold to give the same credit for ground kills that we give for air-to-air kills."

"Sir, that should help. May I make a suggestion?"

"That's one of the reasons I wanted to talk to you was to get your ideas," General Spaatz said with a smile.

"Sir, as soon as it's feasible, I think we should use a portion of our fighters to go out ahead of the bombers, to seek out and engage the *Luftwaffe* fighters before they can get formed up to attack the bombers. I think we'll save a lot of bombers if we do that."

"That's a helluva good idea. We'll do it as soon as we get a few more P-51's." General Spaatz took a sip then inhaled a long drag from his cigarette and stared across the room. "If we don't clear the skies of *Luftwaffe* and whittle Germany's military industry down to size, I don't think the D-day invasion will succeed. Its failure would bring staggering losses and the impact on the war effort could be devastating. It scares the hell outta me to think about it. That's why we've got to start immediately to do everything and anything we possibly can to soften up the krauts before our ground forces launch the invasion.

"In that regard, I want to get Germany's oil industry added to the British controlled list of high priority targets. Tim Tyler says that oil is Germany's weakest link and their refineries are extremely vulnerable. His job in the oil business took him to Germany many times and he got a good look at most of their oil industry. He knows as much about it as anyone in the US or Britain and has convinced me that we need to attack their oil targets as soon as possible. Eliminating most of their oil and gas would severely cripple the Nazis' ability to wage war. Maybe more than any single target system that we can strike.

"But the Brits are not convinced. So this may have to work around them to get the job done. But nothing will keep me from attacking Germany's oil industry as long as I'm running the American Army Air Forces in Europe. I know it's right. I'll go to the mat on this one."

"General, you have a full plate. I'm glad I only have to worry about fightin' the *Luftwaffe*."

"I do have a full plate. But it comes with my job description. Yet the toughest part of my job is sending these young kids into battle day after day. I agonize over that constantly. Just made a really tough decision today that'll be announced shortly. I had to increase our B-17 and B-24 bomber crews' combat tours from 25 to 35 missions. Poor devils have taken a terrible pounding with unbelievably high losses. But I really don't have a choice. Our strategic bomber force is getting larger every day and we've reached the point where the Training Command can't keep up with the demand for new aircrews. So they have to fly more missions. Besides, the ones who make it to 25 missions are rotating to the States about the time they are most proficient. Keeping them here longer might improve our bombing accuracy and maybe help shorten this damned war."

There was a tap on the door. The door opened and Captain Sally Bagby stuck her head inside, "General, your other guests have arrived."

"Okay, Sally. We're on our way." He finished his drink and slid his chair back from his desk. The Colonel followed him down the hall to the large sitting room where the other quests waited.

After dinner they played poker until 2:00 am. Six hours later the Colonel attended General Spaatz's assumption of command ceremony before flying back to Boxted.

£££

After landing, the Colonel drove past the Officer's Club. He noticed the two trucks parked in front and smiled.

Inside his hut, he undressed, rolled back the blankets on his bunk and picked up the phone. "Captain Knight, please."

"Yes sir."

"Stormy, how's the weather shapin' up for tomorrow?"

THE HELLISH VORTEX

"No change sir. The Continent is socked in and will remain that way for at least another three or four days, maybe longer. Happy New Year, sir."

"Thanks, Stormy. Same to you."

The Colonel closed the black out blinds, got into bed and went to sleep thinking about his chat with General Spaatz.

CHAPTER 8

Will-o'-the-Wisp Arena

General "Tooey" Spaatz's air campaign was delayed ten days due to bad weather. Not until the afternoon of January 10th did the forecasters report the possibility of a few hours of good bombing weather over several heavily defended aircraft factories the next day. However, the forecasters warned that the takeoff, en route and landing weather would remain bad. And the good target weather might not hold long enough for the attack.

Spaatz weighed the possibility of high losses and the low probability of success against the necessity of destroying the *Luftwaffe* and reducing Germany's industrial might before D-Day. He had already lost ten days due to bad winter weather and knew there would be more. With time running out, he decided that he had to attack.

On the evening of January 10th a warning order went to all 8th AF units requesting they prepare to strike the Oschersleben's FW-190 plant, Halberstadt's two JU-88 factories and Brunswick's three ME-110 plants the next day. Due to the close call on the weather, Spaatz decided to make the final "go-no go" decision one hour before the bombers were scheduled to take off.

The phone rang and the Colonel picked it up. "Sir, we have a warning order for a maximum effort coming in on the Teletype," Major Hunt said.

"Be right down," the Colonel replied. He marked his place in *The Sun Also Rises* and glanced at his watch. It read 8:30 pm. He slipped into his flight suit, furlined boots and winter jacket and drove through the rain to operations. RAF Lancasters roared east toward Germany as he hurried to Major Hunt's office.

"Sir, we've been tasked to provide 48 P-51's and six spares," Major Hunt said, handing the Colonel a cup of coffee. "We'll provide protection in the target area for 234 B-17's attacking aircraft factories at Oschersleben and Halberstadt. Another 230 B-17's and 138 B-24's will strike aircraft factories at Brunswick. The weather forecast is shaky as hell. I can't see us going in this kind'a weather."

"I'm afraid we will, Bob. The pressure is really on General Spaatz. Our maintenance guys will have to hump to get that many aircraft ready. I'm gonna take a tour of the flight line to see how things are shapin' up," the Colonel said.

Touring the flight line had been part of the Colonel's daily routine since the day he took command of the 345th Fighter Group three months earlier. That day he'd been on a high of highs. After being a "bottle cap" colonel for only four months, General Eaker promoted him to full colonel and gave him command of the group.

On the morning of his arrival at Boxted, he and the adjutant toured the flight line, hangars, shops and offices. They had lunch in the enlisted men's mess hall, a beer in the NCO Club before dinner and finished with dinner at the Officer's Club. By the time the bugle sounded retreat, the 2000 airmen on the field had not only heard stories about their new commander's combat service in Spain, the RAF and Army Air Force, but many had either seen or talked to him.

£££

The Colonel finished touring the flight line and went to bed around 11:00 pm. At 4:30 am, he was awakened by the roar of the first wave of Lancasters returning from Germany. He jumped out of bed, shaved, dressed and hurried to Major Hunt's office.

"Sir, the weather is crummy as hell. If we launch it'll really test our young jocks," Major Hunt said.

"I know. It'll test all of us. Talk to you later. I'm gonna grab a bite to eat." The Colonel stopped at Hot Rod's snack bar, picked up a Spam sandwich and took it to his office. As he sat down at his desk another returning Lancaster passed overhead. He thought about the B-17's and B-24's trying to join-up in the black rain-filled sky and wondered how many midair collisions there would be today.

Master Sergeant Charles Turner, the Colonel's administrative assistant, placed the Colonel's oversized tin cup of coffee on his desk. "It could be a long day, sir. Can I get you another sandwich or some grilled toast?"

"No thanks, Charlie."

Master Sergeant Charles Turner had taught high school history and coached football in Terre Haute, Indiana before the war. For a year he had watched his former students volunteer or get drafted into the military. After Japan's sneak attack at Pearl Harbor, he gave the school two-weeks notice and enlisted in the Army. He declined an offer to go to Officers Candidate School and quickly rose through the ranks to master sergeant.

A bond of mutual respect had quickly formed between the Colonel and Charlie. Charlie admired the Colonel as a leader and the Colonel depended on Charlie to keep the paper work flowing and, more importantly, to make sure the enlisted men were getting what they needed.

£££

THE HELLISH VORTEX

Ted, Robb, Bill and Rocko stopped at the group briefing room door and the MP checked their ID cards, found their names on the mission roster and motioned them inside. The usual thick layer of blue cigarette smoke surrounded the black models of German aircraft that hung from the ceiling.

The red, yellow and green strings marking the bomber's route of flight on the big wall map angled from East Anglia and converged over the North Sea. After crossing Holland, the bombers turned ten degrees right, a course that would take them south of the three targets for a south-to-north bomb run. Berlin loomed just east of the targets.

"Sumbitch!" Rocko brayed. "Gonna rattle the windows in Big B. Should bring *der* master race out a shittin' and gettin'.' "

Ted, Robb, Bill and Rocko sat in the yellow chairs behind the red row that included the Colonel's striped chair. On the back of their hands, they each wrote the mission recall code word, time over target, the flying time and safe heading from the target area to Britain. They waited in the smoky silence as the adjutant stepped off the stage and walked to the door.

"HOFFICERS TEN–SHUN!" he roared. Everyone jumped up and stood at attention.

"Please be seated," the Colonel said as he walked down the aisle. He hopped onto the platform, turned and faced the pilots. "Gents, we're gonna take the scenic route to some of Adolf's finest aircraft factories. You don't have to be a Magellan to see that we'll be headin' toward *Der Fuhrer's* townhouse. And you can bet your cadet pay that the *Luftwaffe*'ll get off their old rusty-dusties for this one. Okay Stormy, see if you can dredge up some sunshine for a change."

"Sorry. sir. You'll earn your flight pay again today," Captain Knight said. "Thick clouds and rain will make the takeoff and join-up tricky. En route there'll be an undercast with a broken deck of clouds at the bomber's flight level and an overcast above. To make it worse for the bombers, their persistent contrails will fill the gaps in between the broken clouds. After a few bomber wings pass along the route, the wings behind will probably lose sight of one another. In addition, there'll be a wall of weather about 100 miles short of the targets. With a lotta luck, a few bombers may make it through the wall. But there's a chance the target weather will turn sour before they can drop.

"The en route winds at 30 grand are roaring out of the west at 70 miles an hour. From the pressure pattern, I'd say they may exceed 100 mph by the time you're headed back to Britain. You'll go like hell to the target and crawl back."

Captain Knight finished and looked to his left for Major Watson where the briefers sat. But Watson strutted across the platform from the opposite side. He was wearing a new tailor-made uniform that had two full rows of ribbons. The word was that he had received all but two of the ribbons from Central American countries while serving in the State Department.

Watson took the cue stick, lowered his eyes and smiled at the Colonel. The Colonel's jaw muscles tightened; he looked straight ahead. Watson's smile disappeared and his left eye and cheek began to twitch.

"Gentlemen," his voice squeaked like chalk grating across a blackboard. He paused, cleared his throat. "Our targets for today." He tapped their locations on the map with the tip of the cue stick, recited the factory's name, the type of aircraft it produced and the production rates.

"Brunswick is 115 miles due west of Berlin. Oschersleben and Halberstadt are 70 miles west and a little south of Berlin." His twitching stopped. "The Germans may think the 700 bombers and 500 fighters are going to attack Berlin. So you can anticipate a stiff fighter defense and there are more than 500 *Luftwaffe* fighters within range of the target areas." He tapped the *Luftwaffe* airfields and gave the fighter types and numbers stationed at each."

The figure 500 German fighters hit Robb like a bolt of lightening. There would be 450 P-47's and P-38's on the mission, but they had limited range and the 48 P-51's in the target area would be outnumbered ten to one. *Shit...two years after we entered this damned war and we have to face these odds. Somebody should have to pay for this...shooting or hanging would be okay.*

"In addition to the German fighters our bombers will encounter extremely heavy flak," Major Watson continued. He tapped the antiaircraft artillery positions along the route and in the target areas, and gave the numbers and types of AAA cannons at each location. He finished and handed the cue stick to Major Hunt.

"Sumbitch, old Geoffrey rides sidesaddle, but he knows his frickin' business," Rocko whispered. Robb nodded, wishing Rocko would be quiet.

"Gotta complicated fighter escort plan, "Major Hunt said. "As one fighter group runs low on fuel, another's scheduled to take its place. It will take near perfect timing and navigation to make it work.

"Spitfires will cover the bombers over the North Sea, going and coming. Five groups of P-47's will take the bombers to within 120 miles of the targets. The bombers'll be by themselves for next 20 miles until we arrive. We'll pick them up 100 miles from the target and remain with them through their bomb drop and withdrawal, until two groups of P-38's pick them up 60 miles west of the targets. More P-47's will cover the bombers when the P-38's leave.

"Gonna divide our 48 P-51's. Half of Hot Rod squadron will go with the Colonel and Snapper squadron to cover the three combat wings of B-17's attacking Oschersleben. Bug Eye and the other half of Hot Rod'll cover the two Halberstadt wings. The Brunswiick strike will not have fighter escort in the target area. It's hoped the Oschersleben and Halberstadt strikes will help screen the Brunswick force.

"These damned 100-mph headwinds will throw a little more shit into this shitty game. We'll be a long way from home and you'll have to watch our fuel like a hawk. According to the cruise charts in the *Flight Handbook* 65 gallons will get you back to Boxted and have enough fuel to make a quick go around in case you screw up your first landing.

"But to get back with 65 gallons, you need to leave the fuel mixture on normal, hold 26 inches and 1600 rpm and make a slow en route descent to 10,000 feet where the winds will be about 40 to 50 mph. At that power setting at 10,000 feet your fuel consumption will be about 40 gallons per hour.

"Sir." Major Hunt handed the cue stick to the Colonel.

"Guys, I think that most of us suspect that the invasion of the Continent will come sometime this spring or early summer. That means that airpower has a lot of work to do before our guys hit the beaches. For the next few months, we're gonna have to fly in lousy weather, fight against tremendous odds and make unbelievable sacrifices. The mission today will give us a taste of what we can expect."

The more Robb heard, the angrier he became. But he knew that it wasn't the Colonel's fault. *If anyone can get us through this mess the Colonel can.*

"Everything about this mission's dicey," the Colonel continued. "The weather will be stinko from takeoff to the target. Even under ideal weather conditions, it's not easy to shuttle fighters in and out and get 'em at the right place at the right time. In addition, there'll be *beaucoup* kraut fighters and we're gonna have to play our fuel down to the fumes. Should be a good day to pickup a Distinguished Flying Cross." He paused and smiled, but there was a stony silence.

"We're gonna take off five minutes early in case the weather delays our join-up or slows us down en route. Don't want to be late for our rendezvous with the bombers because the krauts normally attack 50 to 100 miles short of the target. Once again, we're gonna stick close to our Big Friends like they're in heat and we're jealous lovers.

"Bob mentioned that we have to split the group in half. We could use at least 200 P-51's at each target, but we gotta do the job with 24. Okay gang, let's get strapped-up and have at the bastards."

Low black clouds and rain delayed the gray dawn as they taxied onto the runway. Robb watched the Colonel and Red flight roar down the runway inside their vapor cylinders and trailing muddy plumes. Before he and Ted took off he prayed for some of Dr. Jekyll's renewal potion. As they climbed through the rough clouds, he wondered if flying in horrible weather would ever become routine. They finally broke out at 9500 feet and saw the Colonel and Red flight about one mile ahead.

"Shotgun will orbit between cloud layers at ten grand," the Colonel transmitted as he reduced power and started a level turn. After completing two 360-

degree turns, the 48 P-51's and six spares were in formation. The Colonel rolled out on course and began to climb. The P-51's entered the clouds at 14,000 feet and broke out at 22,000 feet.

To the north Robb saw a maze of twisting contrails where the bombers had joined up. He had always considered a single white contrail spanning the blue sky to be a thing of beauty. But the twisting maze seemed an ugly intrusion.

Flying east the sun was hidden by endless rows of cirrocumulus clouds. Robb recalled the rare cloud formation from one of his many weather classes. The instructors called it a mackerel sky and said it got its name from its pattern that resembled the stripes on a mackerel's back. They also said many old pilots thought the cloud formation looked more like curdled milk and signaled trouble ahead.

Ten miles ahead the contrails of the 700 B-17's and B-24's converged over the North Sea. The imperfect union of 700 white contrails stretched east beneath the foreboding sky, further than the eye could see. Only the faint hum of German radar in Robb's headset broke the stony silence.

The Colonel leveled off at 28,000 feet. A squadron of Spitfires descended toward Britain after completing their escort duties. A few minutes later Robb saw the coast of Holland through a small break in clouds.

South of Amsterdam four P-47's crossed overhead to take their first look at the new P-51's. The P-47 pilots probably wondered how the sleek P-51's, without external fuel tanks, could fly so far. Seeing the fat-bellied P-47's up close, Robb knew why they'd been given the moniker "Jug." They resembled milk bottles with wings and tails

Without the sun to help warm the cockpit, frost formed on the left front side of the canopy and windshield. Robb rubbed a clear spot and checked the sky to the north for German fighters, then glanced at the aircraft clock. It read 8:44. They were about to cross into Germany. He thought about the 500 German fighters and quickened his scan of the sky while he stomped his feet and clapped his hands trying to remove the aching cold. The hum of German radar got louder and Robb felt a knot in his gut similar to what he had always felt on the football field just before the opening kickoff.

"Big Friends, at eleven o'clock. We'll pass a mile south of 'em." The Colonel's transmission interrupted the eerie hum.

Robb rubbed more frost off the canopy for a better look at the B-24's. Their big twin oval tails, narrow wings and bloated fuselages made the B-24 look boxy compared to the smooth and traditional lines of the B-17. Everyone knew that the B-24 was more difficult to fly close together and their loose formations invited *Luftwaffe* fighter attacks.

Aircrews crowded the windows to look at the P-51's as their young bomber pilots struggled to hold the overloaded B-24's in formation. Behind each of B-

24's four engines, superheated gases shot from their exhausts into the 50 below zero air. The clashing extremes of hot and cold exploded into four steamy contrails. The steam quickly expanded while being churned by prop wash and aircraft wake. Soon the four contrails became one.

Two-miles east, a wing of B-24's entered a cloud that had been partially hidden by contrails. Blinded, the wing commander turned south to avoid a collision with the B-24 wing ahead of him.

Beyond the B-24 air division, the first wing of 63 B-17's came into view. They were in tight formation and Robb could clearly see the three separate formations of 21 bombers in each combat wing. The 21-bomber formation was called a combat box and resembled a geometric progression shaped like an arrowhead. Its pointed tip was 200 feet from the trailing edge and the trailing edge was 750 feet from top to bottom. The building block for the combat box was the three ship V. The seven V's were stacked and staggered to provide maximum firepower against enemy fighters.

The second combat box in each wing flew 1000 feet above and to the right of the lead box. The third box positioned its 21 bombers 1000 feet low and to the left. En route, the high and low boxes flew well forward on the lead box to allow mutual fire support during fighter attacks. On the bomb run, when flak replaced enemy fighters, the high and low combat boxes moved back in a semi-staggered formation so that each box could aim their bombs.

"Shotgun, this is Bugeye. We're holding hands with our bombers," the squadron commander called. His squadron and the other half of Hot Rod set up their zigzag escort pattern above the two bomber wings that would attack Halberstadt.

"Shotgun copies," the Colonel replied.

Three miles ahead, Robb saw the lead combat wing. He had counted eleven combat wings in the 50-mile bomber stream. *It's hard to believe there are 700 bombers ... carrying 7000 men...armed with 8400 fifty-caliber machine guns...millions of rounds of ammunition...and 1400 tons of bombs.* He never dreamed he'd see so many aircraft in the same sky at the same time. He recalled how excited he had gotten as a child, each time an occasional airplane passed overhead.

Robb stomped his feet and slapped his hands again, then rubbed frost off the canopy. The rock-hard dinghy felt like a block of ice on his aching butt and he shifted from cheek to cheek to ease the pain.

"Ringo, Shotgun is approaching at your five o'clock with 24 chicks," the Colonel transmitted to bombers' mission commander who was leading the three wings scheduled to attack Oschersleben.

"Ringo here. I was hopin' to hear your voice Shotgun. Maybe prayin' would be a better choice of words."

"Shotgun copies. Ringo, do you have that wall of weather up ahead?"

"Roger. I've been scanning it with my binoculars and just spotted a break that we can pass through. Turnin' 15 degrees right, now."

"Shotgun copies."

"Ringo, Blackbeard here," the commander of the Brunswick strike called. "With these contrails I'm having trouble keeping you in sight, but I'm gonna try to follow you through the break before your contrails close it. I have only one wing remaining. My other wings got separated in the soup and went for alternate targets."

"Ringo copied."

No one spoke as the bombers and P-51's started through the wall of clouds. The contrails from the Brunswick wing completely closed the break like the gates of a Roman amphitheater being slammed shut behind its gladiators.

Inside the amphitheater, the mackerel sky continued to block out the sun, while thick snow blanketed the ground except for a railroad track and a few scattered clumps of evergreen trees. In every direction the clouds and snow came together and their white-on-white nothingness obscured the horizon.

Robb felt like he was flying into a will-o'-the-wisp arena with no top, no bottom and no sides—where today men would die, and tomorrow the sun would shine. The thought of dying in oblivion made death seem scarier. *At least in the ground war battlefields can be marked to honor the dead.*

Insidious vertigo tweaked his senses and his pucker string jumped a notch tighter. He knew that trying to crosscheck the flight instruments while looking for 500 kraut fighters was a good way to spin in from vertigo or get his ass shot-down. *Everyone else is in the same boat. Just keep your cool and just maybe you'll make it back to Britain for dinner.*

He scanned the sky and hurriedly glanced at his flight instruments, then surveyed the ground to the northeast. Hanover appeared as a jagged black smudge in the snow with three connecting railroad tracks. One set of tracks went north to Hamburg, one ran south toward Kassel and Frankfurt, and the third ran east past Brunswick to Berlin.

When the bombers passed due south of Brunswick, Bug Eye and half of Hot Rod squadron quietly followed their B-17's as they turned ten degrees left toward a turn point south of Halberstadt. The Colonel and his 24 P-51's continued to follow Ringo's three wings as they flew toward the Oschersleben turn point. Blackbeard's lone wing followed two miles behind.

Forty-five miles southeast of Hanover, Blackbeard's wing turned to the northwest toward Brunswick. Without fighter escort, their contrails reminded Robb of the cowboy movies where the telltale trail of dust marked the path of a small unit of horse cavalry alone in the wilds of the old southwest.

"Ringo has a gaggle of bandits at 12 o'clock high comin' this way!" The transmission shattered the eerie silence like a rock shatters a glass window in the still of the night.

"Shotgun has 'em," the Colonel replied.

"Ringo, again. Spotted two more gaggles with my binoculars. FW-190's, wearin' external fuel tanks, orbiting southwest of Magdenburg. Another gaggle of ME-110's is holding due east, probably wearin' rockets."

"Shotgun copied," the Colonel replied. He knew that with external fuel tanks the 190's could wait them out and clobber the bombers when his 51's left. *If we had more 51's and external tanks...we could stay and take 'em on.*

He recalled how the Army Air Forces Headquarters and Wright Pat types had ignored the P-51's superior performance reports. He would have liked to see all of those guys strapped inside bombers and sent on every damned mission.

"Snapper Red and Yellow, Shotgun here. Spread out, go line abreast, 2700 rpm, full throttle and double check gun switches hot. We'll scatter this gaggle at 12 o'clock with a game of chicken. Snapper White, keep the rest of Snapper and Hot Rod with the Big Friends."

"Snapper White, roger," Major Brown replied.

Speeding toward the German fighters, Robb counted 30 contrails. They marked the bottom of the mackerel sky like a second coat of white paint. The thought of charging into the 30 German fighters at a combined speed of 800 mph—about half the speed of a rifle bullet—scared the hell out of him.

Head-on passes during P-40 training had taught him that the slightest mis-calculation could result in a midair collision. Even when they were pre-briefed that both fighters would break away to their right, midair collisions occasionally occurred when the pilots misjudged their break-aways. Two of his classmates had been killed making a head-on pass during simulated combat.

Black dots appeared ahead of the 30 contrails much sooner than Robb expected. Cold sweat ran down his forehead and into his eyes. He blinked to clear them and rubbed at the canopy frost. The dots got bigger.

"Snapper Red and Yellow, Shotgun here. Pick one out, hose 'em down."

Robb looked back to make sure there were no Germans sneaking in behind them. Then he looked forward, turned toward a black dot, lowered his head and looked through his gunsight. Before he could put the gunsight pipper over the dot, the dot sprouted wings and the FW-190's guns spit fire.

Robb squeezed the trigger and his four 50 caliber machine guns clacked like air hammers. The 190's big round nose got bigger; the fire from its guns got brighter.

Robb squeezed harder on the trigger, as if it would make his guns fire faster.

RICHARD M BAUGHN

The 190's big round nose filled the 51's windshield. Every muscle in Robb's body turned to rock. He jammed the control stick forward. His butt left the seat; his head hit the canopy, his feet flew off the rudder pedals, and his shins banged the bottom of the instrument panel.

WHOOOMP! The 190 streaked past a few feet above. Robb's 51 bounced through the 190's prop wash. Before he could get his feet back on the rudder pedals, the ragged phalanx of FW-190's filled the sky in front of him. He squeezed harder on the trigger; 190's shot past—above, below and on each side.

In an instant they were gone, but his 51 continued to buck like a wild bronco through their prop wash.

The air suddenly got smooth. Robb's guns were still clacking; he released the trigger and felt himself shaking. He took a deep breath and tried to swallow, but his mouth was too dry.

He took another breath and thanked God for sparing him. *If you hadn't pushed over you would've been creamed. And in a few days you would've been staring up at daisies in a kraut cemetery provided the Nazi bastards had taken time to find and bury your body parts.*

£££

"Good shooting, Shotgun, " Ringo transmitted. "You nailed one, scattered a bunch of 'em."

"Thanks Ringo." The Colonel pulled up into climbing turn.

Halfway through the turn Robb spotted the smoking 190 the Colonel had hit. It was in a steep spiral and trailing black smoke. Three miles west and 4000 feet below, two 190's that had gotten separated during the head-on attack were trying to catch their formation.

The Colonel rolled his 51 into a diving 4-G turn. Ted, Robb, Bill and Rocko racked their 51's around to stay with him. In the turn, Robb's 189-pound body felt like he'd donned a 600-pound suit of concrete.

The Colonel rolled out on a westerly heading and raced toward the two 190's. Beyond them, Robb saw the twisting contrails of the remainder of Snapper and Hot Rod battling the gaggle of 190's the Colonel had tried to scatter.

"Shotgun here, Snapper Yellow, let's tap these two stragglers. I'm takin' the one on the right," the Colonel transmitted. API's sparkled near the 190's nose and moved back along its fuselage to its tail. A big chunk of tail blew off. The 190 cartwheeled like a wobbly boomerang while shedding flaming chunks.

Ted opened fire on the second190; API's sparkled as they ripped into its engine; flames shot back toward the cockpit and the pilot bailed out.

"Shotgun's bendin' it around to the left." The Colonel turned back to the east. "Shotgun has contrails at two o'clock headin' this way. Snapper Yellow, take a peek at 'em. I'll keep the gaggle of 190's with drop tanks entertained in case they decide to join the fight."

"Snapper Yellow, wilco," Ted replied and turned toward the contrails.

Black dots quickly formed ahead of the contrails. Robb glanced behind, looking for more German fighters. Seeing none, he hurriedly looked back. The dots had sprouted wings. *Shit...I don't need another head-on pass.*

"Snapper Yellow One, they're ME-110's. I'm pulling high to the left. We'll swing in behind them," Ted transmitted.

Following Ted through the steep climbing turn, Robb watched the 110's approach low and to the right. They had two formations, each with twelve aircraft flying line abreast. The second formation was two miles behind the first.

"Snapper Yellow, we'll attack by elements," Ted called. "Yellow Three and Four, take the second formation."

"Yellow Three, copy," Bill Spencer replied.

Ted rolled into a dive and came down behind the first row of 110's. He leveled a few feet below the 110's contrails so the rear gunners couldn't see to fire. Robb slid to Ted's right side, checked the sky above and behind, then looked back at Ted. Three hundred feet from the 110's, Ted popped above the contrails. Robb jerked the stick back and followed. All twelve of the 110's rear gunners opened fire with their double-barreled, 7.9-millimeter machine guns.

Robb hunched lower in the cockpit, hurriedly checked the sky behind and looked back at Ted.

Ted's four 50-caliber machine guns belched fire and smoke. API's sparkled on the 110's right engine and pieces blew off; the engine exploded. Flames shot out like a blowtorch.

The rear gunner's machine guns stopped spitting fire. The 110 pulled up sharply, twisted away from the formation trailing fire and smoke. Two crewmen tumbled out and their yellowish-brown chutes blossomed.

"Snapper Yellow's skinning' it back, rolling left." Ted pulled his throttle back to idle and rolled his 51.

Robb snapped his throttle back, jammed the stick to the left, stomped on the left rudder and rolled with Ted. Before Robb could roll level, API's from Ted's machine guns ripped into another 110. Its canopy glass shattered; the rear gunner slumped forward, his double-barreled machine gun stopped spitting fire.

More API's sparkled on the 110's tail. A big chunk broke off. The 110 flipped out of control. The pilot bailed out and his yellowish-brown chute blossomed.

WHOOOSH! Two balls of fire burst from beneath each of the remaining ten ME-110's wings and 20 rockets streaked toward the bombers. All of the 110's pulled up sharply. Half turned left. Half turned right. Each half dived away in opposite directions.

Robb watched the smoke trails of the big 21 centimeter rockets. One of them exploded into a B-17's fuselage and flames engulfed the giant bomber.

A huge secondary explosion blew pieces in all directions. A crewman, with his clothes burning, plummeted from the flaming wreckage—without a chute. His arms and legs flailed as he fell. Robb could see he was still alive. *Wonder if he'll burn to death or die from fright before he slams into the ground?* Robb's stomach tightened.

Ted pulled up sharply, turned back toward the second group of 110's. Robb yanked hard on the control stick and followed. In the turn he saw the second line of 110's passing 3000 feet below. Behind them a smoking 110 that Bill had clobbered twisted out of control.

"Snapper Yellow Three, slide to the right," Ted transmitted. "We'll take the left side. Let's all four shoot at this second wave."

"Yellow Three, rog."

Ted and Robb swung in behind as Bill and Rocko slid to the right. Before anyone could take a shot, the eleven ME-110's fired their 22 rockets. Immediately two 110's turned right; four turned left; three pulled up. The last two 110's slammed together and exploded. Chunks of their wings, tails and fuselages flew from the fused fireball as it tumbled like a jagged mass from hell.

"YELLOW THREE, BREAK RIGHT!" Ted shouted.

Bill and Rocko racked their P-51's up sharply to the right and two FW-190's overshot them.

Ted rolled his 51 in behind the 190's. Robb followed while checking the area behind for more 190's. The pilot of the first 190 tightened his turn, but his wingman swung wide. Ted closed on the lead 190 and opened fire. API's sparkled on the 190's nose and pieces blew off, then flames shot from the engine back to the tail. It flipped upside down; the canopy flew off and the pilot tumbled out. Just as his chute started to open, a fuel tank exploded. Burning gas ignited the chute. As flames consumed the canopy, the pilot plummeted earthward, clawing at the sky.

The second 190 pilot continued his loose turn as if submissiveness would exempt him from the deadly game. He passed in front of Robb.

"Snapper Yellow Two, take 'em. I'll cover." Ted pulled up sharply and rolled in behind Robb.

"Repeat lead," Robb couldn't believe his ears, knowing the German would make Ted an Ace.

"He's yours, Yellow Two. Take 'em!"

"Roger." Robb turned his 51 and lined up behind the 190. He lowered his head, looked through the fixed gunsight and tightened the turn until the sight's pipper was on the 190's cockpit. As he got closer to the firing range, he wondered why the German hadn't tightened his turn or taken evasive action. *Must be one of the 100-hour green beans intelligence told us about, or he could be scared shitless like old Ned.*

"Whack the bastard!" Rocko roared.

THE HELLISH VORTEX

Robb tightened his turn, moved the pipper forward along the 190's fuselage until it was about ten feet in front of its nose and held it steady. At about 15 degrees angle-off, he squeezed the trigger. The four 50-caliber machine guns clacked like air hammers, his 51 vibrated and he smelled a trace of gun smoke. API's sparkled on the 190's nose, pieces blew off the engine nacelle, black smoke poured from the engine and the 190's propeller froze. Its big blades dug into the air like giant speed brakes.

Robb snapped his throttle back to idle and pulled high to keep from overshooting. He rolled his 51 upside down and looked down through the top of the canopy. The German looked up; a small flame leaped from behind the 190's instrument panel. He tried to jettison his canopy but nothing happened. He pounded on the glass with his fists. More flames shot into the cockpit; his pounding slowed, then stopped. His head slumped forward. The 190 rolled slowly to the right and started downhill. Robb watched the burning 190 spiral earthward. *The poor...scared...bastard.*

"Snapper Yellow One's passing Two on the left," Ted transmitted. "Snapper Yellow, skin 'em back to cruise power and give me a fuel check."

Bill waited several seconds for Robb to answer. When he didn't, Bill transmitted, "Yellow Three has 86 gallons."

"Yellow four, 84 gals," Rocko answered.

"Snapper Yellow Two, One here. You copy?"

"Roger ...Two has 83 gallons."

"Yellow One, roger." Ted turned and flew north toward the target to rejoin the Colonel.

As the second and third combat boxes in Ringo's wing adjusted their positions for the bomb run, AAA cannons flashed on the south side of Oschersleben. A bevy of 48 dirty orange fireballs exploded among the wing's remaining 60 B-17's. Like magic, devil's magic, the fireballs changed to black puffs of smoke while thousands of pieces of jagged shrapnel burst in all directions.

Another bevy of fireballs changed to black smoke and more shrapnel shot through the sky. Small pieces sliced through bombers and airmen. Larger pieces ripped gapping holes in the aircraft and butchered them. Tiny pieces of spent shrapnel pinged on the bombers' aluminum skin like hail and rattled souls.

AAA gunners on the north side of Oschersleben joined the shoot. More fireballs exploded; more black puffs darkened the pockmarked sky and more shrapnel killed or maimed. The sky looked like the devil had invaded heaven.

Flames poured from two B-17's; both twisted out of control. Only six white chutes appeared. A third bomber trailed heavy black smoke and fell behind the formation. Flames suddenly shot from its fuselage. Its nose popped up and its right wing dropped. The burning bomber flipped upside down and spun out of control. There were no chutes.

The remaining 57 B-17's opened their bomb-bay doors and stabilized their altitude and airspeed for the bomb drop. Another B-17 exploded and fell. Flames trailed from one more B-17 before it spun out of control. Only three white chutes blossomed. A third B-17 twisted from the flak-filled sky and now there were 54.

Robb thanked God that he was a fighter pilot as he watched the wing of bombers fly through the sooty-abyss. *They've lost nine bombers and 90 men. Poor helpless bastards...at least they can shoot back at German fighters.*

At the bomb release point, each B-17 in the lead box dropped its eight 500-pound bombs. A few seconds later, the second box dropped, followed by the third. All 432 bombs streaked toward the target. Before their bomb-bay doors closed, the 54 B-17's turned west to escape the trail of death. In the turn, pilots of the battered bombers who'd been using emergency power on their good engines to hold formation, throttled back and fell behind. The remaining pilots eased their bombers forward to fill the gaps left by their fallen comrades. After closing ranks, the second and third combat boxes moved line abreast with the lead box. Aircrews bandaged their wounded, covered the dead and readied their 50-caliber machine guns to fight their way back to Britain.

Crews of the battered bombers who had fallen behind knew the Magdeburg gaggle of FW-190's would hit them first. They hurriedly cared for their wounded, covered the dead, while keeping an eye on the sky for German fighters. Then they checked and double-checked their guns and prayed.

Robb watched the battered stragglers limp to the west, falling further and further behind. *Germans'll slaughter the poor bastards...like the Japs slaughtered the sick and wounded who couldn't keep up during the Bataan Death March.*

In his peripheral vision, he saw orange explosions as the first of the 432 bombs hit the snow-covered ground. Each bomb's explosion sent dirt and debris shooting skyward, while rings of shock waves rippled across the white snow. Soon the target area looked like a chunk of the earth had been blown away.

"Pay back time," Robb sighed.

Before the last bomb had exploded, the second wing entered the gates of hell and started down the deadly trail. Despite the efforts of the P-51's, German fighters had shot down four of the second wing's bombers, leaving 59 B-17's. Several of the 59 had been badly mauled. AAA cannons flashed, more orange fireballs exploded, more black puffs darkened the sky and deadly shrapnel took its toll. A B-17's wing exploded and half of it broke off. It fell like the tip of a spear through the devil's hellhole. The rest of the bomber tumbled wildly. Again—there were no chutes.

Bombardiers of the lead combat box released their bombs. Seconds later, the second and third boxes released. All 464 bombs from the 58 B-17's streaked toward the target. The second wing turned, closed ranks, cared for their wounded, covered the dead and prayed as five crippled B-17's fell behind.

THE HELLISH VORTEX

To the south, P-51 and FW-190 contrails suddenly stopped twisting above the third bomber wing. "Shotgun, Snapper White here," Major Brown called. "Kraut fighters headin' home. Must be outta ammo and low on fuel. But after this runnin' gun fight, so are we. I'm headin' west, with eight Snappers and eight Hot Rod's.

"Shotgun copies, Brownie."

Seconds later the third bomber wing's remaining 59 B-17's started its trek into the blackened sky. Two of its B-17's took direct hits and their burning wreckage fell. Two more trailed smoke but held formation. The three combat boxes dropped in turn and 456 bombs streaked toward the fiery black thicket. The 57 bombers banked sharply to escape the flak and headed west. As the wing closed ranks, the two smoking B-17's and four more wounded giants fell behind. Once again aircrews cared for their wounded, covered the dead, readied their guns and prayed.

Seeing the last bomber wing depart the target, the Colonel totaled the fuel in each of the three tanks. He had 71 gallons remaining. At these power settings he knew they were burning about a gallon a minute. Based on Yellow's fuel check 17 minutes ago, he figured they had a few gallons less. "Shotgun gang, it's checkout time. Let's head for home." He turned southwest toward the target to pass by the bombers, hoping to delay the FW-190 attacks against the stragglers.

In the turn, Robb checked his fuel gages. He had 66 gallons and knew that with these headwinds his fuel would be close. He glanced south toward Oschersleben. There were nine scorched spots in the snow around the target areas where nine B-17's had fallen. He counted six more scorched spots along the deadly trail leading to the target. *That's 26 bombers and 260 men lost so far. Wonder how many'll get clobbered on the way home.*

"Shotgun's skinin' it back to 1600 rpm and 27 inches. Startin' down, headin' west. We'll get below these high winds." The Colonel flew past the third bomber wing and swung close to a straggler from the second wing. The B-17 had large holes in its right wing and tail. Two of its engines were shutdown and another was smoking. The crew was throwing out equipment to lighten the load, trying to keep the wounded giant in the air.

Ahead, the second wing entered the wall of weather. Robb looked back and saw FW-190's contrails swarming around the third wing's crippled stragglers like hungry hyenas. Two smoking B-17's were already twisting earthward.

"Shotgun here, close it up. Peter heat on," the Colonel transmitted as they approached the wall of weather. The eight P-51's zoomed into the dark gray clouds and exited the will-o'-the-wisp arena. Five minutes of bouncing through the rough clouds brought them out the other side.

"Top Hat, Shotgun here," the Colonel called the P-38 group leader.

"Shotgun, Top Hat copies."

"Are you getting' close, Top Hat?"

"Top Hat is runnin' a little late. Lost a chick on takeoff, delayed our departure a few minutes."

"Shotgun was a few minutes early, Top Hat. Krauts snookered our asses. They had a gaggle of 190's with external fuel tanks to wait us out. Big Friends have been clobbered by fighters and flak and are still payin' a heavy price. Can you hustle it up? Every second counts."

"Top Hat gang, let's push it up. We're balls to the wall, Shotgun."

"Thanks, Top Hat," the Colonel transmitted as he continued his en route descent. "Shotgun gang, run your right main and fuselage tanks dry and save the left main for last."

The Colonel finally leveled off at 10,000 feet. After 27 minutes, he checked his aircraft clock. "Sunshine, this is Shotgun with eight chicks, about ten minutes out. What's the weather like?"

"Sunshine has a 700 foot ceiling, two miles visibility and light rain. Altimeter is 29.90."

"Shotgun copies. Gang, set your altimeters at 29.90 and we'll letdown below the clouds over the water." The Colonel checked the left main tank. It showed 17 gallons. "If anyone in Snapper has less than 15 gallons, sound off and we'll let you land first."

Robb glanced at his left main. It showed 16 gallons.

The Colonel waited but no one called. "Shotgun, here. When we get below the clouds, we'll fly by two ship elements with a half-mile spacin' between elements, make straight in approaches and land in formation. Any questions?" The Colonel waited a few seconds. "Okay, follow me. Sunshine, Shotgun is counting for a steer. One, two, three, four, five, five, four, three, two, one. Over to you Sunshine."

"Sunshine here, steer 302 degrees."

"Shotgun steering 302."

Ted and Robb landed and Bill and Rocko touched down a few seconds later. As Robb followed Ted along the taxiway, he glanced at his left main tank. It showed less than five gallons. *Shit. . .we played that one close.*

Robb turned into his revetment and pushed the stick forward, released the tailwheel and spun his 51 around. Sergeant Edgington, his crew chief, chocked the wheels. Robb pulled the throttle back, cut the engine, turned off the mags, radio and battery switches, then opened the canopy. The rain felt good on his face.

"Rough mission, sir?" Sergeant Edgington asked. The tight oxygen mask had left deep lines on Robb's face.

"Tough day at the office." Robb disconnected the oxygen hose and radio cord, unlocked his safety belt and shoulder harness, then unsnapped the rock-hard dinghy from his chute. He climbed out of the cockpit onto the wing, stepped onto the tire of the left wheel and hopped to the ground. He stretched, then rubbed the cheeks of his butt. "Chief, P-51 pilots should be issued leather asses."

Sergeant Edgington nodded and smiled. The squadron truck roared into the parking revetment and Robb climbed inside next to Rocko. Sergeant Edgington saluted as the truck pulled away.

"*Amigo*, we earned our lousy $75.00 a month flight pay on that sumbitchin' ball-buster. I don't know about you, but I taxied in on frickin' fumes," Rocko growled as the truck raced toward operations. "But I'll take fighters any day. The route to heaven for those poor frickin' bomber crews passes through hell."

"Yeah. If the birth of Christ were ever celebrated in hell, the devil's Christmas tree would be decorated with dirty-orange fireballs and ugly black puffs. Thank God our combat pass starts tomorrow. I can stand a few days away from this place," Robb said, thinking about Joyce.

"Amigo, I think I'm gonna get shit-faced for three days."

£££

Following the mission debriefing, the Colonel made his tour of the flight line and returned to his office. Charlie placed the big, half-filled coffee cup and the preliminary mission summary on the Colonel's desk. Then he turned on the desk lamp and added a scoop of coal to the fire in the potbellied stove.

The Colonel opened the bottom desk drawer and pulled out the bottle of Red Label and a glass. He poured three fingers of Scotch into the glass, added some to his coffee and handed the glass to Charlie. They raised their drinks and nodded.

"Thank you, sir," Charlie said, then downed the Scotch. "Need anything else, sir?"

"Nothing Charlie, thanks. I'll leave this summary in group ops when I go to dinner. Take the rest of the day off," he said with a smile.

'Will do, sir." Charlie smiled, turned off the overhead light and closed the door behind him.

The Colonel took another swig of his Scotch-coffee and picked up the mission summary.

£££

**SECRET
8TH AIR FORCE
PRELIMINARY MISSION SUMMARY**

I   . Due to bad weather and combat losses, only 263 bombers reached their primary targets. Bombing results varied from fair to poor...

2.   Approximately 60-rocket firing ME-110's, 40 ME-109's and 70 FW-190's attacked the two strike forces near Oschersleben and Halberstadt. More FW-190's, with external fuel tanks, waited in the target area for the P-51 escort fighters to leave before attacking....

3.   German fighters and heavy flak downed 60 bombers. Another 179 bombers received heavy to moderate AAA battle damage. In addition to the 600 men who went down, returning bombers had ten dead, 34 wounded and 27 with severe frostbite, bringing the casualty total to 671.

4.   The P-51's shot down 15 German fighters without a loss. The P-47's shot down 16 and lost four. The P-38's shot down none and lost one.

£££

The Colonel laid the report on his desk and finished his Scotch-coffee, thinking about the 671 casualties. He didn't need a squadron of sleepy-eyed PhD's to tell him that more 51's would have probably saved 200 men today.

He recalled his first P-51 flight at North American's Mines Field near Inglewood, California in April of 1941. The XP-51, even with its underpowered engine, performed better than any airplane he had ever flown. After the flight he sent a special report to Army Air Corps Headquarters, but the staffers were pushing the P-38 and P-47. Although two XP-51's were eventually bought and sent to the Test Center at Wright Field, Ohio for evaluation, little interest was shown in them until the Japs bombed Pearl Harbor. Only then were a few ground attack versions of the P-51, called the A-36, purchased for the North Africa and Mediterranean campaign. Their air-to-air capability was ignored.

In November 1942, the Colonel had three flights in the RAF's Mustang with the Rolls-Royce Merlin engine. It improved the Mustang's superior performance even more. He sent letters to 8th Air Force and Army Air Forces Headquarters, but still the staffs took no action. A few months later, after seeing the RAF's flight evaluation report, General Arnold directed the Army Air Forces to buy 2200 P-51's with the Merlin engine. Eventually 14,490 were bought.

£££

"Amigo, what's the movie tonight?" Rocko asked as they finished dinner.

"I don't know. I'm gonna skip it and hit the sack. wanta get an early start for London in the morning," Robb said.

"Okay, amigo. If I don't see you in the morning, get one for me."

Robb hurried inside the hut and added two scoops of coal to the fire, undressed and got into his bunk. He was exhausted, but each time he closed his eyes he saw burning bombers and bodies falling through the flak in the will-o'-the-wisp arena.

He opened his eyes and stared at the flames through the crack in the door of the stove and thought about today's mayhem. *Young men and teenagers dying without the right of appeal. . .serial killers have more merciful deaths.*

Exhaustion finally brought fitful sleep.

CHAPTER 9

A Tale of Two Loves

Robb awakened to the roar of P-51's taking off for Germany. He checked his watch; it read 8:15. *Oh shit...I overslept.* He jumped out of bed, put on his pants, shoes and flight jacket, ran to the latrine, showered and shaved in the icy water. After dressing, he packed his musette bag, went to the club and waited for the next truck to Colchester.

Sitting in front of the fireplace, he stared at the cold ashes and recalled the burning B-17 crewman that plummeted through the will-o'-the wisp arena with his arms flailing. *Poor bastard must've died a thousand deaths before he slammed into the ground.*

He hoped that a couple of days with Joyce would blur the sights and sounds of war. She had written twice and both letters ignited his vivid memory of her beauty, velvet body and their unbridled sex. He remembered how she had made him feel so wanted and needed. Sometimes he felt like he could have easily fallen in love, but he knew that would be a mistake.

£££

The warm train compartment felt good after the cold ride to Colchester in the GI truck. Within minutes Robb dozed off and didn't awaken until he felt the train slowing on the outskirts of London. Outside, meadows, hedgerows, winding lanes, small thatched roof houses, green double-decked buses and scattered cyclists gave way to solid rows of brick houses, factories, office buildings, red double-decked buses, black taxis and a steady stream of cyclists.

A few blocks from the Liverpool Street Station, the train's speed became agonizingly slow. Three weeks of pent-up desire boiled inside him. It cleansed his mind of combat—like a spring storm washes away the ugliness of winter.

When the train stopped, he grabbed his musette bag, bolted from his compartment and ran through the crowded station to the line of black taxis outside. Despite Robb's urging to speed it up the unflappable taxi driver continued his slow weave through traffic until he came to 52 Knightsbridge Court on Sloane Street.

Robb dashed inside and stepped into the elevator. The white-haired elevator operator pushed the brass handle to UP and the ancient elevator barely moved. Robb wished that he'd used the stairs. As the elevator inched its way up he recalled his abrupt departure from the Red Cross Hotel. *Don't do something dumb again*

The elevator finally reached the seventh floor. The old operator moved the handle to STOP but overshot the floor several inches. He moved the handle to DOWN and stopped a few inches below the floor. On the third try, he stopped level with the floor. The old man slowly opened the elevator door. Robb brushed the sweat off his upper lip, bolted out of the elevator and hurried down the hall to Joyce's apartment.

Before he could knock twice, the door opened. Joyce smiled and her blue cat-like eyes sparkled in the dim light. Her hair flowed below her bare white shoulders. The sheer blue negligee revealed more than it screened. She was more beautiful and desirable than he had remembered.

"Robb, darling," she purred taking his hand and pulling him close.

He dropped his musette bag. His arm circled her waist and held her tight.

Joyce cupped his face in her warm soft hands and pulled his head down. Her fingers slid past his ear and rested on the back of his neck, while she pressed her soft body against him. Her lips parted; her tongue sought his.

He grabbed the cheek of her butt and squeezed. His heart pounded, blood surged through his body and thundered in his ears like an approaching spring storm.

BRAANG! BRAANG! The phone in the entrance hallway rang. Joyce backed away, took Robb's hand, pulled him inside, closed the door and led him past the ringing phone to the bedroom.

By the time the third spring storm passed, darkness had spread over London. Only the red glow from the coal fireplace lighted their naked bodies on the rumpled bed. Robb lay on his back with his legs spread and breathed deeply while Joyce lay on her side looking at him. For the past six hours, they had ridden a roller coaster and each ride had taken them a little higher.

Robb's eyes closed. "Darling, wasn't it wonderful?" she asked.

"Yeah. It was great," he answered struggling to keep his eyes open.

"Darling, I have lady friends who say they often endure sex just to maintain their marriage or keep an affair alive. Can you imagine anything so delight-ful—so fulfilling—having to be endured?"

"No," he replied wanting to go to sleep.

Suddenly he felt her ease out of bed. She noisily added coal to the fire and closed the blackout drape then climbed back into bed. "I love your body, dar-ling," she said snuggling closer.

"I love yours too," he said opening his eyes and gently patting her thigh.

"Darling, do you know your eyes have changed?"

"Yeah, they have crow's-feet from looking into the sun...and dark circles from the lack of sleep," he added hoping she would let him sleep.

"No, there's something else. They have that deep invisible wound of combat. I've seen it in others, so many times. It's this damnable war. It makes us behave like animals not humans. Many animals treat their own better. The more civilized we become the more clever at killing we get. If the egocentric politicians who shield themselves behind self-anointed divinity had to do the fighting, there'd be no wars. I'm sorry, darling. But I'm so angry. I just hate the Germans for starting this damnable war."

Robb gently patted her thigh as the new coal started to burn and the reflection of its flames danced on the ceiling. Suddenly, his hand stopped and his eyes closed.

Her fingers glided across his chest and she gently blew into his ear. "Darling, wake up," she purred.

He squinted with one eye. "I'm awake. Phone's ringing again," he added, hoping she'd answer it so he could sleep.

"Never mind, darling." She let her fingers glide down across his chest to his waist then circled them around his stomach before gently sliding them inside his thigh. She kissed his ear, his neck, then his chest, while her fingers continued their frolic. The fourth spring storm passed and they collapsed into each other's arms and went to sleep.

£££

"Darling," Joyce said as the mantel clock in the living room chimed nine o'clock.

Robb opened his eyes, rubbed them and then stretched. Through the window he saw the gray light of day. Buses and taxis rumbled on Sloane Street. He sat up and Joyce handed him a mug of tea. "Thanks." He raised the cup and took a sip.

She leaned down, gently kissed him. "I'm heating water, darling. We can bathe when you finish your tea."

"Sounds good."

"I'll check the water." She turned and walked toward the door.

Robb watched her. She not only had cat-like eyes, she moved with feline grace. In a few minutes, she passed the bedroom door carrying two steaming pails of water. "Joyce, let me do that," he yelled.

"Never mind, darling. You can pour."

He placed the cup on the nightstand next to the slender crystal vase that contained a fresh yellow rose, slipped into his GI shorts, grabbed his toothbrush and Ipana from his musette bag and hurried to the bathroom. He poured the two pails water into the tub while Joyce turned on the warm tap water.

She checked the water's temperature with her finger. "Just right," she said, turning off the tap and slipping out of her robe. "Come, darling."

RICHARD M BAUGHN

Seeing her naked in the bright light made his heart pound and he swallowed noisily. Neither of them spoke as he pulled her close. She thrust her body against his and her breathing deepened. Their lips met, their tongues searched wildly. He lifted her onto the sink and she wrapped her legs around his hips and put one arm around his neck and the other around his waist. Another spring storm slowly passed.

£££

"Darling, we need to bathe before the water gets cold," she finally whispered after catching her breath.

"Okay." He lifted her off the sink.

She reached into the tub. "It's still warm. Hurry, darling," she said climbing into the tub. He climbed in facing her. She took the bar of soap and worked up lather in her hands and passed the bar to him.

"Do you call everyone, darling?" he asked as he lathered the soap.

"Only people who interest me," she answered while slowly washing his neck and shoulders. "You have a beautiful body, darling," she added as she moved to his chest.

"Not as beautiful as yours," he replied as he placed the bar of soap on the tray and slowly lathered her firm, round breasts. "Your skin's smoothest I've ever touched," he added as he began to feel another urge.

She gently removed his hands from her breasts. "I'm famished. We had better stop this and wash ourselves."

"If you say so," he said with a smile.

Joyce finished bathing, got out of the tub and dried herself slowly, obviously enjoying Robb's stare. He wondered how many men she had bathed with and felt a tinge of jealousy and anger. *It's none of your damned business. . .so forget it.*

"Better get out of the water darling. You might take a chill, darling." She handed him a towel and slipped on her robe. "Get dressed while I demonstrate my domestic side."

While he dressed, he could smell bacon cooking. He slipped on his shoes and hurried to the dining room. Joyce had placed two plates of bacon and eggs, garnished with slices of tomatoes on the table. She returned from the kitchen carrying a pot of tea and a silver toast holder with four pieces and placed them in the center of the table next to the slender crystal vase containing a fresh yellow rose. "Sit, darling."

"Like yellow roses, huh?"

"My lucky flower. Always carry a pressed one."

"Where'd ya get the bacon, eggs and tomatoes?" Robb asked, spreading orange marmalade on his toast.

"I have contacts," she said with a smile.

118

THE HELLISH VORTEX

When they finished, Robb cleared the table, scraped the plates onto an old newspaper then stacked them in the sink while Joyce dressed. In the hallway leading to the second bathroom he passed an open closet. On the floor was a case of Johnnie Walker Red Label, a case of Beefeaters gin, four bottles of Harvey's Bristol Cream and an assortment of liqueurs. On the back wall, bottles of French wine lined the eight racks. *She really has contacts. But I'm not gonna ask.*

£££

It was cold and misty when they left the apartment and walked down Sloane Street. Even in the gray light she looked stunning and passersby tried hard not to stare. Robb felt like he was on center stage and perspiration formed on his upper lip while drops trickled across his ribs. She tightened her grasp on his arm and leaned closer. "I love the American uniform and you look so handsome in yours."

He looked down and tried to think of something to say. Finally he smiled and touched her hand. She tightened her grip and smiled back. People continued to stare as they passed through Belgrave Square toward Grosvenor Place. He kept trying to think of something to say that wouldn't sound dumb, but nothing came out.

As they approached Buckingham Palace, Joyce said, "I never tire of looking at the Palace."

"First time I've seen it. Saw pictures of it, but never the real thing," Robb replied. He wondered how that sounded. She smiled and gently gripped his arm. He was certain that she knew he had a case of nerves.

Near Saint James Park three white-haired men in squarely mounted bowlers approached. Time had turned their white celluloid detachable collars yellow and well-worn institutional ties circled their wrinkled necks. Even the gray day couldn't hide the wear and shine of their black coats and striped pants. They swung their folded umbrellas back and forth at their sides. On each forward swing, a flick of the wrist sent the tip of the umbrella waist high. Then like maestros, they snapped it down, tapped its metal tip on the sidewalk, keeping time with the presto beat of their leather heels. They were old and few in number, but their manner left no doubt that what had been—would be again. As they walked briskly past, each of them surveyed Joyce with a twinkle in their eyes. One jauntily tilted his bowler and smiled and Joyce smiled back.

"They couldn't take their eyes off you," Robb said with a smile.

"Aren't they darling," she replied. After several minutes she asked, "Robb, have you had a serious romance?"

The question surprised him. "One," he finally replied.

"Tell me about it."

He never told anyone how his girl friend had dropped him shortly after he had entered flight school. But by then flying had become his number one love and the loss was less painful. Now he rarely thought about Beth. Yet, it was just another part of his past that he didn't like to talk about. "It's a dull story."

"I'd really like to hear it, Robbie," she coaxed.

"Well, I was going with this girl while in school. Dated for nearly two years before I entered the service. A few weeks after I started my flight training, she wrote and said that she'd gotten engaged to some guy. He's 4-F, failed his military physical. I later found out that she'd been seeing him for two months before I left. They'd meet after I took her home. She told me that she loved me, but she was fooling around with him. She writes occasionally and once she said that she still loved me. I don't pay any attention to that crap."

"I don't mean to pry. But have you really stopped loving her?"

The question annoyed him. He had known Joyce for only a few weeks and had spent less than 36 hours with her. *It's none of her business. I've told her enough.* "I really don't care to discus it anymore."

"Darling, have you been to the American Officer's Club at the Grosvenor House?" she asked.

"Heard about it, but I've never been there." He hoped she wouldn't call him darling in front of anyone.

"We could go there and have a drink before lunch. They have some kind of canned meat almost every day." Due to wartime rationing in Britain what little meat that was available to civilian restaurants came from the black market, where horsemeat was normally sold as beefsteak.

"That sounds good."

"We can take a taxi," she suggested.

£££

An elderly doorman stood beneath the Grosvenor House's grand marquee. He was dressed like a circus ringmaster, but had the demeanor of a field marshal as he directed the flow of taxis and military staff cars with a nod or snap of his fingers. He opened the taxi door. Robb could tell from his eyes that he recognized Joyce. Inside, the concierge watched her with a knowing smile as she crossed the lobby.

Robb and Joyce climbed the stairs and entered the mezzanine, which circled the huge ballroom one story below. Thick carpet covered the mezzanine floor; gold framed paintings and hand-woven tapestries hung from the cream-colored masonry walls. To the right was the longest bar Robb had ever seen. It was crowded and eight bartenders were busy fixing drinks.

Joyce led Robb to the opposite side of the room across from the bar. They sat at a table for two, next to the banister where she could see and be seen from the mezzanine, the bar and the grand ballroom below. Heads turned as they sat down.

Every table in the ballroom was taken. Robb looked for, but couldn't find another second lieutenant. All he saw were colonels, majors and captains, including three WAF captains. They too were staring at Joyce. Suddenly Robb wished they had gone somewhere else. His face felt hot; he started to sweat. *Ignore 'em... most of 'em are noncombatants.*

Joyce noticed his uneasiness, reached across the table, and gently gripped his hand. "Are you all right, darling?"

"I'm okay." A waiter approached; Robb pulled his hand free.

"*Aperitif*, suh?" the old waiter asked, looking down his long nose. His white coat and shirt, black tie and black pants were immaculate.

Robb wondered what the hell *aperitif* meant.

"I'm chilled to the bone, darling. Shall we have a nice sherry to warm us?"

"Okay," he consented. "Two Sherries, please."

"Lovely club, don't you think, darling?"

Robb didn't answer. The place looked like a Hollywood movie set to him. *What a way to fight a war.* Less then 48 hours ago, he had faced death in the real war. And at that very moment, five to six miles above Germany, more than 7000 Americans battled the Nazis in the 50 below zero sky. *More men could die today than died at General Custer's "Last Stand," but the loss probably won't make it to the history books.*

The waiter placed two Sherries on the table. "Fifty cents please." Robb handed him a fifty-cent scrip note, with a ten-cent note for a tip. The waiter turned and left.

"Cheers, darling." She looked at Robb like he was the only one in the room.

They touched glasses and he took a sip. The sherry tasted good and he downed half of it. Its warmth flowed to his stomach. "I like this stuff." He downed the rest.

"It's my favorite, darling."

"Ready for another?"

She nodded and took another sip.

Already feeling the effects of the first sherry, he signaled the waiter for two more. By the time the second drink arrived, much of his uneasiness had disappeared. He looked down and surveyed the grand ballroom.

"See something, darling?"

"Just counting bird colonels. Never've seen so many. Enough to start a chicken ranch."

She smiled. Robb watched her scan the tables and make eye contact all around the room. Glenn Miller's *"Blue Champagne"* began to play on the jukebox. Robb's mind shifted gears; he thought about Austin, Texas, high school dances, movies, Walgreen's, hamburger joints, spiked-cokes, parked cars and Beth. It was hard to believe how much his life had changed in the past 18 months. He wished Beth could see him now.

"Darling, you look oceans away."

"One of my favorites. Reminds me of home."

"It does take one back. It reminds me of the last night I spent with my husband before he went to North Africa." She paused and took a sip. "I've never discussed it with anyone before." She touched his hand and looked into his eyes. "Do you mind?"

By now the sherry had kicked in and had completely relaxed him. "I'd like to hear about it." He was curious and it would keep her from asking questions.

"That night we had attended a concert at the Royal Albert Hall and were on the way back to our Sloane Street flat when there was an air attack. Some of the bombs were dropping quite close but we decided not to go to an air raid shelter and hurried back to our flat. For nearly an hour bombs fell while searchlights scanned the sky and antiaircraft guns roared. Afterwards noisy ambulances and fire trucks raced up and down the streets all night long. It turned out to be one of London's worst bombings and it was a night I'll never forget."

She told Robb that after Dunkirk her husband had served in London on the staff at Whitehall. She said it had been like a second honeymoon but freely admitted to occasional affairs with other men. Finally, she paused and took a sip. "Darling, I do love my husband. He's the kindest, gentlest man I have ever known. I hope I haven't shocked you."

Robb didn't know what to say. He had heard many British married couples took a more liberal view of their sex lives. But Joyce was so beautiful and so proper that her admissions stunned him.

"I have shocked you, haven't I?" she asked.

"It's none of my business," he finally replied. "I'm just happy to be with you."

"I'm happy to be with you too, darling."

The waiter placed the two sherries on the table. Robb paid him and raised his glass. "Cheers."

"Cheers, darling."

He took a sip of sherry as his mind continued to struggle with what she had said. He had never dreamed he could ever love a woman who had slept with so many men, but her beauty and unbelievable sex made him have doubts about the importance of virginity. There was something else about Joyce that attracted him, something more than sex and beauty and he didn't know what it was. *You'd better back off junior. . .you know damned well that she's way outta your league.*

"Darling, you're drifting away again," she said grasping his hand.

He glanced at the bar, then back to Joyce. "Big ballroom, Texas size," he said, and quickly took another sip. *Now that was really brilliant. You're a helluva conversationalist.*

"Yes, darling," she said with a smile. "One of London's largest."

"Could loop the group in it."

She smiled. "I'm feeling a little tiddley. We'd better eat."

£££

Following lunch, they walked through Hyde Park toward Sloane Street. Elderly men and women were vacating the park to get home before the gray day faded into night. A few eager Hyde Park lovers had already selected their favorite benches.

When Robb and Joyce reached the apartment building the white-haired operator coaxed the ancient elevator to the seventh floor. After unlocking the door she led Robb to the bedroom. Exhausted sleep finally followed three spring storms that night.

£££

"Wake up, darling," she purred. Robb struggled to open his eyes, but couldn't hold them open. She gently shook him. "Darling, wake up. You said you wanted to take the 2:30 train to Colchester and it's noon."

He opened his eyes and struggled to sit up in bed. Two days and nights of strenuous sex had stiffened the muscles in his back, neck and arms. She handed him the mug of tea. The sheer negligee revealed her beautiful body. He took a sip of tea and smiled.

"Darling, why are you smiling?"

"I was just wondering if you could die from too much sex."

"Maybe we should try," she said climbing in bed next to him.   A f t e r another spring storm and prolonged bath, Robb dressed and packed his musette bag while Joyce prepared their breakfast. As they ate, she asked, "Couldn't you take a later train?"

"I really have to get back because I'll be flying tomorrow and I need time to get adjusted after London."

"I understand, darling. I've enjoyed our time together...so much," she said, grasping his hand across the table.

He pulled his hand free and stood up. She stood and pulled him close. Her parted lips met his and her tongue searched wildly. He finally pulled his head back, "Joyce, I really have to get going." He knew that if he didn't leave now they would be back in bed within minutes.

"Yes darling. Will you promise to write?" she asked as he put on his trench coat.

"I promise."

£££

The London to Colchester train pulled from the Liverpool Street Station and accelerated smoothly until the faint clickity-clacks of its wheels reached a steady beat. In the warm compartment, Robb stretched out across the long comfortable seat and closed his eyes. He never realized that he had been capable of so much sex. He thought about the other men who had slept with Joyce and felt a pang of jealousy. He opened his eyes and quickly reminded himself that their relationship was all about sex.

£££

After getting a jeep from the motor pool, Big John hurried to the Post Exchange and bought a dozen Hershey Almond bars. He hoped the Heinz catsup bottle filled with Scotch and the Hershey bars would keep Veronica quiet about the egg money he owed her.

He wheeled the jeep through the gate to Veronica's chicken ranch. He slammed the gearshift into second and floorboarded the accelerator. The jeep's rear wheels spun and the gravel flew as he sped up the drive. He whipped the jeep in behind the house and skidded to a stop.

Veronica stood in the open doorway. As Big John approached, she grinned and blood oozed from the crack in her chapped lips. She grabbed the front of his leather A-2 jacket with her meaty left hand and pulled him toe-to-toe. Before he could say anything, she wrapped her big right arm around his neck, licked the blood off her lip and planted her mouth over his.

Big John put the heel of his hand on her forehead and pushed hard to unseal their lips. "Ease off," he gasped. "Breakin' my frickin' neck...ain't gonna get ya laid."

"Sorry, Ducky. Ah've missed ye." She removed her arm, took his hand, pulled him inside, kicked the door shut, led him to the living room and stopped in front of the sofa. "What ye have in bags, Ducky?"

"Brought you some chockie and Scotch." He handed her the bag of Hershey bars and the catsup bottle of Scotch.

She sat them on the table, grabbed a Hershey bar, ripped off the wrapper, stuffed the bar into her mouth and chewed wildly. With chocolate leaking from the corner of her mouth, she grabbed the bottle, unscrewed the lid and took a big swig of Scotch. "Ye 'didn't bring much Scotch, Ducky."

"Got some moose-juice in the jeep. We can drink that later."

"Do ye 'ave to 'urry back to the field?" she asked, unsnapping the bib of her blue overalls.

"Can spend the night. But gotta get a load of eggs back to the field in time for breakfast." He took off his 50-mission crush garrison cap, carefully placed it on the table and started to undress. "You promised me you'd trim your toe nails," he said, glancing at her bare feet.

"Ah've been busy, Ducky." She stepped out of her overalls, sat down on the sofa. "Sit here, Ducky." She patted the sofa cushion. As he started to sit, she grabbed his hand and pulled him down on top of her.

£££

WHAM! The back door slammed shut. Big John opened his eyes. Veronica thundered across the kitchen floor in her big rubber Wellington boots and the dishes in the hutch rattled. She banged a bucket into the sink and ran some water, then thundered down the hallway to the living room and stopped next to Big John.

Big John held his nose. "Why do you wear those frickin' boots in the house?"

"Ah've been gatherin' our precious ieggs." She sat down on the edge of the sofa. With both hands, she pulled off a Wellington and let it thump to the floor. Then she pulled off the other one, dropped it and wiped her hands on the legs of her overalls.

"Move those damned boots outside. Then wash your frickin' hands and pour us some moose-juice."

"Stop usin' that word frickin.' Ye know ah 'ates it."

"Yeah, yeah. Just get your butt in gear."

"Right'o, Ye Majesty." She picked up her Wellingtons, bowed from the waist, then did an about-face and marched out of the room. Her bare heels banged the wooden floor like a bass drum.

Veronica returned, bowed from the waist, thrust her arm toward Big John and handed him his drink. "Ye drink, Ye Majesty."

"Did ya wash your hands?"

"Smell, Ducky," she said, clamping her big hand over his face.

"God damn it." He pushed her hand away, spit and wiped his mouth on his forearm, then took a swig of his moose-juice.

Veronica took a big swig. "Ah don't know 'ow we drink this bloody rot. Wish we had more Scotch."

"Damned good moose-juice, Queenie." He took another big swig.

"Stinks like moose's piss." Veronica lifted her glass and held it to the light. "Even looks like moose piss. Ruddy awful. Ta, Ducky." She downed the drink in one gulp. "Blimey! Even tastes like moose's piss. Ye 'ave mooseys at the field, Ducky? "

"Only two, for blendin' our juice." He grinned and took a sip.

"Bloody moose-juice, knocks me for a loop. Makes me cushy too."

"You got that right, queenie."

"But ah feels all puffed-out the next day. Ducky, where's me iegg lolly?"

"Bring it next time, Queenie."

"Like bloody 'ell you will. Ah gets paid now or no more ieggs, mate."

"Relax Queenie. Got a deal cookin'. Need some cash to swing it. We'll make a killin'. Big bucks. Be patient."

"Patient me bloody arse. Ah'm no bloody muggins. Ah wants me lolly."

"Trust me, Queenie." He took her hand and pulled her close.

"Aye-aye, none of that, mate."

He pulled her hand under the blanket.

"Oooh blimey. But ah gets me lolly next time, Ducky. Or ye get bugger-all. Chockie or no chockie. Careful Ducky. You're 'urtin me charlies."

£££

Robb's train arrived at Colchester and he hurried from the station and boarded the GI truck going to Boxted. The frigid North Sea wind howled through the gaps in the canvas top and he hunched behind the collar of his trench coat. Last night at this time he and Joyce had been in her nice warm bed. That now seemed like another world, another time.

The truck stopped at the front gate and the two MP's checked everyone's ID cards, then let the truck pass. Robb got off at the central bus stop and walked down the lane leading to his Nissen hut. From the flight line came the growl of Merlin engines and the rat-a-tat-tat of machine gun fire as crew chiefs and armament crews readied their P-51's for the next morning's mission.

Chilled to the bone, Robb hurried inside the hut, groped through the darkness, dropped his musette bag on his bunk and found his flashlight. He closed the blackout blinds, turned on the overhead light bulb, took an old *STARS and STRIPES*, wadded its pages and stuffed them inside the potbellied stove. He placed scraps of wood and added a few chunks of coal, opened the stove's draft and lit the paper. As the flames danced, he turned on the radio to the American Armed Forces Network. Tommy Dorsey's recording of *"I'll Never Smile Again,"* with Frank Sinatra, started to play. It reminded him of Austin and Beth.

BAAM! The door slammed against the steel bunk, "Damned wind!" Ted forced the door shut. "It's colder than hell. Just came from operations. Our flight's on the schedule for tomorrow."

"Yeah...that figures."

"Have a good time in London, Robb?"

"Uh huh. A couple of days in London dulled my killer instincts."

"I wish could say the same."

"What did you do for excitement?" Robb asked, as he added more coal to the fire.

"Called a London friend several times, but never got an answer. So I gave up, went to High Wycombe to see dad."

"What's going on in the rarefied air of higher headquarters?" Robb asked, sitting on the edge of his bunk and staring at the orange light coming from the stove's open draft.

"Dad confirmed the rumor about requiring us to strafe airfields after we escort the bombers out of the high-threat area. Moguls at 8th know our losses will be extremely high because most airfields are loaded with flak and automatic weapons. So they're gonna give the same credit for aircraft destroyed on the ground as air-to-air kills. A lot of Americans will become aces, but so will a lot of kraut gunners."

"Yeah." Glenn Miller's *Sunrise Serenade* began to play and reminded Robb of his high school graduation dance. The band had played it three times that night because of all the requests.

"Our bomber crews will be getting some bad news, too. Their tours are going to be increased from 25 to 35 missions."

"Poor bastards. They've had such high losses. A lot of 'em never completed 25," Robb said as he continued to stare at the flames.

"Yeah, it was really a tough decision for General Spaatz. Dad said Spaatz didn't have a choice. But that's only one of his problems. Some senior RAF types have been bad-mouthing our American daylight bombing effort. They're saying it hasn't accomplished much and claim the *Luftwaffe* is stronger now than before we started our bombing effort. Others are saying our B-17's and B-24's are worthless and should be limited to submarine patrol. If this stuff ever leaks to the press and gets to our heavy bomber crews, morale will be shattered."

"That kind'a talk is gross. They know how many guys we're losing every day. I wonder what the hell they're trying pull?"

"Dad says a few blokes are sanctimonious bastards who think we are a bunch of inferiors who couldn't make it in Britain."

"That really pisses me off. The Americans have done more in 200 years than the blokes have in 2000." Robb added more coal to the fire, kicked the stove door shut, got into his bunk and pulled the blankets up under his chin.

"You got that right, Robb. And I'll lay even money that we'll widened the gap even faster in the future." Ted turned off the radio and the light and got into his bunk.

Robb stared through the darkness at the orange light coming from the stove's draft. He never dreamed there had been so much high level bickering between the British and Americans. The two RAF fighter pilots he had met were very friendly and happy the Americans had joined them in the fight against Germany. *Someday...if I survive this damned war...I'm gonna learn more about the key players and what hell went on behind the scenes.*

CHAPTER 10

The Armed Forces Staff College
Norfolk, Virginia
February 21, 1955

The Army Air Forces and 8th Air Force during World War II

By
Major Robb Baines, USAF
Class 55A

Part II (of III parts).

"The only thing worse than fighting with allies is fighting against them."
Winston Churchill.

£££

A. Bastard – First to Fight in Europe
    I.   After Japan's sneak attack on Pearl Harbor, President Franklin D. Roosevelt and Prime Minister Winston S. Churchill held their first wartime conference in Washington, D.C., December 24, 1941 through January 14, 1942. Their military chiefs agreed that Germany should be defeated first, with a cross-channel invasion of the Continent in 1943. The initial phase of the "Germany First" strategy called for the Army Air Forces (AAF) to immediately "...operate offensively in collaboration with the Royal Air Force, primarily against German Military Power at its source." The US Army's bastard would be the first American force to take the battle to the Nazi's homeland.
    2.   General Henry H. "Hap" Arnold believed that Germany's military and industrial complex would be an ideal system of targets to prove the AAF's daylight precision bombing concept. Consequently, he planned to make the British-based 8th AF the largest strategic air force in the world. He was determined to overwhelm the *Luftwaffe* and bring Germany's war-making capability to its knees before the invasion.
        a.   Arnold hoped to have 66 combat groups (3600 aircraft and 200,000 airmen) in Britain by March 1943. His chief lieutenant, Major General Carl A. "Tooey" Spaatz would command the 8th AF, with Brigadier General Ira C. Eaker in command of the bombers and Brigadier General Frank O. D. "Monk" Hunter commanding the fighters.

£££

B. Everybody Wants a Piece of the Bastard
    I.   Unfortunately, in early 1942 the Japanese swept through Malaya, the Netherlands East Indies and Northern Burma, threatening India and Australia. At the same time, Nazi forces were poised to push to the Nile and it seemed likely that they would make another thrust from the Caucasus to east of Suez. The possibility of a Nazi and Japanese linkup put the Middle East and much of the Pacific in jeopardy. As a result, air units earmarked for Britain had to be diverted to the Middle East and Pacific, delaying the 8th AF's buildup.

C. 8th AF Team Moves To Britain
   I. General Eaker went to Britain in February 1942 to understudy the RAF's Bomber Command and prepare for the arrival of 8th AF units. Although some work had started, Eaker faced a myriad of operational, maintenance and administrative problems—all with short fuses.
       a. More than 100 airfields and smaller stations had to be readied or constructed. An integrated communications system had to be developed to tie the American airfields together and link them to the RAF. A large aircraft maintenance and supply organization had to be established to support the huge force of aircraft, motor vehicles and people.
       b. To expedite the U.S.'s presence, General Spaatz directed that 8th AF units be sent to Britain as soon as they were capable of making the flight across the Atlantic. Consequently, Eaker had to plan a six-week combat training program to get the aircrews combat-ready in bombing, gunnery, instrument flying, and high altitude formation.
   2. General Eaker had the full cooperation of the RAF. They made bombing and gunnery ranges available, trained the AAF air intelligence personnel, taught their weather forecasters the peculiarities of European weather, did everything possible to help ready their fellow airmen for combat.
   3. General Spaatz arrived on June 16 and General Hunter in July. By August, 164 P-38's, 119 B-17's and 103 C-47's had flown to Britain via the North Atlantic. More than a hundred bombers and fighters were scheduled to arrive each month thereafter. Although the Middle East and Pacific continued to compete for forces, the 8th AF buildup appeared to be under way.

£££

D. Game Plan Changes
   I. Many Americans disagreed with the military buildup in Britain while the Pacific war was being fought on a shoestring. Feeling the political pressure in an election year, President Roosevelt believed that he had to get American ground forces engaged in combat against Germany by 1942 to preserve the "Germany First" strategy.
       a. In July, Roosevelt and Churchill decided to invade Northwest Africa. An invasion would accomplish three things: (1) ease the political pressure at home, (2) allay Stalin's demands for a second

front, and (3) take pressure off the North African British Eighth Army by threatening the German's rear.

2. On August 16, 1942, the day after the 8th AF's first B-17 combat mission, General Eisenhower ordered General Spaatz to transfer his best combat units to the new African-bound 12th AF. Two heavy bomb groups, two P-38 groups (the only long-range fighters in Europe), two 8th AF Spitfire groups, one light and three medium bomb groups and a troop carrier group were reassigned to the 12th AF. Much of the 8th's maintenance equipment and 75% of its spare aircraft parts were also given to 12th AF units. By October the 8th AF had provided the 12th AF with 3,198 officers, 24,124 enlisted men and 1,244 aircraft. General Eisenhower also took Spaatz to Africa to command American Air Forces.

3. When General Eaker assumed command of the 8th AF on December 1, 1942, it had lost most of its trained flying units, many key people and much of its critical support equipment and supplies. At the same time, the pipeline of men and equipment to the 8th AF slowed to a trickle while the North African requirements were being satisfied.

£££

E. General Arnold Battles to Keep 8th AF Alive

1. Although the North Africa operation sidetracked the planned 1943 invasion of the Continent, Generals Marshall and Arnold never wavered in their belief that the decisive blow against Germany must come with a cross-channel invasion.

2. Everyday, General Arnold battled the Army and Navy numbers-crunchers who wanted to send more B-17's and B-24's to Asia and the Pacific. Many of the crunchers were the same people who had tried to kill the heavy bomber program before the war. The constant battle to protect the integrity of his forces probably helped hasten Arnold's first heart attack.

£££

F. General Eaker's Problems

1. While General Arnold fought daily battles in Washington, General Eaker struggled to mount a strategic bombing campaign against Germany, which had the strongest air defenses in the world.

   a. For over a year, 8th AF bomber aircrews suffered some of the highest losses of any service during all of World War II. One of the bloodiest missions occurred on August 17, 1943, when 376 B-17's and B-24's struck the Schweinfurt ball bearing plant and

Regensburg Messerschmitt factory. (As planned, Colonel Curtis LeMay's 146 bombers struck Regensburg and landed in North Africa. Due to losses and battle damage, only 84 of LeMay's bombers made it back to Britain a week later). Sixty-three of the 376 bomber force were shot down and another 116 received substantial battle damage, some of which never flew again.

b.   A comparison of AAF casualties (killed, wounded and missing in action) by theater illustrate the intensity of the air war in Europe. In Germany-France there were 63,410 casualties and the Mediterranean had 31,155 casualties. In the China-Burma-India theater there were 3,332 casualties and 682 were lost in Alaska.

2.   Eaker's second major problem was a lack of a "blind bombing" (radar) capability. As a consequence, bad weather reduced the number of missions flown and accounted for about 50% of 8th AF's ineffective sorties when missions were flown.

a.   Although Generals Spaatz and Eaker started looking for a blind bombing capability in the summer of 1942, it was not until the fall of 1943 that the British-developed H2S airborne radar became available. Eaker managed to borrow eight sets. He wanted more, but the British manufacturer couldn't meet the demands of the RAF. The Radiation Laboratory at MIT developed an American version of the H2S called the H2X.

b.   The 8th AF first bombed with the borrowed H2S radar on September 27, 1943, and started using the H2X on November 2, 1943. The limited number of radar-equipped B-17's, called "path finders," led formations to the target and signaled the other bombers when to drop their bombs. Although much less accurate than visual bombing, radar permitted more frequent attacks. When General Spaatz took command of the US strategic air forces in Europe (USSTAF) on January 1, 1944, the 8th AF had only 12 of the B-17's radar equipped and none of the B-24's.

3.   Overseas combat training of replacement aircrews remained a requirement in the 8th AF throughout the war. In some theaters, aircrews could be sent into combat with minimal training, but not in Europe; the stakes were too high.

a.   In the beginning, bomber pilots needed high altitude formation flights with maximum bomb loads. Aerial gunners lacked proficiency; some bombardiers hadn't yet dropped bombs from their B-17's or B-24's. Fighter pilots needed high altitude tactical training, and air and ground gunnery training. All pilots required more instrument flight training to cope with the bad European weather. Later, improved training in the US eased the problem but never eliminated it.

4.   The fourth major problem was a lack of a long-range escort fighter, which was due in part to the "invincible bomber doctrine" that prevailed in the Army Air Corps before World War II. The doctrine was strengthened with the arrival of the B-17 in 1935. The B-17 was called the Flying Fortress because of the number of guns it carried. In addition, it was faster than most of the antiquated fighters of the day. The invincible bomber theorists considered the Flying Fortress to be a near perfect solution.

  a.   By 1940, some Army airmen recognized the need for bomber protection, but it appeared that fighters might never have enough range to escort bombers. When it became obvious in Europe that the bombers needed protection from fighters to survive, the YB-40 (an armor plated B-17 with extra machine guns) was developed for bomber defense. Fourteen YB-40's were built and tested by the 8th AF in 1943. Their added weight made them too slow to keep up with the regular bombers after they dropped their bombs. In addition, their defensive capability proved to be negligible. The YB-40 program was such a flop, the YB-41 (the B-24 escort version) was cancelled.

  b.   When 8th AF's long range P-38's were sent to North Africa, the relatively new P-47's had to be used. But it had equipment problems and its escort range, without external tanks, was only 175 miles. More P-38's were requested for the 8th AF, although 9th AF units were scheduled to be equipped with the P-51 to be used as ground attack fighters.

(1).   Designed by North American Aviation of California for the RAF, the P-51 first flew in October 1940. Even with an inferior low altitude engine, the performance of the P-51 (RAF called it the Mustang) was superior to other American fighters. But in the Army Air Force Headquarters and the Wright Field Test Center, the P-51 suffered from the NIH (not invented here) factor.

(2).   In the fall of 1942, the RAF installed the British Merlin engine in the P-51, which vastly improved the 51's overall performance, especially at high altitude. The RAF's P-51/Merlin engine flight test data eventually reached General Arnold and he immediately ordered 2200 P-51's with the Merlin engine. But the USAAF remained oblivious to the P-51's full potential.

(3). Ironically, the 1943-production cost of the P-51 was $58,824 per aircraft, versus $104,258 for the P-47 and $105,567 for the P-38.

    c. Not until the 9th AF's 354th Fighter Group demonstrated the P-51's superior range and fighting ability against the *Luftwaffe*, was the P-51 considered for the 8th AF escort mission. Consequently, General Spaatz ordered the bulk of the 9th AF P-51's be sent to the 8th AF and that the 9th AF be given P-47's and some of the P-38's.

    d. A comparison of fighter **escort ranges** reflects one part of the P-51's superior performance.

(1) After numerous modifications and the addition of two 108-gallon external wing tanks, the P-47's escort range eventually reached 475 miles.

(2) The P-38, with the two 108-gallon tanks, could escort out to 585 miles.

(3) The P-51 with no tanks could escort out to 475 miles. The addition of two 108-gallon tanks took the P-51 out to 850 miles.

£££

G. Royal 'Bad-mouthing'

    1. Because high losses forced the RAF to give up daylight bombing, many in Britain believed the Americans couldn't hack it either. But American airmen knew the majority of military targets were small and required daylight, precision bombing to destroy them. Furthermore, the *Luftwaffe*, like all air forces of World War II, operated primarily during daylight hours. As a result, the bulk of the fighting to win air superiority would have to be fought during daylight.

    2. At the January 1943 Casablanca Conference, General Arnold anticipated that Winston Churchill would recommend to President Roosevelt that the 8th AF be switched to night operations. To help sway Churchill, Arnold summoned Eaker to Casablanca.

        a. General Eaker impressed Churchill with his enthusiasm for and knowledge of precision daylight bombing. Eaker closed his presentation by saying, "We'll bomb the devils around the clock." Churchill agreed not to broach the subject with Roosevelt and later used variations of Eaker's closing remark in some of his speeches.

        b. But some Britains remained critical of the US Army Air Force's daylight concept and their heavy bombers. A Peter Masefield from the *Sunday Times* reported that many in the RAF believed the B-17's and B-24's were capable of neither night nor day operations and should be used for submarine patrol. This story must have put a smile on every Nazi's face. It definitely undermined the morale of 8th AF bomber crews who were laying their lives on the line. For General Spaatz and other American air commanders, Masefield's story smacked of treason.

   c.   After the war, Albert Speer, Germany's Minister for Armament and War Production, stated that the 8th AF not only cleared the *Luftwaffe* from the sky, but also destroyed much of Germany's capability to wage war. Speer's statement helped corroborate the irresponsibility of a few in the RAF, Masefield, the *Sunday Times* and much of the British Press.

£££

H.   The Royal Backseat Drivers.

Student comments: Understandably, the Americans accepted the "British way" when the US first entered the war. But after America's military might overshadowed Britain's and the Yanks had honed their fighting skills, Americans sometimes saw a better way. But it's difficult to break an imperial bulldog's hold, once he's sunk his teeth.

£££

Student comments: As I reviewed the European air war, my respect for General Dwight D. "Ike" Eisenhower and General Carl A. "Tooey" Spaatz deepened. Despite a constant imperial undertow, Eisenhower and Spaatz maintained their balance, kept their eye on the ball and got the job done. Lesser men would have been pulled under.

   I.   Churchill ceded the Supreme Commander's slot to the Americans for the cross-channel invasion, but cleverly installed British commanders of the allied tactical air and naval forces. The British would also command all Allied ground forces during the early stages of the invasion, but they hoped the command arrangement might eventually become permanent.

      a   . The British had used a similar scheme in North Africa and the Mediterranean. Referring to the North African command relationship, Field Marshall Viscount Alanbrooke, Chief of the British Imperial General Staff, noted in his diary,

"We were pushing Eisenhower into the stratosphere and rarefied atmosphere of a Supreme Commander, where he would be free to devote his time to the political and inter-allied problems, whilst we inserted under him one of our own commanders to deal with the military situations and to restore the necessary drive and coordination which had been so seriously lacking."

2. General Bernard L. Montgomery, Churchill's choice to command the ground forces for the cross-channel invasion, never concealed his disdain for Americans, while American generals believed Montgomery to be an overcautious and plodding egomaniac.

    a. Even Churchill said of Montgomery, "In defeat unbeatable; in victory unbearable." Air Chief Marshall Sir Arthur Tedder, Eisenhower's deputy, once said of Montgomery, "He is a little fellow of average ability who has had such a build-up that he thinks of himself as Napoleon. He is not."

3. To further limit Eisenhower's authority, Churchill told him that as the hosting nation, the British would retain control of the RAF Bomber Command, Fighter Command and Naval Coastal Command as symbols of British prestige and independence. Churchill even suggested that Eisenhower's authority, as a Supreme Commander, be terminated as soon as a lodgment in France had been achieved after D-Day.

4. Although Eisenhower had to walk a diplomatic tight rope, he seldom permitted the British to command large numbers of American ground forces and when he did, it was normally for short periods. But in the case of the US Army Air Forces, Eisenhower let General Spaatz and his 615,000 airmen get buried beneath three layers of British control.

    a. The top layer started with Churchill, because the RAF never hesitated to use him as their trump card whenever Spaatz disagreed. The second layer was Air Chief Marshal Charles A. Portal, Chief of the Air Staff of the RAF, who acted as the senior allied airman for all allied air forces in Europe and Mediterranean. General Eisenhower's deputy, Air Chief Marshal Arthur W. Tedder, provided the third RAF layer.

    b. Although the command arrangement usurped much of General Spaatz's authority, the resolute Spaatz subordinated his personal feelings and worked within the imperial system. After Spaatz left North Africa and returned to Britain as the senior US airman in Europe and the commander of all American strategic air forces in Europe (USSTAF), he dug in his heels or worked around the British when the "imperial ways" made no sense.

£££

I. The Royal Square Peg Enters

    I. The British installed Air Marshal Sir Trafford Leigh-Mallory as the tactical air force commander for the invasion without Eisenhower's approval or coordination. On paper, Leigh-Mallory's credentials looked good, but his degree of arrogance was on a par with General Montgomery's.

a. Leigh-Mallory was also a charter member of the "Royal Order of Egotists" and had never developed the art of listening. As a key fighter commander during the "Battle of Britain" Leigh-Mallory had difficulty dealing with both his RAF peers and superiors and barely escaped a "sacking." Even some of his supporters described him as haughty, tactless, pompous and completely without finesse. As the allied tactical air commander, he eventually alienated his RAF and American Tactical air force commanders, his American deputies, as well as Air Chief Marshal Tedder and others.

2. Leigh-Mallory's assigned forces were the RAF's 2nd Tactical Air Force and the US's 9th Tactical Air Force, which had twice the strength of the 2nd TAF. Due to vague guidance and a well-honed presumptuous manner, Leigh-Mallory assumed himself to be the "Supreme Allied Air Force Commander." As such, he believed that he could take charge of the USAAF and RAF strategic bombers whenever he desired to support his preinvasion air attacks.

a. Without consultation with either the American or British strategic air force commanders, Leigh-Mallory decreed he'd take control of all strategic air forces on March I, 1944. He specified that the strategic bombers would attack transportation targets (rail centers and lines of communications) until further notice.

3. General Spaatz, Air Chief Marshall, Sir Arthur "Bomber" Harris, head of RAF Bomber Command and others voiced strong objections with both Leigh-Mallory's target selection and his timing for the use of the strategic bombers.

a. Transportation experts from British intelligence, who had not been consulted either, stated the *Wehrmacht* and *Luftwaffe* needed only a fraction of the vast German-French railroad net for their use, making it extremely difficult to stop the flow of supplies and troops for extended periods. Others believed that the large number of transportation targets would require an inordinate amount of air effort that could better be spent on more crucial targets. Most important, tactical air experience had proven that attacks on transportation targets were most effective when the ground forces were in a position to immediately exploit their destruction.

4. Spaatz had always agreed that his strategic bombers would provide direct support for the invasion, but not until about 60 days before D-Day, giving him time to first win air superiority.

    a. Spaatz rightly believed that winning air superiority would be a slow bloody battle of attrition that would have to be fought during daylight hours over Germany. The winner would be the one who could sustain the losses and continue unremitting air attacks against the enemy's most crucial military targets.

    (1) Since *Luftwaffe* fighters had forced the RAF strategic bombers to operate at night and the RAF had very few long-range fighters, the battle for air superiority would be predominantly an American fight.

    (2) After the "Big Week" (see paragraph J. below), there were unmistakable indications the Germans were husbanding their fighter forces. Spaatz knew his strategic bombers had to hit vital Nazi targets to bring the *Luftwaffe* up to fight. Common sense told him that it would be virtually impossible, highly wasteful and extremely illogical for the *Luftwaffe* to attempt to defend the extensive German-French rail net.

    (3) As stated in paragraph 3.a (above), attacks against rail and other lines of communications would only make sense if they occurred just before and during the D-Day invasion, when the Allied ground forces could take advantage of attacks.

    b. With these factors in mind, Spaatz argued that bombing transportation targets too soon would allow the Germans time to repair the damage, while permitting the *Luftwaffe* to rebuild their fighter forces—making them a greater threat during D-Day and putting the invasion in jeopardy.

5. Leigh-Mallory countered that striking rail centers would bring the German fighters "aloft." When Spaatz asked, "What if the Germans don't defend the rail centers? How will air superiority be won?" Leigh-Mallory responded that the fight to win air superiority could wait until the troops were crossing the beaches.

6. Spaatz, a quiet man, whose motto was, "I never learned anything by talking," couldn't believe that an airman, who had commanded RAF fighters during the "Battle of Britain," could downplay the importance of air superiority before **the largest and riskiest military invasion in history.** From then on, Spaatz viewed the obdurate Leigh-Mallory as a loose cannon with an endless supply of faulty ammunition.

7. Fortunately, Leigh-Mallory's inept handling of his "transportation plan" created such a donnybrook that the proposal had to be put on hold while it got "committeeized." In late February, Churchill entered the fray because of his concern for the number of French civilians that might be killed during the bombing of railroad targets. Churchill's

concerns delayed approval of the plan until April, allowing Spaatz more time to win air superiority and reduce Germany's industrial might.

a.   Spaatz approved the use of a portion of the fighters to act as a "freelance fighter force." They would be free to seek out the *Luftwaffe* before they could assemble and attack the bombers. He believed such action would reduce the B-17 and B-24 losses.

b   . To expedite the destruction of *Luftwaffe* fighters, Spaatz requested that the fighters strafe German airfields, after they had completed their escort duties. Knowing most airfields were heavily defended and losses would probably triple, the 8th AF provided an incentive for strafing attacks by giving ground kills the same credit as aerial kills, As it turned out, the strafing losses were five times higher than air-to-air combat losses.

c   . By February, Spaatz's 8th Air Force had 2295 heavy bombers and enough H2X radar equipped bombers to attack with a large force when visual bombing was not possible. They also had sufficient P-51's and P-38's to provide limited escort to Berlin and beyond. His relatively new 15th Air Force had 1292 heavy bombers, but no H2X capable bombers and only four fighter escort groups, none of which were P-51's. Consequently, the 15th couldn't bomb in bad weather, and with inadequate fighter protection, they suffered high losses to enemy fighters whenever they attacked the high-threat targets in Germany and Yugoslavia.

d.   The bad winter weather remained the main obstacle to Spaatz's aerial offensive and in one of his messages to Arnold, he stated, "...with a few days of visual precision bombing of aircraft plants, a giant step would be taken towards air superiority. Losses will be heavy, but the price has to be paid some time and will result in fewer losses later...."

£££

J.   The Big Week

I.   A break in the weather finally came on February 20. For five of the next six days, the weather permitted Spaatz to attack critical German targets with a total of 3300 heavy bombing sorties from the 8th AF and another 500 from the 15th AF. RAF Bomber Command also flew 2351 night sorties against some of the same targets. The 8th AF dropped more bombs during these five missions than had been dropped during their first year of operation. The five days of attacks became known as "The Big Week."

a.   The 8th AF lost 137 heavy bombers and the 15th AF lost 89 bombers. The RAF lost 157 bombers due in part to the improved German night fighter operations. Their five-day loss rate exceeded that of the 8th AF.

    b.   The 8th fighters also launched 2548 escort sorties, 712 of which were provided by the 9th Tactical Air Force. The 15th AF launched 413 fighter sorties to protect their bombers. The 8th and 15th AF's lost 28 American fighters. German records for the five days stated that 131 *Luftwaffe* fighters were shot down and more than 100 were heavily damaged. (Their records also reported that the *Luftwaffe* lost 533 fighters during the month of February.)

    c.   As usual, the B-17 and B-24 aerial gunners' claims were high because in the heat of battle, 10 to 15 gunners could be firing at the same fighter when it went down. One thing is certain: the number of claims by aerial gunner's always reflected the intensity of the battle.

2.   But the most important contribution of the fierce aerial combat of January and February 1944 went unnoticed by the Allies: 30 percent of the *Luftwaffe's* fighter pilots were shot down or severely wounded. Included were many of their experienced flight leaders.

    a.   Fighting on three fronts (Russian, Mediterranean and European), the *Luftwaffe's* pilot training program could not keep pace with their losses. When the 8th and 15th Air Forces' increased their attacks, Luftwaffe losses jumped. By February of 1944, the shortage of German fighter pilots became critical and the *Luftwaffe* had to limit their defensive operations. A few months later, a shortage of aviation fuel also limited combat flying and forced the Germans to begin reducing the number of flight training hours given their new pilots. Consequently, from February 1944 to the end of the war, the Luftwaffe had to fight with a relatively small force using increasing numbers of inadequately trained pilots.

£££

K.   Record Breaking Air Attacks

    I.   During February, March and April, while the committee and Churchill continued to "fine tune" the transportation plan, strategic bombers from the 8th and 15th Air Forces almost doubled their attacks against critical German targets.

    a.   The 8th launched 9884 heavy bomber sorties in February, another 11,590 in March and 14,464 in April. 8th AF escort fighters (with help from the 9th AF) launched 10,295, 14,659 and 14,072 sorties.

(1). February had its Big Week, but the intensity of the aerial combat in March 1944 could be termed as "The Big Month." Despite bad weather, the 8th AF's limited radar bombing capability permitted the bombers to fly 23 missions. On four of those missions, the *Luftwaffe* came up with over 200 fighters and engaged in some of the fiercest aerial combat of the entire war.

(2). Twice, bad weather kept the 8th AF from reaching their targets in Berlin. But on March 6, a force of 653 heavy bombers struck the German capital. The *Luftwaffe* attacked repeatedly with over 200 fighters. Most German fighters landed, refueled, and rearmed, and the *Luftwaffe* flew about 400 sorties. A record-breaking 69 heavy bombers were shot down along with 11 escort fighters. German records indicate the *Luftwaffe* lost 83 aircraft that day, mostly to American fighters.

(3). The 8th AF struck Berlin targets a second time on March 8 and lost 37 heavy bombers and 17 escort fighters, while the *Luftwaffe* reported losing another 80 fighters.

(4). On March 16th and 18th, approximately 700 bombers attacked aircraft plants in southern Germany each day. The two strikes cost the 8th Air Force 66 bombers and 13 fighters, while the *Luftwaffe* reported the loss of 83 fighters.

    (a). An example of the pounding the *Luftwaffe* took was found in the March 16 records of a ME-110 group. On that day, 43 of their ME-110's attacked and shot down 5 bombers before American fighters entered the battle and shot down 26 of the ME-110's. Another ten battle-damaged 110's crashed before they could make it back to their field. The group's seven remaining ME-110's had to be taken out of combat for several months until the group could be re-equipped with the newer ME-410 and provided with minimally trained replacement pilots.

(5). During April, the 8th Air Force bombers attacked twelve German targets, including another Berlin attack on the 29th. They also struck V-weapons sites eight times. The 8th AF fighters conducted seven low altitude fighter sweeps across Germany when the weather wouldn't permit high altitude bombing. The pace of 8th AF fighter's dive bombing and strafing activity increased from 83 sorties in February to 887 in March and 3803 in April.

    b. The 15th Air Force launched 3981 bombing sorties and 2628 fighter sorties in February, 5996 bombing and 4487 fighter in

March and another 10,182 bombing and 6050 fighter in April. But only a fraction of them were against strategic targets because they were tasked to support the beleaguered ground forces in Italy. They were also hampered by the lack of a radar bombing capability in bad weather.

(I). The 15th AF attacked one target in Austria, one in Bulgaria and one in Yugoslavia in the month of March. In April they struck German and Yugoslavian targets ten times. Two of the Yugoslavian strikes were against the oil refineries at Polesti (see paragraph M., 4,below). Whenever the 15th AF heavy bombers attacked German and Yugoslavian targets, they suffered very high losses from German fighter attacks because of a shortage of escort fighters. On April 16, the 15th AF finally received a P-51 group, its fifth operational fighter escort group....

£££

L. Morale

1. Fighting the fiercest combat in the history of aerial warfare took a high toll. The 8th and 15th AF lost 457 heavy bombers in February, 424 in March and 683 in April. The 8th AF fighter sweeps and air to ground attacks increased fighter losses from 172 in January and February to 232 in March and 338 in April. (A few 9th AF losses are included in these figures because they were flown in support of the 8th AF.)

2. Army Air Force casualties (killed or missing in action) in Europe and the Mediterranean numbered 4653 in February, 4744 in March and 7214 in April for a total of 16,611. By comparison, they had 22,176 casualties during the first 25 months of combat with the Germans.

   a. The heavy bomber crews continued to suffer the majority of the losses. On top of that, their combat tours had been lengthened. The crews knew that many of them would be shot down or killed before they completed their combat tours.

(I). One of the indicators of lower morale was the increased number of heavy bombers landing in Sweden and Switzerland due to battle damage. During the period December 1943 through February 1944, only five crews landed because they believed their damaged bomber wouldn't make it back to Britain. In March, 37 landed and another 52 landed in April. Most had extensive battle damage and probably wouldn't have made it back to Britain, but some could have.

3. Because B-17 and B-24 aircrews in Europe and the Mediterranean

suffered one of the highest loss rates of any service during World War II, their morale was always a primary concern. Aircrews were provided several special amenities, including a week of plush living at a British estate to give them a break from the war. To demonstrate leadership by example, a general officer flew on most combat missions. Colonels commanding fighter and bomber groups normally flew more than their share of combat missions as well. Several generals and many colonels were lost in combat.

£££

L.   The RAF's Harpoon
   1.   On April 12, 1944, RAF Headquarters, for reasons known only to them, announced to the press that despite all the 8th AF's bombing and fighter attacks, the strength of the *Luftwaffe* fighter forces protecting Germany proper had increased by "200 to 300 machines." They went on to say that the *Luftwaffe* fighters were now numerically stronger than they ever had been. Naturally, the British press gave the RAF news release front-page coverage.
   2.   Reporting a stronger *Luftwaffe* ran counter to what the Americans were experiencing in combat. It had been obvious to the 8th AF that the *Luftwaffe* had been husbanding their fighter forces by limiting their defenses to only the most critical targets. Such activity rightly suggested that the *Luftwaffe* fighter force had to be on the wane, which Spaatz's intelligence people believed and had reported.
      a.   Lieutenant General Adolf Galland, Commander of the *Luftwaffe* fighters protecting Germany, told the Reich Air Ministry in April 1944 that over 1300 aircraft and 1000 pilots had been lost in the past 90 days. Galland said that 511 fighter pilots were lost in March, which was 21.7 percent of its fighter pilot force. He said his fighters were outnumbered 7 to 1 by a superior enemy fighter force that was getting stronger every day. "...Since American fighters have gone on the offense, no place in Germany is safe from attack...the American air forces now enjoy near air supremacy."
   3.   To make matters worse, the witless RAF news release came the day after the 8th AF had lost 64 heavy bombers, its second highest single-day loss of the war. (That day nine bombers landed in Sweden.) To many, including Generals Spaatz and Doolittle, the news release seemed part of a continuing and sinister anti-American bombing effort by some of the RAF and British press.
   4.   An irritated General Spaatz voiced strong personal objections to the

RAF and also prepared an unsigned letter, which he sent directly to Air Chief Marshal Portal, Chief of the RAF's Air Staff, and hand carried another copy to the US Ambassador, John G. Winant. Winant forwarded Spaatz's letter on to Churchill. Ambassador Winant was sympathetic, because his son, a heavy bomber pilot, had been shot down in October 1943 and the British press ran the story about his son before Winant could inform the rest of the family.

5.   The RAF did eventually apologize for their "machine count" press release about the Luftwaffe strength, but the damage had been done. Their "no brainer" statement to the press had planted the seeds of doubt and many AAF bomber crews wondered if their sacrifices were justified. As a result, Generals Spaatz, Doolittle, Twining and all of their subordinate commanders had to spend an inordinate amount of time trying to convince their aircrews that the RAF announcement had been less than accurate.

£££

M. Spaatz's Oil Plan

1.   After February, when it became apparent to Spaatz and his staff that the *Luftwaffe* had been hurt, and they knew that more critical targets had to be found to keep the Germans coming up to fight. Spaatz recognized that oil was the lifeblood of the German military, just as it was in the American military. There were 54 German fuel plants and refineries (23 synthetic oil plants and 31 oil refineries) that processed 90 percent of Germany's in-country fuel. All were vulnerable to bombing and most were located away from population centers, which made them easy to find and reduced the possibility of civilian casualties. With good weather, the 54 vulnerable targets could be destroyed in a matter of days.

2.   Spaatz believed attacking the oil industry would be a decisive one-two punch. American fighters would shoot down the defending *Luftwaffe* fighters, while the bombers destroyed one of Germany's most critical military resources. He knew that the lack of fuel would soon ground much of the *Luftwaffe*, help to immobilize the *Wehrmacht* and beach a large part of the Nazi Navy. He also believed it might force the *Luftwaffe* to use their night fighters during the day to help defend the oil targets, which would help reduce RAF bomber losses. But Portal, Tedder and Eisenhower refused to increase the priority of oil targets.

3.   The Polesti oil refineries provided Germany with 25 percent of its fuel, making Polesti one of the most important targets in Europe. In Spaatz's mind, its destruction was the logical first step in reducing

Germany's supply of fuel. He made separate requests to bomb Polesti oil refineries with his 15th AF since the 15th wouldn't be part of the D-Day force. But Portal refused each of Spaatz's requests.

4.   About the same time, Portal bypassed Spaatz and directed the 15th AF to bomb some highly questionable political targets. Fed up with the arbitrary, stiff-necked British control, Spaatz decided to attack Polesti oil under the guise of striking the Polesti rail yards, which were located close to the refineries.

      a.   On April 5, the 15th AF accidentally bombed, with great accuracy, an oil refinery instead of the nearby railroad yards. Several more Polesti "transportation missions" were flown in April and more would follow. Polesti oil shipments to Germany dropped from 186,000 tons in March, to 104,000 tons in April and 40,000 tons by June.

5.   On April 19, Spaatz sought Eisenhower's permission for the 8th AF to make two visual strikes against oil targets in Germany to test the *Luftwaffe*'s response. After a heated discussion, Eisenhower gave Spaatz verbal approval, but bad weather delayed the test strikes until May 12 and 28.

6.   The day after the May 12th oil strike, the Allies intercepted a German message that ordered AAA guns pulled from both the Eastern Front and aircraft factories to protect oil refineries. In another intercepted German message after the May 28th oil strike, the Wehrmacht directed that training be reduced to conserve fuel. They also ordered more vehicles converted to wood burning propulsion.

      a.   Albert Speer, Germany's Minister for Armament and War Production, told Hitler after assessing the two oil strikes in May, "The enemy has struck us at one of our weakest points. If they persist at it this time, we will soon no longer have any fuel production worth mentioning. Our one hope is that the other side has an Air Force General Staff as scatterbrained as ours!"

7.   Following the two oil strikes in May, Eisenhower and the British finally saw the light and jumped on the oil bandwagon. The logjam was broken and the lifeblood of the German war machine finally made it to the "Royal" target list.

      a.   By June, German fuel production had been reduced by almost 50%. The *Luftwaffe* had also been forced into using their emergency fuel reserves and placed more limitations on their combat operations. They also had to drastically reduce their pilot training program, which exacerbated their pilot shortage problem, and the quality of their new pilots went from bad to worse.

8. Thanks to a tenacious "Tooey" Spaatz, a major Allied boo-boo was corrected, albeit a little late.

£££

N. (*Vergeltungsnaffes*) Vengeance Weapons
I. The British first learned about Germany's "futuristic" V-weapons development program in 1939. By February 1943, it became clear to British intelligence that the threat had to be taken seriously. For the next 11 months, nearly 40 percent of all reconnaissance sorties were devoted to taking pictures of V-weapon installations and activities.
   a. There were two V-weapons: the V-1 and the V-2. The crude looking V-1, which many referred to as the "buzz-bomb," was a small pilotless airplane that resembled a torpedo with wings. It weighed 4800 pounds, was powered by a ram jet engine and carried 1000 pounds of explosives. The V-2 was a 12-ton rocket, the forerunner of modern day rockets, and carried 2000 pounds of explosives.
   b. In May 1943, an aerial photo of Peenemunde gave the British their first look at a V-1. Other photos showed a huge unexplained concrete structure on the French coast near Watten, which alarmed the British due to its nearness. Eventually, seven Watten type structures were located. The French underground confirmed their unorthodoxy, but not their purpose. Then several long (300 feet), narrow, ski shaped concrete ramp-type structures were spotted, with their axis pointing at Britain. Ninety-six ski sites were eventually started, but only 22 were ever completed.
2. As bits and pieces of information trickled in, accurate estimates of the Vengeance Weapons capabilities got lost in a maze of "frantic guesstimations." The V-2 rocket's weight soared to 100 tons, while the V-1's weight went as high as 20 tons. Some believed the V-weapons were capable of spreading a "Red Death" that could kill every living creature in Britain. Knowing the Germans had used poison gas during WWI, politicians and scientists feared apocalypse in reverse.
3. The British finally revealed most of what they knew about the V-weapons to the Americans on December 1, 1943, when they asked the 9th AF to help bomb the concrete sites. On December 15, they asked General Eaker to use the 8th AF strategic bombers against the sites. The day before Christmas, the weather opened and the 8th AF made its first V-weapons attack near Calais, with 722 bombers and nearly 600 fighters. But many more missions would follow.
4. Although annoyed by the late revelation, the Americans quickly evalu-

ated Britain's unsuccessful efforts to neutralize the V-weapons sites on the coast of France. General Arnold and Spaatz believed the main reason for the lack of success was the failure to determine the best aircraft, weapon and tactics to destroy the concrete sites.

 a. Arnold and Spaatz were also concerned the V-weapons threat would become a major diversion of USAAF strategic air power, keeping their bombers from striking vital military targets in preparation for the D-Day invasion.

5. With General Marshall's approval, General Arnold ordered the Commander of the Air Proving Grounds at Eglin Field, Florida to build a duplicate V-weapons site, then conduct a test to determine the best aircraft, weapon and tactic combination to neutralize the installation. Arnold told the Eglin commander to get the job done "In days, not weeks."

 a. All available concrete within hundreds of miles of Eglin was required to construct the missile site. Military and civilians crews worked in twelve-hour shifts, seven days a week. Army Ground Forces provided a camouflage unit, and an antiaircraft battalion was sent to simulate German defenses. As soon as the concrete had set on the reinforced site, the bombing started. All bombers and fighters were tried with every type bomb-fuse combination and bombing tactic.

 b. The test proved the best combination to be high-speed, low altitude fighter attacks, using 1000 or 2000-pound bombs with delayed fuses. This combination was the most accurate, achieved the most damage with the least amount of exposure to ground defenses and required a relatively small number of sorties to do the job.

£££

O. More Royal Backseat Driving

 1. For reasons that are still unclear, Leigh-Mallory and others in the RAF refused to adopt the Eglin Field tactic and insisted that USAAF strategic bombers be used. Leigh-Mallory claimed fighters were ineffective and too vulnerable to ground fire. He had supposedly arrived at this conclusion based on some RAF dive bombing missions using 250 and 500 pound bombs (small bombs that would do little more than chip the reinforced concrete). Larger bombs with delayed fuses could penetrate the concrete before exploding, causing substantial damage. Dive bombing also exposed fighters to AAA gunfire for at

least 30 seconds, while low level attacks (25-50 feet) reduced their exposure to less than half that time.

2. On May 6, 1944, the Americans ignored the British and sent four P-47's from the 365th Fighter Group to attack one of the missile sites using the Eglin plan. They penetrated heavy ground fire and completely neutralized the site. Leigh-Mallory eventually relented and tried the Eglin tactic, but continued to ask for heavy bomber attacks.

    a. Postwar analysis showed that on average, it took about 70 heavy bombers, dropping 250 tons of bombs, to achieve the same level of damage that low altitude fighters could do with 45 tons and about 10 to 15 fighter sorties. Equally important, the Eglin Field low altitude tactic also permitted attacks beneath low clouds that kept bombers out and allowed more frequent strikes.

    b. During the war, a total of 25,150 sorties were flown against a wide range of V-weapon targets, at a cost of 771 American airmen and 154 aircraft. One hundred and seven missile sites were supposedly neutralized. The 8th AF and 9th AF were credited with 74, and the RAF neutralized 33. Had the Eglin Field low level tactic been used, the same job could've been done better, faster, and with fewer forces, fewer bombs and fewer losses.

3. The first V-I struck London on June 13, 1944. The first V-2 struck a Paris suburb on September 8 and a few hours later the second V-2 landed in London. Although there are variances in numbers, it appears the Germans launched about 13,000 V-I's and 2800 V-2's at France, Belgium, Holland and Britain.

    a. Less then 20% of the V-I's intended for Britain ever reached their target. Many blew up en route, 1866 were shot down by anti-aircraft fire, 1847 were destroyed by fighters, 232 collided with barrage balloon cables and about 20 were downed by Naval forces.

    b. Approximately 9000 Britains were killed by V-weapons. In the cold calculus of war, RAF and USAAF bombers supposedly killed more than 35,000 Germans at Dresden, Germany, in one 24-hour period.

£££

Student comments: Maybe the V-weapons greatest contribution to the Nazi' war effort was the number of heavy bombing sorties and other attack sorties they diverted from Germany. Hitler supposedly said (and if he didn't he should have), "Bombs dropped on missile sites in France reduce the number of bombs dropped on critical targets in Germany."

CHAPTER 11

The Big Week

Late in the afternoon of February 19, 1944, the Colonel and Ted departed the Amersham Hill Station and hurried through the afternoon drizzle to the shiny, old black taxi. A tall gray-haired driver, who wore two rows of World War I ribbons on the lapel of his black suit coat, jumped out of the front seat and opened the rear door. He stood at attention and gave his best British salute. "Colonel, suh."

"Bryon. How've you been?"

"Spiffing, suh. And yourself?"

"Just fine."

Ted tossed his musette bag on the backseat, climbed in and slid across to make room for the Colonel. Headquarters 8th Air Force had asked the Colonel to chair a two-day tactics meeting and he had selected Ted to be his assistant. They would prepare a tactics pamphlet to be used as part of the combat indoctrination for new fighter pilots. Ted looked out the window at the low hanging clouds. He hadn't seen the sun for days and began to wonder if winter would ever end.

"Stopping by the Green Goose for a pinter, suh?" Bryon asked, as he sat down behind the steering wheel.

"Yes, Bryon," the Colonel replied with a smile.

Bryon smiled back as he eased his ancient taxi from the curb and drove slowly up the street. After two blocks, he stopped in front of the Green Goose. They each downed a pinter before continuing on to Wycombe Abbey where the 8th Air Force headquarters was located. Wycombe Abbey had been a posh girl's school before General Ira Eaker selected it for his headquarters.

At the gate, the guard saluted, checked their ID cards, saluted again and motioned them on. Bryon continued down the macadam drive toward the imposing gray stone manor house.

Battlements lined the roof and corner towers. Large mullioned windows overlooked acres of velvet green lawn that surrounded the abbey. The Americans had added a volleyball court and softball diamond next to the two tennis courts. Beyond the lawn lay lush pastures with scattered clumps of beech, oak and chestnut trees.

Bryon stopped near the front door where two staff cars and a jeep were parked. The old man jumped out and opened the door for the Colonel. "When will you be leaving, suh?"

"Hopefully, on the 21st." Knowing the old man was caring for his wife, invalid daughter and the three children of his son who had been killed in Burma, the Colonel handed him a pound note. "Keep the change, Byron."

"Thank you kindly, suh. Here's my card. If you should need me anytime before, please call." Bryon saluted and climbed into his taxi, shifted into low gear and stepped on the accelerator. The exhaust belched blue smoke as the old taxi chugged slowly up the macadam drive toward the guardhouse.

"Ted, you probably want to see your dad. Let's rendezvous in the conference room tomorrow morning at 0830. Will you prepare an outline for the tactics manual, so we can start the discussion right away."

"Yes sir." Ted saluted and the Colonel turned to go inside.

Ted always enjoyed the serenity of the Abbey. He walked out onto the grass where he could see the chapel behind the manor house and more of the grounds. They were beautiful and peaceful, another anomaly of the war.

To his left, stately white swans floated in the Abbey's emerald pond, just as their ancestors had for a hundred years. Five cygnets, in V formation, glided in the water behind their orange-billed mother. Their regal manner left little doubt they knew the royal pecking order.

Another reason Ted enjoyed visiting Wycombe Abbey was that he got to see Technical Sergeant Darlene Bradford, his father's chief clerk. A tall, dark-haired beauty with olive skin and radiant green eyes, her only makeup was lipstick—she didn't need more.

Darlene had studied journalism for three years at Colorado University before joining the Woman's Auxiliary Corps. In the summer of 1943, she turned down her appointment to Officer's Candidate School and volunteered for the first WAC shipment to Britain. She wanted to be close to her youngest brother, a bomber pilot assigned to the 96th Bomb Group at RAF Station Swetterton Heath.

"Captain Tyler, so nice to see you." Her voice was deep like Lauren Bacall's. Erect breasts gave her GI shirt a new dimension. Her long shapely legs and symmetrical hips made the drab Army skirt look like something out of Abercrombie & Fitch. Ted would have asked her for a date three months ago if she hadn't worked for his dad.

"How've you been, Darlene?" He enjoyed the scent of her Chanel Number 5.

"Fine, thank you. How's it feel to be the first P-51 ace in the 8th Air Force?"

"Haven't had much time to think about it."

"Your dad's so proud. Never says much, but I can tell."

"How's he doing?"

"He's been working very hard. Been sneaking off more often to fly combat. He gets the eyes every time he reads a mission report with your name in it. I sometimes think he's trying to keep up with you. General Doolittle asked him to slow down. But you know your dad."

"Is he busy?"

"Talking to a Shell mogul, trying to scrounge some aviation fuel, to make up for two freighters the U-boats sunk. Should be finished soon. I think I just heard him hang up. Go on in, I'll make some fresh tea."

Ted tapped on the open door. His father looked up, "Ted, how long have you been here?"

"Just a few minutes."

"Had a flap goin.' Had to fix it right away," he said, coming from behind his desk. He put an arm around Ted's shoulders and squeezed. "Great seein' you son."

"Nice to see you dad. Sounds like you're keeping busy."

"Yeah. We're finally getting the forces we were promised a year and a half ago. In the last few days a P-38 group became combat ready. Two more P-51 groups and another 38 group'll be ready sometime this week. Then we can cover the bombers over any target in Germany with about 150 long-range P-51's."

"That's great news, dad."

"It's been a struggle. General Arnold had to fight like hell to keep our forces coming to Britain, especially the heavy bombers. Sailors have been bustin' the buttons off their bell-bottoms, trying to get more B-17's and B-24's in the Pacific. But when the war's over, you can bet your poop deck pantaloons, the Canoe U boys'll fight like hell to deep-six our heavy bombers again."

"Why would they want to do that? Don't they know by now that there's always enough fighting to go around in a war?"

"You would think so. But it comes down to the battle for the buck. The war has put Army Air on center stage and the Navy and Army ground pounders are scared shitless. They're afraid we'll become a separate air force after the war and really steal some of their thunder at budget time.

"The Navy's jitter count has been off the chart ever since the Japs creamed their fantails at Pearl Harbor and the American public saw what airpower could do...with a bunch of little peashooters. Imagine what a gaggle of B-17's or B-24's would've done to 'em at Pearl."

"I know what you mean, Dad. Even at West Point some instructors pooh-poohed the potential of airpower and if you disagreed with them, you could end up being docked a grade."

"Ted, isn't it amazing that we're the only major power in the world that hasn't put the airplane on an equal footing with rifles and rowboats?"

"It's hard to believe. Dad, you and my boss sound a lot alike. Does the Army Air Force have talking papers for all full colonels?" Ted asked with a smile.

"Nope. But those of us who've been around the block and suffered through the lean years sing from the same sheet of music. We defied death in the same flyin' coffins, survived on the same lousy pay, drank the same cheap booze and feasted on canned pork and beans the last week of every month."

"I'm old enough to remember the beans. In grade school we use to compare our mothers' recipes. Mom had some of the best."

"Your mother still datin' that guy from North American Aviation?"

"Yes, she is," Ted replied, then quickly changed the subject. "Dad, how's the D.C. pressure these days?"

"Not too bad. Tooey Spaatz's is a good buffer. He's one of the few people Arnold doesn't try to bully."

"When I was a kid and General Spaatz came to the house, he always impressed me as being a cool head. I'm sure he can handle pressure."

"He can and will. Speaking of pressure, our cloud watchers think we've got a break coming in the weather over Germany. May happen the day after tomorrow and could last five or six days. Be no holdin' Tooey Spaatz if we get some decent bombin' weather. Each day he'll send close to a thousand bombers deep inside Germany to clobber their aircraft industry."

"I just hope our fighters can provide enough cover to hold down the bombers losses," Ted added.

"So do I. Even with our increased fighter support, our numbers massagers say we could lose 200 bombers the first day. The thought of losin' 2000 men in a few hours scares the shit outta all of us. We could have five or six days of the heaviest losses of the war. Could lose more than 600, maybe 700 bombers. You can imagine how the press would play the loss of 7000 men in just five or six days. They're on our asses if we don't launch missions and when we do, they moan about the losses. Many of the press who covered World War I know enough about wars to understand the problem. But some of the young liberal bastards think you can win wars without payin' the price."

"Dad, sometimes I wonder whose side they're on."

"Yeah. We've always had that problem, but it seems to be gettin' worse. It ain't gonna be easy for Tooey to keep launchin' missions in the face of high losses. Each mission takes a lot out of him, but he knows that the job has to be done." Colonel Tyler suddenly stopped.

Ted caught the scent of Chanel Number 5.

"Excuse me, gentlemen, tea." Darlene placed Colonel Tyler's cup between two stacks of paper.

"Darlin', Thank you." He looked into her eyes.

Darlene's cheeks brightened. She avoided his eyes, handed Ted his cup of tea and departed.

"Dad, are you doing much combat flying?"

"God dammit. Don't you start. I've been catchin' hell from all quadrants. I've flown a few. But no more than my share."

"Just thought I'd ask."

Ted and his father had an early dinner. Afterwards Ted went to his room to prepare a discussion outline for the tactics manual. The next morning, he and the Colonel had breakfast and started the meeting at exactly 8:30. During the afternoon session the Colonel was called out of the meeting. He returned 45 minutes later and told Ted that he had been ordered back to Boxted to get ready some big missions. Then he announced that Ted would take charge of the meeting.

£££

The Colonel changed trains in London and boarded the Colchester train at 10:00 pm. He hoped the 8th AF weathermen were wrong about freezing drizzle and heavy clear icing in the morning.

Nine years of flying had taught him that fog, thunderstorms and ice were nature's three deadliest flying hazards. You could take off in dense fog, but you never attempted to land in it except as a last resort. Thunderstorms were to be avoided in flight because the severe turbulence and hail could severely damage your airplane. When a thunderstorm was over an airfield, you always waited until it moved on before taking off or landing, due to the strong and unpredictable winds. The Colonel had had two friends who ignored this last rule and were killed when the winds suddenly changed direction during landing.

Icing was the insidious killer. It could build up on the flight surfaces and reduce their aerodynamic qualities while adding weight—a combination that could cause the airplane to spin out of control.

Bombers and cargo aircraft had deicing equipment that prevented ice or removed it from their flight surfaces. But the fighters had no deicing capability. They had enough power to carry some ice until they climbed above or descended below the icing level. Not even the design engineers knew how a heavy load of clear ice would affect the new laminar flow wing on the P-51.

The train pulled into the Colchester station and the Colonel hurried to his staff car.

"Hello, Freddy," he said to the driver who was holding the open door of the 1942 Chevy.

"Hello, sir," Freddy replied, before he closed the door and climbed into the driver's seat.

155

"Run into any ice on your way in?" the Colonel asked.

"No sir. I had nothing but drizzle. But the temperature is getting close to freezing so I've been driving very slow, just in case."

Freddy eased the Chevy away from the curb and drove slowly down the street. The Colonel took off his hat and leaned back in the seat. Neither of them spoke as they drove toward the airfield.

"Sir, we're approaching the front gate," Freddy warned seeing the Colonel had fallen asleep.

The Colonel sat up and put on his hat. The guard saluted, checked their ID cards, motioned them through the gate and saluted again.

"Freddy, stop by group ops, please."

"Yes sir."

Freddy stopped in front of group operations and got out and opened the door. The Colonel thanked him and went inside. Major Hunt and Captain Knight were talking in front of the map of Europe. The clacking keys of the Teletype machines told the Colonel that General Spaatz had released the warning order.

"Sir, we have a maximum effort. We're tasked for 48 P-51's with six spares," Major Hunt said as the Colonel approached.

"Stormy, does it still look like we'll get freezing rain?"

"Yes and it will start anytime now, sir."

"Bob, how we fixed for aircraft?"

"Sir, we have 48 primaries and three spares ready now. Three more spares will be ready in two hours."

"Looks like things are under control. Guess I better get some sleep. See you guys in a few hours."

£££

"Maximum effort, gentlemen," the duty sergeant said, turning on the overhead light. "There's freezing drizzle and it's covering everything with a layer of ice. It's like trying to walk on a skating rink. So be careful when you go outside."

Robb kicked the blankets back and hurriedly dressed. Today would be his first combat mission without Ted and the first time he would lead an element. *Why does the weather get double shitty whenever I face something new?*

After finishing in the latrine Robb, Rocko, Bill Spencer and Bernard "Matt" Mattson, a new pilot, boarded the flight line truck. The driver left the gearshift in low and drove slowly along the icy road to operations, where they got out and made their way along the slippery sidewalk leading to the entrance.

Glenn Miller's *"I've Got A Gal in Kalamazoo"* was playing as the pilots filed into the lounge. Big John started breaking a dozen eggs, two at a time, and

156

dropped them gently onto the kerosene grill, then added twelve slices of Spam and bread. He grabbed his spatula and scraped hot grease onto the sizzling eggs before he scooped two of them onto each of the six plates next two thick slices of Spam and bread. Then he banged the grill hard with his spatula. Corporal Perkins spun around, grabbed the plates and placed them on the snack bar and quickly filled six tin cups with grapefruit juice.

As Robb and Rocko started across the room with their plates and juice as Glenn Miller's *"In The Mood"* boomed from the snack bar radio.

"Won a jitterbug contest in Hoboken, dancin' to that little jump tune." Rocko said with a big grin. He shuffled his feet and wiggled his butt as he held his plate and balanced his cup of juice. "Not bad, huh, *amigo?"*

They continued across the room, sat down and started to eat. Glenn Miller was Robb's favorite band and he kept time with the music while he ate. *In The Mood* ended and without a break, *Autumn In New York* started to play.

"Sumbitchin' song gives me a giant case of red ass. It reminds me of neckin' up a storm with one of my steadies in the back seat of my dad's new Buick." He looked at his watch. "With the time change, I might be makin' out in the back seat right now, if the sumbitchin' Japs and krauts hadn't started this frickin' war."

Bill, Matt, Robb and Rocko finished eating and hurried to the group briefing room and sat in the row of green chairs.

"Sumbitch. Look at those frickin' targets! Gonna be a white knuckler."

The colored strings on the big map stretched from East Anglia, across Holland and went deep inside Germany. The smokers snatched cigarettes from their packs and lit up when they saw the targets. Within minutes, a layer of blue smoke began to obscure the ceiling.

"HOFFICERS, TEN—SHUN!" the adjutant shouted.

"Sumbitchin' adj gets his jollies off yellin' like that. Wish he'd get a new frickin' line."

Robb was on edge and the shouting annoyed him too. He had been thinking about leading the element in combat and wondering how the ice would affect his P-51 on takeoff and what he'd have to do to counter it. *I wish Ted was here.*

"Gents, please take your seats." The Colonel stepped up onto the platform, walked to the lectern and picked up the cue stick. "If any of you think the mission'll be scrubbed because of this ice, I suggest you forget it. We're gonna launch because the cloud watchers say that today will be the first of several days of good bombing weather over Germany. General Spaatz can't afford to miss this opportunity. We've gotta destroy nazi aircraft factories and clear kraut fighters from the sky so our ground pounders can sample some of that French wine.

"Last night, 700 Halifaxes and Lancasters pounded Leipzig and Berlin. You can bet your next month's cigarette ration that the kraut gunners and *Luft-*

waffe are gonna be pissed after losin' sleep. They'll get off their old *wiener schnitzels* for our visit. Stormy, give us your woeful tale."

"Sir, we've got a wedge of high pressure moving south from the Baltic. It's a granddaddy and should clear the sky over Germany for at least four days...maybe five. Got another one near Iceland movin' this way, which should give us a few more days of good bombing weather. Unfortunately for your takeoff you'll have freezing drizzle and heavy clear icing that'll go up to about 6000 feet."

Captain Knight covered the en route and target weather, then gave the winds aloft. "Weather here will be better when you return. Ice will be gone, ceiling will be up around 700 to 800 feet and the visibility will be about two miles."

"Eight hundred and two. C-A-F-B in blokeland," Rocky snorted.

"What the hell's C-A-F-B?" someone shouted.

"Clear as frickin' bell," Rocko shouted back.

Everyone looked at the Colonel. When he smiled, they smiled.

Major Watson took the cue stick from Captain Knight and glared at Rocko before he spoke. "Bombers are attacking twelve ME-I09, JU-88, JU-188, FW-190 factories and assembly plants. First nine targets are located here in the Brunswick-Leipzig area." He tapped their location on the map with the cue stick. "Other three are near Posen and Tutom." He moved the cue higher on the map and tapped their locations.

"These twelve targets produce about half of Germany's aircraft. They are all heavily defended by flak and fighters." He tapped each red flak circle, then the black fighter circles and recited the number and types of guns and fighters at each location....

"B-26's from the 9th Air Force will attack tactical targets in Holland and France, trying to draw some of the *Luftwaffe* fighters away from us. The 15th Air Force is supporting ground operations at Anzio and will not be attacking in southern Germany today. Questions, gentlemen?" He waited, but there were none. He handed the cue to Major Hunt, glared at Rocko and sat down.

Rocko nudged Robb. "Be nice if we could strap that old sumbitch to a bomb shackle, drop his ass in one of *Der Fuehrer's* honey-buckets."

Robb held his finger to his lips without shushing.

Major Hunt walked to the center of the platform as spoke, "This will be our first thousand-bomber raid, making February 20, 1944 a red-letter day for the 8th AF. We'll be getting additional fighter support from the 9th AF and RAF, which'll give us about 850 escort fighters today. To make our job a little easier, the bombers will reduce the spacing between combat wings and follow the same route as long as possible, before splitting to hit their individual targets.

"We'll also have a new P-51 group that just came on line to help us in the target area, the 357th. So make damned sure you're shooting at a ME-I09 and not another P-51. Colonel, sir." Major Hunt handed the cue back to the Colonel.

"Gents, as you've heard, we're gonna plow more new ground today," the Colonel said. "In addition to a 1000 bomber raid, we're gonna take this slick-winged little beauty into clear icin' conditions for the first time. Unlike rime ice it's hard to see, but it'll be there. Bob and I worked up a few procedures to counter it. We'll taxi five minutes early, so the ground crews can de-ice the canopy, wings and tail again, just before we takeoff. As an additional safety factor, I'm gonna takeoff one minute early and make sure it's okay. If it's, I'll call back and clear the rest of you for takeoff.

"Before you roll, get your peter heat on and pipe hot air to the carburetor. Don't forget to turn off the carburetor heat when you're above the icing level or you won't get full power at high altitude.

"Be sure to retract your landing gears as soon as you're safely airborne because too much ice might keep the gear from locking into place. Hold 57 inches and 3000 rpm for your climb, which'll get you above the icing level faster.

"If you have to abort, don't tool around in the clouds any longer than you have to. Add a little airspeed on final, because you'll be carrying a load of ice.

"I've had the taxiways and a thousand feet on each end of the runway sanded, but they could still be a little slick, so be careful taxin' out. Okay, gang, let's get strapped up and wait for the launch order." The Colonel leaned the cue stick on the lectern.

"Sir, we don't have to wait. We just received it." Major Hunt handed the message to the Colonel.

"This is it, guys. It reads as follows:

£££

'Headquarters United States Strategic Air Forces Europe.
Personal from Spaatz to Doolittle 8AF, Brereton 9AF, Twining 15AF
Info: all air divisions, wings and groups
Time/Date: 0630 hours, zulu, 20 February, 1944.
Text of message:

LET 'EM GO.

Spaatz

£££

The Colonel handed the message back to Major Hunt. "Let's get strapped up and have at the bastards."

£££

Bug Eye and Snapper squadrons waited near the end of the runway as the Colonel and Hot Rod lined up for takeoff. The Colonel quickly checked his engine and roared down the runway. One minute later he called, "Shotgun, here. Launch 'em. I'll give you a call when I find a clear flight level for join up."

Hot Rod's two ship elements roared into the air, two seconds apart, while Bug Eye pulled onto the runway. Seconds later Bug Eye began to takeoff and Captain Draper led Snapper onto the runway. Before Robb finished his engine checks, Captain Draper and his wingman took off and others quickly followed. Finally Bill and Matt rolled. Robb and Rocko waited two seconds and raced down the runway. After take off, Robb quickly retracted the landing gear and started a climb.

"Shotgun's level at seven grand in between layers. I'm skinnin' it back for join up," the Colonel transmitted.

While climbing Robb held his 51 steady and hurriedly glanced at the wings, but saw no ice. He and Rocko zoomed out of the clouds tops. A thin layer of clear ice covered the windshield and leading edge of the wings, but his 51 was flying okay. He looked at Rocko and Rocko gave him an okay signal. *So far, so good.*

Robb saw eleven flights with 44 aircraft at 10:00 o'clock and turned toward them. Due to the windshield ice, he had to lean to the right to see Bill and Matt. They were at one o'clock and moving in close to the group. "Snapper Green, Three and Four are closing at your seven o'clock."

"Snapper Green, roger," Bill replied. A few seconds later he called, "Snapper lead, Green's sliding into position."

"Shotgun here. Carburetor heat off and go climb power."

As the 48 P-51's climbed, the windshield and wing ice slowly disappear. Halfway across the North Sea, they passed through the bomber's contrails. At 29,000 feet, the Colonel leveled off and had the group spread out in combat formation.

Robb saw the last combat wing in the bomber stream crossing the coast of Holland. Although the spacing between wings had been reduced, the 1000 bombers stretched east beyond the horizon.

None of the 10,000 airmen in the 1000 B-17's and B-24's knew that the numbers crunchers had guessed that 2000 of them might be lost today. But their anxiety levels always ran high before they entered the risk-filled sky to face an enemy with a lust for killing.

But the bomber crews sweat-jobs started early. They sweated every takeoff, because one cough from any of the four engines at lift-off could cause their overloaded bomber to crash. Many of them had watched a faltering giant slam into the ground, spewing thousands of gallons of high-octane gasoline. In an instant, a once sturdy bomber became a blazing inferno.

THE HELLISH VORTEX

After takeoff, aircrews sweated mid-air collisions when hundreds of bombers circled and climbed through black sky and clouds trying to join up. Each time two of them collided the flames burned a hole in the blackness and bug-eyed aircrews quickened their scan for other bombers and prayed.

At high altitude, they sweated the insidious hypoxia that could lead to a most blissful death. Everyone agreed there was no better way to die.

In the 50 below zero sky, they sweated frostbite which could take fingers, hands, toes, feet—or worse.

Then came the tough part. Over enemy territory, every other fear gave way to the dreaded German fighters and flak. Most believed flak to be the worst, because they were defenseless—like targets in a shooting gallery. At least they could shoot back at German fighters.

No one sweated more than the crewmen in the bowels of the bomber who couldn't see ahead. Their first clue of impending disaster was a blinding flash—a deafening explosion—a taste of blood.

And their sweat jobs didn't end after they'd fought their way back to Britain. Bad weather could cause a mid-air collision or a dangerous near blind landing.

Ninety miles from the target, Captain Draper led Snapper squadron to the third bomber wing and began the escort weave above them. Seconds later, Bugeye took the second wing while the Colonel and Hot Rod continued to the lead wing. Two minutes later, a short transmission indicated the new P-51 group had joined the fourth, fifth and sixth bomber wings.

Robb clapped his hands and stomped his feet to warm them, then rubbed some frost off his canopy. Looking through the clear spot, it seemed impossible that 1800 aircraft had flown across Holland and half of Germany with so little radio chatter.

"Snapper Green One has eight contrails, high, five miles south." Bill's transmission shattered the icy silence.

"Snapper Red One here, look 'em over Green," Captain Draper replied.

"Snapper Green turning right, 2700 RPM, full power." Bill headed directly at the contrails.

Robb whipped the nose of his 51 a few degrees left. *Damn it. . .another head on pass.* He lowered his head and put the sight pipper on the black dot that appeared ahead one of the contrails. The black dot got larger and fire shot from its nose.

Shit. . .they're ME-109's! Robb knew their 20-millimeter cannons could reach out further than his 50-caliber machine guns. He squeezed the trigger; the four 50-caliber machines clacked like air hammers.

A flash appeared off to Robb's right. Bill's 51 had disappeared inside a 100 octane fireball. *SHIT.* Robb's gut wrenched. He squeezed harder on the trigger.

WHOOOSH! The 109 zoomed past, a few feet to Robb's left.

For an eternal instant, the shock of Bill's exploding 51 caused Robb's mind to freeze. *Get with it dumb shit. . .before the krauts nail your ass.*

"Green Three's coming up and to the left," Robb transmitted, as he yanked his 51 into a tight climbing turn. But the Germans continued on toward the bombers.

Robb lowered the nose to regain airspeed while he glanced in the direction of Bill's 51 hoping to see a white chute. But there were only burning pieces of the plane tumbling earthward. *Damn it!*

"GREEN THREE, BREAK LEFT!" Rocko yelled.

Robb yanked the stick back and stood on the left rudder pedal. His 51 whipped into a tight climbing turn. G-forces pulled his oxygen mask down across the bridge of his nose; his body felt like a chunk of lead. He tightened his stomach muscles to keep from blacking out and glanced at his rearview mirrors. Two ME-109's were closing fast.

Going straight up, Robb rolled his 51 and its nose dropped toward the horizon. He snapped the throttle to idle and jammed the stick forward to maintain level flight and quickly lost airspeed. He looked down through the top of the canopy; the two 109's shot past 50 feet below.

He lowered the nose, slammed the throttle forward to full power, then rolled right side up and pushed the stick forward slightly. At zero G, he quickly gained airspeed and banked steeply to cut off the turning 109's. As he closed on them, he held the pipper of his gunsight on the last one. When he was about 300 feet out, he tightened his turn and placed the pipper ten feet in front of the 109's nose and squeezed the trigger. Nothing happened. He double-checked that the gun switch was on and squeezed the trigger again. Still nothing.

Everyone had been told that the four 50-caliber machine guns in the P-51 B/C's had been tilted to one side to facilitate the hook-up of the ammunition feed chutes, a configuration that often caused spent casings and links to jam the guns. But it was the first time it had happened to Robb.

"Green Three's guns won't fire!" Take 'em, Four!" Matt had joined with Rocko and Robb pulled up sharply and rolled in behind them.

"Got 'em *amigo*." Rocko opened fire; API's sparkled along the fuselage of the last 109. Flames shot from the engine; the German pilot flipped his 109 upside down and bailed out. The other 109 dived away.

"Nice shooting, Green Four. You keep the lead. Let's hold max cruise and swing back to rejoin Snapper and our bomber wing," Robb transmitted.

"Copy, *amigo*."

Rocko, Matt and Robb turned east. Thirty miles ahead, more than 100 fighter contrails twisted around the first three wings of B-17's like loose spaghetti. Terse radio chatter confirmed the savageness of the twisting and turning dogfights. A smoking B-17 turned away from the formation. It suddenly flipped out of control. Two white chutes appeared. Two more burning B-17's were spinning earthward. There were no chutes.

The first wing of B-17's started their bomb run and the ME-109's broke away before the sky filled with orange bursts and black puffs. A B-17 exploded. There were no chutes.

Seconds later, the second wing of B-17's started their bomb run and the attacking ME-109's broke away. Some turned east to attack the third wing which Snapper was protecting.

"Snapper Red One here. Let's take these new guys head-on." Captain Draper's deep Mississippi drawl never wavered as his flight of four raced toward the ten ME-109's and open fire.

"Red Lead, here. I took a hit. Two, look me over," Captain Draper transmitted when the third wing started its bomb run and the ME-109's broke away.

"Red Two, here. Lead you took a hit in the bottom of the fuselage near the air scoop. But I don't see any leaks."

A mile east orange fireballs and black puffs filled the sky around the third combat wing of B-17's as they released their bombs.

"Red One, copied." Captain Draper knew some of the coolant lines had to be damaged and could break anytime. Without coolant the engine would overheat and quit within minutes. "Let's head back. I'm reducing power and starting a slow descent."

"Green Three, here. We're down to 75 gallons. I'll take the lead and we'll follow Red," Robb transmitted.

"Roger, *amigo*."

"Thanks for the company, Green Three," Captain Draper replied.

For the next 32 minutes the seven 51's headed west descending at 500 feet per minute. Through a break in the clouds near Amsterdam Robb saw the North Sea where death could come in a few minutes in the icy waters. Although Captain Draper's engine could quite anytime, he continued on instead of bailing out over Holland and being captured by the Germans. Robb wasn't surprised because Draper was West Point graduate and came from a family of military patriots.

"Purple Stick, this is Snapper Red One. I crossed the coast of Holland five minutes ago. I have battle damage and could lose my engine anytime."

"Purple Stick copies Snapper Red One. Please make your parrot squawk and state your angels and heading, suh," the RAF radar controller replied.

"Red One is squawking, angels 14 and heading 290," Captain Draper said, turning on his IFF transponder.

"Purple Stick has you 60 miles east, Red One. Strangle your parrot and hold your heading, suh. I have dispatched one of our patrol launches. He is presently heading east and is about 55 miles from you."

"Red One, copies. Do you know what the ceiling is over the water?"

"Purple Stick, here. Our patrol launches are reporting 700-foot ceilings with two miles in rain and choppy seas."

"Snapper Red copies. Snapper gang, close it up, I'm going to throttle back and start a gradual descent and get below this stuff."

Captain Draper reduced power and the seven 51's descended through the thick clouds. Twelve minutes later, they broke out at 700 feet.

"Red Lead, Two here. You're leaking coolant, sir."

"Snapper gang, move out and look around. Purple Stick, do you have us?"

"Purple Stick, here. I have you, suh. Launch is two miles west of your position. His call sign is Happy Bottom."

"Red One, copies. When the coolant temp needle hits the red, I'll pull up into the clouds and bail out."

"Red Three here. I'll stay with you."

"Red Three, negative. Everyone remain below the clouds. When I bailout, circle and look for me in my chute so you can guide the launch in for the pick up."

"Red Three, copies."

"Red One's coolant temp just hit the red. Purple Stick and Happy Bottom, I'm squawking and pulling up. I will be bailing out in a few seconds."

"Happy Bottom here. I copy, suh."

Robb watched Captain Draper's 51 disappear into the undercast. That familiar feeling of being so close and not being able to help gnawed at Robb's gut.

"Red One's engine just quit. I'm flipping upside down and for a little dip. Save some dinner for me tonight."

"Happy Bottom here. Red Three, I have a tally ho on your six chicks. We are looking for your flight mate's chute, suh."

"Red Three copies. We're all low on fuel, but we'll circle twice and look for the chute."

"Happy Bottom here, I copy, suh."

Robb, Matt and Rocko followed Red through two circles, but saw nothing. Robb guessed that Captain Draper had hit the tail on bailout or his chute had opened.

"Red Three, here. Happy Bottom, we're down on fuel and have to leave."

"Happy Bottom, roger suh. We'll continue our search."

"Red Three, roger. Red and Green, let's go Sunshine channel and head home." Everyone checked in on Sunshine's channel and Red Three requested a steer to the field. Robb, Rocko and Matt followed one mile behind Red and all six of them landed with less than 15 gallons of fuel.

Major Brown met with all of the pilots after the mission debriefing. "Guys, Air Sea Rescue never found Captain Draper and we may never know what happened." He paused and swallowed. "Losing him and Lieutenant Spencer, two of our best in one day...is really tough. Unfortunately, it's all part of this damned war. But they would have been proud of their contribution today. We downed 61 kraut fighters and damaged another 37, while helping to hold the bomber losses to 21.

"Now we've got to move on. And in that regard, I have a couple of announcements. Lieutenant Tyler has been promoted to Captain and will take over operations when he returns tonight. Second Lieutenant Baines is now First Lieutenant Baines and will take command of D flight, with Flight Officer Fazzio as his assistant.

"Let's all rendezvous at the bar in an hour and knock one back for Captain Draper and Lieutenant Spencer. Services will be held in the chapel at 2000 hours. Tomorrow's warning order is in and we have another max effort. Suggest we all hit the sack early."

Following the services, Robb, Rocko and Matt walked back to their hut and went to bed. As Rocko snored and smacked his lips, Robb stared into the darkness and wondered why Bill and Captain Draper had been killed and he had been spared. *Both were married and had their futures secured. Doesn't make sense that I should live and they should die.* He knew their bodies would never be found and knew it would make things more difficult for their families. When sleep finally came, not even the roar of 600 RAF bombers heading for Germany awakened him.

February 21 brought another maximum effort with 861 heavy bombers and 679 fighters attacking aircraft factories and airfields. Fog held the 15th AF on the ground and it also hampered the 9th AF's medium bomber strikes in the Low Countries. Once again, the 8th Air Force bombers flew a common route as long as possible and reduced the spacing between combat wings. The bombers lost 16, while the fighters lost five. Two P-51's from the new group were lost and one from Hot Rod squadron. US fighters destroyed 33 and damaged 18 more. Before many of the weary aircrews had gone to bed that night, all 8th Air Force units had received a warning order the February 22nd mission.

£££

"Another max effort, gentlemen," the sergeant announced after turning on the light bulb.

Robb struggled to open his eyes, then rolled onto his back. Every muscle in his body seemed to ache and the cheeks of his butt felt like two chunks of raw meat that had been pounded for hours on a butcher's block. Overhead came the rumble of returning RAF bombers. *Shit. . .I'd give anything for another three hours of sleep.*

"Sumbitch, it seems like I just hit the sack. Another four hours in that refrigerated Spam-can, sittin' on that frickin' concrete dinghy'll end my sex life… that's for sure," Rocko grunted.

Like sleepy robots, Robb and Rocko took their towels, toothpaste and tooth brushes and walked wearily down the dark lane to the latrine, oblivious to the icy wind and rain.

"Wait *amigo*." Rocko stopped, unbuttoned his fly and peed. "I can't hold it any longer in this cold air. Besides, if I'm gonna work like a God damned horse, might as well piss on the road like one. Wasn't so shit-eatin' cold, I'd drop my drawers, fertilize the King's Royal Limestone."

£££

Robb, Pete Langer, Rocko and Matt filed into the briefing room and sat in the green chairs. Pete was a new 19-year-old pilot from Boone, Iowa who had arrived from Goxhill two days earlier. He was the only one without a tanned eye mask—the fighter pilot's badge of honor. *I wonder if I ever looked that young. A few max efforts will take care of his boyish looks.*

"Sumbitch, we're the last flight in the last squadron again. Seems like we're always bringin' up the frickin' rear," Rocko snorted.

The adjutant smiled, looked at the wall clock and marched down the aisle toward the door. "HOFFICERS, TEN—SHUN!"

"Take your seats, please." The Colonel stopped next to his striped chair. "Stormy, give us your sad tail," he said before sitting down. Nearly three years of combat had made the Colonel's eye mask darker and the crows-feet so deep that it looked like a tattoo.

Captain Knight took the cue stick. "Sir, weather's still not cooperating today. Some of our bomber fields are socked in and it will be damned tough for them just to taxi, let alone get off the ground. Those that do get off will have difficulty joining up. And some targets may have too much cloud cover for visual bombing and the radar pathfinders will have to be used. Bad weather may force some bombers to attack their alternate targets...." Captain Knight finished and passed the cue to Major Watson.

"We have 800 bombers, with 600 escort fighters, attacking aircraft factories at Schweinfurt, Gotha, Bernburg, Oschersleben, Aschersleben and Halberstart. A small diversionary force, using radar jamming, will attack the Aalborg Airfield in Denmark. They hope to confuse the German radar controllers and disperse the Luftwaffe's fighter defense. In addition, the 15th AF will attack Regensburg with 185 bombers. Hopefully, this attack will further complicate the Luftwaffe's fighter defense plan...." Major Watson finished and handed the cue to Major Hunt.

"The targets are spread out today, which will make it tougher to cover our big friends. Be even tougher if any of 'em have to hit their alternate targets.... Colonel, sir."

"Krauts have takin' a bashin' for two days. It's time for 'em to try somethin' new. So we've got to expect the unexpected and try not to let them snooker our asses. Okay, let's get strapped up and have at the bastards."

£££

Snapper pilots hunched behind the fur collars of their flight jackets and waited to board the truck taking them to their P-51's.

WHOOMP! An orange fireball lit the clouds, two miles north.

"Oooh shit...a midair," a voice whispered, as in prayer. Everyone turned, raised their heads and watched in silence. A flaming B-17 with its tail missing, fell like an inverted cross. Three seconds later, another flaming B-17, minus its nose, twisted from the bottom of the clouds. There were no chutes from either bomber.

BAA-ROOM! BAA-ROOM! The two bombers slammed into the ground.

WHUMP! WHUMP! WHUMP! Bombs exploded and the ground quivered under Robb's feet.

"Jesus, Joseph, and Mary," the same voice whispered. "Twenty men down the tubes...and the game hasn't even started."

"It's a wonder there aren't more midairs," Major Brown said, staring in the direction of the explosions. "East Anglia is wing tip to wing tip with airplanes. Flown by green kids." He paused and took a deep breath. "Kids doing things that seemed impossible for the old timers only three years ago." He continued to stare for several more seconds. "Okay, guys. It's time to snap to and do the impossible." He climbed into the truck and sat on the wooden bench.

£££

After take off, the Colonel held his heading for three minutes and climbed through the clouds to the west before starting a left climbing turn. Due south of the field he found a clear area between cloud layers at 9000 feet. He leveled off and began to orbit. One by one the flights joined behind his flight.

Robb and Pete broke out of the clouds and turned toward the group. Rocko and Matt joined in the turn and the four of them eased in behind White. "Snapper, Green's in formation."

"Shotgun copies," the Colonel answered, knowing they were the last flight in the group. "Let's go climb power."

In the climb, Robb saw scattered B-24's searching for their units over the North Sea. *Weather's playing hell with their join up.*

Below, a B-24 skimmed through the clouds, struggling to get on top. Five hundred feet ahead, the faint silhouette of another B-24 appeared in the clouds—on a collision course with the first.

RICHARD M BAUGHN

WHOOOM! The two slammed together and a huge fireball mushroomed above the clouds. Chunks of aluminum and debris flew in all directions.

Four engines from one B-24 tore loose from their mounts. For a split second, they zoomed forward in a ragged formation, across the top of the undercast before tumbling into the white clouds. By then, the wreckage of both B-24's was gone. A fleeting puff of black smoke marked the spot—where 20 men had died.

Over Holland, the Colonel swung a mile south of a lone B-24 combat wing. Robb finally spotted more contrails 20 miles east. As they got closer, he counted five combat wings of B-17's and realized one whole air division was missing. *Damned this weather!*

"Shotgun, Salt Peter, here," the P-38 group commander transmitted.

"Shotgun, go Salt Peter."

"We've just crossed into Germany with the lead bomber wing and have two gaggles of bandits approaching. One from the east and one from the south. More than enough to go around. Bastards gonna hit us early."

"Shotgun, copies. Let's push 'em up to 2700 rpm and full throttle. Double check sight on, gun switches hot, keep your eyes peeled."

Ten miles east, fighter contrails swarmed around the first wing of B-17's. Two smoking bombers spiraled down from the formation. Four white chutes appeared.

"Shotgun gang, select a full tank. Could be a long fight."

"Snapper Green. Has eight bandits, five o'clock, high, comin' our way," Robb transmitted while turning the fuel selector to the fullest tank.

"Snapper Red, here. Take 'em Green," Major Brown transmitted.

"Green's pulling up and to the right." Robb pulled his 51 into a near vertical climb and rolled left. The FW-190's passed beneath and continued on toward the bombers. Robb came down behind the last 190 and opened fire; API's sparkled along its fuselage.

"SNAPPER GREEN ONE—BREAK RIGHT!" Rocko shouted.

Robb yanked hard on the stick. He and Pete climbed steeply, but the FW-190's followed.

Going straight up, Robb waited until his airspeed dropped through 70 mph and rolled right. His 51's nose shuddered toward the horizon. Inverted, he looked down through the top of the canopy. Pete was gone and there was only one FW-190 behind him. "Snapper Green Two, you okay?"

"Green Three and Four are passin' Two. He's okay. Two, join on my right wing," Rocko directed.

"Where's that second 190?" Robb asked.

"Sumbitch spun-out. It's just you and that hot-rock Nazi. Fricker has a yellow chevron on the side of the fuselage. Must be a kraut squadron commander."

"Green One, rog." Robb snapped the throttle back to idle, slammed the stick and rudder to the right and twisted through the air. The sky and earth flip-flopped back and forth then back again. After the third roll, he stopped upside down, yanked the stick back in his gut, pulled hard and dived. In the rearview mirror, he saw the 190 low and behind.

Robb jammed the throttle to full power, tightened his stomach muscles and yanked back on the stick and started to climb.

Seven-G's turned his body to lead; his vision narrowed, then turned gray and he blacked out. *Ooooh shit...hope that kraut's lights have gone out too.*

In the blackness, the 51 shuddered and Robb released some stick pressure. It shuddered again and he released more stick pressure. He was losing airspeed fast. *Must be goin' straight up. Wish I could see to roll.* He rolled anyway, hoping the kraut would overshoot.

He rolled to the right and continued pulling. His 51 shuddered again and he released more stick pressure. As the G's lessened, shades of gray replaced the blackness, then a fuzzy outline of his windshield appeared. In the rearview mirror, he saw the 190 low and behind.

Robb pulled harder on the stick. The 51 shuddered and its wing dropped. He eased in the rudder to keep from spinning. In the rearview mirror, he saw the 190 low and behind.

Shit...gotta do something to get this guy off my ass! Robb knocked the flap handle down to 20-degrees. He snapped the throttle back to idle, stomped on the rudder and shuddered through a tight roll.

When he looked up, the nose of the FW-190 was 50 feet above his head. *Bastard overshot a little. Keep rolling!*

Robb jammed hard on the rudder, his 51 rolled and shuddered. While up side down, he bent his head back and glanced through the top of his canopy. The 190 was 30 feet below. The cold blue eyes of the German pilot met Robb's glance. *The bastard knows that he has the advantage. Keep rolling or he's gonna nail your ass.*

Robb moved the stick to the right and kicked right rudder. His 51 rolled and the 190 rolled with him. Three times, the fighters twisted around each other, passing canopy to canopy, eyeball to eyeball. But on each roll, the 190 inched further back.

Robb kept his 51 twisting and turning, with and without flaps, at full power and idle, many times on the edge of a spin. He tried every move that Ted had taught him—and more. But the German matched him trick for trick.

The sky and earth flip-flopped as they corkscrewed down. It was like twisting through a kaleidoscopic centrifuge. Soon, they were no more than 100 feet above the ground where the margin for error dropped to zero. Robb looked in the rearview mirror. The German was moving into position for the kill.

"GOTTA...ROLL!" Robb shouted to himself. He whipped the stick to the right and stomped on the right rudder. His 51 flipped on its back; its nose dropped and the ground leaped up at him.

Robb's heart pounded in his chest and blood thundered in his ears as the world around him suddenly went into slow motion.

Oooh shit...this is it. GOD DAMN IT! DON'T GIVE UP!

He jammed the stick forward to keep from slamming into a hill. His 51 shuddered on the edge of a stall as it rolled right side up, a mere 30 feet above the ground. Then his 51's right wing dropped and he kicked the left rudder to stop it. His chest heaved as he tried to catch his breath and each instant became an eternity.

He blinked sweat from his eyes and glanced in the mirror. The 190 was sliding into position for the kill.

Roll again and you'll hit the ground. Sit here and get your ass shot down.

That dreaded fighter pilot's adage that they used at the bar when discussing air-to-air combat exploded in his ears like a death knell: *outta altitude, airspeed and ideas.* His gut wrenched; he tasted bile.

He glanced in the rearview mirror. The 190's prop suddenly stopped spinning and the plane quickly dropped from sight. An orange fireball mushroomed and loomed in the mirror.

"Sumbitchin' kraut's engine quit and he splattered his ass," Rocko shouted.

"Rog." Robb's mouth felt like it was filled with sand. His arms and legs trembled as he tried to think what he should do next. *Adjust the power and retract the flaps dumb ass.* A few seconds later, warmth flowed through his body like he'd chugalugged a double martini on an empty stomach.

"Sorry *amigo*, I couldn't get in a shot. You and that hot-rock Nazi never held still long enough. Sumbitch must've been Red Barron's son."

"Rog on that." Robb swallowed some sand and started a shallow turn. In the turn he released his death grip on the stick and throttle, opened and closed his aching hands, then shifted from cheek to cheek on the rock hard dinghy. The bridge of his nose hurt from the pull of his oxygen mask. He unfastened it and rubbed his nose, then put it back on. *Never wanta tangle with another guy like that! Ted taught me a lot but that kraut gave me a postgraduate course.*

Up ahead a column of black smoke rose from the crash site where the 190 had struck the ground at the base of a huge tree. Its engine was jammed back toward the cockpit and one wing had broken off. The crumpled fuselage looked like an accordion and the stripes of the yellow chevron were rippled. Flying past, Robb dipped his wing and saluted.

"I'm down to 85 gallons. Let's head on back," Robb transmitted as he turned west and started to climb.

THE HELLISH VORTEX

"Sumbitchin' kraut must've run outta gas."

"Rog," Robb sighed. If the Colonel hadn't put them on a full tank, it could have been him in that field instead of the kraut. *The Colonel saved my ass.*

At debriefing, they were told that due to bad weather, only 255 bombers had struck their assigned targets. The 8th AF lost 41 bombers and the 15th AF lost 14. American fighters destroyed 59 and lost 11. Captain Knight said the weather would be too bad for a mission the next day.

"Amigo, since we have tomorrow off let's go to the bar for a blabber mouth," Rocko said to Robb as they finished dinner.

"I'm bushed. Gonna hit the sack," Robb replied.

Robb trudged down the lane to his hut, went inside and added a scoop of coal to the fire and undressed. He had never felt so tired. Wracking fighters around the sky was always very physical and a five-minute dog fight left you exhausted. But his life or death struggle today had gone well beyond that. He felt as though a portion of his life had been stripped away.

He climbed into the bunk and as soon as his eyes closed the FW-190 appeared, low and behind. He snapped them open and stared at the fire in stove. *That kraut had your ass. You should be dead.* Once again, he wondered why he had been spared and the German had died. He recalled what his aunt always said when pressed for answers about the riddles of life, "Sometimes God works in strange ways." *One thing is certain. . .I'll never forget February 22, 1944.*

After a day of rest, the 8th AF launched 809 bombers and 767 fighters. Bombing results ranged from fair to excellent. Forty-four bombers and ten fighters were lost, versus the destruction of 38 German aircraft. The 15th AF sent 114 bombers and lost a whopping 27.

Early on the morning of the 25th, the 8th AF launched its fifth maximum effort in six days. They sent 754 bombers and 899 fighters, including three P-51 groups to attack more aircraft factories. The target weather was good and the bombing results were excellent. Thirty-one bombers and three fighters were lost versus the destruction of 26 German aircraft. The 15th AF launched 400 bombers and lost 33.

That evening, exhausted 8th AF aircrews trudged from the debriefings to their chow halls. Even the excitement of surviving another day of fierce combat hadn't produced enough adrenaline to offset their weariness. With the promise of bad weather the next day, all they wanted was to have dinner and hit the sack. Overhead, thick clouds blanketed Europe as the he curtain fell on "The Big Week," the largest series of air battles of World War II—so far.

"Sumbitch. I'm maxed out. . .on max efforts," Rocko said, following Robb, Matt and Pete through the door of the hut. "Frickin' sex life's gone to hell. Gonna get dressed and head for Colchester to down a couple of brews, eat some fish and chips and get laid."

Robb, Matt and Pete had a cold shower and went to the club. They had a beer before dinner and went to the movie.

£££

The Colonel completed his tour of the flight line and returned to his office. He sat down his swivel chair, opened the bottom drawer of his desk and pulled out the bottle of Red Label Scotch and a glass. Charlie placed the half-cup of coffee and the 8th Air Force's recap of The Big Week on the desk, while the Colonel poured three fingers of Scotch into the glass, then poured a like amount into his coffee cup. He handed the glass to Charlie and they raised their drinks and nodded.

"Anything else, sir?" Charlie asked, after downing his drink.

"No thanks," Charlie."

"Cold night, sir." He shook some of ashes down, added a scoop of coal to the fire and left.

A gust of wind whistled through a crack in the Nissen hut. The Colonel thought about the maintenance crews still hard at work in the freezing cold. They had worked all night every night during the Big Week to keep the group flying. Each morning, they stood at attention in dirty fatigues, their uniform of the day. They raised their greasy hands with bloodied knuckles and saluted—as *their* aircraft roared down the runway. Then they ate and tried to sleep a few hours before their aircraft returned. "God, how I love those guys," he whispered to himself and took a big sip of the Scotch-coffee. He scanned the Big Week recap starting with the loss the loss columns. The 8th and 15th Air Forces lost nearly 2400 men, missing, killed or wounded. Every group had felt the sting of death. His group had lost three.

He took another swig and recalled the first 8th AF heavy bomber mission, on August 17, 1942. His squadron of Spitfires had helped escort *twelve* B-17's to the Marshaling yards at Rouen-Sotteville, France. After the Big Week, it didn't seem like much.

He was glad the press had given the Big Week extensive coverage, but wondered how history would judge it. He knew the airpower detractors would concentrate on playing it down. But he was certain that the airmen who did the flying, fighting, bleeding, fixing and dying would know the Big Week had been a giant step toward victory in Europe.

The Colonel downed his Scotch-coffee and turned off the desk lamp. Then he leaned back in his chair, put his feet up on the desk and went to sleep.

CHAPTER 12

A Trip to London

"Robb." Ted nudged him a second time. "Robb, wake up."

Robb opened his eyes, raised his head. "What's...goin' on?"

"Weather's bad. The Continent is going be clobbered in for two days. Gotta flight to Northholt. Going to see my dad for a few hours. After the Big Week, I thought you might like to go and have a change of scenery. I've gotta get back tonight, but you can have a night in London."

"Uh...yeah...okay." He stretched, rubbed his eyes and looked at his watch. "Nine o'clock. How soon do we leave?"

"In about an hour. Meet you at Base Ops."

"I'll be there."

On the way to the latrine, Robb thought about Joyce. *Maybe I can find her.* She hadn't written for more than two weeks. Three days ago, he'd called the Red Cross Hotel and was told she'd taken a leave of absence. He called her apartment twice, but never got an answer.

£££

Robb and Ted pulled the collars of their trench coats up around their necks and stepped outside Base Ops into the blowing rain. They sloshed across the macadam-parking ramp toward a dumpy looking, high-winged monoplane that had a bulbous nose, bloated fuselage and a bulky bowlegged landing gear.

"What the hell's that?" Robb asked.

"UC-64," Ted replied.

"Ugly old bird."

"Double ugly," Ted smiled. "That narrow gear has a built-in ground loop."

"Yeah." Until now, Robb had referred to all aircraft in the feminine gender, but this old bird barely rated an it.

They climbed aboard and the second lieutenant taxied the UC-64 to the end of the runway. He pushed the throttle to takeoff power. The engine gave a thunderous roar and the bowlegged old bird struggled to inch down the runway.

"I built airplane models whose rubber bands gave them better acceleration." Ted said.

Robb smiled.

A gust of crosswind sent the old bird swinging to the left toward the grassy quagmire off the side of the runway.

Robb and Ted grabbed the armrests, braced themselves and waited for the crash.

The young pilot stomped on the right rudder and brake, twisted the mulish yoke and over-corrected to the right. He kicked the left rudder, stomped on the left brake, twisted the yoke and over-corrected to the left. After another zig and two zags, he finally got the UC-64 headed straight down the runway.

"Give me combat anytime," Ted grumbled, tightening his safety belt.

Robb nodded and tightened his safety belt as the UC-64 gained enough speed for its tail to rise. Another gust of crosswind sent it skipping across the runway to the left toward the bottomless sod. Robb grabbed the armrests and braced his feet.

Just before the UC-64 skipped off the edge, the pilot yanked back on the yoke. The old bird shuddered into the air with its wheels skimming the green morass.

"Junior birdman's a mile behind this old goat," Ted grunted.

Robb nodded.

Dead ahead a small building loomed like a skyscraper.

"Oh...shit," Ted muttered.

Robb tightened his grip on the armrests and braced himself for the crash.

The pilot muscled the yoke to the right and raised the left wing; it missed the building by inches.

He then rolled the wings level and the old bird staggered through the turbulent air until it gained enough speed to climb. Climbing at 200 feet per minute, it wallowed into the bottom of the black clouds.

WHOOSH! A violent downdraft sent the UC-64 plunging earthward. Robb and Ted's butts left their seats; their feet dangled above the floor; the safety belts dug into their guts. A Mickey Mouse comic book, a pencil and pieces of safety wire hung in midair in front of them.

WHOO-OOMP! An updraft flung the old bird skyward. Robb and Ted's butts slammed back into their seats; their feet banged the floor; the safety wire, pencil and Mickey Mouse comic book plunged from sight.

After a seemingly endless climb, the pilot leveled the UC-64 at 1500 feet and throttled back to cruise power. For the next 30 minutes, he wrestled the cantankerous old bird through the bumpy clouds while the Northolt controller directed him toward the field.

The pilot throttled back and started to descend. With the reduced power, Robb could hear the rain pinging on the metal and fabric skin. At 400 feet, the old bird broke out of the clouds over RAF Station Northolt. The pilot lowered the flaps, increased the prop pitch, and turned left to line up with the runway. Then he reduced the power slightly, held the airspeed at 70 mph and the old bird growled down the final approach for landing.

Three feet above the ground, he reduced power once more and the aircraft shuddered, hit the runway, bounced and tried to ground loop to the left. The pilot kicked the right rudder and twisted the yoke. After a zig and zag, he got it headed straight down the runway.

"Junior birdman's making better recoveries," Ted sighed.

Robb nodded, happy to be on the ground.

The pilot taxied to the parking area and muscled the UC-64 in between two sleek Spitfires. When he cut the engine, its pistons slapped, the connecting rods clanked, the engine wheezed then burped two puffs of blue smoke and stopped.

"Can see why Noorduyn Aviation call this thing a Norseman," Ted said. "Takes Viking courage just to get into the damned thing. Never gonna get inside one again unless I'm driving. Let's get the hell outta here."

They caught a ride in a jeep going to Wycombe Abbey. "Robb, I've got to warn you, my dad's gonna talk a lot of shop," Ted said, getting out of the Jeep.

"Won't bother me. I enjoy that kinda stuff," Robb replied, admiring the Abbey, the emerald pond and the lush grounds. "What a beautiful place. Looks like something out of a Hollywood movie."

"Yeah, it's a little nicer than Nissen huts. I love this place. It's like being in a different world," Ted said, holding the door for Robb.

"Look at the WAC's," Robb whispered, as they walked down the hall toward Colonel Tyler's office.

"A little Americana up front. Look good, don't they?"

"Do they ever," Robb smiled. "Did you hear about Rocko and the WAC lieutenant?"

Ted shook his head.

"He met her in London and coaxed her to have a drink. After a few, he called her a split-tailed lieutenant and asked her how many short-arm inspections she'd given. She stood and dumped her drink on his head. Rocko looked up and grinned, 'Playin' hard to get, huh baby?'"

"Can't understand why any red-blooded American girl wouldn't go for Mr. Couth," Ted said with a smile.

"Hey. Look at that one," Robb whispered. "What a beauty."

"That's Darlene Bradford, my dad's chief clerk."

"Sherman would've never said war's hell with a chief clerk like that." Robb liked everything about her, even her braided hair. The braids ringed her head like a tiara.

Her greens sparkled as she looked up and smiled. "Captain Tyler, so nice to see you."

"Always nice seeing you, Darlene. I'd like to introduce Lieutenant Robb Baines."

"Nice to meet you, Lieutenant," she said. "I've seen your name in a number of combat reports."

"My...pleasure." Robb felt intimidated by her beauty and poise. She studied his eyes like other older women had before telling him he looked too young to be a fighter pilot.

"Your father's waiting, Captain Tyler."

Colonel Tyler pushed his chair back and came from behind the desk. He put his arm around Ted's shoulder and squeezed. "This must be Robb Baines," he said, extending his free hand. "So nice to meet you, Robb."

"My pleasure sir," he replied, wondering if he should have saluted before shaking Colonel Tyler's hand. He was taller than Ted and handsome enough to be a movie star. Although his thick black hair and neatly trimmed mustache had a few flecks of gray, he looked too young to be Ted's father.

"You guys did one helluva job durin' The Big Week. Even Hap Arnold and his Pentagon kibitzers are pleased. Our air attacks might even help quiet the rooskies about openin' another front against Germany. Strategic bombin' effort is another front. We know for sure it's already drawn thousands of men and artillery and many critical supplies from the Russian and Mediterranean fronts."

"I warned you, Robb," Ted said.

"Warned him about what?"

"That you like to talk shop."

"I can't help it. "It has taken us 30 years to get Army Air to this point. Today the 8th and 15th Air Forces can hit Germany with 1500 B-17's and B-24's, along with 1000 fighters. In a few months we'll be able to launch more than 2500 heavy bombers and 1500 fighters. That's a force of more than 26,000 men—about the same as two ground divisions. Largest, fastest, most devastating cavalry charge known to man. A hellish vortex that'll soon level the Nazi war making machine. But the grunts don't think you can have a cavalry charge without litterin' horse shit."

Robb was struck by Colonel Tyler's use of the words "hellish vortex" when referring to the huge air attacks against Germany. He wondered if the combat would get worse.

"Dad do we have any firm intelligence about the results of The Big Week?"

"Some message traffic verifies that the Luftwaffe is startin' to hurt and indicates they plan to defend only Germany's most critical targets. That means to get the Luftwaffe up to fight, we've got to avoid pissin' away our strategic bombing effort on tactical targets like the missile launching pads on the French coast. Tactical fighters and medium bombers can do a much better job against them.

"To get ready for the invasion, our strategic bombers should be used to attack targets like Germany's aircraft and oil industries. The oil industry for example has a very low priority and should be moved up near the top of our strategic target list. I know for a fact that oil is one of Germany's most critical assets and the krauts will fight like hell to defend it.

"If we destroy their oil and fuel industry, it'll ground the bulk of the air force, beach much of their navy and immobilize a lot of their army. General Spaatz agrees, but so far he hasn't been able to convince General Eisenhower or the blokes. But General Spaatz is not about to give up. He'll skin this cat, one way or the other."

"Robb, you probably recall that I told you that dad was a chemical engineer and worked for Standard Oil. He made many trips to Germany before the war. In 1931, he met a Gerhard "Max" Schulz, a German fighter pilot in World War I, who was also a chemical engineer working for I.G. Farben."

"That's really something to meet someone you fought against," Robb said, wanting to hear more.

"That's right. Old Max and I had a lot in common. He spoke perfect English and we hit it off right away. Max had many contacts and took me through most of Germany's major refineries, including the Fischer-Tropsch laboratories. They're the prime mover for producing synthetic fuels and rubber from coal. After several visits it became apparent that Germany's huge effort in synthetic fuel indicated that oil was their Achilles' heel. I reported what I had learned to the American Embassy several times."

"I wonder why the Americans haven't made it a priority target?" Robb asked.

"I'm afraid my reports may have gotten buried in our illustrious State Department."

"Sir. Do you know what happened to Max Schulz?" Robb asked.

"He was accused of treason in January 1941 and put before a Nazi firin' squad." Colonel Tyler paused a few seconds. "Let's get somethin' to eat," he said, glancing at his watch.

Colonel Tyler, Ted and Robb sat at a table in the corner of the dining room eating their dehydrated potatoes, Brussels sprouts, canned ham and chopped raw carrots with raisins.

"Dad, seems like the bad-mouthing of General Eisenhower in the British newspapers is getting worse."

"It is. Lot of it is instigated by the bloke army. They want one of their own to be the Supreme Allied Commander. They would like to see their chief Yank hater, his eminence Bernard L. Montgomery, in Eisenhower's job.

"Our generals are not the least bit fond of Montgomery. They have nick-named him "Slow Motion" because the old fart's so concerned about his winning image that he won't make a move unless he's got endless supplies and overwhelming numbers of equipment and men. I'm convinced he's constipated about half the time, cuz he's afraid to take a crap unless he's got a year's supply of toilet paper stacked outside the crapper."

"Sir, how long has this been going on?" Robb was shocked to hear about the high command bickering.

"Bloke army has been tryin' to run everything since before North Africa. Back then, they argued their combat experience made 'em more qualified. At one meeting, our General "Pete" Quesada asked, 'What experience are you referring to...Dunkirk, Crete, Greece or Singapore?' Their most famous defeats shut 'em up for a while.

"Senior bloke army officers are a snooty bunch...they even have their own dialect. They speak in a clipped manner, where their lips barely move, and sometimes their words sound more like indistinguishable grunts, which only they can understand. I'd say it's highly cultivated, because it's not apparent in either the RAF or Royal Navy."

"It's a damned wonder that we get anything done, with all of the bickering," Ted said with a smile.

"Yeah. Fortunately, we don't have a lot of problems at the fightin' level because there's more than enough fightin' to go around." Colonel Tyler paused and took a sip of coffee. "Robb, where in Texas are you from?"

"Austin, sir."

"Pretty little city. I landed there once durin' one of my reserve cross-country trainin' flights. Spent the night in the Driskill Hotel. It still there?"

"Yes sir. What kind of plane were you flying, sir?"

"I had a P-12 that time. Another time I led a flight of three 0-52's over Austin, during a flood in the summer of 1935. Was at Kelly Field for two weeks of training. Flew some Corps of Engineer types up to check on the flood. Got some legal buzzin.'"

"I saw you! My aunt's house is on a hill overlooking the Colorado River. I was on the back porch. Looked straight out at the formation. Seeing that flight of 0-52's was the thing that convinced me to become an Army pilot. Had my first ride in an airplane shortly after that. A red and white Waco."

"Glad we kept you outta the Navy. Always liked flying around central Texas. Use to do some flying with Claire Chennault. He helped the city of Austin find the location for their airport."

"Dad," Ted interrupted. "I've gotta catch my flight back to the field and Robb's going to spend the night in London."

"Understand. Didn't mean to be such a motor mouth. I'll get a staff car to take ya to Northolt. You can drop Robb off at the station on the way."

£££

"Your dad's a real tiger," Robb said getting into the staff car.
"Yeah. He's still flying combat. Has flown over thirty bomber missions. Admits to a lesser number, but Darlene keeps score. He went with Curt Lemay on the Regensburg mission."
"Wow. Keeps that up, he'll finish a combat tour."
"Yeah, that's his goal."
"Looks young."
"Plays squash or runs almost every day. Can still rack a fighter around the sky with the best of 'em. Taught me a lot."
"Must be tough on him being away from your mother?"
"They've been divorced for five years."
"Sorry. That Darlene's some kind of looker. She have a steady?"
"Dad's never said."
"I can't believe I saw your dad fly over Austin."
"Yeah, quite a coincidence."

£££

In June of 1935, three days of heavy rain had filled the central Texas streams and rivers, sending them over their banks. From the back porch of his aunt's house on West 7th Street, Robb had watched the Congress Avenue Bridge disappear beneath the raging Colorado River.

On the morning of the fourth day, the sun burst through the dark clouds. Robb heard the distant roar of aircraft engines. He grabbed his balsa wood aircraft model, a P-12, and rushed to the back porch. A flight of three 0-52's roared past at eye level. They were heading northwest and passed close enough for Robb to see the heads of the pilots and observers moving.

After they disappeared up the river, Robb waited, hoping they'd return. Thirty minutes later, the roar of engines came from the northwest. The 0-52's passed closer than the first time.

Robb raced across the porch, with his balsa model, trying to hold formation. He'd never been so close to an airplane in flight, nor seen a formation. From that moment on he began coaxing his aunt for an airplane ride. Two weeks later she took him to Robert Mueller Airport. With two dollars that he had earned mowing lawns, Robb paid Pinkey Hutchins for a fifteen-minute flight.

Pinkey gave him an old leather helmet and goggles to put on and Robb stared at himself in the broken mirror. In a few minutes he would join the ranks of his heroes like Eddie Rickenbacker, Frank Luke and Charles Lindbergh.

Robb and Pinkey walked across the grass, to the Waco, a beautiful red and white biplane. Its open cockpit was an aromatic delight, a combination of doped fabric, gasoline, wood and leather.

Robb climbed in and Pinkey helped him buckle and tighten his safety belt. Robb's stomach tingled; his legs quivered.

"Any questions?" Pinkey asked.

Robb shook his head no.

Pinkey smiled and climbed into the rear cockpit.

From the aviation magazines he'd read, Robb recognized the airspeed indicator, altimeter, tachometer, oil gauge and needle-ball indicator on the black instrument panel. Below his feet, steel cables ran from the stick and rudders back to the tail and out to the ailerons. Only the wooden fuselage ribs and fabric protected him from the outside world. His stomach tightened.

"Switches off!" the mechanic shouted.

"Switches off!" Pinkey yelled back.

The mechanic pulled the prop through, "Contact!"

"Contact!" Pinkey shouted, turning the magneto switch to 'both.'

With two hands, the mechanic swung the prop. The engine kicked over, belched fire and a puff of blue smoke from its exhaust, then cracked like gunfire and the Waco shook all over.

Pinkey held up a clenched fist, with its thumb extended outward. The mechanic yanked the chocks from in front of the wheels and jumped clear.

They taxied to the end of the grass runway, turned the Waco into the southerly wind and stopped. Pinkey pulled the stick back; pushed the throttle forward, ran the engine up, checked the mags, then throttled back. He moved the stick around the cockpit, pushed the rudders full travel, checking that the flight controls were free.

Robb heard a slap on the fuselage and looked back. Pinkey pointed at his goggles, reminding Robb to pull them down. Then Pinkey yelled, "Ready?"

Robb legs shook as he nodded.

The throttle went full forward and the engine boomed a deafening roar. The Waco rocked on its landing gear and the fabric buzzed against the wooden ribs of the fuselage. Prop wash blasted Robb's face and ripped beneath his helmet's earflaps; he grabbed the chinstrap, yanked it tighter. A knot formed in his stomach.

Pinkey released the brakes. The Waco leaped forward.

Robb's back pressed hard against the seat. He grabbed the armrests. His feet slid off the wooden footrests and dangled above the cables, ribs and fabric. The knot in his stomach tightened.

The balloon tires and tail wheel bumped across the grass and dirt. The Waco's speed increased; its tail rose and the bumps softened. The Waco skipped once then leaped into the air.

The end of the runway shot beneath them. As they climbed toward the southeast, a field lined with live oaks and pecan trees slid past. Ahead, the Colorado River made a big loop around another field covered with dried mud left by the flood. On a dirt road off to the right, an old Ford Model-T truck passed a wagon being pulled by a team of mules.

At the loop in the river, Pinkey banked the Waco to the right and turned toward the northwest. He leveled off at 1000 feet, throttled back and the engine's exhaust cracked a steady beat. Flying through the smooth blue sky was like a dream come true and the knot in Robb's stomach disappeared.

Ahead, the Capitol's dome dominated the downtown skyline. A few blocks north, the UT tower anchored the southwest corner of the University of Texas campus that contained its cream-colored buildings with red tile roofs. Houses, half hidden beneath green oak trees, surrounded the campus and the football stadium buttressed it to the East.

Pinkey banked the Waco to the left and turned south over the Capitol. The American and Texas flags on its dome rippled in the breeze. Robb felt a newfound freedom—a freedom from the earthly fetters of traffic lights, speed limit signs and other man-made restraints. They were far below, out of sight, not allowed.

People looked out the windows of the Stephen F. Austin Hotel and Scarbrough Building and waved. Pinkey rocked the Waco's wings. A few blocks south of the Colorado River, he banked the Waco and turned toward the north. Barton Springs swimmers and sunbathers shaded their eyes, looked up and waved. Pinkey and Robb waved back at the earthlings.

Pinkey added power; the Waco climbed. Above the summer haze, the sky got bluer, the air cooler. On the West 7th Street hill, Robb saw his aunt's house. Further west, lay the hill country, whose valleys and crests were covered with the greenness of live oaks and cedars.

As they got higher, the horizon broadened, the green hill country seemed flatter, city blocks looked shorter, buildings got smaller, cars moved slower and people became mere specks.

Pinkey pulled back the throttle. Above the engine's slow lope and rush of air, Robb heard a slap on the fuselage and looked back. Pinkey smiled, then shook the stick and yelled, "You've got it, son!"

Flying the Waco through the cool, clear blue sky of Texas, free of man's shackles, was more exciting than Robb imagined. Nothing on earth could come close—it was a heavenly encounter.

£££

"Robb. We're at the station," Ted said as the staff car stopped in front of the South Ruislip Station.

"Uh…guess I dozed off. Did I snore?"

"No. Just a quiet nap."

"Still a little tired after The Big Week. Thanks for the lift. See ya tomor-row."

The possibility of seeing Joyce made the taxi ride to the Red Cross Hotel seemed agonizingly slow. But he couldn't forget Colonel Tyler had said and the words hellish vortex started a tug of war with his thoughts about Joyce. *With the increased fighting this could be my last chance to see her.*

He paid the driver and ran up the steps, hoping Joyce would be stand-ing behind the counter. Instead, a woman in her 40's, with a large nose, brown horn-rimmed glasses and protruding front teeth, greeted him. The vase in which Joyce kept the yellow rose was missing. When Robb inquired, the woman at the counter said she had heard about Joyce, but had no knowledge of where she had gone.

After checking in, he called Joyce's apartment, but no one answered. With-out Joyce, the Red Cross Hotel was just a dreary place to sleep. *Got to get the hell out of here.* He caught a taxi and went to the Grosvenor House.

Glenn Miller's recording of *"Jersey Bounce"* was playing as Robb entered the huge ballroom. He scanned the mezzanine and the floor below, but Joyce wasn't there. He went to the phone booth and tried calling her apartment again, but there was no answer. As Robb sat at the bar and sipped his sherry, he listened to Duke Ellington's recording of *"Don't Get Around Much Anymore."*

"My dear boy, what a pleasant surprise." Major Watson placed his soft leather overnight bag, tailor-made cashmere uniform overcoat and immaculate garrison cap on a chair at an empty table near the bar. "May I join you for a drink?"

"Uh…yeah…yes sir."

"Dry martini with two onions, please," Watson told the bartender. "Been to my tailor for a fitting. Had to stop by for a drink, before going to my hotel. Where are you staying, Lieutenant?"

"Red Cross Hotel."

"How ghastly. I have a suite at Clairidge's. I could arrange a room for you."

"No thank you, sir. Already checked in."

Major Watson stirred the martini with the toothpick containing the two onions. He removed the toothpick, pulled off one of the onions with his teeth and chewed. After placing the toothpick and remaining onion back in the long stem glass, he downed the martini and set the glass on the bar. Then he pulled a white handkerchief from his coat sleeve and tapped his lips. "Do you have any-thing planned this evening, Lieutenant?"

THE HELLISH VORTEX

"Might...uh...meet a friend." Robb took a big sip of his sherry.

"I'm having a few friends in for cocktails and hors d'oeuvres at six o'clock." Watson stuffed the handkerchief back in his coat sleeve. "You and your friend are welcome to join us. Major Charles Pearcey, our famous American ace, will be there."

Robb couldn't believe his ears. The world suddenly seemed smaller.

Major Watson took his coat, hat and overnight bag from the chair. "Please try to join us."

"I'll try." *Like hell I will.*

One of the last people Robb wanted to see was Kitty Lou Pearcy's husband. Kitty Lou was a stunning blond who could have doubled for Betty Grable. Except Kitty Lou was a much better actress. She played to perfection whatever role she desired. She could be a coy, one-dimensional southern belle with enough innocent charm and grace to get what she wanted. During their month of intimacy he learned that she could also be mean as hell, at ease with the language of dockhands.

He first noticed her at the Waycross Army Air Field Officer's Club where she always arrived with married friends and left early, like a faithful and devoted wife. But when they exchanged glances, her eyes and smile told another story. Robb suspected the rumbles about her were true.

He found out the night of the graduation party for the group of P-40 pilots that finished their training a month ahead of him. Kitty Lou gently pressed a note into his hand while he was standing at the bar. "Please call me at 10:00 tomorrow morning. My number is 364," the note said.

She picked him up at the bus stop in her gray 1941 Chevy convertible her "daddy" had given her for high school graduation. They drove to the Suwannee River where her folks kept a motorboat. After placing three large cushions, a picnic basket and a beer cooler in the boat, they went down the river to the edge of the Okefenokee Swamp.

Docked in the shade of the tupelo gum and cypress trees, Kitty Lou handed Robb two bottles of beer and an opener. She placed the cushions in the bottom of the boat, then took off her blouse, unbuttoned her wraparound skirt and laid them to one side. The yellow one-piece bathing suit revealed a beautifully tanned and shapely body. She sat down on the cushions, fluffed her long blonde hair, leaned back and moistened her parted lips. "Take off your uniform, get comfortable," she purred huskily, then took a long sip from the bottle of beer.

Robb gulped down a noisy swallow and beer foamed out of the end of the bottle. Although he had worn his bathing suit under his uniform, his hands trembled as he hurried to undress.

All afternoon, while Robb and Kitty Lou made love the alligators and water moccasins slithered past, leaving ripples in their wake that slapped gently against the side of the boat.

183

4ln9c-1419647679

RICHARD M BAUGHN

For the next four weeks, Robb and Kitty Lou made love, either in the swamp, in her Chevy, or in her parents' house. Two weekends were spent in the Waycross Hotel. But the swamp was her favorite spot. Each time they made love there, Robb had the feeling they were being watched. When he mentioned it, Kitty Lou smiled.

Once in the midst of their lovemaking they heard a rustling in the trees and looked up. A black teenager stared down at them from a cypress tree. Stark naked, Kitty Lou stood up and yelled, "Get your black ass outta here." The teenager swung from the tree into his rowboat and paddled away. Smiling, Kitty Lou laid back and they picked up where they had left off.

She enjoyed talking about her affairs which started when she was thirteen. But she never mentioned her husband. Robb wondered why but never asked.

At his graduation party, Robb saw Kitty Lou pass a note to a P-40 pilot in the class behind him.

£££

When Robb heardTommy Dorsey's *"I'll Walk Alone"* with Frank Sinatra—one of Joyce's favorites--he finished his sherry and ordered another. He took it to the telephone booth on the mezzanine and tried calling again, but there was no answer. He downed his drink and took a taxi to her apartment. The white-haired elevator operator said Joyce hadn't been there for more than a week, but he avoided answering other questions.

Robb walked along the crowded Sloane Street, crossed Knightsbridge and Carriage Roads into Hyde Park. Without Joyce, London was just another faraway and lonely place. He made his way through the park and crossed Park Lane.

"Lonely, Yank?" the Picaddily Commando's voice croaked from the darkened doorway. Robb ignored it and continued to walk, wondering if he'd ever see Joyce again. He hadn't felt so alone since childhood.

BEEP! BEEP! Robb jumped as a taxi entered the drive. It crossed the sidewalk a few feet in front of him and stopped in front of Claridge's. *Could get a free drink from old Watson. . .just for laughs.*

Robb knocked and the door swung open. "My dear boy, so happy you could make it," Major Watson smiled. "Are you alone?" He peeked out the door.

"Yeah...yes sir. Didn't find my friend."

"Please come in."

Small groups of droopy-eyed civilian men and their wives, along with several senior British officers and their wives, were sipping cocktails and nibbling watercress sandwiches or soggy patty shells filled with a yucky looking spread.

"Scotch and soda, Lieutenant?" Watson asked, leading Robb to the table with liquor, mix and hors d'oeuvres.

"Yes sir."

"Feel so uncivilized, fixing drinks," Watson said, pouring some Scotch into a glass. "Tried to get help but couldn't. There's a war, you know," he said with a wink.

Robb forced a smile. *Too bad. So you snooty bunch of bastards have to live like the rest of us.*

Watson gave the Scotch a shot of seltzer and handed the glass to Robb. "Come, meet my friends from the US Embassy and British Foreign Office."

Robb took a big gulp of his drink. *I should've gone back to the Grosvenor House. I don't need this crap.*

Watson stopped at the first group. "May I introduce Lieutenant Baines, one of my young pilots," he squeaked with a trace of the Britisher's la-de-da accent. Except for an attractive, fortyish-looking British wife who acted as though she wanted to more than mother him, they peered down their noses at him through bored eyes. After a perfunctory exchange, Major Watson led him away.

Crossing the room, Robb suddenly stopped—dead in his tracks. From the far corner, Joyce's radiant blue eyes beamed at him.

Major Watson stopped and turned. "Something wrong, Lieutenant?" Watson's eyes flicked back and forth between Joyce and Robb. "Recognize someone?" His eyes continued to flick.

Not knowing what to say, Robb ignored the question. A tall, gray-haired British Army colonel stood next to Joyce. He looked down, saw Joyce staring, then looked at Robb. Robb's face felt like it'd been baked in the hot Texas sun.

"Like to meet the Freemantles?" Watson smiled.

"Uh...what'd you say?"

"Would you like to meet the Freemantles?" He sounded irritated.

"Who are they?"

"The British colonel and his wife across the room," Watson snapped. "Would you like to meet them?"

"Why not." *Get hold of yourself...keep your cool...ride this out.*

"Colonel and Mrs. Freemantle, may I introduce Lieutenant Baines. He's one of my young fighter pilots."

"Hmmm...hmmm," Colonel Freemantle deadpanned his guttural grunts. "American fighter pilot...hmmm." His lips barely moved and the words came out clipped. He thrust his big hand forward and gripped Robb's hard.

"I'm Joyce." She beamed, raising her hand.

Robb jerked his hand free from Colonel Freemantle's steel grip.

"Hmmm...hmmm." Colonel Freemantle grunted with a victory smile.

"So very nice to meet you, Lieutenant." Her hand was soft and warm; her radiant eyes connected with his.

RICHARD M BAUGHN

"Hmmm…hmmm." Colonel Freemantle's eyes turned icy.

The room closed in on Robb; the lights seemed to brighten, like he was standing in a spotlight. Sweat formed on his forehead and upper lip; a drop trickled down the bridge of his nose and slid off the end. He pulled his hand free from Joyce's and tried to think of something to say, but couldn't. *Why doesn't that mouthy Watson say something?*

"Would you excuse us, please?" Watson said finally. "I want to share Lieutenant Baines with the rest of my guests. Come my boy."

"Nice to have met you," Robb struggled.

"Hmmm…hmmm." Colonel Freemantle continued his icy stare.

Robb tried to smile and started to do an about face, but caught himself, Instead, he turned awkwardly and in the middle of the room stopped and downed his Scotch and soda. Then he followed Watson.

"Oh dear me," Watson sighed, stopping at the table. "Help yourself to another drink, Lieutenant, while I get more hors d'oeuvres."

Robb poured a big Scotch, gave it a long squirt of seltzer and downed a gulp. *Finish this drink and leave!* He took another swig and glanced around the room, being careful not to look at Joyce. He thought about Colonel Freemantle's stiff manner and his hard-to-understand clipped speech. *Now I know what Colonel Tyler meant.* Robb raised his glass and glanced to his left to avoid Joyce's eyes. The attractive fortyish British wife smiled; he forced a smile and took a sip.

Major Watson placed two more trays of hors d'oeuvres on the table just as someone knocked on the door. "Excuse me, my boy."

It was Major Pearcy looking even younger than he had on the cover of *LIFE*. His long blonde hair was combed straight back and held in place with hair oil. Except for the tanned area that marked his leather eye mask, his complexion was creamy and his eyes were cold blue. Below his silver pilot wings were two full rows of ribbons, headed by the Distinguished Service Cross, a Silver Star and a Distinguished Flying Cross with six clusters.

The room got brighter and smaller. Sweat oozed from Robb's armpits. *Can't believe I'm in the same room with two husbands whose wives I've slept with. Gotta get the hell outta here!* Robb turned, looked the other way and took a big swig, hoping Watson and Pearcy would bypass him. As he swallowed, he felt a soft touch on his shoulder.

"Lieutenant Baines," Major Watson said. "May I present Major Charles Pearcy."

Robb turned, "It's uh…an honor to meet you…sir."

Major Pearcy extended his limp hand as his blue eyes surveyed the room. "Major Watson tells me you're a fighter pilot," he said, continuing to look around the room.

"Yes sir."

Major Pearcy nodded and smiled at someone across the room. "Geoffery, I see the Freemantles. I must say hello." Without looking at Robb or saying anything, Major Pearcy pulled his hand free and left.

THE HELLISH VORTEX

"Excuse us, Lieutenant," Major Watson said before he hurried after Major Pearcy.

As Major Pearcy held out his hand, Joyce's eyes flashed and her smile broadened. *Good God. She's slept with him too!* Robb chugalugged his Scotch and left.

£££

"Sir, ye 'ave a call," the cockney hotel maid said, nudging Robb's shoulder a second time.

"Okay, okay," he mumbled. His head throbbed from last night's drinking bout and he fumbled with the bottle of APC's. He popped two in his mouth, swallowed some water and stumbled down the hall in his olive drab shorts to the phone. "Hello."

"Darling. Can you come to my flat?"

Robb's heart skipped a beat. "On my way," he heard himself say.

£££

They kissed hungrily in the doorway. "Darling, we better move inside," she said after taking a breath. She led him down the hallway toward the bedroom. Through the door, he saw the orange glow from the fireplace reflected on the waiting bed. A single yellow rose stood in the tall slender vase on the nightstand.

Minutes later their naked bodies lay motionless amid the rumpled sheets. Robb was on his back, trying to catch his breath, while Joyce lay on her side with her right leg and arm across him. He could hardly believe that he'd found her. Like Ted said, "fighting the war from Britain is filled with anomalies."

"Darling, I've missed you," she finally purred. Her fingers floated across his chest and as she kissed his ear, they glided through the hair on his stomach on their way to center stage. She enjoyed the power of her touch. Once again the world around them disappeared.

£££

"Darling, we must talk," she said, blowing gently in his ear until he opened his eyes

"About what?"

"Have you tried to contact me these past two weeks?"

"Yeah. Where have you been?"

"We were at our country home. Freddy wanted to get away from the hustle and bustle of London."

"How long have you known Major Pearcy?" Robb couldn't help himself.

"We met about a year ago at an Anglo-American ball. He was one of the speakers. We sat next to one another during dinner."

187

"Have you been seeing him?"

"Sometimes he calls when he's in London. But that's not what I want to talk about."

"Then what is it?"

"First, I missed you, darling."

"Missed you, too."

"I didn't plan to see you again after Freddy returned, but I couldn't bear telling you. Then when I saw you last night, I knew I had to see you one more time."

Robb listened without comment.

"But this is the last time. Freddy has been posted to the Supreme Headquarters, Allied Expeditionary Force, under your General Eisenhower." She sounded cool and deliberate. "I can't jeopardize his career. I'm truly sorry, but we both knew it had to end. "You do understand, don't you, darling?"

"Yeah."

"In fact, I'm meeting him for tea shortly so you must leave now," she said. "Do you understand?" she repeated.

"Yeah." He pulled her closer.

"Oh, darling. . .you'll make me late for tea."

CHAPTER 13

Big B

General Spaatz considered Berlin to be a "four-for-one target." In addition to being the seat of power, it had a number of key industrial targets including a ball bearing plant, the Daimler-Benz aircraft engine plant and the Bosch electrical plant. There were also several lakes in and around the city, providing a good land-water contrast for radar bombing when the weather was bad. Equally important, Spaatz knew Berlin was a city the *Luftwaffe* would defend.

By March 1, 1944, the 8th AF had four groups of P-51's and three groups with P-38's enough long-range fighters to escort the bombers anywhere in Germany. On the evening of March 2, Spaatz ordered the first American bombing attack against Berlin.

£££

After the guards checked their identifications, Robb, Pete, Rocko and Matt followed Ted and Red flight down the aisle in the group briefing room. "Berlin...Big by God B!" Rocko snorted, when he saw the target on the big wall map. Before sitting down in his yellow chair he thrust his arm up in a Nazi salute and roared. "*Seig heil!* Up *der Fuhrer's* old inner tube!" Some pilots shook their heads; others just sighed. Ted turned and smiled then wrote the time over target, recall word, heading and flight time from Berlin to Boxted on the back of his left hand. All Snapper pilots did the same.

As more pilots arrived there were sighs and groans and the smokers anxiously took cigarettes from their packs of Camels or Lucky Strikes, lit them with their Zippos and filled their lungs with smoke. Once all three squadron were seated, the adjutant looked at his watch, glanced at the wall clock and leaned the cue stick against the lectern. Silence fell across the room as he marched to the rear door.

"HOFFICERS, TEN—SHUN!"

"Take your seats, gentlemen." The Colonel hopped onto the stage, picked up the cue stick, held it horizontally with both hands and looked at the pilots. "Gents, today, March 3, 1944, we're gonna plow more new ground. This will be the first daylight raid on Berlin by American heavy bombers. Waited a long time for this one," he said pensively.

"Secondly, we got our first shipment of external fuel tanks yesterday. Hung 'em last night. Each P-51 is carryin' two 75-gallon tanks that resemble bathtubs. They'll give us *beaucoup* fuel—at least another three-and-a-half-hours of flyin' time. Now we can escort the bombers anyplace in krautland. We've really turned the corner in the strategic air war.

"Spring's gettin' close, but as you saw on the way to work, winter still has the upper hand. Stormy's gonna tell us the weather over krautland is iffy as hell. But we're gonna go. Cuz General Tooey Spaatz wants Berlin...bad. Okay Stormy."

"Sir, you're right about the weather," Captain Knight said taking the cue stick. "Weather over the Continent's not good. Some of the weathermen at 8th Air Force think there may be some breaks over Berlin, but I don't. Bad stuff will start over Holland and I think that it'll get worse the further east you go.

"In addition to the bad weather, the contrails will be thick and persistent all the way from Britain to Berlin. You will probably have to fly through your inbound contrails on your way back. Between the clouds and contrails, it'll not only be tough to navigate, it'll be difficult to keep one another in sight—especially for the bomber wings in the rear end of the stream. Just not a good day to put 1500 aircraft in the same sky...." Captain Knight finished and handed the cue to Major Watson.

"Our targets for today are the V.F.K. antifriction-bearing plant and Bosch electrical plant," Major Watson said, as he tapped their locations around Berlin with the cue stick. "If they can't be struck visually, the radar equipped pathfinder B-17's will lead the bombers to the large rail facilities near the *Friedrichstrasse* section of Berlin." He placed the cue tip on the target.

Watson recited the numbers and locations of AAA guns and fighters along the route and in the target area. "Attacking Berlin will certainly bring the *Luftwaffe* up in force...." He finished his briefing and passed the cue stick to Major Hunt.

"As you can see, the bomber's twelve combat wings are swinging north of Holland. They'll remain over the water and cross the Jutland Peninsula. Near Kiel, they'll swing south to Berlin. We're hoping to confuse the German radar controllers about where we're going to attack while avoiding some flak.

"There'll be 756 bombers and 730 fighter escorts from 8th and 9th AF. In the target area, we'll be joined by three more P-51 groups, which should help even the odds. Three P-38 groups will be just to the west. Second mission for one of the 38 groups. So keep your eyes peeled because those new double-breasted fighter jocks might mistake you for a ME-109. About 500 P-47's will cover the bombers along the route on the way in and out.

"Like the Colonel said, we'll be carrying two 75-gallon bathtubs and their weight will add about 400 feet to our takeoff roll. Their drag and weight will also add about two minutes to our climb to 30-grand. Tanks have been feed checked on the ground, but we need to make sure they're gonna feed in the air. So, turn 'em on as soon as you get squared away after takeoff. Anytime you switch to a bathtub, watch your fuel pressure. If the pressure drops more than 4 psi, switch back to internal fuel. Wait a few seconds and try the bathtub again. If only one tank feeds, that's a go. If neither of them feeds you can stay home from work.

"If you have to abort, you can land with full tanks. Just use a flat, power-on approach and fly 15 mph faster than normal. Make a slow, smooth flare for landing and gradually retard power until touchdown. If for some reason you don't feel comfortable about landing with the tanks, drive to the North Sea and shed 'em.

"For those who continue on the mission, start using the bathtub fuel as soon as you get the fuselage tank down to 25 gallons. Burn 20 minutes of fuel from one bathtub, then 20 minutes from the other, to avoid excessive weight differential. When the bathtubs run dry or if kraut fighters tap us, go to an internal wing tank and shed the bathtubs *muy pronto*. If one or both won't drop, kick the rudders and pump the stick while pulling the bomb-tank salvo levers.

"Sir," Major Hunt handed the Colonel the cue stick.

"Gang, this shitty weather's gonna be like flyin' through a Nebraska blizzard," the Colonel said, taking the cue stick. "We'll be flyin' in and out of the clouds and contrails, fightin' vertigo, while tryin' to keep one another in sight, dodgin' other friendly aircraft and lookin' for krauts. Gonna make ya wonder why ya ever took up flyin'.

"Just drivin' to Berlin and back will make a dogfight with the Red Baron seem like an ice cream social. But remember, we'll be above some of the weather. The bombers will have to wade through most of it.

"Okay Guys, let's get strapped up, head for the murk and have at the bastards."

£££

Robb and Pete broke out of the first layer of clouds at 6000 feet. To the north, crisscrossing contrails filled much of the sky over East Anglia where the bombers had joined up. A few seconds later, Rocko and Matt popped out. Robb turned 180 degrees and rolled out on a heading of east. One mile ahead, he saw Ted's flight moving in behind Bugeye and Hot Rod. Robb turned five degrees left to join with Ted.

"Snapper Yellow, check external tanks," Robb called, switching the fuel selector to the right external tank. The fuel pressure needle dropped from 18 psi to 16, then returned to 18. He let it feed for a few seconds, then switched back to internal fuel. After a few seconds, he rotated the selector to the left external tank. The pressure dropped to 14 psi and he quickly switched back to internal fuel, waited for the fuel pressure to return to 18 psi, then switched back to the left external tank. *Feed, you bastard.* The fuel pressure dropped to 16 psi and returned to 18. *That's better.* "Snapper Yellow One, bathtubs feeding. Goin' fuselage tank."

"Yellow Two, feeding."

"Three samo."

"Yellow Four, feeding."

"Snapper Red, Yellow's moving in at your six o'clock," Robb called.

"Snapper Red copied," Ted answered.

"Snapper White, check external tanks," the third flight commander called.

A few seconds later, White Three transmitted, "Can't get either bathtub to feed. Tried each of 'em three times."

"Snapper White One, roger. Snapper Spare One, fill in for White Three. White Three, take the day off," the flight commander said.

"White Three, rog."

"Snapper Red, White's sliding into position."

"Shotgun, Snapper's tucked in," Ted called.

"Shotgun roger. I'm turnin' to the northeast and goin' climb power."

Over the North Sea, a labyrinth of white vapor contrails marked the northeast route of the 756 bombers. The contrails filled the gaps between the broken clouds and made the gray horizon looked more like dusk than dawn.

"Shotgun gang, close it up, turn on your navigation lights and check that your pitot heat is on. Spares, you can return to the field," the Colonel transmitted.

The 36 P-51's zoomed into the clouds and contrails, and for the next twelve minutes vertigo tweaked Robb's senses. He felt like the world had tilted 45 degrees to the right until they broke out on top at 26,000 feet. The Colonel continued to climb to 28,000 feet and leveled off 2000 feet below the solid layer of cirrostratus.

"Shotgun gang, let's turn off the nav lights and go combat spread. I'm gonna move to the right and parallel the bombers' contrails." The Colonel turned ten degrees right, held the heading for ten seconds, then turned back on course.

Three miles ahead, Robb saw the contrails of the P-47 squadron crisscrossing above the last bomber wing in the stream. He rubbed frost off the windshield and canopy for a better look at the bombers. Each of the 63 B-24's resembled a snowblower, belching huge plumes of pure white snow.

Passing the B-24's, Robb watched the overloaded bombers fly through the clumps of clouds and contrails. The giant bombers bounced up and down and slid back and forth, as the young pilots struggled to hold formation. Their bouncing and sliding resembled a game of crack the whip. The further back in the wing formation they were, the rougher the ride—the higher the bounce and the longer the slide.

Poor bastards have another seven hours of this and this is the easy part. Once again, Robb felt thankful that he had fought so hard to become a fighter pilot.

"Shotgun gang, coastline at one o'clock," the Colonel transmitted.

Robb glanced down to the right. He saw the Dutch coast through a small break in the clouds.

"Shotgun gang, have a gaggle of contrails at three o'clock low, about four miles east. Looks like one of our bomber wings must've gotten separated in the bad weather and turned south to look for an alternate target."

Robb glanced at the bombers and their fighter escorts heading south. He looked back at the bomber wing on his left; it disappeared into a clump of clouds that were partially hidden by contrails. Another wing lumbered out of the same clump of clouds heading south. *Shit...that had to be close! Damned near wiped out two wings of bombers. We shouldn't be flying in this crap.*

The Colonel turned right to continue paralleling the bomber stream to the east. Near the Frisian Islands, the cloud coverage increased and the cirrostratus overcast thickened. The sky ahead darkened like a partial eclipse. *Shit...damned weather's going from bad to worse. Give me clear skies and krauts anytime.*

The Colonel and Hot Rod disappeared in the clouds, then Bug Eye disappeared. "Shotgun gang, I just flew into a band of cirrus," the Colonel transmitted. "Everybody hold your heading, altitude and airspeed. We shouldn't be in it very long."

Blinded, Robb hunkered down and watched his flight instruments, holding his heading, airspeed and altitude steady. He prayed he wouldn't run into Snapper Red, or that Snapper White wouldn't slam into him from behind, or that another group of escort fighters wouldn't slam into the entire squadron.

Seconds later, Robb broke out of the cirrus. His position in relation to Ted's flight hadn't changed and Bug Eye and Hot Rod were a half-mile ahead. *Thank God! We should get the hell outta here before a bunch of us get killed in a mid air collision without accomplishing a damned thing.* He rubbed more frost from his windshield so he could keep Ted in sight.

"Guys, Shotgun has another band of clouds dead ahead," the Colonel called. "Looks like we're gonna be in and outta this stuff for a while. There's not enough clear sky to join in close formation, so just hold what you have until we break out in the clear again."

Robb hunkered down to look at his flight instruments. They zoomed out of the clouds and he glanced ahead looking for other aircraft then shot back into the clouds. *Shit! This half-blind, half-visual flying is a good way to bust your ass.*

"Shotgun's in the clear," the Colonel transmitted after eight minutes of half-blind and half-visual flying that seemed more like 80 minutes. "It looks pretty good up ahead. Don't forget to keep switchin' back and forth on your external fuel tanks."

Thank God were outta that crap. Robb leaned forward to switch the fuel tank selector handle from the right to the left external tank.

"Ringo, Shotgun is closin' at your five o'clock."

"Ringo here, glad you made it, Shotgun."

"Shotgun roger. I only see two wings of bombers."

"Ringo here. That's all we have. The others got separated in the soup."

Robb checked the sky to the east and west, but saw only the two wings. *Shit. . .we all should have turned around.*

"Ringo, Shotgun here. You have that wall of weather dead ahead?"

"Ringo has it, Shotgun. I'm gonna try to get through. Can you stay with us?"

"Can do, Ringo. Shotgun gang, close it up. Double check that your nav lights and peter heat are on."

Robb wobbled the wings, signaling Pete, Rocko and Matt to move in close, then he slid in a few feet behind Ted's flight. *What the hell are they thinking flying into this crap? Gonna get us all killed.*

The two bomber wings plowed into the wall of clouds. Their 126 contrails marked the spot.

With his 36 P-51's in tight formation, the Colonel charged into the wall of clouds, 2000 feet above and a mile south of the bomber's contrails.

The clouds were bumpy and Robb tried hard not to bounce too high or slide too far, hoping to make it easier for Matt, Rocko, Pete and Snapper White. But even Ted had to bounce and slide to hold formation.

WHOOMP! WHOOMP! Two orange flak bursts flashed in the dark clouds, off to the right and ahead of Snapper Red.

"FLAK! Snapper Red Three here!"

WHOOMP! WHOOMP! Two more orange bursts exploded just to the right of Robb.

"Snapper Yellow has flak, three o'clock!" Robb transmitted as his heart held hands with his Adam's apple and vertigo knocked his senses cockeyed. *This is idiotic. . .how can we be so damned dumb?*

WHOOMP! WHOOMP! Two more orange bursts exploded to the right of Snapper White.

"Snapper White has flak burst at three o'clock!"

"Shotgun here. Must be the squatters on Helgoland. Won't last long."

Robb blinked the sweat from his eyes. *Shit. . .it's already lasted too long.*

Bad weather never needed help to send the fear factor off the chart.

It could make a simple takeoff or landing a life or death event.

It could make a routine join-up and rendezvous a deadly 600-mile-an-hour game of chicken.

It could make formation flying a test of wills.

It could conceal *Luftwaffe* fighters, who with the help of radar could attack from out of nowhere.

It could make a target look different on different days and cause a miss.

But bouncing through the soup in a mass formation with vertigo doing a hatchet job on your senses and flak nipping at your ass—could rattle your soul in slow motion.

After what seemed an eternity, the 51's bounced out of the clouds into the open sky. Robb tried to swallow some of the sand in his mouth and licked the crust on his lips as he looked around. There was a gray overcast above and a thick undercast below with scattered potbellied snowmen in between.

"Shotgun's starting a shallow turn to wait for the bombers," the Colonel transmitted.

Robb suddenly realized how cold his hands and feet were and how much his butt ached. He stomped his feet, clapped his hands and shifted from cheek to cheek. *Damned miserable cold and rock hard dinghy. Shit! We're gonna have to fly back through that crap.*

Ringo's wing lumbered out of the clouds, one combat box at a time. The third combat box appeared a half-mile south and it had 19 bombers instead of 21.

"Shotgun, Ringo here."

"Go Ringo," the Colonel replied.

"Weather's triple shitty. We got scattered and lost two in a midair collision. I'm doin' an about-face and headin' west. Startin' a left turn now."

"Shotgun's doin' the same. Close it up, gang."

Robb shook his head, as he moved in close behind Ted. *It's about time we turned around.*

Ringo's second box joined on him in the turn. The third box trailed a mile behind. Ringo's two boxes entered a potbellied snowman, which stood waist deep in a layer of stratus. The third box swung wide to miss the snowman.

A lone combat box that had gotten separated from the second wing charged into the same snowman—from the opposite side.

Orange explosions flashed in the snowman's belly.

Ringo's bombers lumbered out, missing a three ship V from the second box.

The lone box, from the second wing, came out the other side, missing two of its bombers.

Robb knew that no one could have survived the seven midair collisions. *Seventy men killed and we're damned lucky there weren't more.*

"Shotgun here. You okay, Ringo?"

"Ringo's tryin' to count noses," he replied as he continued to turn toward the west.

"Shotgun, roger. Ringo, we're about a mile behind and 2000 feet high. Let's head a little south to avoid some of our inbound contrails and those toads on Helgoland."

"Ringo will do." He held his turn and rolled out five degrees left of his planned outbound heading and entered the wall of clouds.

The 36 P-51's entered the dark gray clouds. The pilots in the first squadron made the usual small bounces and slides to hold formation, which started a ripple effect in the second and third squadrons, and the whip started to crack. Robb hunched down, blinked the sweat from his eyes and struggled not to bounce or slide while watching Ted through the windshield. As they passed through some thin clouds, Robb glanced to his right and left. Pete, Rocko and Matt were still there.

Seconds became minutes and minutes became hours until they finally popped out of the weather. *Thank God we made it.* Robb glanced around and saw Ringo's bombers directly below. A mile north there was another box of bombers.

"Shotgun gang, spread out a little and look around. Let's plan to keep our bathtubs unless kraut fighters tap us. Snapper, cover the box of bombers at two o'clock."

"Snapper Red, copies," Ted replied as he turned north and began crisscrossing above the B-17's while passing in and out of the clouds and contrails. Most contrails were smooth and fuzzy but some were thick and contained propwash indicating an aircraft had just been there.

Each time Robb bounced blindly through a thick one his body turned to rock and his mind froze until he broke out in the clear. The seemingly endless mental whiplash finally ended when the bombers turned southwest and descended into a clear area.

Without the tension, Robb suddenly felt exhausted. He released his death grip on the throttle and stick, one hand at a time, and moved his fingers to get the blood circulating, but that hurt. He became aware of his aching toes and it hurt to move them too. *Shit. . .hope I don't have frostbite.* Descending through 14,000 feet, Robb took off his oxygen mask and gently rubbed the bridge of his nose. It felt like it had been bruised.

"Shotgun, Ringo's leveling at 8000. We're about 50 miles from the coast and have a clear area with no sea traffic. Gonna get rid of our bombs in the water."

"Shotgun, rog."

Robb shook his head, as the bombs streamed from the B-17's bellies. *Bet the krauts never dumped their bombs in the water when Britain was socked in.*

"Ringo, Shotgun's breakin' off."

"Roger Shotgun. Thanks much for the cover. Those external tanks give you fighter jocks a chance to get in a full days work."

"You got that right, Ringo. See ya next time. Shotgun gang, let's go tower frequency." The tower reported a 1000-foot ceiling with three miles visibility. With such good weather the three squadrons landed quickly.

£££

After they were debriefed, Pete and Matt took a nap while Robb and Rocko showered and went to the club. They ordered beers and carried them to the lounge where they stood with their backs to the blazing fireplace and rubbed the cheeks of their butts.

"Colonel's right about shitty weather. Give me clear skies and krauts anytime," Robb said, gently running his finger across the bridge of his nose.

"Rog, *amigo*. Flying in that sumbitchin' weather is work. Never been so frickin' tired," Rocko sighed. They downed the beers. "Innkeeper, two more blabbermouths for two weary warriors with sore asses," Rocko said.

"Make it three," Ted said walking in behind them. "Rough day. Like the Colonel said, playing chicken in that lousy weather takes all the fun out of flying."

"Make an old man out of you in a hurry," Robb said, as they sat down at a nearby table. He noticed crow's feet in the tanned area around Ted eyes. *Never seen him looked so tired. . .wonder what I look like?*

"Frickin' bathtubs," Rocko growled. "Thought the Colonel was gonna escort the bombers all the way to their parking revetments. Four hours and 54 minutes on that frickin' cast-iron dinghy's made my ass feel like two chunks of raw meat. Sumbitchin' moguls should've issued cute little French masseuses with those frickin' tanks."

Ted took another swig of beer. "Where are Matt and Pete?"

"They're baggin' a few Z's before dinner," Robb replied.

"I checked the mission summary before I left ops," Ted said. "We lost eleven bombers, seven fighters and shot down eight Germans today. A few bombers hit some minor targets. Not a very good day. Sounds like we're going to try for Berlin again tomorrow."

"If we go, I hope to hell we make it all the way," Robb said. "Chaps my ass to lose 117 men then watch the bombers drop their bombs into the North Sea."

"Yeah, I know, but it's policy," Ted replied. "If they can't see a target visually or on radar, they're supposed to drop in the North Sea or in a safe area to avoid killing innocent civilians," Ted replied.

"Sumbitch! Who in the hell are the frickin' innocent civilians in Germany?" Rocko snorted. "Are they the frickin' Nazis that work in the cannon factory? Or the Nazi pecker-heads that work in the bayonet plant? Or maybe they're the Nazi farmers who ram pitchforks through the guts of American airmen hanging in their chutes from trees.

"Civilians, that's what 97% of the American GI's were a few months ago. And the ones who don't get killed will become civilians again. Why should four yards of frickin' olive drab wool and some close order drill make Americans more expendable than some mean, patriotic Nazi sumbitch in a pair of lederhosen." Rocko downed a big slug of beer.

"Ain't no reason to kings-X those frickin' Nazis. Bastards started this frickin' war. Frickin' bombin' policy's made by someone that doesn't make his livin' luggin' frickin' bombs to Germany. Probably do-gooders or candy-assed politicians who've never been shot at. Politicians are lowlife sumbitches. Second guessers full of nice little suggestions on how ya should die for your country while they build up big fat bank accounts and chase young secretaries around DC. Can't win wars and worry about killin' the frickin' enemy."

"You're right, Rocko," Ted sighed. "God forbid if we ever go to war and become too timid or humane to win. Besides, someone once said, 'It's only elementary decency to hate your enemy.'"

"Speakin' of the frickin' enemy, look who's comin'. That old fart looks like a frickin' field marshal with all those phony ribbons on that tailor-made uniform."

Major Watson had a martini in each hand. "May I join you, gentlemen?" he asked, while placing both long stem glasses on the table.

"Sure Geoffrey. Have a seat," Ted said.

"Just returned from London. Caught a flight down and back on the UC-64. Had the most unpleasant *tête-à-tête* with my Bond Street bootmaker. He treated me rudely just like any other American."

"Dear me...sounds excitin'," Rocko interrupted. "But I gotta go to Colchester for a couple half-and-halfs, some fish and chips, and get my ashes hauled. Want'a tag along Geoffrey, old boy? My friend's gotta an old brawdy bout your age." Rocko grinned and pushed his chair back from the table.

"Hardly, Mister Fazzio." Watson's close-set, beady eyes steadied beneath their droopy lids, like a snake ready to strike. Seeing Ted and Robb smiles annoyed him as much as Rocko's remarks. "Such a crude and uncouth person," Watson said, after Rocko left.

"He has many good qualities," Ted countered.

"Really?" Watson's left eye and cheek twitched, then steadied. "As I was saying, before I was so rudely interrupted, my boot maker upset me today. He made my first pair of shoes in 1937 when I served in France with the State Department. The same year I became acquainted with a most interesting young British couple, Mr. and Mrs. Derek Ashmore. You've both met the former Mrs. Ashmore. Joyce Freemantle."

Robb couldn't believe what he was hearing. He avoided looking at Ted.

Major Watson's eyes flicked back and forth, checking their reactions. He took the toothpick with the two onions from one of the martinis, pulled an onion off with his teeth, chewed, then washed it down with some of the martini.

Watson's pointed red tongue swept back and forth, to the corners of his mouth, as he got ready to speak. "After Joyce completed five years of study in France, she took a job as a tour guide. She's fluent in French, knows Northern France as well as her beloved Devonshire. On one of her trips, she met Derek Ashmore who was a British Foreign Service Officer serving in Cherbourg."

Robb finally glanced at Ted; his blue eyes had turned icy.

Watson took a cigarette from his gold case, closed it and tapped the cigarette on the lid. He placed the cigarette between his lips and lit it with his gold Benson lighter and filled his lungs with smoke. As he exhaled, his beady eyes returned Ted's icy glare.

Robb took a sip of his beer. *Boy...I'm happy to be on the sidelines.*

"I spent a holiday with the Ashmores in the spring of 1938," Watson continued. "They took me on a tour by car. Joyce knew every inn owner from Calais to Brest. She made the drive on those ridiculous French roads without a map," he took another sip from his martini, then continued.

"Joyce and Derek were in southern France and missed the Dunkirk evacuations. They eventually obtained false papers from the underground, returned to Cherbourg and joined a resistance group while trying to arrange a way home.

"Derek got killed one night while attempting to sabotage a German troop train near Nantes. After his death, Joyce continued with the resistance group. Incidentally, Joyce is half Jewish, still has many relatives in Germany. She hates the Nazis with a passion.

"One day, two demented Frenchmen in the underground held her captive in the cellar of a remote farm house and abused her for several days. She finally slashed the throat of one and escaped." Watson plucked one of the onions from the second martini, chewed, then washed it down. His pointed tongue swept back and forth before he filled his lungs again and slowly exhaled.

Ted's jaws tightened.

Watson's smirk annoyed Robb. *The old son of a bitch...is he making all this up?*

"After Joyce escaped from the renegades, she traveled by night, made her way to Dieppe where she had close friends. She hid in a cellar of an inn for a week until the weather and channel permitted crossing in a small skiff. A few miles from the British coast, the little boat swamped. Although she had a life preserver, she nearly died from exposure before she was rescued and taken to the hospital at Brighton. That's where she met Colonel Freemantle. He had been convalescing from serious wounds he'd received in France before Dunkirk."

Watson downed the remainder of the second martini. His pointed tongue swept to the corners of his mouth once more as he pulled a handkerchief from his sleeve and stared at Ted.

"Very interesting story, Geoffery. Thank you for sharing it with us. Robb, let's have dinner. Excuse us, please."

In the dining room, Ted and Robb sat quietly at an empty table and ate their dinners.

"Do you believe that story about Joyce?" Robb finally asked.

"Oh, it's true. Joyce told me all about it."

£££

"Gentlemen, the operations truck will depart in one hour," the duty sergeant said, turning on the hut's ceiling light.

Robb stretched, rubbed his eyes and ran his finger back and forth across the tender spot on the bridge of his nose. He thought again about Watson's story wondering how long Joyce and Ted had known each other and whether Joyce brushed him off too. *Forget it. . .you've got other things to think about.*

"Short frickin' night," Rocko grunted.

Robb grabbed his pants, shirt and a second pair of socks, then dressed under the blankets. He kicked the blankets back, sat up, swung his feet out, held them above the cold concrete and slipped on his GI shoes. His butt still felt like two pieces of pounded-round.

An icy wind swirled the powdery snow across the macadam lane as Robb and Rocko hurried to the latrine. After returning their towels and toothbrushes to the hut, they boarded the GI truck and hunched behind the fur collars of their flight jackets. The truck bounced along the winding lanes and they gripped the wooden bench, using their arms as shock absorbers to ease the impact on their tender butts.

£££

The Colonel walked down the aisle, stopped short of the platform and turned toward the pilots. "It's Big-B again, guys," the Colonel said. "Same targets, different routing. Weather's still iffy, but we're gonna go. General Spaatz's not gonna quit until we plaster Berlin. Stormy, give us the bad news."

"Sir, many bomber fields have blowing snow, some heavy. My guess is, a few units won't get off the ground, and some of those that do get off won't get joined-up due to all of the cloud layers over Britain. Weather over the Continent is gonna be every bit as bad as yesterday, maybe worse...."

£££

THE HELLISH VORTEX

After taking off in blowing snow, the Colonel found a clear area in between cloud layers at 7000 feet and got the group together. Climbing across the North Sea, Robb noticed a B-24 wing circling with about half of its 63 bombers in a tail chase trying to join up. To the north, south and east there were more scattered bombers. Some were single aircraft, others were in pairs and a few had joined in a three ship V's, all looking for their units. Other bombers never found their units and were returning to Britain.

Near the coast of Holland Robb looked down. Five thousand feet below he saw the contrails of two wings that had become separated in the bad weather and turned away to bomb their alternate targets. Their contrails soon disappeared in the clouds. *I'm glad we're above most of this crap.*

Flying across Holland Robb kept looking for the bomber stream, but there were only contrails. He checked his aircraft clock. *We're damned close to Germany and I still don't see any bombers. Wonder how many got off the ground and how many made it this far? There they are!*

"Ringo, Shotgun's approachin' at your five o'clock," the Colonel transmitted.

"Nice to hear your voice, Shotgun. Thought you might have the day off and we'd have to go it alone," Ringo replied.

"Not gonna miss this one, Ringo. I only see two wings."

"That's all I have, Shotgun."

The two wings of bombers disappeared into a huge clump of thick clouds. About a minute later, Robb saw the first wing emerge. He kept waiting for the second wing, but it never appeared. He glanced to his right and saw it turning south.

"Ringo here. Shotgun, we're down to one wing. Second wing lost sight of us and had to turn away."

"Shotgun here. I copy you Ringo. Hot Rod, you stay in close to Ringo. Bugeye you cover the rear and I'll take Snapper and sweep the area ahead."

"Shotgun, this Pink Pants. Do you read?" another P-51 group commander called.

"Shotgun reads you five by, Pink Pants."

"Pink Pants is about three minutes behind. Since our bomber wing had to break away, I'll continue on with you. I'll pass you on your left and press on to the target to see if we can drum up some business and take on a few krauts before you get to there."

"Shotgun roger. Thank you much, Pink Pants."

For the next 50 minutes, Ringo's wing of B-17's flew east through clumps of thick clouds while Hot Rod criss-crossed above them. Bugeye covered the rear and the Colonel and Snapper made sweeping "S" turns about 20 miles ahead of the bombers.

"Shotgun, Hot Rod here. Ringo just penetrated some rough looking clouds and one of his combat box had to break away," the squadron commander reported.

"Shotgun, roger. Ringo, are you okay?"

"Ringo here, we're tryin' to hang in there. In addition to what Hot Rod reported, four more 17's got separated and another two had a midair."

"Shotgun here. Sorry to hear that, Ringo. Hey! Shotgun just broke out in a clear area. You should be there in a few minutes, Ringo. There are a few breaks in the undercast and I can see the ground around the target area." The Colonel started a shallow left turn to check for German fighters around Berlin.

"Ringo just broke out in the clear too, headin' for the IP."

"Hot Rod has 30 plus contrails high and five miles south. They're heading our way. Let's go internal fuel and shed our tanks...ready...now. Going 2700 rpm and full power. Double check your guns hot." Hot Rod's twelve 51's turned to intercept the German fighters.

"Bugeye, let's increase power and shed our tanks...ready now," the squadron commander called as he turned toward the bombers to back up Hot Rod.

"Hot Rod gang, they just opened fire; they're 109's," the squadron commander called, seeing the fire coming from their 20-millimeterr cannons in the nose. "Let's open fire!"

"Hot Rod lead, White one here. Your Red Three just took a hit."

"Hot Rod Lead, roger," the squadron commander replied as the 109's zoomed by. "I'm bending it around. The krauts are heading for the bombers."

"Hot Rod Red Three just bailed out and has a good chute."

"Hot Rod Lead, roger. Bugeye, are you in position to intercept the krauts?"

"Bugeye is a mile behind the bombers. The krauts are hitting them head on now."

The ME-109's raced toward the bombers firing their cannons. When they got closer, they flipped their 109's upside down and fired their 13-millimeter machine guns. Just before they rammed the B-17's, the German pilots split-S and dived away.

Two smoking B-17's spiraled from the formation. Flames shot from the second wounded giant and six white chutes finally blossomed. Fire shot from the first smoking bomber; its wing broke off and the bomber flipped out of control; no chutes appeared.

The 109's recovered from their dive and climbed behind the bombers, getting set for another attack from the rear. Bugeye cut the 109's off, swung in behind them and opened fire. Two 109's in the rear started trailing fire and smoke; two yellowish-brown chutes appeared. The remainder of the 109's continued their attack.

Fire shot from another B-17 and twisted out of control; two more trailed smoke but continued on. After completing their firing passes, the 109's made hard diving turns and headed for the clouds.

"Shotgun, Pink Pants here. We're 30 northeast of target. Spotted about 70 bandits, but lost 'em in the clouds before we could engage. They might be heading your way."

"Shotgun copies. Thanks, Pink Pants. We'll keep our eyes peeled." The Colonel swung back toward the northeast to try and intercept the 70 bandits before they could attack the bombers.

"Ringo is starting a radar bomb run."

The B-17's opened their bomb bay doors, stabilized their altitude and airspeed, and volleys of dirty-orange fireballs detonated around them. A bomber exploded from a direct hit and its burning wreckage tumbled through the formation. A large chunk of its wing collided with another B-17; the 17 snapped out of control and twisted crazily. There were no chutes.

More fireballs and black puffs filled the sky around the 31 B-17's. Their 248 bombs streaked toward the ground through the exploding flak. The bombers quickly started a right turn to head west. In the turn, the crews hurriedly bandaged their wounded, covered the dead, double-checked their guns and prayed for one more dinner.

Through an opening in the clouds, Robb watched the bombs explode; their shock waves rippled across a row of buildings into open fields.

"Shotgun here. Nice goin', Ringo."

"Ringo here. We didn't hit much, but we dumped a small load close enough to let 'em know we were in town and the bastards know we'll be back."

"Shotgun here. Hot Rod and Bugeye, stay with the bombers. I'm gonna make a couple of orbits and bring up the rear in case those 70 krauts show up."

Halfway through the second orbit, Robb saw Pete's 51 starting a shallow turn away from formation. "Snapper White Two, you okay?" Robb asked. There was no answer.

Robb moved in closer. Pete's head was tilted forward. "White Two, if you read or see me, nod your head." Pete sat there in frozen silence.

"Snapper White Two, go emergency oxygen!" Nothing. "White Two, go emergency oxygen!" Pete's head quivered, then his chin dropped to his chest; his body slumped forward against the shoulder straps. His 51's nose lowered and its turn steepened. *Shit. . .he's hypoxic!*

During flight training, all aviation cadets were taught the insidious effects of hypoxia when flying at high altitudes. In a low-pressure chamber that duplicated high altitude conditions, each cadet took turns removing his oxygen mask to experience the initial sensations of hypoxia. They then watched one another lose useful consciousness—in a matter of seconds—while displaying a sense of well-being. When the cadet started to shake, the instructor quickly replaced the mask. And once back on oxygen, none of the cadets recalled his inability to perform or his false sense of well-being.

Experiencing and observing the insidious effects of hypoxia had been a convincing lesson. Everyone agreed that dying from a lack of oxygen would be an ideal way to go, the high of highs.

"Snapper White Two, go emergency oxygen!" Robb yelled in desperation.

Pete depressed his mike button, but nothing came out except his labored breathing. Having his mike button depressed blocked his radio's receiver.

Shit. . .can't talk to him. I'll give 'em some prop wash. . .maybe that'll rouse him. Robb passed in front of Pete and watched his 51 bounce through the prop wash while continuing its 300-mph spiraling descent.

Robb moved back in formation. *Shit. . .I'm so close yet so far away. If I could just reach inside the cockpit. . .a simple flip of the oxygen lever to emergency. . .or reconnecting the oxygen hose could save 'em.*

Pete's breathing became guttural; his shoulders jerked; his head trembled.

"Snapper White One, Three here," Rocko called. "We're approachin' the undercast."

"Snapper White, Shotgun here. You've done everything you can do. Don't get yourself in trouble."

"Snapper White One, roger, sir. I'm breaking away."

Pete's 51 zoomed into the undercast. Seconds later, there was a choking sound, followed by strained breathing—then a throaty gasp. Robb wondered if it was part of the Cheyne-Stokes respiratory cycle. He had heard it when he had been at his aunt's bedside the day she died.

Only the transmitter buzz remained. An instant before the buzzing stopped, Robb thought he heard the beginning of a crash. Anyway, that's the way he'd always remember it.

£££

Johnny Mercer's *"And The Angels Sing"* was playing on the jukebox as Robb, Matt and Rocko raised their glasses of beer.

"To Pete," Robb said, and they all took big sips. Robb stared at his beer for a couple of seconds before speaking. "Seeing a friend get clobbered by the krauts is one thing. Watching someone die from a lack of oxygen is something else. Just a simple flick of the emergency oxygen lever or reconnecting his oxygen hose could've saved him."

They each took another sip of beer and stared at the floor.

"Think I got some sumbitchin' frostbite on the cheek of my frickin' ass."

"Maybe you should see Doc Herny," Robb suggested.

"Wouldn't ask that sumbitchin' chancre mechanic for nuttin'. Bastard got straight A's in Egomania. Probably gets a hard-on just lookin' in the mirror."

"Heard that second 51 group lost 11 out of 33 today," Robb said to change the subject. "Sounds like they were letting down in a group formation and flew into the ground. Leader probably misread the altimeter like those two P-38's did last week."

"Frickin' weather. Wonder it doesn't get more of us."

"Stormy says Continent's gonna be clobbered in tomorrow. Should be a day off. But he says the weather'll open up over Berlin the next day."

"That means that March 6th could be a frickin' ball-banger," Rocko grunted.

"We better drink up and get to Pete's memorial service." Robb finished his beer and pushed his chair back to leave. Rocko and Matt joined him and they headed for the chapel. That night Robb found a quiet spot in the club and started a letter to Pete's parents.

CHAPTER 14

A Bomber Mission

On the evening of 5 March 1944, Colonel Timothy Tyler and Technical Sergeant Darlene Bradford boarded the train to Bedford. For the past three days, he had watched the weather, waiting for the break that would allow the first big American strike against Berlin. He wanted Berlin to be his 35th and last combat mission.

Tim Tyler had read John Bunyan's 'Pilgrim's Progress' while at Cornell and had first visited Bunyan's home in Bedford and his birthplace in nearby Elstow during World War I. Bunyan's allegorical presentation of an awakened soul, with intolerance for those with the form of prayer rather than the spirit of prayer, had sparked Tim's interest. When the 379th Bomb Group arrived at RAF Station Kimbolton near Bedford, Tim decided to fly the rest of his combat missions with the 379th.

Eight months earlier, he and Darlene spent two nights in Bedford at a small inn on High Street. Beneath the roar of B-17's and Lancasters, they visited the haunts of John Bunyan and went punting on the River Ouse, going as far as St. Neots. Most Americans in the area called it St. Nuts.

Although Tim and Darlene had visited Bedford several times, she had never come with him when he flew combat. This time he wanted her there to celebrate his last combat mission.

£££

Colonel Tyler and Colonel Maurice "Moe" Preston, the group commander, entered the briefing room and took their seats in the front row. Everyone else sat down and the intelligence officer pulled the curtain that covered the huge map of Europe. For the third time in the past four days, the green, red and yellow strings led to Berlin.

"Oh shit...not again!" someone groaned in the back of the room.

Colonel Preston turned and smiled. Silence fell across the room because everyone knew he had been on all previous attempts to bomb Berlin. He nodded and the weather officer began to brief. He finished and turned to Colonel Preston. "Sir, it looks like we've finally gotten a break in the weather. Any questions, sir?" Colonel Preston shook his head and the weatherman passed the pointer to the intelligence officer.

"Gentlemen, 730 bombers will strike the Bosch plant, the Erkner bearing plant and the Daimler-Benz aircraft engine plant." He covered the production rates for each target and how their destruction would impact Germany's war effort. "There are approximately 700 FW-190's and ME-109's along the route that can attack our bombers," he tapped the black circles marking their locations. "The RAF haven't bombed for several nights, so up to 150 night fighters could also be launched against us. Heavy concentrations of 40's, 88's and 105 AAA cannons are here, here and here...." He finished and handed the pointer to the group operations officer.

"Today, there'll only be three P-51 groups in the target area. The fourth P-51 group, the one that lost 11 of their fighters in the weather two days ago, won't be going. En route, three groups of P-38's will pick us up from the P-47's and the 38's will hand us over to the 51's about 70 to 100 miles short of the target area." He finished and turned toward Colonel Preston, "Sir."

Colonel Preston stood and faced the crews. "Gentlemen, gonna be another tough mission, but I know you'll do yourselves and the 379th proud."

He and Tim walked down the aisle. At the rear of the room, the Catholic chaplain made the sign of the cross and bowed his head. They nodded back.

In Moe's office, they put on their electrically heated flight clothing, gathered their flak vests, 45 automatics, escape and evasion kits, steel helmets, parachutes, leather flight helmets, oxygen masks, Mae Wests, furlined flight boots and loaded them into the trunk of Moe's 1941 Chevrolet staff car.

Moe eased the Chevy along the taxiway behind three of the GI trucks taking the aircrews to their B-17's. He turned into the second aircraft-parking revetment and stopped next to the lone B-17.

The staff car's dim blackout headlights shined on the bomber. *Urgin Virgin* was painted in large yellow letters just below the navigator's window. To the right of her name were four swastikas, indicating her crew had shot down four German fighters. Below the swastikas were three groups of small bombs. A yellow group of 25 indicated the *Urgin Virgin's* first assigned crew had completed their 25 mission combat tour. The second group of 31 white bombs showed that her present crew had four more missions to go to complete their required 35. A third group of 43 orange bombs, indicated the old bomber had carried other crews on another 43 combat missions.

"Moe, this old girl's been around."

"She's flown more missions than any B-17 in the 8th Air Force...probably the entire Army Air Force."

"Hope her luck continues. See you in about ten hours," Colonel Tyler said, picking up his flight gear.

"Drinks'll be on me, Tim," Moe said before driving away.

"Give you a hand, sir?" the crew chief asked, coming from the *Urgin Virgin's* bomb bay where the armorers were working. "Just starting my exterior preflight check. Would you like to follow along, sir?"

"That'd be great, chief. I'll leave my gear here." They walked toward the *Urgin Virgin's* 19-foot-high tail. Unpainted aluminum patches angled across the tail's vertical and horizontal stabilizers. "She got shot up by a FW-190 last week, sir."

After checking the other side of the tail, the crew chief shined his flashlight on the fuselage and walked toward the right wing. Colonel Tyler noticed more patches on the fuselage. They checked the flaps and trailing edge of the wing out to the tip then followed the leading edge of the wing back toward the fuselage, checking the de-icer boots, engines, access plates and props. The crew chief swung back under the inboard engine, checked for hydraulic leaks in the wheel well and inspected the landing gear and tire.

"Chief, the bombs are hung, fuses set and arming wires installed. All 50-caliber ammo's been loaded and all guns have been checked," the lead armorer said as his crew crawled out of the bomb bay.

"Thanks, guys," the crew chief replied as the armorers got into their weapons carrier. "Best damned gun plumbers in the group," he said, turning to Colonel Tyler.

"That's good news, chief."

The crew chief shined his flashlight on *Urgin Virgin's* nose. There were more unpainted aluminum patches below the copilot's seat.

"Old girl's really been battered," Colonel Tyler said as they finished the exterior preflight checks.

"She's no virgin, sir. But she's a classy lady...won't let you down. I've been her crew chief since she was first assigned to the group. I got special permission to go on five combat missions so far, and I'll fly in her anytime, sir."

"Good enough for me, chief."

A GI truck squeaked to a stop; the *Urgin Virgin's* crew jumped out. The young pilot saluted, "Sir, thank you for filling in for my copilot. He lost four fingers on his right hand from frostbite."

"Sorry to hear that. How is he?"

"He's doing okay. He'll leave for the states in two days."

Colonel Tyler and the pilot stuffed their flight gear into the small hatch below the cockpit, then climbed through the hatch. They stored their gear in the cockpit, then checked that the switches were off and the circuit breakers were set. The pilot turned and pulled on the yoke ensuring the flight controls were free. Then he set the trim tabs for take off.

As the pilot continued his checks, the bombardier, navigator and top turret gunner climbed through the hatch. The navigator and bombardier went forward to the nose of the aircraft, while the gunner climbed to the top turret behind the cockpit. In the nose, the navigator hung his sextant, unfolded his maps and laid out his plotter and supply of sharpened pencils, while the bombardier checked the bombsight, connections and zeroed the settings. They both double-checked their guns and belts of ammunition.

Aft of the top turret, the radio operator, belly turret gunner, two-waist gunners and tail gunner stored their flight gear. The gunners double-checked their 50-caliber machine guns and ammo, while the radio operator secured his coded radio data and visually checked that his radios were turned off and their cables were secure.

Gear loaded and checks complete, the crew assembled in the dispersal tent next to the revetment, to await the start engines signal. Colonel Tyler stretched out on one of the canvas cots and closed his eyes. He always hated the wait before takeoff.

Following the Jap's sneak attack on Pearl Harbor, Colonel Tyler decided to become the only World War I combat pilot to complete a combat tour in World War II. But after he'd fallen in love with Darlene, each mission got a little tougher. During the bloody October 14, 1943 mission to Schweinfurt, when 60 of the 230 attacking bombers were shot down and more than half of the force received battle damage, he thought about stopping. But something wouldn't let him.

"GOT OUR WARNING FLARES! START ENGINE TIME!" the crew chief shouted through the tent flap. The crew scrambled through the darkness to the *Urgin Virgin*. In less than two minutes the second set of flares disappeared into the low overcast and the 96 engines of the 21 primary bombers and three spares coughed smoke, spit fire and cracked a steady beat.

To escape the noise, the curious cows standing along the fence next to the parking stand scurried to the opposite side of the pasture. Ground crews pulled the battery carts and snatched chocks from in front of the wheels and the 24 B-17's pulled slowly from their dispersed parking stands and waited their turn to get on the taxiway.

Loaded with 2500 gallons of 100-octane gasoline, eight 500-pound bombs, 2000 rounds of 50-caliber ammunition, ten men and their equipment, the tired old 25-ton *Urgin Virgin*—the matriarch of the group—creaked onto the taxiway behind Moe Preston's B-17. One by one, the other giant bombers pulled in behind and taxied nose to tail. They resembled a herd of elephants, walking slowly along a trail.

Moe taxied his B-17 onto the runway. He waited for 30 seconds, then pushed the throttles forward. The four 1200-horsepower radial engines spit blue flames from their exhausts and gave a thunderous roar.

"Rough House is rolling!" Moe released the brakes; the big bomber rolled forward through the blackness. The blue flames from the four engine exhausts resembled torches from hell.

The *Urgin Virgin*'s pilot gunned the engines, pulled onto the runway and eased the throttles forward to takeoff power. The engines roared; the old bomber shook and rattled.

Colonel Tyler tightened the throttle friction, checked that all of the engine instruments were in the green, then tapped the pilot's hand to indicate that all four engines were set and ready for takeoff.

"We're rolling," the pilot called over the intercom as he released the brakes. The ancient bomber inched forward through the blackness.

Colonel Tyler held his left hand behind the four throttles to make sure they didn't slide back. He called out their speed over the intercom, while his eyes flicked back and forth between the airspeed indicator and the lights marking the far end of the runway. "TAKEOFF SPEED!" he yelled into the intercom as the end of the runway disappeared beneath the old bomber's nose.

The pilot pulled back the yoke; the *Urgin Virgin* quivered into the black sky like a battered woman, reluctantly submitting to another day of abuse.

"GEAR UP!" the pilot yelled over the intercom when the rate of climb indicator showed 300 feet per minute.

Colonel Tyler raised the gear handle; the left landing gear chattered and thumped into the wheel well, then the right wheel thumped into its well.

"FLAPS UP!" the pilot shouted.

Colonel Tyler retracted the flaps, rechecked the engine instruments and adjusted the throttles and prop pitch. "Climb power set."

At 300 feet, the *Urgin Virgin* entered the soup. Her red and green wing tip lights glowed in the heavy clouds like they were shining through huge frosted windows.

For eight minutes, the ancient bomber rattled, creaked and wallowed through the bumpy clouds. Suddenly, the air got smooth; the red and green glow disappeared and wing tip lights glistened in the blackness. They were above the first layer of clouds.

Colonel Tyler spotted the wing tip lights and engine exhausts of Moe's B-17. "Lead's dead ahead."

"Got 'em," the pilot answered.

"Rough House is turning left turn." Moe started a left climbing turn, using the group's radio beacon as the anchor point. The Urgin Virgin's pilot eased the ancient bomber into formation on the right side of Moe.

All across East Anglia, Colonel Tyler saw clusters of red and green wing tip lights as the 730 bombers joined-up. It was an amazing sight. Three years ago no one dreamed the Army Air Force would be capable of getting so many aircraft up in the same sky at one time, especially at night and in bad weather. Colonel Tyler wondered if the Nazi sympathizers near each airfield had radioed the takeoff times and bomber count to *der* fatherland.

Periodically, Moe's left waist gunner fired a combination of one red and two green flares to help guide his group's aircraft to the right formation. Suddenly a huge explosion lit the sky to the north where two bombers had slammed together. Colonel Tyler quickened his scan to look for other aircraft and wondered how many more would be lost during join-up.

"Ten thousand feet, everybody on oxygen," the pilot called.

Colonel Tyler checked his mask, hose connections, oxygen regulator and pressure. He recalled his second combat mission when the radio operator failed to answer one of the periodic oxygen checks at 27,000 feet. The unconscious radio operator would have died if a fellow crewman hadn't immediately gotten him onto emergency oxygen.

Moe continued circling through the darkness until the other two groups had joined and all 63 bombers of his combat wing were in formation. Then he turned toward Great Yarmouth to take his place behind the first wing in the bomber stream.

Racing across the North Sea after the stressful takeoff and join-up there was the usual lull before the fury of battle allowing time to think. Colonel Tyler recalled how small and poorly prepared the Army Air Forces had been before the war and all of the people who had sacrificed their lives in combat while building a viable air force. The 8th Air Force would soon have nearly 1500 long-range P-51's, which could escort the bombers anywhere in Germany. But he recalled how shocked he'd been when his old friend Gehard "Max" Schulz told him four years ago that the *Luftwaffe's* had flown their first jet fighter. He suspected the Germans could unleash their jet fighters any time now. If they did, the U.S. bombing effort and the D-Day invasion would be in jeopardy.

Near the coast of Holland, the dawn's gray half-light dimmed the red and green wing tip lights and the crews turned them off. Minutes later, a group of P-47's arrived and started crisscrossing above the first combat wing. A few seconds later, another group of P-47's crisscrossed above Moe's wing.

Approaching the German border the tail gunner called when the P-38's arrived to replace the P-47's. Droning deeper into Germany everyone maintained a stony silence as they scanned the sky for enemy fighters.

"Tail gunner here, got P-51's passing at three o'clock." The 51's continued on to replace the P-38's with the first wing of B-17's.

"Pilot here. Let's check oxygen masks, hose connections, pressure and regulators," he said trying to sound calm.

"Nav's checked."

"Bombardier check."

"Belly checked."

"Left and right waist checked."

"Tail checked."

"Got Big B 74 miles on the nose," the navigator called.

"Tail here, our P-51's are just arriving."

Colonel Tyler looked at his watch and nudged the pilot, "P-51's are right on time." He glanced at the pilot and wanted to say his son flew P-51"'s, but didn't. The pilot's young eyes were locked onto the ship ahead. He was just a kid, no more than 19 or 20. Colonel Tyler thought about how the war had surrounded him with kids and given him Darlene who made him feel like a young man again.

"Rough House here, got bandits, 3 o'clock," Moe transmitted. "Our fighter escorts are going after 'em." Overhead, two flights of 51's dropped their external fuel tanks, whipped into a steep turn and headed south toward the eight contrails.

£££

"Snapper White and Yellow, check switches hot," Ted transmitted as he turned into the eight German fighters. "They're flying line abreast. Probably ME-110's, carrying rockets. Let's pull high, swing in behind 'em. White'll take the right half. Yellow, take the left half."

"Yellow, roger." Robb pulled his 51up into a steep left turn. Bob Hermanes, Pete's replacement was on his wing while Rocko and Matt following close behind. Robb reversed his turn and came down behind the ME-110's on the left. Their twin barrel machine guns sparkled as the rear gunners opened fire. Robb rolled out behind a 110 and placed his gunsight's pipper on the fuselage. He squeezed his trigger; API's sparkled along the fuselage and worked forward to the canopy. It shattered and the 110's rear guns stopped firing.

Robb released his trigger, kicked the right rudder and his 51 skidded right. He placed the pipper on the 110's right engine, squeezed the trigger and API's sparkled on the engine. The engine exploded; fire and black smoke shot into the air.

Robb snapped the throttle back, pulled up sharply, rolled his 51upside down and looked down through the top of the canopy. The German pilot tumbled out the left side and his yellow chute opened. *Damned thing has radar. . ... It's a night fighter.*

Robb rolled right side up and looked back. Rocko had shot the tail off another 110 and it was spinning out of control. Ted and his flight had shot down two more 110's which were twisting earthward, trailing black smoke.

WHOOOSH! Balls of fire erupted under the wings of the remaining four 110's. Eight rockets streaked toward the bombers and the 110's executed a break away. Two 110's made steep diving turns to the left and two dived to the right.

"Snapper White, let's head back and join with Shotgun before the 190's and 109's attack," Ted transmitted.

£££

"Rockets, three o'clock, comin' our way!" Colonel Tyler called over the intercom. He watched the rockets streak toward Moe's wing of bombers. Two rockets flew a twisted course, indicating poor stabilization and uneven propellant burning. Two more rockets stopped smoking, nosed over and went straight down, when their propellant stop burning. He spotted a rocket holding a steady course with its nose centered on its smoke. It was heading right for them.

"ROCKET!" Colonel Tyler yelled over the intercom as he jerked back the yoke. The overloaded *Urgin Virgin* shuddered a few feet higher and the rocket zoomed past, just missing the old bomber's belly.

"SHEE-IT!" the belly gunner yelled. "Frickin' fence post peeled a layer of skin off my ass."

"Nice goin', Colonel," the pilot said over the intercom, as he watched the rocket head for the lower box of bombers. It slammed into a B-17's wing and exploded. A big chunk of wing tore off and the bomber snap rolled into another 17. A huge fireball engulfed the two giants as they dropped below the formation.

"Oh, shit...lost two," the pilot sighed into the intercom, knowing that 20 men had just died.

Near the tailend of the wing formation, another rocket plowed into the belly of a 17. A fireball mushroomed and pieces shot out.

"Tail gunner, here. Another 17 behind us just took a hit. Don't see a single chute from it or the other two."

The P-51's covering the first combat wing dropped their external tanks and turned toward a large gaggle of ME-109's coming from the north. The 51's and 109's charged at one another head on with their guns blazing.

The two fighter forces came together and swarmed like mad bees. Their three-dimensional contrails marked the sky, as individual air battles decided who would live and who would die.

Within seconds, three fighters corkscrewed toward the ground, trailing black smoke—their banner of death.

Some of the ME-109's broke away and headed toward the B-17's. As usual they opened fire with their 20-millimeter cannons until they got closer and fired their 13-millimeter machine guns. Just before ramming the bombers, the 109's flipped up side down and dived away.

Three burning B-17's twisted out of control; two more trailed smoke but held formation.

A 109 pilot who had fallen behind his formation came at the bombers. He turned a few degrees to the left, then turned back without firing. Suddenly, he flipped his 109 upside down, opened fire and slammed into a B-17. A huge fireball erupted and spewed wreckage in all directions, then fire and wreckage dropped from the sky.

The Colonel and his 51's turned toward another gaggle of 109's coming from the southeast. The two groups of fighters zoomed at one another with their guns blazing. But instead of staying to fight, the 109's headed for Moe's wing.

"Rough House has bandits eleven o'clock high, headin' our way," Moe called as the 109's approached.

RATTA-TAT-TAT! The *Urgin Virgin*'s top turret gunner opened fire with his two 50-caliber machine guns. Colonel Tyler felt the gun vibrations in his seat and feet.

WHOOOMP! One of the German's 20-millimeter cannon shells ripped into the *Urgin Virgin*'s right wing and the ancient bomber's nose jerked right.

"Right wing's hit! Near the outboard engine!" the waist gunner yelled.

Colonel Tyler snapped his head to the right and saw the jagged hole.

Every muscle in his body tried to knot. "SHIT!" he grunted to himself, hoping the shell hadn't hit the main wing spar. He knew that if the spar broke, the wing would break away and the B-17 would flip out of control and they would all be trapped inside.

He had experienced such a failure in 1929 while testing a Curtis P-1 at McCook Field, Ohio. He had started a full power dive from 23,000 feet and at 12,000 feet the main spar in the biplane's top wing failed. Half of the wing broke away and sliced off the horizontal tail and the P-1 did a series of violent snap-rolls before tumbling out of control.

His arms, legs, shoulders and head slammed the sides of the cockpit. Through blurred-vision, he saw the sky and ground flip-flopping back and forth. It was like being mauled in the jaws of a hug tiger. A feeling of helplessness fell over him and he waited to die.

After a seemingly endless wait, the P-1 began to slow down and the body slamming eased. Through the haze of fear, he struggled to reach the buckle on the safety belt and unsnapped it, expecting to hit the ground any moment.

WHOOSH! He flew out of the cockpit, saw a flash and everything went black.

When he regained consciousness, he was hanging from a tree branch in his chute, about ten feet above the ground. The right side of his head felt like it had been hit with a sledgehammer and he couldn't see out of his right eye. A stabbing pain ran the length of his right arm up through his shoulder.

A small branch, holding a shroud line, broke and he dropped a few inches. Pain shot through his arm and shoulder like a lightening bolt and he passed out.

Sometime later, he heard voices. Through his left eye, he saw a farmer and his wife climbing onto the bed of their Model T truck, which they had parked directly below him. He groaned from the pain as they unfastened his chute, eased him down and gently stretched him out on the truck bed. The farmer's wife ripped two strips of cloth from her slip while her husband cut two small branches from the tree. Without removing his flight jacket, they put a crude splint on his right arm to immobilize it. To protect his head, the wife cradled it in her lap while her husband drove slowly to their farm house.

The farmer cranked the old wall phone and called McCook Field. His wife cleaned and bandaged the gash on his head, then dabbed iodine on his cuts and scratches. She told him they had heard his plane and looked up just before the wing come off and hit the tail. Seconds later, they saw him fly from the cockpit. She said his chute opened immediately.

Ever since the accident, Tim had thanked God that the P-I had an open cockpit. But every time he flew in a closed cockpit airplane he thought at least once about a catastrophic failure and getting trapped inside of an out-of-control aircraft.

£££

WHAP! WHAP! WHAP! The ME-I09's machine gun bullets raked the *Urgin Virgin's* nose.

"Bombardier's been hit!" the navigator shouted.

"How bad is he?" the pilot asked. There was no answer. "Nav, how's Bomber?"

"He's...dead."

"You okay, Nav?" Again, there was no answer. "Nav, you okay?"

"I'm...okay."

"Rest of crew check."

"Top turret okay."

"Radio okay."

The belly gunner didn't answer.

"Belly, pilot here. You read?" There was no reply.

"Left and right waist are okay. Left waist'll check on Belly."

"Tail's okay."

Colonel Tyler scanned the engine instruments; all four were in the green. He looked out at the right wing and prayed that it wouldn't fail.

"Left waist here. Belly's dead and the turret is damaged and won't move. He's pinned inside and I can't even touch 'em."

"Pilot roger. We'll be starting our run on Berlin in three minutes. Nav, take over for Bomber and pickle our bombs. Hang in there, guys...we're almost halfway home."

One mile ahead, AAA cannons flashed on the outskirts of Berlin as the first combat box of the lead wing started its bomb run. Within seconds, volley after volley of dirty orange fireballs exploded in and around the 21 B-17's. Their ugly black puffs dotted the sky while thousands of jagged chunks of shrapnel sliced through many of the B-17's. Three B-17's trailed smoke but held formation.

More volleys followed and one B-17 took a direct hit. Its fuselage broke in half and the two burning pieces tumbled from the formation. There were no chutes. A few seconds later, the 20 B-17's released their 160 bombs and turned west.

Like a chain reaction, dirty orange fireballs and black puffs continued to fill the sky as the second combat box started its run with the 19 remaining bombers. Two more of its B-17's took direct hits, exploded and fell through the pockmarked sky. There were no chutes.

Another B-17 trailed smoke, but held formation. Now there were just 17 remaining. They released their 136 bombs and started to turn west just as flames erupted from the smoking B-17's wing. The wing exploded and tore off; the bomber flipped out of control. Now there were 16 heading west. Two white chutes appeared, then a third.

By the time the third combat box with 20 B-17's started its run, the sky over Berlin looked more black than blue. Two bombers immediately took hits and trailed smoke, but both held formation. All 20 B-17's pickled and 160 bombs streaked past the three white chutes.

Seeing the three airmen dropping through the battle-scarred sky filled with falling bombs and exploding cannon shells, Colonel Tyler was reminded of a combat report he had read about a year earlier. A waist gunner who had bailed out over a heavily defended target in France and been lucky enough to have survived and made it back to Britain had written it.

£££

"....As I hung in my chute, bombs whistled by," the gunner's report said. "Some so close I could see their fuse propellers spinning. At the same time, AAA cannon shells cracked skyward and exploded overhead. I looked up. Some spent shrapnel had cut holes in my chute. I prayed that the chute would hold together.

"As more AAA shells exploded and more bombs streaked past, I suddenly remembered that there were some lower formations of bombers behind. I looked back. They appeared to be coming right at me. I was certain I'd be crushed by a wing or tail—or chopped to pieces by spinning propellers. By the grace of God, the bombers passed above me.

"The closer to the ground I got, the louder the thunder from the exploding bombs and cannon fire became. I looked down and saw the cloud of smoke and debris that hid the ground. It was like falling into an active volcano, while the devil pounded out his favorite opus.

"When I entered the cloud of smoke and debris, the noise from the exploding bombs and cannon fire reached a crescendo. I thought my eardrums would burst, as the explosive shock waves pounded my body and dust filled my eyes and nose.

"I begged for God's help—and died a thousand deaths. I don't think I could have gotten any closer to hell without dying.

"Before I knew what had happened, my feet slammed onto the brick street. Somehow my chute collapsed. More bombs exploded; more cannons fired. Chunks of timbers and bricks thundered around me. My eyes and chest burned from the dust and cordite.

"Suddenly the bombing stopped, then the cannons stopped firing. The silence was deafening. As the dust settled, I just sat there. I guess I was too scared to move. Then I started laughing. Don't know why. It didn't make sense to me then and it still doesn't. But I couldn't stop. I continued laughing until a man and woman from the French underground grabbed me and took me to a safe house. . . .

"It took two and a half months to make it across France through Spain and back to Britain. . . .

"Since my bailout, not a night has passed that I haven't had nightmares about that mission. Each nightmare seems to get a little worse. I am hoping that by the time the war ends and I get back to my high school teaching job, the nightmare will stop."

£££

"Starting the bomb run," the *Urgin Virgin*'s pilot called.

WHUMP! WHUMP! WHUMP! Three orange bursts exploded just to the right of the old bomber's nose. The fireballs changed to black puffs—shrapnel sliced through her fuselage and wings.

"I'm hit!" the left waist gunner groaned.

"Right waist, take care of 'em!" the pilot shouted.

WHUMP! WHUMP! WHUMP! The *Urgin Virgin*'s right wing popped up; the yoke twisted in the pilot's hands. Colonel Tyler grabbed the yoke and helped the pilot level the old bomber's wings.

"Taken another hit in the right wing!" the top turret gunner yelled. "Hole, size of a basketball, between the engine and wing tip!"

Colonel Tyler's head snapped to the right. "Hang in there wing," he prayed.

WHUMP! WHUMP! WHUMP! More orange fireballs exploded; more shrapnel sliced through the ancient bomber's skin and the ping of spent shrapnel could be heard rattling along the top of the fuselage.

WHUMP! WHUMP! WHUMP! "Number three's losin' oil pressure!" Colonel Tyler shouted, wishing he could crawl inside his steel helmet.

"Keep it turnin' till we unload these bombs," the pilot answered.

"Nav here, bomb bay doors comin' open." The *Urgin Virgin* yawed, as one door opened before the other.

WHUMP! WHUMP! WHUMP!

The pilot had a full nelson on the yoke to hold the *Urgin Virgin* level.

"Bombs away!" the navigator shouted.

The *Urgin Virgin* leaped skyward as the 4000 pounds of bombs dropped from her belly. The pilot jammed the yoke forward to counter her leap.

WHUMP! W-h-o-o-s-h! WHAAM!

Colonel Tyler's head slammed against the side of the cockpit. He saw a blinding flash and felt freezing air blast his face and eyes. He groped for his goggles and pulled them on. They were splattered with blood. He readjusted his oxygen mask. When he straightened his steel helmet, he felt a rip on the edge of it where a piece of shrapnel had sliced through. He touched his head, looked at his gloves; there was no blood. "Close," he whispered.

The *Urgin Virgin* was in a turn to the right. Colonel Tyler looked at the pilot, did a double take and winced.

The pilot was slumped forward, against the yoke. A jagged piece of shrapnel had sliced through his helmet and stuck deep inside his forehead. In the 50-below-zero air, half-frozen, jelly-like blood covered the exposed shrapnel. It resembled a scarlet sepal.

More jelly-like blood covered the pilot's forehead, eyes and oxygen mask. Red icicles had started to form on each side of the mask like a red Fu Manchu mustache.

Colonel Tyler tried to roll the *Urgin Virgin* out of the turn, but the pilot's body held the yoke. He attempted to push the pilot back in his seat, but couldn't. While pushing, he felt a sharp pain and an electrical shock in his left side. He unplugged his electrically heated suit and looked down. Near his waist, blood oozed around a jagged piece of shrapnel that had ripped through his flak vest.

"This is the copilot…pilot and I have been hit. Need help in the cockpit."

"On my way, sir," replied Technical Sergeant Richard M. Caughlan, the radio operator. In the cockpit Sergeant Caughlan disconnected his walk-around oxygen bottle, hooked up to the aircraft system and plugged in his radio headset.

"Push the pilot back in the seat; tighten his shoulder harness and lock it. Cover his head," Colonel Tyler motioned.

Sergeant Caughlan forced the pilot's body back, locked the shoulder straps and tightened them. He grabbed a canvas equipment bag and put it over the pilot's head.

Colonel Tyler rolled the *Urgin Virgin* out on a heading of 270 degrees, pulled one end of his white scarf from around his neck and wiped the pilot's blood off his goggles. His elbow bumped the shrapnel in his side. "Sergeant, get a bandage from a first aid kit."

Sergeant Caughlan grabbed one of the first aid kits behind the seat and took out a bandage.

"Yank that shrapnel out."

Colonel Tyler flinched as Caughlan pulled out the jagged piece of steel and dropped it to the floor.

Colonel Tyler loosened his shoulder harness, unsnapped his parachute harness and loosened his "Mae West" and his flak jacket. He unzipped his flight jacket and flight suit and raised the top of his long underwear to expose the wound. Sergeant Caughlan shook some sulfa onto the bandage, placed it over the wound and pulled down the underwear to hold it in place.

Colonel Tyler zipped up his flight suit and jacket and pulled the flak jacket as tight as he could to keep pressure on the bandage. He readjusted his 'Mae West,' then rebuckled his chute and tightened the shoulder straps. "Keep an eye on the engine and hydraulic gauges and let me know if any get outta the green."

"Yes sir."

"Nav, close the bomb bay doors."

"Roger, sir."

"Sir, oil pressure on number three's in the red," Caughlan called.

"Copilot to the crew, number three's losin' oil, shuttin' it down and featherin'." He wanted to streamline the blades before the engine lost all of its oil. He knew that an unfeathered prop on a dead engine would act like a giant speed brake.

"Number two engine's runnin' a little hot, Colonel," Caughlan shouted.

"Throttlin' it back slightly. Keep your eye on it. Crew, gonna start a slow descent, keep our speed up, use the bomber stream to screen us as long as possible. Right waist, how's left waist?"

"Left waist is doing okay, sir."

For the next 30 minutes, Colonel Tyler held a 500-foot per minute rate of descent, remaining beneath the bomber stream.

"Levelin' at ten grand. We'll use these broken clouds for cover," he transmitted.

WHUMP! WHUMP! WHUMP!

"Flak! Dead ahead!" the top turret gunner shouted.

Colonel Tyler twisted and pulled back on the yoke, with all of his strength. "Hang together old girl," he whispered, feeling a sharp pain in his side. The old bomber's nose and right wing came up and she started a climbing left turn.

WHUMP! WHUMP! WHUMP! Her rudder pedals banged the soles of his boots; the yoke tried to jump out of his hands.

"Headin' for that cloud at one o'clock," Colonel Tyler grunted over the intercom, as he jammed the yoke forward and dived into the cloud, praying the old bomber would hold together.

"Took hits in the tail!" the top turret gunner yelled. "Part of the elevator and some of the rudder's shot away! Tail, you read? Tail, ya read?" The tail gunner didn't answer.

"Top turret, keep your eye on the tail, let me know if it starts sheddin' pieces," Colonel Tyler transmitted.

"Top turret has two 190's six o'clock high comin' down on us!"

"Give me a call just before they get into firing range."

"In range now, Colonel!"

"Everybody hang on!" He snapped the throttles back and pushed the yoke forward. The negative G's pulled his feet off the floor; his butt left the seat; the safety belt dug into his gut; he felt another shot of pain in his side. A yellow pencil, pieces of safety wire, two cigarette butts, a small nut and a Dick Tracy comic book floated to the ceiling of the cockpit.

"Krauts missed!" the top turret gunner shouted, as the two 190's passed overhead. "Good goin', Colonel."

"How's the tail look?" Colonel Tyler asked, glancing at the right wing and pushing the throttles forward.

"What's left of it...still there. Sir, 190's comin' back!"

Before the *Urgin Virgin* could enter the cloud, the 190's opened fire. A burst of machine gun fire tore into the number three engine near its mounts and the engine drooped about 20 degrees.

"Engine mounts on number three shot away!" Colonel Tyler shouted, as the *Urgin Virgin* yawed to the right and shook like she was being dragged across a giant washboard. He tried to counter the yaw with trim, but the trim tabs were shot out and nothing happened. "Shit...trim tabs shot out. Gonna take all my strength...just to keep her pointed toward Britain" he whispered to himself.

"Here they come again!" the top turret gunner yelled as the *Urgin Virgin* entered the cloud.

Inside the cloud, Colonel Tyler reduced power on the outboard engines. "Gang, trim tabs shot out. I'm slowin' her down to make it easier to hold a heading and give us more time in this cloud. It should also ease the shaking. Nav, what's our location?"

"Nav here, Amsterdam's five miles due west."

"Copy. Top turret, keep an eye on the right wing, rudder and elevators in case they start to shed. Anything else happens to this old girl, might not be able to keep her in the air. Since the left waist gunner is wounded and can't bail out, I plan to stay with her...set her down...if she decides to quit flyin'. The rest of ya may wanna bail out. Give it some thought, while we have time before we get over the North Sea. Meantime, throw out everything we don't need to lighten our load."

"Top turret here, don't need time to think. I'm stayin', sir."

"Right waist gunner's stayin' too, sir."

"Nav, I'll stay."

"Radio, I'm stayin'," Sergeant Caughlan said.

"Roger gang. With any luck, should make it to Manston."

Two minutes later, the *Urgin Virgin* came out of the clouds. Eight miles ahead, the dirty-green North Sea looked more ominous than ever before.

£££

"Snapper Yellow One, here. Big friend popped out of a cloud, one o'clock low, a few miles from the coast. Let's go bomber common," Robb transmitted.

"Gotta flight of four, at 5 o'clock high, Colonel," the top turret gunner called.

"Keep your eye on 'em. This far west, let's hope they're friendly," Colonel Tyler replied.

Robb waited for the VHF radio to cycle to the new channel. "Snapper Yellow, check."

"Yellow Two."

"Three."

"Four."

"Four bogies are Little Friends," Colonel Tyler said over the intercom.

"Yellow Three, ease down and check our Big Friend. I'll remain high for cover and radio relay if we need it," Robb transmitted.

"On my way." Rocko and Matt lowered 15 degrees of flap and moved closer to the bomber, being careful not to point their noses at the crippled giant.

"Top turret, here. They're sliding in close."

Rocko moved underneath and pulled up on the left side. He saw the form of the pilot with a bag over his head. "Lone B-17 named *Urgin Virgin*, ya read Snapper Yellow Three?"

"Snapper Yellow Three, Rough House 36 reads you five square."

"How ya doin', Rough House?"

"Son we've had better days. Got three dead and two wounded. Lost contact with the tail gunner. Don't know his status. We're headin' for Manston."

"Rough House, your right inboard engine's shakin' like it has the heebie-jeebies. Looks like it's about to drop off."

"Wish it would and reduce the drag. Can you slide back, check out our tail gunner?"

"Rog." Rocko moved back toward the B-17's tail. The fuselage was lined with shrapnel and machine gun holes. The belly turret's shattered glass was covered with blood and half of the rudder and a third of the elevators had been shot away. "Tail gunner's not movin' and his compartment is shot to hell."

"Rough House copied. Could ya have your high element contact Country Club. Give 'em our status, get their weather. At this speed, we're estimatin' Country Club in about an hour."

"Snapper Yellow One, wilco," Robb replied.

"Cylinder head temperature on number two's in the red, sir," Sergeant Caughlan called over the intercom.

"Guys, shuttin' down number two. Anyone who'd like to change their mind and bail out, better do it now, while we're still over land," Colonel Tyler called. No one answered. "Guys, gotta throw out everything that's not nailed down, includin' guns and ammo. Save the rear fire extinguisher, throw the other three out. Nav and top turret, when you finish, move on back to the waist area. Everyone get set for a crash-landing."

"Dear God...could use some help," Colonel Tyler whispered to himself. He had lost track of the number of aircraft emergencies he'd had during the past 27 years, but each time he had prayed for help. He had learned that fear was a great motivator for prayer and he thought maybe that's the way it ought to be. He also believed that we should pay our respect to God but not to bother Him all the time. He compared praying to good radio discipline: transmit only when it's necessary and to save your requests for the Slough of Despond.

"Yellow One's back on freq, Rough House. Country Club has your status. Their ceiling's 500 feet, visibility's one mile with rain. Wind 260 at 10. You're cleared for a straight-in."

"Snapper Yellow, Rough House's gonna start a slow descent and get underneath this lower deck of clouds."

"Yellow One, copy. I'm droppin' 15 degrees of flaps and slidin' down, joinin' on your right wing." Robb and Bob eased into position on the *Urgin Virgin's* right wing.

"Yellow Three, here. Rough House, your good engine on the left is startin' to smoke."

"Rog, it's runnin a little rough but runnin'. Keep me posted, Snapper," Colonel Tyler replied.

They descended for the next 16 minutes and finally broke out of the clouds at 600 feet. Colonel Tyler looked down at the North Sea. Wind whipped the big waves, changed their foaming white caps into a steamy spray. He knew surviving a water landing would take a miracle. He checked the temperature on the smoking engine. The needle was just below the red line. "Should've made 'em bail out over Holland," he whispered. "Dear God, stay tuned..."

"Ah say, Rough 'Ouse 36, this is Purple Stick. Do you read, suh?"

"Purple Stick, Rough House 36, reads you five-square."

"Jolly good, Rough 'Ouse 36. Make your cockerel crow, suh."

"Cockerel crowing, Rough House 36," Colonel Tyler said, turning on the IFF transponder.

"Purple Stick 'ere, strangle cockerel, suh. Painting you on my radar. Vector 250 for 15."

"Rough House 36, cockerel is strangled. Steering 250."

"Rough 'Ouse, Purple Stick 'ere. State angels, suh, and are you popeye?"

"Purple Stick, Rough House is level at 600-feet with four little friends."

"Rough 'Ouse, Purple Stick 'ere, say your status, please."

"Got four dead, two wounded; two engines out, a third with a giant belly ache and it may quit anytime. With wounded on board, we'll ditch if the last good engine konks."

"Understand, suh. You've a bit of a sticky wicket, Rough 'Ouse. Sea's choppy, but rescue launch proceeding your direction. A bit of good news, suh. Just heard on the wireless, your strike today was bang-on! Good show, mates."

"Copied, Purple Stick." Colonel Tyler swelled with pride. He swallowed the lump in his throat and blinked the tear from his eyes. "Snapper Yellow, how's that engine look?"

"Yellow Three here. It's smokin' more, Rough House."

"Rough House, Yellow One here. Our fuel's mighty low, almost down to fumes. We'd better head for home."

"Copy, Snapper. Thank you for your support."

"Our pleasure. Good luck, Rough House."

"Suds are on us in London Town, Snapper."

"You're on, Rough House," Robb answered, turning north to follow the coastline to Felixstowe. From there, he would turn west and follow the inlet and railroad to Boxted. "Yellow Three remain this frequency, monitor Rough House's progress. Yellow One's going to tower freq.'"

"Yellow Three, Rog."

"Rough 'Ouse 36, Purple Stick 'ere. I hold you two out. Country Club is standing by this frequency, suh."

"Purple Stick, thanks much. Country Club, Rough House 36, do you read?"

"Country Club reads you five-by," the Manston tower replied. "Ceiling's 500, visibility one mile with light rain, wind 260 at 10. Transmit for a steer, please."

"Country Club, Rough House 36, one, two, three, four, five...five, four, three, two, one. Over to you, Country Club."

"Country Club here, steer 280."

"Rough House 36 turnin' 280. CAN'T...HOLD...IT!"

"Rough House 36, Country Club here, do you read?" There was no reply. "Rough House 36, Country Club, do you read?"

"Purple Stick 'ere, they dropped off my radar scope."

"Country Club copied. Rough House 36, do you read? Rough House 36, Rough House 36, do you read?"

£££

Rocko changed to Boxted Tower frequency, "Snapper Yellow Three's on. You read, Yellow One?"

"Read you five square Yellow Three. How's Rough House?"

"He augered."

"SHIT!"

CHAPTER 15

A Dead-Stick Ace

"LEFT OUTBOARD ENGINE BLEW!" Sergeant Caughlan yelled into the intercom.

With only the right outboard engine running, the *Urgin Virgin*'s right wing pulled up; her nose twisted down and to the left. Colonel Tyler stood on the right rudder pedal, wrestled the yoke with both hands, but he couldn't stop her diving turn. "CHOP THE POWER ON THE RIGHT OUTBOARD ENGINE!" he yelled to Sergeant Caughlan.

Sergeant Caughlan yanked the right outboard engine throttle to idle.

Colonel Tyler strained to turn the *Urgin Virgin* back toward the Manston runway. He saw flames coming from the left outboard engine. "Hit the fire button on the left outboard engine and feather the prop."

Sergeant Caughlan pushed the fire extinguisher button. As the extinguisher started to put out the fire, he pushed the feathering button, but nothing happened. He pushed the feathering button again, but the prop didn't feather. "Got the fire out, but the prop won't feather, sir."

"Shit!" With one engine at idle and three dead engines, one with an unfeathered prop, another with a 20-degree droop, Colonel Tyler knew the added drag would make the *Urgin Virgin* drop like a rock.

He checked the altimeter. They we're already down to 300 feet. "Crew, this is the copilot, prepare for a crash landing."

During the scramble in the cockpit, the bag covering the pilot's head had gotten knocked off. Four hours of death had removed the hue of life from his young face and replaced it with a deadly gray. The caked blood on the jagged chunk of shrapnel sticking out from his steel helmet and the Fu Manchu mustache on his oxygen mask looked more purple than red. Colonel Tyler winced and looked back at the runway.

Sergeant Caughlan grabbed the bag and placed it over the young pilot's head.

The altimeter needle swung past 225 feet. Without the roar of the engines, the slipstream whistled through the *Urgin Virgin*'s riddled skin. It reminded Colonel Tyler of the guide wire buzz on the World War I bi-planes when their engines failed.

The whistling suddenly dropped an octave, like the bi-plane just before it stalled. Colonel Tyler checked the airspeed indicator; it read 70 mph. He released backpressure on the yoke and the airspeed increased to 75. But the altimeter needle swung past 150 feet.

Through the rain, he saw the lights marking the end of the runway. He rechecked the altimeter; it read 100 and he realized there was no way he could make it to the runway. He'd be damned lucky to reach the overrun.

But to reach the runway overrun, the *Urgin Virgin* had to pass several small green fields, none of which were large enough for a crash landing. And thick hedgerows, which could stop a tank, surrounded every field.

The whistling deepened again and Colonel Tyler lowered the *Urgin Virgin*'s nose. She regained gliding speed but lost more precious altitude. "Don't get ham-handed now you old fart," he whispered.

He checked the altimeter; it read 75 feet. From here on he had to perform a precarious balancing act. Even if he managed a perfect trade-off between altitude and airspeed, the *Urgin Virgin* could still land short of the overrun. "Stand by to lower flaps," he yelled to Sergeant Caughlan.

"Yes sir."

The altimeter needle swung past 50 feet. Hedgerows shot past like wattled hurdles. Colonel Tyler eased back on the yoke, trying to stretch her glide. The altimeter needle passed 25 feet.

"Everybody get ready for a belly flopper," he grunted over the intercom. Sweat ran into his eyes, he blinked to clear them, trying to hold the yoke steady and not waste a foot of altitude. "Dear God, it's me again," he prayed. "Could use some help."

The final hedgerow rushed at the *Urgin Virgin*.

"FLAPS NOW!"

Sergeant Caughlan flicked the switch. The *Urgin Virgin*'s flaps started down and her rate of sink slowed.

"BRACE YOURSELVES!" Colonel Tyler shouted over the intercom.

With all the finesse he could muster, he held the matriarch bomber level. She quivered ever so slightly.

SCRUNCH! The top of the last hedgerow scraped her nose turret.

SCAAR—RUMP! The hedgerow ripped into her aluminum belly.

The *Urgin Virgin* shuddered and Colonel Tyler yanked back the yoke trying to slow her fall.

WHOOMP! She belly flopped onto the overrun, slid through the water-logged sod, leaving a wake of muck and mud.

Just as she stopped, her tail rose a few inches and her nose dipped slightly, like a tired old lady of grace struggling to take her last bow.

Silence filled her riddled fuselage. Colonel Tyler turned off the radio, ignition and battery switches, then unsnapped his oxygen mask. He continued to hold the yoke like he was grasping the hand of a close friend. Finally, he bowed his head and closed his eyes. "Dear God, thank you for letting two old warhorses finish their last charge."

A gentle breeze swished through the holes in the *Urgin Virgin's* riddled skin and broke the placid calm.

"I'll get the door!" someone shouted from the rear.

"Colonel, we'd better hurry and get out," Sergeant Caughlan urged.

Colonel Tyler nodded. He reached for his steel helmet, lifted it off his head, saw the shrapnel hole. His hands started to shake. He gripped the helmet, hoping the shaking would stop.

"Sir, you okay?"

"I've flirted with death many times and never had the shakes. Maybe it's some kind of psychological aftershock. Probably take a squadron of shrinks a year of guessin' to figure it out. Maybe I'm just too old for this," he said with a smile.

"You did one helluva job, sir."

"Thanks. Couldn't have done it without your help." Colonel Tyler wanted to hug Sergeant Caughlan, like a father would hug a son. Instead, he unsnapped his safety belt and parachute.

"Colonel, we'd better hurry."

"Yeah. Let's pull the pilot out."

"Better let the crash crew do that, sir."

Colonel Tyler nodded, pushed himself out of the seat. He felt dizzy and sat back down.

"Can I give you a hand, sir?"

"I'll be okay. Just a little woozy. Sudden movement tilted my gyros. Guess my age's showin' again. Go ahead, I'll be right behind you son."

"You go first, sir. I'll follow."

"Fair enough." Colonel Tyler got out of the seat.

"Sir, you've lost more blood."

"Yeah. Felt some pain, during my wrestlin' match after the engine blew. Crew may need help with the wounded in the rear. Let's go back and see."

They made their way through the bomb bay and radio compartment. The top turret and right waist gunners were huddled next to belly turret where the gunner's body was trapped.

"Sir, we can't get the belly gunner out," the wounded waist gunner said looking up at Colonel Tyler. He was holding the fire extinguisher in his right hand and the left sleeve of his flight jacket and flight suit had been cut so his wound could be bandaged. Several layers of blood soaked gauze held the bandage in place.

"I know, sergeant. Let's let the crash crews take care of him," Colonel Tyler replied.

"Okay, sir. You're bleeding, sir. You okay, Colonel?" the waist gunner asked.

"I'm okay."

Further back, the navigator kicked and pushed on the rear door, trying to force it open through the mud. "Nav, let me give you a hand with that door," Sergeant Caughlan said, hurrying past the others.

"Got the door open!" the navigator shouted after he and Sergeant Caughlan pushed the door wide open. "Let's get the hell outta here!"

The crew sloshed across the sod, hurrying to get away from the *Urgin Virgin*. At the edge of the runway, they stopped to catch their breaths as sirens wailed and the fire trucks and ambulances raced toward them.

"Sir, that was a great piece of flying," the navigator said. "You got everything outta her. We all owe you, sir."

"Yes sir. Red Baron couldn't have done any better," the left waist gunner added, still holding the fire extinguisher. "We'll fly with you anytime, Colonel."

"Thanks guys. Makes an old man feel good. My fifth dead-stick landing. Guess that makes me a dead-stick ace," he smiled.

The crew smiled and nodded.

"Guys, let's take a minute of silent prayer to thank God that we made it and pray for the rest of the crew who didn't," Colonel Tyler said. A few seconds before the minute ended, the screeching brakes of the fire trucks and ambulances broke the silence.

"Nav, will you tell the crash crew that four of our crew are inside the *Urgin Virgin*, so they can recover all the bodies," Colonel Tyler requested before climbing into the ambulance.

"Will do, sir," the navigator replied.

Once all the crew were inside, the ambulance sped down the runway toward the RAF dispensary.

"Sir, what'll they do with the *Urgin Virgin*?" the top turret gunner asked.

"Can't let 'em junk her, sir," the left waist gunner added. "She's seen too much action to be turned into junk. Besides, four of our crew were killed inside her."

"Be no junkin' her if I can help it," Colonel Tyler replied.

The crew nodded.

After getting his wound cleaned, stitched and bandaged, Colonel Tyler called 8th Air Force Headquarters, requested airlift to take the crew and the four dead members to RAF Station Kimbolton. The aircraft would drop Colonel Tyler off at Northolt enroute. "Our fighters lose many?" he asked the duty officer before hanging up.

The duty officer knew what he wanted. "The party in question got two more kraut fighters."

Relieved, Colonel Tyler called Darlene at the Hogs Breath Inn. "Darlin, we had engine problems and had to land at Manston. I'll be flyin' into Northolt in a few hours. See ya at High Wycombe."

"Are you alright, Tim?"

"I'm fine."

"Are you sure?"

"Positive."

"Tim, I love you."

"Love you too, Darlin.' Gotta hurry. See ya in a few hours."

The C-47 stopped in front of Northolt Base Operations and left its engines running. Colonel Tyler went forward to say good-bye to the left waist gunner who was lying on a stretcher.

The gunner looked up, "Sir, thanks again. Damned few pilots could've done what you did. You kept the *Urgin Virgin* flyin' when others would've augered-in."

"Wish I could've done more, son." Colonel Tyler swallowed the lump in his throat and patted the gunner's shoulder.

"Sir, don't forget the *Urgin Virgin*."

"I'm gonna do everything I can. You have my word."

"Thank you, sir," he said smiling.

"Sergeant Caughlan has given me the names and home towns of all the crew. Maybe we can all get together after this damned war is over," Colonel Tyler said giving his shoulder another pat.

"That'd be great, sir."

"Let me help you, Colonel," the young flight nurse offered as Colonel Tyler started toward the rear of the C-47.

"I'm okay. Thank you, Lieutenant."

Colonel Tyler stopped at the four wooden coffins, faced them and saluted.

At the large cargo door, the *Urgin Virgin*'s five remaining crewmen shook his hand and thanked him once again. Then Sergeant Caughlan and the navigator held the big door open while the C-47's flight engineer installed the small metal steps.

The flight engineer jumped out and helped Colonel Tyler down the steps. Colonel Tyler hurried through the rain to the waiting staff car. Before he got in, he turned toward the C-47 and saluted and the *Urgin Virgin*'s crew returned the salute. The flight engineer closed the door, the pilot gunned the engines and the C-47 pulled away.

Colonel Tyler got into the staff car and said, "Wait a minute, please." He watched the C-47 taxi to the runway and check its mags. After it took off and roared into the clouds, he said, "Okay, let's go."

As they pulled away, Colonel Tyler suddenly felt very lonely. He recalled the cold dark dispersal tent, as he and nine total strangers waited to enter the risk-filled sky. That long wait seemed like it had happened days ago, not this morning. He would never forget the crew, nor the *Urgin Virgin*, nor this day—surely the longest day of his life. He had spent ten hours of it riding with death, waiting his turn to die. Four men had been killed and the mission ended with a crash landing that could've easily taken the rest and made it an even ten. "Dear God, thanks again," he sighed.

He leaned back in the seat, felt the pull of the stitches in his side. He had finally achieved his goal of flying 35 heavy bomber missions, a complete combat tour. But so far, being the only pilot in the Army Air Force to have completed combat tours in World War I and II hadn't brought the exhilaration he had expected. Instead, he felt guilty that four young crewmen had been killed on his last mission.

Before he dozed, he recalled all his friends who'd died in combat or aircraft crashes during the past 27 years while he'd been spared. None of it made sense and he wondered if it ever would.

The staff car stopped at the front door to High Wycombe. Colonel Tyler hurried to the operations center. The duty officer, a young captain who'd completed his combat tour in bombers, handed him a copy of the mission summary. "Sir, sit at my desk. May I get you a cup of coffee?"

"Thanks, coffee sounds great."

"Congratulations on your 35th mission, sir. You did a helluva job nursing that old bomber home, then coaxin' her across those cabbage patches."

"Thank you. Had a little luck and a lotta help from the crew." Colonel Tyler sat down, took a swig of coffee and started to read the mission summary.

£££

SECRET
8th Air Force
Preliminary Mission Summary
March 6, 1944

£££

I.   The 8th Air Force attacked Berlin with 730 B-17's and B-24's, escorted by thirteen groups of 8th AF fighters and four groups from the 9th AF. The bombers dropped 1648 tons of 500-pound bombs on targets in Berlin. Broken clouds covered some aiming points and degraded bombing accuracy. Firm damage reports will be sent when reconnaissance photos are evaluated...

2.   AAA over Berlin was extremely heavy and the *Luftwaffe* launched their largest and most determined fighter attacks since the Big Week. Single

engine and many twin-engine fighters were employed. About half of the twin-engine fighters were night fighters....

    a.   Sixty-nine bombers did not return. Forty-one were shot down by German fighters, 22 were downed by AAA fire and four badly damaged bombers crashed landed in the North Sea (only 16 of the 40 crewmen were rescued). Another six bombers landed in Sweden. One badly damaged B-17 crash-landed at RAF Station Manston. Four of its crewmen were killed and two were wounded. Twenty-six aircrews returned to Britain with disabling wounds (14 with serious frostbite and 12 were hit by AAA shrapnel).

    b.   Brigadier General Russ Wilson, the 4th Combat Wing CO, was lost when his aircraft was shot down over Berlin....

    c   . Of the returning bombers, six were unrepairable and will be junked and 347 had varying degrees of battle damage. Complete battle damage assessment will follow. The continuing rise in AAA losses/damage reflects Germany's increased dependency on AAA defenses....

3   During the fierce *Luftwaffe* fighter attacks, B-17 and B-24 gunners claimed 97 destroyed, 28 probably destroyed and 60 damaged. Claims are being analyzed and firm figures will follow....

4.   A total of 801 escort fighters launched (615 P-47's, 86 P-38's and 100 P-51's). One group of P-38's returned early because of excessive engine failures. Eleven American fighters were lost (five P-47's, five P-51's and one P-38)....

    a.   Eyewitness reports and gun camera film confirmed 81 *Luftwaffe* aircraft destroyed by our fighters. The P-51's destroyed 43, had one probable and 20 damaged; P-47's destroyed 36, had seven probables and 12 damaged, while the P-38's destroyed 3, had no probables and damaged 1....

    b.   A strafing attack on an airfield, resulted in the destruction of another German aircraft and damage to 12 more. In the future, more fighters will conduct strafing attacks against airfields, trains, trucks and other military targets when they complete their escort duties....

5.   Total casualties for the mission were 755 ....

£££

Colonel Tyler handed the report to the duty officer, then checked his watch. It was 7:30.

"May I get you anything else, sir?" the Captain asked.

"No thank you. Awfully tired. Think I'll go to my room and stretch out."

Colonel Tyler entered his room, undressed, took a sponge bath, put on his pajamas and lay down. He started to read the *STARS and STRIPES* and went sound to sleep.

£££

Darlene returned to High Wycombe at 10:15 pm. She stopped in the headquarter's kitchen, made two cheese sandwiches, poured two glasses of canned grapefruit juice and brought them to Tim's room. She sat down on the edge of his bed and he opened his eyes.

"Brought something to eat."

"Not hungry, darlin.' Just need sleep." He held out his hand.

She placed the tray on the table and lay down beside him. When she put her arm around him, she felt the bandage. "Tim, you've been wounded."

"It's nothin', darlin'. Just snuggle. Not much of a celebration, is it? Not sure I ever wanta celebrate today's mission."

"Tim, being with you is all I want. I've been worried sick all day." She snuggled closer, being careful not to touch the bandage.

At 2:00 am, she got up and hurried down the hall. She hated the sneaking around, but they both wanted to wait until after the war to get married so they could have a proper wedding back in the States with her family.

The next morning, Colonel Tyler had the doctor check and rebandage his wound, before going to the office. He called the 379th Bomber Group to get the history on the *Urgin Virgin*, then drafted a letter for General Spaatz's signature and had Darlene type it.

£££

Headquarters
USSTAF
APO. 621

7 March 1944

Subject, Restoration of B-17 serial number 42-0106

To: USSTAF Deputy for Service and Supply

1. Request that B-17F serial number 42-0106 (*Urgin Virgin*) assigned to the 379th Heavy Bomb Group, which crash landed at RAF Station Manston, on 6 March 1944, be restored. The *Urgin Virgin* has completed 157 combat missions, more missions then any B-17 or B-24 in the 8th AF.

a. Her first assignment was with the 305th Heavy Bombardment Group. While there, she flew 76 combat missions, received major battle damage eleven times, minor damage twelve times and had only three maintenance aborts.

b. After a major overhaul and modification update at the Burton-wood Depot, the *Urgin Virgin* was assigned to the 379th Heavy Bombardment Group, Kimbolton. Since then, she has flown another 81 combat missions without a single maintenance abort, while receiving major combat damage seven times and minor damage four times.

2. This gallant lady deserves a permanent place of honor before she's lost in our "throw away society." After her restoration is complete, it is directed that she be retired from combat, assigned to administrative duty and flown by only the most qualified crews. When the war ends in Europe, the *Urgin Virgin* will be returned to the United States, assigned to a permanent Army Air Force airfield and put on public display.

£££

Carl A. Spaatz
Lieutenant General

£££

The morning of March 14th, 1944 was like most. Colonel Tyler was at his desk by 6:00 am, making the first of several daily checks on the arrivals of freighters with aviation gas. His next call was to transportation to check on the truck movement of the gas from the ports to the airfields and storage sites. Then he reviewed the daily status reports of the fuel on hand at every airfield. His last call was to the civil engineer to get the construction status of the additional storage tanks.

At the time, there were 7000 combat aircraft in the 8th and 9th AF's, consuming nearly 36 million gallons of gas a month. In a few months, there would be 10,000 combat aircraft. A month before the D-Day invasion, it was anticipated the monthly consumption of fuel would shoot to more than 80 million gallons and would continue at that rate for at least six months. Only bombs and ammunition approached the shipping requirements of aviation fuel.

"General Doolittle would like to see you right away," Darlene said, entering his office. "General's aide said to bring your coat and hat."

"Thanks, darlin'. Love ya," he said, patting her hip on the way out.

"You're going to get caught one day," she smiled.

Colonel Tyler entered General Doolittle's outer office. The aide jumped up and opened the door. "Sir, go on in, he's waiting."

"Tim, Tooey wants to see us right away. Didn't say what was on his mind, but he seemed anxious," General Doolittle said as he put on his coat and hat.

£££

"General Spaatz is expecting you, gentlemen," Captain Sally Bagby, Spaatz's executive officer said opening the office door.

General Spaatz stood to greet them. "Hi Jimmie, Tim. Glad to see ya," he said. "Tim, how ya feeling?"

"Still a little tender, but I'm okay."

"Tim, Moe Preston sent a note to Jimmie and me. Said your effort on the March 6th Berlin strike was absolutely superb. Saved the lives of five crewmen."

"Just doin' my job, sir."

"Speaking of jobs, gotch'a new one. Ain't a combat command, but it's an important one. And tough."

Same old Tooey, Colonel Tyler thought. Tooey never was one to waste a lot of time on small talk.

"General Eisenhower's got the toughest combat job in the entire war. Gotta platoon of prima donnas working for him, including me," Spaatz smiled. "Also has Churchill breathing down his neck.

"As you know, Ike's senior staff is overloaded with blokes and ground-pounders. Consequently, the employment of Army Air comes as an afterthought or as a result of some half-baked idea by some ground-pounder. Some of these half-baked ideas could be dangerous and take a lotta undoing.

"I've been working on Ike for a long time to get a senior Army Air Force pilot on his personal staff. Someone with combat experience who'll be close to him and see him almost every day. He finally bought it two weeks ago. Nobody around with better credentials than yours. You have strategic and tactical combat experience, know logistics and you can't be intimidated. Besides, you know how to hold a stiff pinkie on the cocktail circuit," Spaatz with a smile.

"Tim, Ike's the most evenhanded person I know. His position and power haven't made him the least bit arrogant. You can be honest with Ike and he won't have your rations. Only other guy I know that can handle power better is George Marshall.

"Enough of that. Have something else for you," Spaatz said, pushing the button on his desk. The office door opened. "Sally, we're ready."

Sally Bagby came in with three blue leather boxes and a small black box. A technical sergeant with a camera followed her.

"Jimmie, Tim, let's go over by my flags. Sally, will you remove those eagles from Colonel Tyler's shoulders?"

Colonel Tyler stood in front of the American flag and Captain Sally Bagby started taking off his colonel's eagles. He realized he was about to be presented with some medals, but couldn't figure out why his eagles were being removed.

General Spaatz took two stars from the black box and handed one to General Doolittle. "Jimmie you take his left shoulder. Tim, we figured you were over-age in grade so we decided to promote you," General Spaatz said with a smile as he pinned the star on the epaulet of Colonel Tyler's uniform coat.

Tim Tyler couldn't believe what was happening. If he hadn't known Tooey Spaatz so well, he would have sworn it was some kind of joke.

"Tim, Hap Arnold gave me these stars when I made BG. Sergeant get some pictures of this," Spaatz said.

General Spaatz and Doolittle pinned on the stars, while Sally read the promotion order signed by President Roosevelt. Tim knew that Tooey had to have cut through a mountain of red tape to get the promotion approved so fast.

After the stars were on, Sally handed Spaatz the Distinguished Service Cross from the first blue box and read the citation while he pinned it on. They repeated the procedure for the Distinguished Flying Cross and the Purple Heart. Then Generals Spaatz and Doolittle shook his hand while the sergeant took more pictures.

"Sally, I want good background coverage on General Tyler's combat experience, especially for the British press," Spaatz said. "Sergeant, get a few more pictures, then let's get back to work." The sergeant took two more pictures and followed Sally Bagby out of the office.

"Tim, you'll need a good aide. Have anybody in mind?"

"Yes sir, my chief clerk, Sergeant Bradford."

"Okay. We'll get him commissioned."

"It's not a him, sir. Sergeant Bradford's a WAC."

"Jimmie, what'a you think?"

"I can't see anything wrong with it, sir," General Doolittle answered. "Sharpest NCO in my headquarters."

"I guess Ike wouldn't mind. He's got Captain Kay Sommersby working for him as his secretary and driver. I know Sally'll be pleased. She's always hounding me to use more WAC's in key positions. Okay, prepare the paperwork to give her a commission and I'll sign it. Tim, not to beat a horse to death, but a lot's ridin' on how well you handle this job. I know you won't let us down. That's enough singin' to the choir.

"Tim, Jimmie and I have decided to let Colonel Green take your old job. Think he can handle it?"

"Yes sir."

"Good. Incidentally, I signed your letter on the *Urgin Virgin*."

"Thank you, sir. Thank you for everything." Tim saluted. As he followed General Doolittle out of the office, he felt like he was walking on air.

On the drive back, Tim glanced out the side window. From the corner of his eye he could see the new star beaming on his epaulet. It looked damned good and Brigadier General Tim Tyler sounded good too. Two years ago he was a major and now he was a one button general going to work in the front office of the Supreme Allied Commander. He would get a firsthand look at General Eisenhower's key players like Tedder and Bradley, maybe see some of Patton's antics, or suffer through some of Montgomery's self-centered monologues. More importantly, he would have a front row seat to witness the final results of the bloody two year air war that would set the stage for largest, riskiest and most crucial military operation in history, the D-Day invasion of France. He knew the invasion would overshadow everything, but he hoped that one-day historians would recognize the importance of the Army Air Force's sacrifices and contributions to its success.

CHAPTER 16

The Armed Forces Staff College
Norfolk, Virginia
February 21, 1955

The Army Air Forces and 8th Air Force During World War II

By
Major Robb Baines, USAF
Class 55A

Part III (of III Parts)

Student comments: Winston Churchill's tribute to RAF fighter pilots following the Battle of Britain seems appropriate for the British and American airmen who paid a high price to make the invasion of France possible. "Never in the field of human conflict was so much owed by so many to so few."

During the two years of aerial combat that preceded the D-Day invasion of France, the 8th, 9th and 15th Army Air Force lost more than 30,000 men who were either killed or taken prisoners. The RAF paid an even higher price because they fought longer.

A few weeks after the June 6, 1944 D-Day invasion, General Dwight D. Eisenhower, supreme allied commander, while standing near the beach and surveying the Normandy bridgehead, said, "If I didn't have air supremacy, I wouldn't be here."

£££

A. *Der Dummkopf* and the *Luftwaffe*

1. Although a few Hurricanes and Spitfires had demonstrated the necessity of air superiority, Adolf Hitler, Germany's self-anointed military genius, believed the aircraft's only *raison d'etre* was to carry bombs. Like most ground-bound, one-dimensional military experts, *der dummkopf* failed to understand the third dimension of war.

2. Following the Battle of Britain, General Galland, the *Luftwaffe*'s fighter commander, explained the reasons for the German Air Force's defeat: A fighter force too small for the job, fighters with limited range, and faulty tactics (not allowing fighters to leave the bombers). But *der dummkopf* and Reichsmarshal Hermann Goering viewed Galland's reasons as excuses for failure. Later, when the *Luftwaffe* faced growing Allied air forces in Russia, the Mediterranean and Europe, Galland continued to ask for a larger fighter force but his pleas fell on deaf ears.

3. After the great American/German air battles in February, March and April 1944, Galland made his strongest plea yet. He reported extremely high pilot losses, including many flight captains, squadron and group commanders. Galland said the *Luftwaffe*'s pilot training program had fallen hopelessly behind. He asked for more instructors, more aircraft and more airfields to train new fighter pilots. But *der dummkopf* and Goering ignored him.

4. When General Spaatz's oil strikes created fuel shortages, the *Luftwaffe* had to decrease the flight training for their new pilots from 260

to 110 hours. Before the war ended, *Luftwaffe* pilots received only 50 hours flight training versus Allied pilots' 300 hours. Fuel shortages also forced the *Luftwaffe* to limit their combat flying. Badly outnumbered and inadequately trained, the new German pilots became easy prey for the more numerous and better trained Allied pilots.

5. While the *Luftwaffe's* fighter pilot strength withered, Germany's monthly fighter production increased, peaking at 4000 in September 1944. But due to the lack of pilots and a shortage of fuel, hundreds of new ME-109's and FW-190's sat on the ground. The lack of adequately trained fighter pilots became the Achilles heel of the *Luftwaffe* and gave the Allies air superiority.

6. Even as larger and more frequent Allied air attacks sent Hitler and his mistress scurrying deep inside the bowels of their reinforced concrete bunker. Hitler refused to admit the need for a larger fighter force. Instead, he ordered additional anti-aircraft cannons to protect cities and key targets. His no-brain, point defense, strategy ceded most of the German sky to the Allies.

£££

B. Allied Air Strength on D-Day

I. By D-Day, Allied air forces had nearly reached their full strength. The 9th U.S. Tactical Air Force had 2600 fighters and medium bombers, while the RAF had 1300. The 9th AF had 1400 cargo aircraft and the RAF possessed 200. The U.S. and RAF combined possessed 400 Reconnaissance and 2700 gliders. The 8th and 15th Air Forces had 4200 heavy bomber and 1800 fighters, while the RAF had 1800 heavy bombers and no fighters. The Allies' grand total was 13,750 aircraft, more than enough to perform both the tactical and strategic missions.

£££

C. The *Luftwaffe* On D-Day

I. On D-Day, the *Luftwaffe's* fighter strength in Europe was down to 1100 fighters and only 170 were in France. When the Wehrmacht suffered staggering losses from Allied air attacks, German ground commanders defending against the invasion begged for help from their once powerful *Luftwaffe*. The Nazi high command ordered 300 air defense fighters sent from Germany to France to support the Wehrmacht.

 a. Many of the 300 pilots were inexperienced and their flight to France gave an indication of what was to follow. Some got shot down en route, some got lost and others crashed while trying to land on the hastily prepared airstrips. Once in France, many German fighters were damaged or destroyed on the ground by Allied aircraft, while a shortage of parts and fuel grounded more. The few *Luftwaffe* fighters that took off on D-Day were shot down or chased from the sky by the 2700 American and 1000 British fighters. By June 16th, what was left of the battered *Luftwaffe* in France was ordered back to Germany. During the German retreat across France, the *Luftwaffe* seldom posed a threat and many Allied soldiers went through the entire war without seeing a German aircraft in the air.

£££

D.   Bold Decision

I   . General Eisenhower's decision to launch the invasion of France was the toughest military decision of World War II. His forces numbered 2,876,000 soldiers, sailors and airmen, the largest force ever assembled under one commander for a single operation. Sending a huge force across a 60-mile wide span of the hostile English Channel to break through the heavily fortified German coastal defenses of France seemed an impossible task.

2.   Because the invasion force needed a full moon and low tides, June 5, 1944 was selected as the invasion day (D-Day). But when the final decision time arrived at 4:00 AM, on June 4th, a storm approached from the Atlantic. One group of weather experts said the bad weather would improve in 36 hours, making June 6th an acceptable invasion date. Other weather experts believed the bad weather might not improve.

a.   If Eisenhower delayed beyond the 6th, he'd lose the favorable tides and moon, forcing at least a two-week delay—with no assurance the weather would be any better then. Such delay would have dulled the fighting edge of his forces, caused innumerable logistic problems and lost valuable summer weather for fighting.

b.   Eisenhower undoubtedly recalled the words of Dennis Hart Mahan, a military engineer and author, who said, "Even the very elements of nature seem to array themselves against the slow and over-prudent general."

3.   At the June 4th conference with his senior commanders, Eisenhower made a preliminary decision to invade on June 6th. At 4:15 am on June 5th, while the wind whipped the channel waves into mountains

of foam and rain pounded his headquarters building, Eisenhower made his final decision to go.

   a.   It's interesting to note that as Eisenhower agonized over his high-risk decision, Churchill and his team of military experts maintained an unaccustomed silence. Failure would be Eisenhower's alone.

£££

E. D-Day

Student comments: No amount of words or pictures could adequately portray D-Day. The aerial view of thousands of aircraft overhead, with hundreds of vessels carrying the invasion force across the Channel to storm the beaches, left one awestruck.

£££

1.   Shortly after midnight on June 6, 1944, under the watchful eye of Army Air Force night fighters, 1600 cargo planes and 512 gliders started taking off with the first of two waves of paratroopers and equipment. A few hours later, three airborne divisions the US 82nd and 101st, along with the British 6th had dropped behind German lines.

2.   At the same time, 4200 landing ships and craft, 1200 merchant ships and1200 naval ships, which included 7 battleships and 23 cruisers, moved toward Normandy. The initial assault force of 185,000 men was jam-packed on the troop ships and landing craft. They bounced and rolled in the rough seas knowing that in a few hours the stench of vomit would be replaced by the stench of death.

   a.   Behind the invasion armada, 100 tugs towed huge reinforced concrete structures that would be used to build two man-made harbors for off-loading men and supplies.

3.   At 3:14 am, Allied bombers began two hours of continuous attacks on the German beach fortifications. Naval gunfire then took over and continued until a few minutes before 6:30 am when the first landing craft came ashore. Their loading ramps slammed open; thousands of troops charged into a crescendo of German gunfire and exploding landmines. Soon bodies were being tossed about in the surf or lay cold in the bloodstained sand.

4.   More planning went into the D-Day invasion than any operation in the history of warfare. But due to the elements, the enemy, and human error combat seldom goes as planned. Darkness, fog patches,

enemy ground fire and human error, caused drop zones to be missed and many paratroopers got widely separated. Neither the aerial or naval bombardments silenced the coastal defenses. Assault landing craft missed their designated spots on the beaches and units became separated.

    a.   But disciplined junior officers, non-commissioned officers and privates rallied and avoided chaos by organizing scattered groups into fighting units. They fought their way across the blood soaked beaches, up the steep banks and through the tough German defenses.

5.   While the ground forces slugged it out, 13,750 Allied fighters and bombers swarmed overhead. Some acted as a protective umbrella against enemy aircraft, while others bombed and strafed enemy troops, trucks, trains and bridges and kept German replacements from reaching the beaches.

    a.   *Luftwaffe* records indicate they attempted to launch 250 sorties on D-Day, but almost all were turned back or shot down before they could reach Allied forces. Only three FW-190's appeared over the beach and were quickly chased away. That night, 22 German aircraft attacked some ships and inflicted slight damage.

    b.   A German soldier wrote home, "The American fliers are chasing us like hares." The commander of Panzer Lehr Division later described the road from Vire to Beny Bocage as a *Jabo Rennstreche* (an Allied fighter-bomber racecourse). General Galland said, "From the very first moment of the invasion the Allies had absolute air supremacy."

6.   By nightfall, more than 100,000 Allied soldiers were on French soil to stay.

£££

F. Montgomery's 'Administrative Tail'

1. Three weeks of fighting took the Americans and British inland 15 to 20 miles, along a stagnant line from Saint-Lo east to Caen. Montgomery was supposed to attack in the vicinity of Caen and capture an area he should have taken days before. It was hoped his assault would draw German forces from the American sector, allowing Bradley to break out at Saint-Lo and capture the port of Cherbourg. Bradley would then make an end run to the south and east and encircle the German forces in front of Montgomery.

    a. The slow moving Montgomery delayed his attack to "tidy up his administrative tail," a much used excuse that annoyed Eisenhower, Air Chief Marshal

Tedder (Eisenhower's deputy) and others. Finally on July 7-8, after thousands of Allied aircraft bombed and strafed the Germans in front of him, Montgomery made the first of two unsuccessful attempts to take the ground around Caen.

b. He scheduled his second attack for July 18th and boasted to his superiors and the press that his second attack might cause the entire German defense to collapse. Once again, a massive air attack preceded Montgomery's assault. First, RAF heavy bombers dropped 6,000 half-ton bombs and another 9,600 500-pound bombs. Then the 8th AF's heavy bombers dropped 13,000 100-pound and 76,000 20-pound fragmentation bombs. After Montgomery's attack started, 4000 medium bombers and fighters provided continuous direct support. The earth in front of Montgomery's forces looked like the backside of the moon.

c. Field Marshal Gunther von Kluge, who replaced von Rundstedt as the German commander, told Hitler about the air attacks. Referring to the air attacks, he said, "My conference with the commanders of the units at Caen held just after the last heavy battle forced me to the conclusion...that there is no way in which we could do battle with the all powerful enemy air forces...without surrendering territory. Whole units were attacked...they emerged from the churned earth with the greatest difficulty, sometimes only with the aid of tractors...."

3. Despite the near collapse of German defenses, Montgomery failed a second time. His failure generated a firestorm of criticism from both the American and British.

a. Air Chief Marshal Sir Charles Portal, Chief of the RAF, predicted that American and British people would soon question, "...tying up tremendous air power to plow up fields in front of an army reluctant to move." Eisenhower's deputy, Air Chief Marshal Tedder. believed that Montgomery should be replaced. An irritated Eisenhower noted that the air forces had dropped 1000 tons of bombs for each mile of Montgomery's advance. At that rate, he wondered if the Allies could afford to support Montgomery's advance across France. Eisenhower complained to Churchill and Churchill seemed to agree, but Montgomery was still too popular with the British public to fire. (Only a man like Harry Truman had enough guts to do something like that.)

b. Montgomery suggested his comments regarding the second assault had been misunderstood by the press and senior Allied military officers. He claimed he had overstated his objectives in order to get adequate air support an absurd, childlike excuse that flew in the face of the facts.

c.   General Eisenhower had fought hard to gain control of the strategic air forces so he would have all Allied Air Forces available for direct support of the ground war. Moreover, the strategic air commanders were eager to use their massive airpower to help the ground forces break through the German defenses and regain the initiative, so the strategic bombing program could be resumed. By July 18th, Eisenhower, Bradley, Spaatz and all other Allied airmen would have given "Slow-motion" Montgomery almost anything to get him off his "administrative tail."

d.   General Bradley thought Montgomery had not overstated his objectives. Bradley believed Montgomery was hoping for a much-needed victory to improve his tarnished image and give him a chance to keep his temporary job as the "Grand Ground Commander."

£££

G. Airpower Opens the Door for Saint-Lo Breakout

I   . General Bradley planned to make his breakout a few days after Montgomery's second assault. Like Montgomery, Bradley wanted massive air strikes to soften the German defenses. Following several weather delays, Air Chief Marshal Leigh-Mallory, who was in charge of the Allied tactical air forces that temporarily included the 8th Air Force's heavy bomber, launched a heavy bomber attack on July 24th in highly questionable weather. (This would be one of many mistakes made during the battle of Saint Lo air/ground attack. See paragraph H., below.) The mission eventually had to be recalled minutes before the bombs were to drop. The weather improved the next day and 1600 B-17's and B-24's, 380 medium bombers and 600 fighters laid a carpet of bombs that shattered the German defenses, permitting Bradley's forces to break out.

a.   Lieutenant General Fritz Bayerlein, commander of the *Panzer Lehr Division*, reported that as a result of the Sain Lo air attacks, 1000 of his troops were killed and three battalion command posts were destroyed. He added that all but a dozen of his armored fighting vehicles were knocked out and an attached parachute regiment got mauled so badly it had to be taken out of action. General Bayerlein said later, "It was hell... The planes kept coming overhead like a conveyer belt, and the bomb carpets came down…at least 70% of my personnel were out of action—dead, wounded, crazed or numb."

b. Field Marshal Guenther Hans Kluge stated that Allied air power alone came close to breaking the German front. He told Hitler, "It is immaterial whether such a bomb carpet strikes good troops or bad, they are more or less annihilated. If this occurs frequently, then the power of endurance of the force is put to the highest test, in-deed it becomes dormant and dies."

c. After the war, Field Marshal Gerd von Rundstedt said the aerial attack at Saint-Lo was the most effective use of air support he saw during the war.

d. Referring to the Saint-Lo bombing, Bradley said, "The bombing had done far more damage than we could possibly imagine."

e. The official Army history confirmed all the above. It said, "… About one-third of the total number of combat effectives…were probably killed or wounded, the survivors dazed. …Only local and feeble resistance was possible against the attacking American infantrymen."

£££

H. Goofs At Saint Lo

£££

Student comments: the Saint-Lo breakout was the greatest air/ground operation of World War II, but serious errors were made in its planning and execution.

£££

I. General Bradley made heavy bombers the "nutcracker" for his breakout, but there is no evidence that heavy bomber experts were consulted before the plan was finalized. By the time Bradley presented the specifics of his plan to Generals Spaatz and Doolittle on July 19th (two days before the strike was set to go), it had already been approved by Eisenhower and Montgomery. pompous Leigh-Mallory, who knew next to nothing about USAAF heavy bomber operations but would control the mission, completely dismissed the expert's reservations. For some unexplained reason, the Americans didn't press the issue further and the disagreements were never resolved. Consequently, since Leigh-Mallory was the air boss for the mission, Bradley believed it would be flown as he had requested.

d. American airmen, eager to demonstrate their airpower but faced with Bradley's time restriction, wrongly decided on their own to make the bomb run perpendicular to the front lines to fulfill the time requirement.

e. Despite a highly questionable weather forecast, on the evening of July 23 Leigh-Mallory decided to launch the first strategic bomber attack the next day. In the morning the weather was so bad he delayed the takeoff for two hours, hoping it would improve. Then, once the 1600 B-17's and B-24's were airborne, he canceled the mission seven minutes before they were to start dropping their bombs. Since Leigh-Mallory had gone to France to observe the bombing and hadn't established direct communications with them, some of them dropped before they received the cancellation order. A number of bombs landed short, killing 25 Americans and wounding another 113.

f. Understandably, an irate Bradley raised hell when he heard about the losses and the perpendicular bomb run. Although he knew it would be risky, Bradley reluctantly agreed to another perpendicular bomb run on July 25th because he needed the bombing effort to facilitate his breakout. Unfortunately, more bombs were dropped short in that attack, killing another 111 Americans and wounding 490 more.

2. Leigh-Mallory and his staff (which included Americans) committed a fundamental error when they allowed General Bradley to finalize his plan without the advice of the 8th Air Force heavy bomber experts. The experts would have pointed out the problems and trade-offs could have been made, which would have greatly reduced the risk to friendly forces while accomplishing Bradley's objective.

a. There was nothing scientific or magic about using 1600 heavy bombers; that just happened to be the maximum number the 8th AF could put up at the time

b. To survive *Luftwaffe* fighter attacks during daylight hours in the "high threat area" over Germany, the 8th AF had to employ their bombers using 21 aircraft formations. This allowed for maximum firepower against German fighters while permitting essential en route maneuverability. To maintain their mutual firepower protection, the 21 bombers had to release their bombs on a signal from the lead bombardier. But because the formation was approximately a half-mile wide, even a perfect run by the lead bombardier still produced a 2000-to-3000 foot error for some bombs.

c.　Saint-Lo was not in the "high threat area" and a smaller formation could and should have been employed, which would have improved bombing accuracy. Improved accuracy would have reduced the number of bombers needed to do the job and permitted a bomb run parallel to General Bradley's troop line. Had the heavy bomber experts been consulted during the initial planning stage, they would have had time to make such an analysis and institute the obvious changes in tactics.

3.　General Spaatz, as the senior American airman in Europe, should have made the strategic bomber's position clear at the July 19th meeting and demanded that the problems be resolved before the mission was flown. American lives were at stake and it was time to ruffle wool. Spaatz admitted later that the perpendicular bomb run was a mistake.

4.　Despite General Bradley's legitimate anger and sadness over the two tragic losses, he wrote to Eisenhower a few days after his breakout and said, "This operation could not have been the success it has been without the close cooperation of the Air..."

£££

I.　Jet Development

1.　In 1935, three completely independent jet engine design efforts began in England, Germany and the US. But the capable and more determined Germans, using a jet engine developed by Pabst von Ohain, demonstrated a clear lead in 1939 by flying the world's first jet aircraft, the Heinkle 178. An Italian jet flew in August 1940 and the British Gloster E28/39 jet with Frank Whittle's engine made its first flight on May 15, 1941.

2.　An American, Vladimir Pavlecka, submitted his 1935 engineering proposal for a jet engine to Douglas Aircraft Corporation. Douglas sent the proposal to Pratt & Whitney, who consulted with MIT. Neither of them believed the engine would work, nor did they see a need for jet engines. Even after the Europeans had proven the feasibility of jets, the US Army Air Forces and the Navy didn't see a need for jet aircraft. The Navy was afraid jets would burn the wooden decks of their aircraft carriers. The Army Air Force staff was struggling to get enough money for thirteen B-17's couldn't be bothered with "pipe dreams" and rejected jets without checking with the boss.

a.　In June 1941, General "Hap" Arnold watched the RAF Gloster E28/39 fly. He immediately planted shoe leather in the right spots and got the US effort off the ground. Arnold obtained a couple of British Whittle jet engines, along with British technical data, then saw to it that development contracts were awarded. Bell Aircraft built the P-59 which made its first flight on October I, 1942, but it was under-powered and didn't perform much better than propeller aircraft.

b. Lockheed got a contract in June 1943. In just 145 days, they built and flew their new P-80A on January 8, 1944. It reached a speed of 500 mph, a little less than the British Meteor and Germany's ME-262.

c. In 1944, after Spaatz expressed fear that ME-262's might soon be employed in mass, General Arnold assigned top priority to P-80 production. But the first 500 P-80's delivered until the end of 1945, with 3000 more scheduled for 1946. When the war ended, production schedules changed, but eventually 1731 P-80's were produced.

£££

J. *Der Dummkopf* Goofs Again
   I. In August 1940, after the bloodless victories and lightning *Blitzkriegs*, Hitler envisioned a short war and put a stop order on all research and development projects requiring more than 18 months to complete. Ernst Udet, Chief of Air Supply for the *Luftwaffe*, ignored the order, but the pace of the program became slower.

   2. Several jet fighters were eventually developed, but the *Luftwaffe* selected the ME-262. It first flew on July 18, 1942, setting a record-breaking 530-mph without a problem. The next ten flights were nearly trouble free and each flight reached speeds of 530 mph. The Messerschmitt test pilot and engineers were convinced it was ready for production. But in August, a military test pilot crashed on takeoff, which delayed the program for several months.

      a. General Galland flew the ME-262 in May 1943 as part of an effort to gain Hitler's approval for production. Galland immediately saw the ME-262's superior performance as the solution to both the shortage of pilots and fuel. Since jet engines could burn most fuels, from low-grade kerosene to aviation gas, jets would have eased the fuel shortage problem. Due to the ME-262's superior performance, fewer pilots would have been needed to do the job. A relatively small number of jets (300 to 500) could have raised havoc with all Allied air and ground operations. Galland said, "I would rather have one ME-262 than five ME-109's." He recommended building 100 immediately for tactical tests and starting mass production as soon as possible. Everyone agreed. Production could have started within six months at a rate of 60 aircraft per month, quickly increasing to 200 per month. But the mulish *Dummkopf* demanded more tests.

3. Albert Speer, one of Hitler's closest henchmen, said that in September 1943 Hitler arbitrarily ordered a halt to preparations for large-scale production of the ME-262. Then on January 7, 1944, after hearing about British experiments with jet aircraft, Hitler flip-flopped and ordered immediate production of as many ME-262's as could be built. BUT, he demanded the ME-262 be modified and used as a bomber.

4. Changing the world's greatest fighter into a Band-Aid bomber delayed the ME-262's entry into combat again. The delay occurred at a time when the ME-262 offered Germany its only real defense against Allied bombing attacks and the invasion. While the first 125 ME-262's sat on the factory ramp undergoing *der dummkopf's* "Blitz Bomber" modifications, about half were destroyed by 8th AF bombers. Attempts to use the ME-262 as a bomber were nonevents. Finally in March 1945, in one of his many mood swings, Hitler ordered that all ME-262 fighter-bombers be converted immediately to fighters.

5. ME-262's first attacked two RAF Mosquito fighters in July 1944. The same month, two American P-51 pilots were attacked by a ME-262 near Munich. In September, formations of ME-262's taunted the US strategic bombers and fighters. Although they never attacked, their superior performance struck a chord of fear in Generals Spaatz and Doolittle.

6. Some pundits considered the V-2 rocket as Germany's only WWII weapon of the first magnitude, but the ME-262 was the only weapon that could have made an impact on the war. Without Hitler's no-brain decisions, the ME-262 could have easily entered combat before the spring of 1944. Even with Hitler's interference, the Germans still produced more than 1400 ME-262's, 500 of which were built in 1944. Several hundred ME-262's would have challenged the invasion and extended the war until the Allies produced enough jets to regain control of the sky.

£££

Student comment: If Allied political leaders had exercised the same degree of control over the military during WWII as Hitler did, the war might have ended in a stalemate.

£££

K. Summer and Fall 1944

    I. By D-Day, Spaatz's oil attacks had reduced German oil production to 23% of its capacity and gasoline production had dropped to 19-20%, resulting in severe fuel shortages. At Caen, during Montgomery's failed assaults, German tanks were stranded, unable to move due to the lack of fuel. At the Saint-Lo breakout and during their sweep across France, the Americans encountered thousands of abandoned tanks and military vehicles that had run out of fuel.

        a. Intercepted German communications reflected the Nazis' concern about the oil strikes. Speer was promised, but never received, 2000 *Luftwaffe* fighters to protect the oil industry. But he was given another 200,000 people to help repair the bomb damage inflicted on the oil refineries and synthetic fuel plants.

    2. Throughout the summer and fall of 1944, the 8th AF devoted much of its bombing effort attacking missile sites, airfields, bridges, and railroads, and hauling urgently needed gas and supplies to the ground forces. From August 29 through September 30, 1944, 225 B-24's carried nearly three million gallons of gas and 244 tons of supplies from Britain to France.

    3. In September, Air Chief Marshal Tedder added German transportation targets (rail lines, marshaling yards, canals and barges) to the strategic target list. Tedder correctly reasoned that, unlike the French railroads where the *Wehrmacht* needed only 20% of the rail capacity, the loss of transportation facilities in Germany would ultimately choke the life out of the country's industry, just as Spaatz's oil attacks had strangled much of the German war machine.

£££

L. The Ho-Hum Air War?

£££

Student comments: My research of the air in Europe (France and Germany) revealed that when the *Luftwaffe* failed to appear on D-Day, many historians adopted the attitude that the air war had all but ended and gave it the ho-hum treatment. But the Army Air Forces attacks to destroy the Nazi war machine at its source and to support our ground forces raged on at an even more rapid pace and American airmen continued to suffer very high losses.

£££

    I. Army Air Forces in Europe lost 7272 aircraft before D-Day compared to 11,246 lost after D-Day. Monthly losses remained high up to the very end and 825 aircraft were lost in April 1945.

2. B-17 and B-24 attrition remained high and accounted for nearly 62% of the 11,246 losses. In July 1944, the 15th AF lost more men than the entire ground forces fighting in the Mediterranean. RAF Bomber Command losses exceeded those of the entire British Second Army in July. The *Luftwaffe* also suffered from the intense fighting. It lost 13,000 airmen in the five months, June-October 1944, as compared to the 31,000 lost in the previous four years. Many of the German losses occurred while attacking 8th and 15th AF strategic bombers and fighters.

3 When the Luftwaffe lost some of its defensive sting, Germany quickly doubled its AAA force to more than 300,000 people. By late 1944, more than 2,000,000 German soldiers and civilians, plus thousands of prisoners from occupied countries were forced to help man the Nazi's AAA defenses.

   a. The Germans also added 135-mm cannons to their arsenal of 88 mm and other smaller caliber cannons. Radar modifications allowed the Germans to detect and track the bomber's H2X radar, which improved kill capability in bad weather. Proximity fuses and electronic sensors that detonated shells when they came within 140 feet of aircraft also improved their kill capability.

4. High AAA losses proved that air-to-air combat is not always the best gauge for determining the intensity of aerial warfare—a fact that every airman that humped bombs in the air-to-mud mode knew all too well. For example, the 8th AF fighter losses jumped five times higher when they began strafing in early 1944. The invasion of Europe did not end the air war against Germany.

£££

M. *Luftwaffe* Gets a Temporary Boost
   1. In September 1944, General Galland finally got approval to rebuild his fighter forces, but he was not told the reason why. He eventually generated a force of about 2500 ME-109's and FW-190's, but had only a five-day supply of fuel. Since he believed his primary mission would be the air defense of Germany, he used some of his precious fuel to give his minimally trained pilots a scant 15 hours of air-to-air combat training.
   2. Galland planned to attack the 8th AF bombers with 1000 fighters

the first time the Americans struck a deep target with a large force in good weather. He hoped to destroy 400-500 bombers at a cost of no more than 400 of his fighters and 150 pilots. While waiting to launch his "Great Blow," Galland attacked a number of times with up to 200 fighters and several times he launched about 500 fighters.

3. But Galland's plans for a massive attack got scrubbed in late November 1944 when he was ordered to send the bulk of his fighters to the Western Front for Hitler's counteroffensive, The Battle of the Bulge.

£££

N. The Battle of The Bulge (Surprise?)

1. While the Allies looked for a knockout blow, *Wehrmacht* forces and equipment were being repositioned for Hitler's counteroffensive. Although bad weather hampered flying, 9th AF flew more than 500 aerial reconnaissance missions during the 30-day period preceding the German attack. Aerial photos and visual reconnaissance on nearly every mission confirmed the ever increasing and widespread movement of trains, tanks, trucks, supplies and troops toward the west and the Ardennes. Ground intelligence also confirmed German activity closer to the frontlines. Yet, when General Eisenhower's operations officer briefed the air commanders about the ground situation in the Ardennes on December 15th, the briefer said, "Nothing to report."

a. It has been suggested that many believed the German activity was posturing in anticipation of the Allied offensive. But such extensive German deployments should have triggered increased security by any prudent commander.

2. In the early morning darkness of December 16th, strong German forces attacked in the lightly defended Ardennes. Eisenhower and Bradley scrambled to reinforce the surprised and badly outnumbered troops.

a. Slow-motion Montgomery, smarting from his recent airborne debacle in Holland, but still harboring visions of being "The Grand Ground Commander," sat on his administrative tail, did an in-place wiggle and waggle, then demonstrated what was probably his strongest forte—a verbal hatchet job on Eisenhower and Bradley.

3. The Nazi breakthrough and the ground fighting that followed has been thoroughly documented. But little mention has been made of air power's contribution before and during The Battle of The Bulge.

£££

O. Battle of The Bulge (Behind The Scenes)

    I. The Battle of the Bulge shattered Allied confidence. But had the Allies been decrypting the thousands of Nazi commercial messages that were available to them, they would have learned that Spaatz's oil offensive and three months of relentless air attacks on Germany's transportation system had nearly choked the life out of Germany's industry. Overall industrial production had dropped to about 25% of normal.

        a. Because marshaling yards could be detected by radar, the B-17's and B-24's could strike them in bad weather. These continuous attacks had made it impossible for railroad repair crews to keep up and by December 1944, about 2000 locomotives and nearly 100,000 rail cars stood idle. Consequently, more than 70% of all rail shipments had stopped.

        b. Because of the drastic reduction in transportation, coal supplies fell to less than 25% of normal (eventually, Germany suffered a coal famine). Iron ore deliveries to the smelters were only 20% of normal. Due to the lack of coal and iron ore, iron and steel production had tumbled to 30% of normal. Some critical areas had completely stopped. For example, the ball bearing industry had collapsed.

        c. Monthly tank production had dropped from 114 to 65; the supply of rifles went from ten days to three; the level of assault rifles slid from four months to three weeks; stocks of 88mm cannon shells fell from a month to two weeks. Poor distribution caused shortages to some German units and many commanders had to fight with a strict hand-to-mouth rationing system, which forced them to limit their firepower.

    2. Because oil and gasoline production had been reduced to about 20% of normal, an important part of The Battle of the Bulge included capturing Allied fuel supplies to sustain the German drive. When they failed to do so, a lack of fuel forced the *Wehrmacht* to abandon fighting vehicles by the hundreds.

        a. As an important aside, Spaatz's oil attacks also contributed to the success of the Russian winter offensive. At one bridgehead in Silesia, 1200 German tanks were immobilized due to a lack of fuel and the Russians overran the tanks. Stalin later admitted that the Spaatz's oil campaign played an important part in the success of the Russian winter offensive.

    3. Although airpower's direct contribution to the ground battle is seldom mentioned by historians, the following should be noted. Dur-

ing The Battle of the Bulge, Allied Air claimed the destruction of 11,378 motor transport vehicles, 1161 tanks and armored vehicles, 507 locomotives and 6266 rail cars. They also eliminated 472 gun positions, made 974 rail and 421 road cuts, knocked down 36 bridges and dropped supplies to Allied ground forces.

4.   Airpower critics say the claims are high and its contribution was minimal at best. But General Omar Bradley reported that "Field Marshal Gerd von Rundstedt, the commander of the attack at the Bulge, stated] that the main reason for the failure of the Ardennes offensive was his own lack of fighters and reconnaissance planes and the tremendous tactical airpower of the Allies." Bradley also learned after the Bulge that the 9th SS Panzer Division had to delay its attack on Liege, Belgium after a single Army Air Force fighter-bomber blew up a fuel truck carrying three tons of gasoline, delaying the overall German advance for two days. "German General Hasso von Mateuffel, Fifth Panzer Army commander at the Battle of the Bulge wrote, "Allied air forces found worthwhile targets throughout the whole area of our offensive. Bomb carpets were laid down on roads and railways behind the front, and our already inadequate supply system was throttled. The mobility of our forces decreased steadily and rapidly." German Major General F.W. von Mellenthin, chief of staff of the Fifth Panzer Army during the Bulge, said, "The Ardennes battle drives home the lesson that a large-scale offensive by massed armor has no hope of success against an enemy who enjoys supreme command of the air." After the war, Bradley said in reference to the interviews of German ground forces, "From the high command to the soldier in the field, German opinion has been agreed that airpower was the most striking aspect of the Allied superiority."

£££

P.   The Bulge and The *Luftwaffe*
1.   Weather permitting, the *Luftwaffe* normally launched 100 to 150 aircraft during The Battle of the Bulge. Its largest strike came on January 1, 1945, when more than 800 aircraft made a daring low-level attack against Allied airfields on the Continent. The raid cost the RAF 160 aircraft and the US 36, most of which were destroyed on the ground. But the *Luftwaffe* also lost 220 aircraft—its worst day of the war. In three weeks during "The Bulge," the it lost nearly 600 aircraft.
a. For many Allied ground forces, The Battle of the Bulge was their first and only encounter with the *Luftwaffe*. As a result, nervous Allied ground gunners sometimes shot at all aircraft and a num-

ber of RAF and American aircraft, including one of the 8th AF's leading aces, Major George Preddy, was shot down by friendly fire.

2. On January 12th, the German high command decided to move many of the *Luftwaffe* aircraft from the Western to the Eastern Front to help counter the Russian's winter offensive. From then on, German aircraft on the Western Front were restricted from flying over enemy territory or attacking the bombers except under the most favorable conditions.

£££

Q . ME-262

I. General Galland eventually fell out of favor with Goering. In December 1944, Galland was relieved of his command and put under house arrest. Later, Hitler allowed Galland to recruit top-notch pilots and form a ME-262 fighter squadron. A month later, more than 20 of Galland's jets zoomed in and shot down 12 heavy bombers without being touched by 8th AF escort fighters.

2. The January jet attack came on the heels of an intelligence report that estimated 400 ME-262's could be operational by April. A nervous Spaatz immediately got Eisenhower to move jet targets higher on the bombing list. Because much of the jet industry had dispersed or moved underground, Spaatz decided to attack jet engine facilities and operational jet fields. He also increased the number of escort fighters for bombers striking targets within range of the ME-262's.

3. Galland's squadron shot down 14 bombers in February and another 63 in March. His ME-262's knocked down their last two 15th AF bombers on March 24th. On April 17th, some 8th AF fighters followed the jets back to their airfields and shot them down in the landing pattern, strafing others on the runway or in parking revetments.

    a. The last jet attack against the 8th AF occurred on April 20th. On April 26, General Galland led the last significant jet attack against the 9th AF when his jets shot down six B-26's. Galland destroyed one B-26, but minutes later his jet was badly damaged by Ist Lt. James J. Finnegan in a P-47. Wounded, Galland crash-landed and narrowly escaped death.

4. Those airmen who encountered the ME-262's learned firsthand the potential of jet aircraft. They didn't need a high-powered study to tell them what a force of 400 ME-262's would have done to Allied air and ground forces a year earlier. Thanks to Adolf, *der dummkopf*, it never happened.

£££

R. The End

  1. By February 1945, German industry and transportation was in near paralysis. The *Wehrmacht was retreating so fast that the Luftwaffe* had to scramble from airfield to airfield to remain ahead of the tidal wave of Allied ground forces. Eventually, many *Luftwaffe* aircraft had to be hidden in the woods and flown from the *Autobahn.*

  2. By April, many of the *Wehrmacht* began surrendering. On one occasion, two flights of P-47's (eight aircraft) from the 9th AF strafed a convoy until Germans waved white flags. The P-47's continued to circle the Germans and called for American ground forces to take charge of the Air Force's prisoners.

  3. The 8th AF flew its last strategic bombing mission on April 25, 1945 when 589 bombers struck the Skoda arms plant and airfields at Pilsen, Czechoslovakia. Six bombers were shot down and four more were damaged beyond repair. The same day, the 15th AF sent 519 bombers to Linz and lost 15. The 15th AF flew one more mission the next day and bombed targets near the Austrian Alps.

£££

S. More Stats

  1. When the US Army Air Force (USAAF) and RAF reached their full strength in Europe and the Mediterranean, they numbered more than 1,300,000 and had 28,000 aircraft.

  2. As has been mentioned before, one of the most startling facts that I discovered during my research was the number of USAAF airmen killed while fighting the Germans. It warrants repeating. There were 41,802 airmen killed from a force that never exceeded 100,000 pilots, navigators, bombardiers and aerial gunners, versus the 36,950 Naval personnel that died from a force of 3,380,817 and the 19,733 Marines who lost their lives out of a force of 475,604.

£££

T. United States Strategic Bombing Study (USSBS)

  1. In April 1944, Generals Spaatz and Arnold took action to form a team of unimpeachable experts to evaluate the Army Air Forces' bombing effort in Europe. Eventually it became a National effort and on September 1944, a team of high-powered civilians, along with Army, Navy and Air Force representatives was approved by President Roosevelt to evaluate the European bombing effort.

  2. The USSBS stated, "...Its (Allied air) power and superiority made possible the success of the invasion. It brought the economy which

sustained the enemy's armed forces to virtual collapse although the full effects of this collapse had not yet reached the enemy's front lines when they were overrun by Allied forces... By the beginning of 1945, before the invasion of the homeland itself, Germany was approaching a state of helplessness. Her armament production was falling irretrievably, orderliness in effort was disappearing, and total disruption and disintegration were well along. Her armies were still in the field. But with the impending collapse of the supporting economy, the indications are convincing that they would have had to cease fighting—any effective fighting—within a few months."

a.   Field Marshal Herman Goring, Grand Admiral Karl Doenitz, other senior military commanders and German industrial giants believed Allied air to be the decisive factor in Germany's defeat.

b.   The report found that by 1944 Germany had two million soldiers, civilians and prisoners manning and maintaining the ground AAA defense force against air attacks—people who were urgently needed in the frontlines and elsewhere.

3.   The bombing report also stated that 72% of the bombs dropped on Germany were dropped after July I, 1944 when Allied air power reached its full strength. This fact makes one wonder how many Allied soldiers would have been spared if the strategic bombing forces had reached full strength sooner. At the very least, it makes a case for preparedness.

4.   While assessing the bomb damage, the report rightly pointed out the large number of bombs that missed their targets, something Air Force critics are quick to cite. But if the hits and misses were ever tallied for the cannon, rifle and machine gun fire of the land and sea forces—the miss columns would make the World War II Army Air Forces look like worlds greatest sharpshooters.

5.   The report included an estimate of the number of German civilians killed by Allied air forces during WWII, which some say was an ugly display of brute force. But we had a powerful weapon system, which even in its infancy could make a major contribution to the war effort. We could either use it to its fullest and save Allied lives, or restrict its use and save the lives of the enemy. I suspect all the ground forces in Europe, as well as the people in nations occupied by the ruthless Nazis and the Jews awaiting execution in the Nazi gas chambers, fully supported the massive strategic bombing effort.

£££

U. Now What?

1. During WWII, urgent military requirements caused the technological genie to burst from its bottle. From now on, technology will revolutionize the military and all of civilization at a breathtaking pace. So-called backward countries can become major threats to world peace in a matter of a few years. Since our ability to predict the time, location, and intensity of the next war is zero, we must remain strong. Only a continuing US military research and development effort will provide superior aircraft and weapons for a first rate air force.

2. The one thing we can predict with 100% accuracy is—that if we don't maintain a high level of preparedness, our military will become an obsolete relic, just as it was before WWI, WWII and the Korean conflict.

3. Unfortunately, Americans have notoriously short memories and a propensity for living in a dream world, a recipe for repeating past mistakes.

CHAPTER 17

One Pass and Haul Ass

"Sunshine, Shotgun here. I just crossed the coastline with Bugeye Red and I'm countin' for a steer. One, two, three, four, five, five, four, three, two, one. Over to you, Sunshine," the Colonel transmitted. Looking into the late afternoon sun through the thick haze made it impossible to see the water in front of him. He had to look straight down or behind to see it.

"Sunshine here. Steer 317," the tower replied.

"Shotgun's steerin' 317 and levelin' at 1000 feet with Bugeye Red. Yellow and White are in trail with one-mile spacin' between flights. Snapper and Hot Rod are several miles behind Bugeye."

The Colonel was tired and he knew his pilots were exhausted after playing five hours of high-speed chicken in the clouds and contrails with 1200 aircraft. Low clouds and thick haze had kept them from strafing and his group hadn't lost a single P-51 today. Yesterday had been a bad day; he had lost two pilots from Bugeye and the 8th Air Force had lost 64 B-17's and B-24's—the bombers' second worst day of the war. More than anything, he wanted get everyone back safely today.

"Shotgun just passed the railroad." He watched the Colchester-Ipswich railroad pass beneath him. The haze seemed thicker over land as he started looking for the A-12 highway that ran just east of the field. "Shotgun, here. Give me a call when you see us, Sunshine."

"Sunshine has Shotgun in sight. You're about a mile out and look like you're lined up with the runway."

"Shotgun, rog. I'm crossin' the A-12, got the end of the runway."

"Sunshine, roger. Shotgun, you're cleared to land with Bugeye."

"Shotgun, here. Guys, I'm gonna bend it around to keep the field in sight. So stay close to me. Shotgun on the break."

The Colonel snapped the throttle to idle, flipped his 51 into a vertical bank and made a tight descending turn, while lowering his landing gear and flaps. The thick haze worried him, because vertigo was a real threat in this steep landing pattern. After 360 degrees of turn, he rolled his 51's wings level over the end of the runway and touched down. He let his 51 roll to the far end and turned onto the taxiway. Looking down sun, he could see one flight on the landing roll and another in the pattern. "Get 'em all on the ground in one piece. Sure's as hell don't wanna lose any in the damned landin' pattern," he whispered to himself.

In the parking revetment, he swung his 51 around and cut the engine. He jumped out of the cockpit and stood on the wing to watch Snapper and Rod Rod land. The crew chief placed the Colonel's flight gear in the back seat of the staff car and started the car's engine.

When the last flight in Hot Rod landed, the Colonel got off the wing and climbed into the car. Although it was April 12th, a penetrating winter chill was still in the air and the car heater felt good as he pulled onto the taxiway and drove toward operations.

Major Hunt and Charlie were waiting in the Colonel's outer office. When they heard the Colonel's car stop in front, they both got to their feet and Charlie opened the door.

"Thanks Charlie. What's up, Bob?" the Colonel asked Major Hunt, noticing the STARS and STRIPES in his hand.

"Sir, you'd better be sitting when you read this."

"Come on in. Let's have a drink first," the Colonel replied leading Major Hunt into his office. Charlie poured coffee into the large cup and followed them inside. He placed the half-filled cup on the Colonel's desk and turned on the lamp.

The Colonel took a bottle of Red Label and two glasses from the bottom drawer. He poured three fingers of Scotch into the glasses then filled his coffee cup and put the Red Label back in the drawer. "Lousy weather. Been a helluva long day." The Colonel raised his cup and nodded.

The Colonel and Major Hunt took big drinks and Charlie downed his.

"May I get you anything else, sir?" Charlie asked, holding his empty glass.

"Nothing right now, Charlie, thanks." Charlie did an about face and walked out, closing the door behind him.

"Sir, you won't believe this." Major Hunt handed him the STARS and STRIPES. "Look at that God damned headline."

£££

RAF AIR VICE-MARSHAL SAYS
LUFTWAFFE STRONGER TODAY
THAN FIVE MONTHS AGO

£££

(London, April 12) Air Vice-Marshal Richard Peck, public information deputy for the RAF said, "Since November 1943, the *Luftwaffe* fighter strength, assigned for the protection of the Reich, has increased by 200 to 300 machines."

He also stated, "The onslaught against the German Air Force on the ground and in the air has certainly succeeded in reducing the reinforcement of the enemy's air defenses to a point far below what we had planned. But it has not prevented some continued strengthening...."

Peck went on to say the reason for the *Luftwaffe's* reduced opposition in recent months had been the bad weather....

£££

The Colonel slammed the paper onto the desk. "That limey asshole! Son of a bitch doesn't know shit from Shinola. His stupid press release will rip our fragile morale and damage the credibility of our American air effort."

"Sir, that story makes me wonder what the RAF's motive could be," Major Hunt said.

"I'm wonderin' the same thing. Makin' that statement after the losses we suffered yesterday is either plain stupid or calculated." The Colonel took another big sip and stared across the room. "Even if it were true, and it ain't, there's absolutely nothin' to be gained by sayin' it publicly at this time...unless they're tryin' to make us look bad. And they've given us plenty of reasons to believe that might be the case. Bob, have we gotten any word outta higher headquarters on this?"

"Nothing officially so far. But my contacts at 8th tell me that Generals Spaatz and Doolittle are really pissed off. They told me that General Spaatz is going to bring the US ambassador in on it, hoping he'll bring it up to Churchill."

"Bob, I wanta move fast on this. Try and nip it in the bud. Let's get all the jocks together in the group briefin' room in an hour. Tell 'em I'm sorry to bother them, but that I need to talk about this bloke press release. Maybe that'll keep 'em from being too pissed off about being called out after a long mission."

"Yes sir. I'll get the word out right away."

An hour later the pilots were assembled in the group briefing room. Every seat had been taken by the time Robb and Rocko arrived, and they joined others that were standing next to the wall.

"That frickin' limey air marshal's dumb-ass remarks are gonna interfere with my sumbitchin' sex life tonight," Rocko growled as they waited.

"I don't think the Colonel will keep us that long," Robb said with a smile.

"HOFFICERS, TEN--SHUN!" They all jumped to their feet.

"Please be seated, guys," the Colonel said walking down the aisle. He stepped onto the platform and took the cue stick. "Gents, I apologize for callin' you out, because I know that you are all tired after today's mission. I thought that the RAF news release today might have raised a question or two...or even planted some seeds of doubt about our air effort.

"When that bloke air marshal said the *Luftwaffe* had increased the number of their machines in the past five months, I guess he meant trucks and staff cars." The Colonel paused and smiled and most of the pilots smiled back.

"Those of us who have been goin' to Germany in broad daylight, and kickin' the shit outta the *Luftwaffe*, know that since the Big Week the krauts have not been comin' up to fight as often or with as many fighters. There has to be a reason or reasons for their reduced activity. The bloke air marshal says it's the bad weather. I've been fightin' the krauts for over four years and bad weather has never scared them before. If we can fly in it, so can they.

"It's easy for intelligence types to hang their hats on hardware counts when guesstimating capabilities of an enemy. In that regard, let's assume that the bloke air marshal has pictures of more airplanes sittin' on the ground than there were a few months ago. That might indicate that the Nazis are producin' aircraft faster than we've been shootin' em down. And that could very well be the case.

"But we're encounterin' fewer kraut fighters and more and more of the ones we tangle with are being flown by green beans. That tells me that the experienced krauts we shoot down are gettin' killed or wounded and taken out of action. My guess is the *Luftwaffe* can't train enough pilots to keep up with their losses. Anyone who has strapped a fighter to his ass for more than two semesters knows that it takes a helluva lot longer to train a pilot than it does to build a production line airplane. So all of those fighters sittin' on the ramp at the aircraft factories don't add a thing to the *Luftwaffe's* ability to defend Germany.

"I'm here to tell you that we're kickin' the shit out of the *Luftwaffe*. We are eliminatin' fighter pilots faster than they can train new ones. In addition, I'm convinced that the quality and numbers of Luftwaffe pilots will really take a nosedive when General Spaatz's campaign to destroy Germany's oil industry kicks in. Fuel shortages will force the *Luftwaffe* to train fewer pilots and give them even less flyin' time than they're gettin' now. It's as simple as that.

"For that bloke air marshal to conclude the *Luftwaffe* has gotten stronger—based solely on an aircraft ground count—is dumber than hell. The RAF also used piss poor judgement by releasin' that idiotic machine count crap to the press while we're fightin' the fiercest air battles the world will ever see. Makes me wonder what the limey bastards are up to.

"I'd suggest that the bloke air marshal smarten up and save his wild assed guesses for his chums durin' high tea at Whitehall. Or better yet, he should look for another line of work.

"Any questions, guys, on what I said or about the RAF news release or anything else?" the Colonel asked.

"You hit the frickin' nail on the sumbitchin' head, Colonel. If that frickin' bloke air marshal had two more ounces of brains, he'd have exactly two ounces."

"Thank you, Rocko, for that ringin' endorsement," the Colonel smiled. "Any other question or comments?" There were none. "Okay guys, we already have an alert order for a mission tomorrow, so let's get a good night's sleep. Thanks again for your time. See ya in the mornin.'"

Back in the office, the Colonel signed the stack of papers that Charlie had waiting, then headed for his staff car. He was exhausted and really wanted to go to his hut and get some sleep, but he had to make his tour of the flightline to see his troops. He pulled on to the taxiway and drove toward the aircraft parking revetments. Too tired to talk, he drove slowly past each of them. Busy aircraft maintenance men with greasy faces and hands looked up from their P-51's and waved as he passed. The Colonel waved back and whispered, "God, how I love those guys."

On April 13, the 8th AF sent 566 B-17's and B-24's to attack the Messerschmitt plant at Augsberg and other German industrial sites, while 500 bombers from the 15th AF attacked Hungarian targets. The 8th AF lost another 38 bombers to AAA and fighters.

The next day poor weather held them on the ground and the Colonel spent the morning visiting the fighter squadrons. Since his talk, only four pilots had questioned their squadron commanders about the effectiveness of the American air campaign. But the Colonel heard that the RAF release had created a ground swell of questions and complaints from the bomber crews. General Spaatz and Doolittle, along with every bomber commander had to devote an inordinate amount of time countering the RAF new release.

That night the Colonel stretched out on his bunk to reread Ernest Hemingway's *A Farewell to Arms*. After only two pages, his phone rang. It was Major Hunt.

"Sir, tomorrow the weather will be too bad for high altitude bombing, but good enough to get fighters in below it. So General Spaatz is sending 530 8th AF fighters and 86 fighters from the 9th AF to conduct low altitude fighter sweeps over central and western Germany to strafe Luftwaffe airfields. Our group has been tasked to strafe nine heavily defended fields."

"Only nine. Ain't that lovely. Wonder how we got so damned lucky?" He had trouble going to sleep because he knew that even if his group did everything right, they would still suffer high losses.

£££

"Time to get up, gentlemen," the duty sergeant said as he turned on the dim overhead light.

Robb shaded his eyes and squinted at his watch. It was 5:30. "Shit! I was hoping we'd get another day off." Replacement pilots hadn't kept pace with the group's losses and Robb's flight had flown six combat missions in the past seven days. Even after a day off, he was too tired to feel anxious about today's mission. His mind was numb and he didn't give a shit.

"Sumbitch…one day off and we're back in the saddle. When the hell are we gonna get our replacement pilots? If I don't get down to London soon, my ho's gonna dump me for some frickin' gooney bird pilot or bombardier." Rocko grabbed a sock, stretched it between his big and second toe on his right foot and pulled it back and forth.

Robb stood and stretched then gently rubbed the cheeks of his butt. They felt like they had been pounded with a rivet gun. He noticed Rocko pulling the sock back and forth between his toes. "What the hell are you doing?"

"Gotta little athlete's foot. Ain't even a frickin' jockstrap."

"Why don't you use that GI foot powder?"

"Scratchin' feels too damned good. Takes my mind off my sore ass," Rocko grunted before starting on the left foot. When he was finished he tossed the sock on top of the pile of dirty clothes on the floor. Then he grabbed his duffel bag and emptied more dirty clothes onto his bunk. He rummaged through them and pulled out a wrinkled pair of long johns and two more gray wool socks, then stuffed the dirty clothes back into the bag.

"What the hell are you doin' now?" Robb asked as Rocko exchanged one set of dirty underwear for another.

"Flyin' every frickin' day, haven't had time to get my laundry done. Wearin' everything twice. When I finish, I'll take 'em to Madeline's full service laundry in Colchester and get 'em washed while I get laid."

Robb shook his head, grabbed his towel, toothbrush and Ipana toothpaste and walked to the door. As he opened it, he could hear the roar of a P-51's Merlin engine and the crack of 50-caliber machine guns firing at the boresight target. "Let's get goin', Rocko."

"I'm comin', *amigo*."

£££

The Colonel sat at his desk and munched on his Spam sandwich. After a few hours of fitful sleep, he had awakened wondering what he would say to his pilots about the day's high-risk mission. He recalled the group's first combat mission when they were outnumbered five to one. That morning he had tried to instill confidence and stimulate aggressiveness. But today he had to tell them to control their aggressiveness—to think smart and get the job done without being shot down.

The Colonel took another small bite, washed it down with coffee and looked at his watch. It was time to go. He pushed his coffee cup to one side and threw the rest of his Spam sandwich into the wastebasket and left his office. As he approached the briefing room, he sucked in his gut and walked briskly inside and down the aisle.

THE HELLISH VORTEX

"HOFFICERS, TEN—SHUN!" the adjutant bellowed.

"Sumbitchin' adj is gonna ruin my frickin' hearin' with all that yellin.'"

"Please be seated," the Colonel said hopping onto the platform and picking up the cue stick. "Gents, the weather's too bad for the bombers, but we can get in below it. We're gonna take a page outta General "Jeb" Stuart's tactics manual. We're gonna zip across the North Sea at six grand with our 36 Mustangos and hit the deck at the Dutch coast. Our nine flights will then split and go deep inside Germany to whack the bushes around nine airpatches.

"Sounds like fun, because we all enjoy buzzin.' But strafin' airfields is risky business. So we've gotta keep our heads out and fly smart or we could get tagged and end up in one of *Der Fuhrer's* hog-wallows. Stormy, lay some weather on us."

"Sir," Captain Knight said, taking the cue stick. "A reconnaissance pilot reported a thick layer of clouds covering much of the Continent, with a few breaks along the coast of Holland. By the time you get to Germany, the ceiling will be around 2000 feet and the visibility will be about three to four miles...." Captain Knight finished and handed the cue stick to Major Watson.

"Each flight has been provided a photograph of the airfield it's attacking," Major Watson said, taking the cue stick. "From the photos you'll see that most airfields contain several kinds of aircraft. But the ME-109's and FW-190's are first priority....

"Although parts of Germany are beginning to look like a wasteland from the bombings, these airfields are real hot spots with a lot of sting. Many of them are defended by at least 20 to 30 AAA cannons, numerous automatic weapons and everyone is armed with a rifle or handgun. It's been estimated that some *Luftwaffe* airfields now have more guns per square mile than any place in Germany."

"Sumbitch. Ain't that peachy keen."

Major Watson glared at Rocko and handed the cue stick to Major Hunt.

"Guys, I do have some good news. We'll have 620 fighters attacking Germany from many directions. That combined with the fact that we'll be operating below most of the kraut radar should help keep the *Luftwaffe* and German radar operators confused. One other thing, we won't be carrying external tanks, so we can scoot along a little faster.

"We'll cross the North Sea at about six grand and let down near the coast of Holland. Our route'll take us 18 miles north of Amsterdam, then across the Zuider Zee to the inlet near Kampen. There we'll split the group and let down to 500 feet. Bugeye's three flights will swing northeast toward their three airfields. Snapper will head east toward their three fields and the Colonel will swing southeast with Hot Rod's three flights toward their three fields...."

Major Hunt finished and turned toward the Colonel. "Sir."

"Gents, as Major Watson said, many of the airpatches have *beaucoup* AAA cannons. But if you hug the deck on your attack, the big guns can't fire at you without hittin' some krauts on the other side of the field. The real threat will be small arms fire. Every kraut swinger on the patch will have a machine gun, rifle or *pistole*. If they know you're comin,' they'll fill the sky in front of you with lead and you'll have to fly through it.

"So gents, unlike air-to-air combat where flyin' ability and aggressiveness count, today we've gotta mentally shift gears...think like a guerrilla fighter. Sneak in low and fast...surprise 'em...hit 'em hard and get the hell out.

"With all four aircraft firin' on the attack, each flight should knock out at least two to three kraut fighters on a single pass. And 18 to 27 kraut fighters destroyed is a pretty good day's work for one group. With any luck, we could get a lot more.

"As Bob Hunt said, at Kampen, we'll let down to 500 feet, each flight will head for their airfield at 300 mph, while maintaining radio silence. At 500 feet, we'll be high enough to navigate, but low enough to stay under most radar coverage.

"From the last checkpoint to your airpatch, increase your speed to 400 mph and drop to 50 feet. That means you'll have to hit the last checkpoint on the button and hold a headin' that'll take you to the center of the field.

"Two miles from the airfield, drop to the deck. No 50-foot stuff. I mean get down and cut grass so the krauts can't see you comin.'"

Ever since Robb had learned about the mission, he had worried about navigating on the deck. His one and only "on the deck" mission had been flown 18 months ago in a P-40 at 250 mph and 100 feet. *Today we gotta dodge trees and telephone poles while cutting grass at 400 mph. If I miss the field and have to come back around, the gunners will be waiting to blow us out of the sky.*

"Gents," the Colonel continued. "Before you start your attack, wingmen move forward where you can see and be seen. If you straggle, you may pick up a chunk of lead meant for your leader.

"Durin' the attack, drag your asses across the airpatch and hose down the aircraft in front of you. You should get at least two chances to fire—once when you first cross the field boundary, and again on the other side. Don't worry about savin' ammo. Open fire a little early and walk your shells up to the bird you're shootin' at because you'll only have one chance. Once you cross the field, continue cuttin' grass until you're outta range of the kraut guns.

"When you're clear, come up for air and head for home. Don't think about circlin' the wagons and goin' for more passes. That'd be like havin' a pissin' contest with a herd of skunks...and you'll lose. No kraut aircraft on the ground is worth a pilot and P-51.

"So gents, our golden rule for today is 'one pass and haul ass.'"

"Amen, amen," Rocko grunted his agreement.

The Colonel wanted to say more, but he knew the ones that would heed his advice had heard enough. The know-it-alls would learn the hard way. He also knew that if every pilot followed his advice, some would still get shot down.

£££

Flying at 6000 feet, the Colonel led the 36 P-51's across the North Sea. Four miles short of the Dutch coast he descended through the breaks in the clouds and leveled at 1000 feet. They quickly crossed the Zuider Zee and headed for the Kampen inlet.

"Shotgun squadrons, you're on your own," the Colonel called, approaching the inlet. "Good hunting, gang." He swung southeast with Hot Rod. Bugeye turned northeast and Ted continued east with Snapper and descended.

After a few seconds, Ted leveled off at 200 feet and set course for the Mageburg airfield. Snapper White flight turned toward Brunswick and Robb set course for Zwolle, Holland, his first check point on the way to the Hanover airfield.

To maintain 300 mph, Robb set the RPM at 2500 and the throttle at 42 inches. In a few seconds his speed stabilized; he adjusted the rudder and aileron trims and checked the map on his left leg. Streaking through the sky at five miles a minute, he moved his index finger along the course line on the map and followed his flight path across the ground.

Zwolle appeared dead ahead, then shot past. Robb glanced at the aircraft clock. It had taken one minute and 55 seconds to fly the ten miles from the Kampen inlet.

Goin' a little too fast. He punched the button on the clock, reset the elapse time hand to zero, then punched the button a second time to start the timing for the next checkpoint. He eased the throttle back a tiny bit, glanced at his map and found the next checkpoint, Almelo, which was 25 miles east. *Should be there in five minutes.*

Trees, fields, buildings and roads shot beneath him as his 51 sliced through the smooth morning air. It felt good flying low without the bathtubs and not wallowing through the stratosphere freezing his ass off.

To the right he saw the east-west highway and railroad leading to Almelo. Both the rail line and road would eventually run past Hanover.

He glanced at the compass, then the directional gyro to see if it had precessed. *Looks good.* He checked the needle and ball, then made a slight adjustment in the rudder trim. In his peripheral vision, he saw Matt, Rocko and Bob flying well forward. He checked the engine instruments; they were all in the green.

Almelo appeared to the right of his 51's nose and seconds later houses and buildings shot past his right wing. The rail yard had some bomb craters, twisted track and upended rail cars. He checked the clock. *Five minutes. . .ground speed 300. . .right on the money.*

Robb punched the clock button twice and started the timing again. The next checkpoint was where the east-west highway and railroad crossed the Vechte River, eight miles inside Germany. *Twenty-six miles to go. . .five minutes and twelve seconds.*

He glanced at the directional gyro and compass; they were right on. A north-south road shot past. He checked his map. The road was almost halfway between Almelo and the Vechte River. As his finger slid along the course line, he noticed the note he had made to check the fuel.

He looked down at the left wing tank gauge; it read 60 gallons. He leaned forward, turned the fuel selector from the left wing tank to the right tank. Then as prebriefed, he clicked his VHF radio mike button twice to remind Matt, Rocko and Bob to change tanks. One by one, they clicked their mike buttons to acknowledge the tank change.

Ahead, Robb saw the highway and railroad bridges crossing the Vechte River. Bomb craters dotted the approach to each bridge and the highway bridge had a span in the water. A burned out *Wehrmacht* truck sat on the east bank and a few hundred yards further east a damaged Panther tank was in the ditch next to the highway.

The bridges blurred beneath Robb's 51; he checked the clock. *On time. . .gyro and compass right on.*

He punched the clock button twice and looked at the map. The Ems River and railroad next were one minute ahead. Robb glanced to the left and right. Matt, Rocko and Bob were flying line abreast. He checked the engine instruments; they were in the green.

The single-track railroad, bordering the Ems River's west bank, came into view. Off to his right lay the city of Rheine.

A clump of trees passed under his left wing. Nazi soldiers scurried behind parked trucks and tanks.

He watched the Ems River shoot past, checked the clock and reset it, then looked at the map. *Mittleland Canal. . .two minutes.*

Like the east-west highway and railroad, the Mitteland Canal ran to Hanover. Eleven miles west and a little south of the Hanover airfield, the railroad turned northeast, crossed the canal and passed through the town of Wunstorf, then swung southeast and recrossed the canal. Robb and Rocko had selected the second of these easy-to-find bridge crossings as their final checkpoint.

A hill loomed in front of Robb. He pulled up, zoomed over the hilltop and dropped down into the valley on the other side.

A man and woman were herding three cows into a lot. The roar of his 51's four Merlin engines sent the cows scampering. The startled couple froze in their tracks and watched the fighters speed past.

THE HELLISH VORTEX

The Mitteland Canal appeared ahead. It came from the south, crossed the east-west railroad and highway and ran north two miles, then meandered east toward Hanover.

Approaching the canal, Robb saw the two bridges just ahead. He zoomed past the second bridge and checked his clock. *Right on 300 mph.*

He punched the clock button twice and started the timing for his next checkpoint, Onsabruck, which was 18 miles east. *Three minutes and 36 seconds ahead.*

He glanced at the gyro and compass, then at the engine instruments. *Everything's okay.*

The east-west highway and rail line curved north, closer to his route of flight. Ahead, he saw Ibbenburen, which was half way to Onsabruck.

Ibbenburen shot past. Three miles east, a steam engine lay on its side with 18 crumpled cars behind. Speeding past the train, Robb noticed the cars were ripped and splintered from rocket and strafing attacks by fighters.

He thought about the final run to the airfield and glanced at the map to confirm that he still remembered the heading and time from the last checkpoint. *Got it. . .74 degrees for one minute and 42 seconds.*

Onsabruck's skyline appeared on his right. Seconds later, buildings shot past. The railroad yard had bomb craters but the main rail lines had been repaired.

He saw fire spitting from the muzzle of a lone machine gun off his right side. Its trail of smoking shells came at him, then arched behind. *Thank God. . .he's not pulling enough lead.*

A building blocked the machine gun's line of fire. Robb scanned to the right and left looking for more guns but saw none.

The main north-south rail line and highway running between Onsabruck and Bremen shot beneath his 51. Nothing was moving on either of them.

Robb quickly punched the clock button twice, then checked his map. It showed Minden 28 miles east. *Five minutes 36 seconds.*

He saw Onsabruck disappear in his rearview mirrors.

A ridge came at him. He pulled up and skimmed its top, then dropped down on the other side. Another north-south railroad shot beneath him.

Ahead, the east-west highway swung north, closer to the Mitteland Canal, while the railroad turned about ten degrees right.

Further east, the canal and highway began to converge. Just before they came together, Minden appeared dead ahead. He was right on course.

A few seconds later, Minden shot past; he punched the clock twice and checked his map. *Final checkpoint. . .steer 78 degrees for 23 miles. . .four minutes and 36 seconds.* He turned left to 78 degrees and checked the compass and gyro. They were right on. The engine instruments were in the green. *Check your gun switch.* It was on. He glanced at the gun sight to make sure the fixed reticule and pipper weren't too bright. They looked good.

His route of flight took him between the canal on the left and the highway and railroad on the right. All three were deserted. Further east he saw a barge that had been shot up and noticed a damaged truck off to the side of the road.

Two minutes out of Minden, he let down to 100 feet, hoping to remain below the Hanover radar.

A minute and a half later he saw the rail line crossing the canal on the west side of Wunstorf and strained to see the last check point, the second rail and canal intersection on the east side of town. It was dead ahead.

He started a gradual descent and clicked his mike button three times to signal Matt, Rocko and Bob to increase power. He set the prop at 3000 rpm and pushed the throttle forward to 57 inches. The engine growled and his 51 vibrated as the1490 horses kicked in. The surge of power pushed him back in the seat.

The final checkpoint—shot beneath him. Robb punched the clock twice as he turned to 74 degrees. Seconds later, he leveled at 50 feet. *One minute and 12 seconds to go.*

His speed stabilized at 405 mph. He adjusted the rudder trim, then eased down to 25 feet. Trees, buildings and fencerows rushed at him and blurred as they shot past.

He sneaked a peek at the gyro and the clock. *Heading 74 degrees, 50 seconds to the field.*

A clump of tall trees rushed at him. He pulled up, shot over their tops, eased back down and glanced at the clock. *Thirty seconds to go.*

Robb scanned the horizon, looking for the control tower or hangers on the airfield, but saw nothing. He glanced at the clock. *Fifteen seconds to go.*

A steel tower and its electrical power lines appeared dead ahead. More steel towers appeared to the right and left. High-tension wires sagged in between them.

SHIT. . .God damned map didn't show this power line! It's gonna force us up where bastards'll see us. Could fly under the wires but Matt, Rocko and Bob might not see 'em. Robb's pucker string snapped tight.

The steel tower and high-tension wires loomed in front of him. Robb pulled back the stick. Matt, Rocko and Bob also pulled up. A half mile ahead Robb saw the airfield and its hangers. Aircraft were parked everywhere.

"Air patch, twelve o'clock," Robb transmitted. Matt, Rocko and Bob had moved slightly ahead.

Robb dumped his 51's nose and eased back to 25 feet. The airfield fence rushed at him.

At 405 mph, it would take less than 20 seconds to run the gauntlet of lead. But since they had to pull up to miss the wires, Robb was certain the Germans had seen them. He knew that in 20 seconds of heavy crossfire the Germans would have plenty of time to shoot all four of them down.

THE HELLISH VORTEX

Fear bolted through his body and triggered a voice from his childhood. It was clear and resonant, with a British accent, as it recited the first stanza of Lord Alfred Tennyson's, *The Charge of the Light Brigade at Balaclava.*

£££

Half a league, half a league,
Half a league onward,
All in the valley of Death
Rode the six hundred.....

£££

Robb's fifth grade teacher had played the record of *The Charge of the Light Brigade at Balacava,* over and over. Within a month, everyone in Robb's fifth grade class knew Tennyson's words as well as they knew their names. Robb had always wondered how the "600" felt as they rode into "the valley of Death." Now he knew

WHOMP! WHOMP! The muzzles of two 40-millimeter cannons flashed when two nervous gun crews fired early. Two dirty-orange fireballs exploded above the field and left gray puffs of smoke like greeting cards from hell.

Five streams of burning golf balls from 20-millimeter cannons crisscrossed in front of Robb. Along the edge of the field, flashes of rifle and machine gun fire joined the fray.

Robb's pucker string tightened another notch; he hunched lower in the cockpit trying to make himself smaller as more streams of burning golf balls whizzed past--a few feet above his head.

Directly ahead, a group of parked German aircraft popped into sight. He leaned forward, took aim at a ME-109 and squeezed the trigger.

The four 50 caliber machine guns clacked like air hammers; their armor-piercing incendiary shells sparkled as they ripped huge chunks of sod and macadam from the ground and sent them tumbling through the air. The APIs trenched their way forward to the ME-109. It sparkled and exploded. The flames shot high.

Robb pulled up a few feet, zoomed into the flames and shot out of the other side. He quickly dumped the stick forward, hugging the ground as he crossed the airfield's perimeter road and entered "the valley of Death."

WHOOMP! WHOOMP! WHOOMP! Cannons flashed in front of him, on his right and left and in his rearview mirrors. More 40-millimeter cannons opened fire and their dirty-orange fireballs and their gray puffs darkened the sky. By now a dozen streams of burning 20-millimeter golf balls were coming from different angles, crisscrossing a few feet above him. Two golf balls collided; one deflected skyward, the other shattered and hit the ground.

Muzzle flashes came from behind sandbags, trees and trucks and from windows as the Germans opened fire with hundreds of machine guns, rifles and *pistoles*. They sent a wall of lead slugs through the air.

Knowing he'd reached the deadliest stretch in "the valley," Robb hunkered down to run the deadly gauntlet of lead. Although he was going 405 mph, his speed suddenly seemed no faster than "The Brigade's."

£££

Cannon to the right of them,
Cannon to the left of them,
Cannon in front of them
Volleyed and thundered;
Stormed at with shot and shell,
Boldly they rode and well,
Into the jaws of Death
Into the mouth of Hell

£££

WHAAP! A slug struck Robb's canopy, just behind his head. Air screeched through the hole like a siren.

Robb's body turned to rock; his field of vision narrowed, like he had entered a tunnel. Yet he not only saw cannons flashing and small arms firing ahead--but also from each side. It was like the tunnel had translucent walls.

WHOOMP! In the corner of his eye he saw a huge flash. Bob's 51 had exploded. Flaming chunks of aluminum wreckage tumbled wildly as it rocketed across the ground. Robb flinched, knowing that Bob was somewhere inside.

In an instant, the burning wreckage was left behind.

WHAAP! WHAAP! Two more slugs crashed through Robb's canopy, just above his head. Two more sirens screeched.

He jammed the throttle forward and eased his 51 lower—lower than he'd ever flown—and prayed his prop wouldn't hit the ground.

WHOOM! Flames torched from Matt's 51. It hit the ground, skipped a few feet into the air and exploded. Burning fuel spewed behind the jagged mass of metal that tumbled once and slammed into a hanger.

In an instant, the wreckage was left behind.

WHAAP! WHAAP! Slugs hit the rudder of Robb's 51; the rudder pedals banged the soles of his GI shoes. Fear shot through his body; his heart pounded like a sledgehammer. Blood thundered in his ears as his feet did the familiar dance of death.

WHAAP! WHAAP! The rudder pedals banged again. Certain that "the jaws of Death" were about the slam shut, he hunkered down and waited to die.

276

But his P-51 roared on, deeper "into the mouth of Hell."

Through the hazy tunnel of fear, he spotted another group of aircraft a few degrees to his right. *If I'm gonna die, I'm gonna go down fighting.*

He eased his 51 up to 50 feet, did a shallow bank and turned three degrees to the right, then leveled the wings. Streams of burning golf balls streaked past a few feet above his head.

Robb eased his 51 back to the deck.

The gunners tried to follow him. Their burning golf balls hit the ground and ricocheted into a machine gun nest on the opposite side of the field. Two Germans, in dull green uniforms and shiny steel helmets, flew from the machine gun nest and tumbled through the air. Their arms and legs flailed like rag dolls—until they slammed back into the ground.

WHAAP! WHAAP! Robb's feet did another deadly dance as another burst of machine shells hit his rudder.

He hunkered down and took aim at a ME-109 and squeezed the trigger. His four machine guns clacked, API's sparkled and the 109 exploded. A fireball mushroomed 100 feet into the air. Robb held his breath, zoomed through the flames, came out the other side and crossed the airfield's boundary fence.

WHAAP! WHAAP! The control stick shook as another burst of machine gun fire ripped into his 51's right aileron. *Gotta get outta the line of fire.*

Robb jerked the stick back; his 51 jumped higher and the banging stopped. He eased it lower, hugged the deck and streaked across the pasture next to the airfield.

In his rearview mirrors he saw a 20-millimeter cannon flash. Its stream of burning golf balls shot past a few feet above him. They hit the ground hundreds of feet ahead of him and ricocheted back into the air.

The flashing cannon dropped from sight and the sky and ground suddenly became peaceful as he departed the "mouth of hell."

Fear drained from his body and mind and the translucent tunnel disappeared. In his peripheral vision, he saw Rocko's P-51 and rejoiced. In the endless flight across the "valley of Death" fear had shrouded his mind and he had completely forgotten about Rocko.

But an instant later his joy gave way to grief as he suddenly remembered the gruesome spectacles of Bob and Matt's fiery deaths.

£££

Stormed at with shot and shell,
While horse and hero fell,
They that had fought so well
Came through the jaws of Death,
Back from the mouth of Hell,
All that was left of them,

£££

Robb cut grass for another five seconds before coming up for air. As he pulled up he transmitted, "Yellow One's skinning it back to 36 inches and 1800 rpm. I'm starting a climbing turn to the left to bleed off some of this speed. Check your engine instruments."

"Gotch'a *amigo*. Everything's in the green."

In the climbing turn, Robb blinked sweat from his eyes, unsnapped his oxygen mask, rubbed the tender spot on the bridge of his nose, took a deep breath, exhaled, then swallowed some sand. At 250 mph, the screeching from the bullet holes in the canopy lowered two octaves. He thought about Matt and Bob as he tightened the chinstrap on his helmet to eliminate some of the noise.

"I'm moving in closer, *amigo*. We can check one another's birds." Rocko called.

"Rog. Don't get too close. My tail has been shot up. It might fail and we could slam together."

"Understand, *amigo*. I counted 19 holes in the fuselage and tail of your bird. Tail looks okay and I don't see any coolant spray or oil leaks. Your bird should take you back to blokeland."

"Thanks. Also took three slugs in the canopy, so make the count 22. I'll slide back and check you."

"Okay, *amigo*."

Robb moved back and started counting. "Three, I counted 15 holes but no coolant spray or traces of oil. It looks like your bird's in one piece."

"*Amigo*, they can take strafin' airfields and stick it where it won't get sunburned."

"You can say that again...with gusto."

Robb rolled out on a heading of 270 degrees and looked south toward the airfield. Eight towers of black smoke marked six burning 109's and the crash sites of Matt and Bob. He felt another lump in his throat and more tightness in his gut. All four of them had faced the same threat at the same time, yet two lived and two died. *Shit...it doesn't make any sense.*

At the coast of Holland, Robb turned left. With a damaged aircraft, he wanted to cross the Channel at Calais rather than flirting with the unforgiving North Sea. Watching the coastline pass under his wing, he kept thinking about Matt and Bob. *If that damned power line had been on the map we could've attacked from another direction and remained low and got in and out before they could react.*

£££

Some one had blundered;
Theirs not to make reply,
Theirs not to reason why,
Theirs but to do and die;

£££

THE HELLISH VORTEX

On the landing roll, Robb noticed five fire trucks on the ready line instead of the usual two. There were also three ambulances rather than one. The walkway around the second floor of the control tower had many more watchers.

At the end of the runway, Robb and Rocko turned onto the taxiway. In addition to the crew chiefs, armorers, refuelers, radio repairmen, hydraulic specialists and electricians who normally greeted the returning fighters, there were clerks, military policemen, medical and mess hall personnel in their white work uniforms and administrative officers in pinks and greens. *Never had a turnout like this. Word must've gotten out that we lost a bunch today. I wonder how many?*

Flight line personnel automatically stood at attention and saluted as Robb and Rocko passed. A jerky chain reaction of side-glances started among the others as they took the cue and saluted. It reminded Robb of the Catholic Church where many people stood, sat and genuflected, guided by the few who knew the drill.

Further down the taxiway, a group of British laborers in frayed caps, dirty overalls, muddy rubber boots, greasy shirts and ties and tattered suit coats leaned on their shovel handles and watched the battered 51's pass.

Robb turned into the revetment, taxied to his parking spot and swung his 51 around. He noticed Matt and Bob's empty parking spaces on the opposite side, another lump formed in his throat as he turned off the radio and ran the engine up to 1500 rpm to clear the plugs. After 15 seconds, he chopped the power and pulled the mixture control to idle cutoff. When the engine stopped, he turned off the battery and ignition switches, pushed the fuel shutoff lever and pulled the fairing door release handle. He felt completely drained and sat back in the seat, stretched his legs, stared at the empty parking spaces and swallowed another lump.

"Let me give you a hand, sir," Staff Sergeant Edgington, said removing the shoulder straps. "Sorry about Lieutenant Mattson and Lieutenant Hermanes."

Robb nodded. "How many did the group lose today?"

"Seven, sir. Bugeye lost three, Hot Rod lost two and our two."

Robb's jaws tightened and he shook his head. "Shit! My flight's the only one in Snapper that had losses."

"I'm sure wasn't your fault, sir. Looks like our bird'll be in the barn for a while, sir," Sergeant Edgington said, trying to change the subject.

"Uh...yeah. Didn't take very good care of it, chief," Robb replied, stepping out of the cockpit.

"Made it back, sir. That's all that counts." Sergeant Edgington took Robb's chute and laid it on the wing.

The squadron weapons carrier pulled up. Robb jumped off the wing, took his flight gear and climbed in the back of the weapons carrier. Sergeant Edgington saluted as it pulled away.

After the memorial service, Robb and Rocko went to the bar, ordered a beer and sat at a corner table.

"Frickin' pucker string got so tight today, my fuzzy growler may not growl for a month."

"Yeah. I'll take the stratosphere, freezing cold, kraut fighters anytime."

"Hi guys," Ted said, pulling up a chair. "I'm going to take a walk to group, read the mission recap and check on tomorrow's weather. Wanta come along?"

"I'll go," Robb said, finishing his beer.

"Not me," Rocko grunted. "I'm havin' another blabber-mouth, headin' to Colchester for some fish and chips and get laid."

The 8th Air Force preliminary mission report seemed more cold and impersonal than most. It stated matter-of-factly that 33 fighters had been lost while strafing, seven of which were P-51's from one group. That was it. That was all it said about the group's seven losses.

£££

The Colonel returned to his office after touring the flightline. "Sir, 12 new pilots will arrive from Goxhill tomorrow," Charlie said, placing the cup of coffee on the Colonel's desk. "And eight replacement P-51's will be flown in later tonight."

"It's about time we got some pilots." The Colonel pulled the bottle of Red Label and a glass from his desk drawer and poured their drinks. Just as he handed Charlie his glass the phone rang.

"Group headquarters," Charlie answered. "Yes mam. I'll get him right away." He shielded the mouthpiece. "Sir, General Tyler's aide is on the phone. The general wants to speak to you."

"Yes," the Colonel said taking the phone. "Okay I'll hang on. Hello, sir. Fine, thanks. And yourself?" He listened for the next few seconds then said, "Yes sir, we really had a bad day." He listened again. "Yes sir. They'll be on their way in the morning." He hung up the phone.

"Charlie, get Captain Tyler and Lieutenant Baines some orders for the flak house. I'll tell Captain Tyler tonight."

"Will do, sir."

Charlie finished his drink and left. The Colonel took another big swig of Scotch-coffee, leaned back in his chair and closed his eyes. Today's combat mission was his worst ever. Seven pilots had been killed—more than 20 per-cent of his force. It reminded him of the World War I slaughter Rmarque described in *All Quiet On the Western Front.* He open his eyes and finished his Scotch-coffee and stared at the ceiling. "Young men killin' and being killed while a few old men beat their chests and cry for more," he whispered. "Greedy, arrogant, manipulatin' old bastards satisfyin' their lust for power, tucked safely behind their age. Only my love for flyin' keeps me goin'."

CHAPTER 18

Double Ugly

Big John and Corporal Perkins left to pickup their supplies from the messhall, leaving Robb alone at the snack bar. He sipped his coffee and listened to Glenn Miller's *I've Got A Gal In Kalamazoo* and wondered why he had been taken off today's mission.

Merlin engines suddenly growled and howled as the first two P-51's roared down the runway. For nearly two minutes their thundering drowned out the radio and rattled the stack of tin plates on the snack bar.

When the roar of the last two P-51's faded, the tin plates stopped rattling and even the radio became silent as disk jockey changed records. In the stillness of the empty room, Robb suddenly felt all alone and lonely. He wished Ted would hurry back.

Glen Miller's *"Sunrise Serenade"* started flowing from the radio. It reminded him of Austin, of Beth, of double dates, jukebox dances and necking in parked cars. That all seemed so long ago and far away.

"Lieutenant Baines, Captain Tyler just returned from group and he would like to see you," the operations sergeant said.

"Thank you, sergeant." Feeling relieved, Robb quickly placed his coffee cup on the bar and headed for Ted's office.

"Come on in, Robb," Ted said, looking up. "Close the door, sit down. I don't know what the hell's going on. The Colonel called me late last night. Said we were both overdue R and R's, so he was sending us to the flak house and the group adjutant would have our orders this morning. Also said my dad wanted us to stop to see him on the way. An aircraft will pick us up this morning at 8:30. That's all I know. As soon as I finish signing these reports, we'll get packed."

£££

General Tyler waited for Darlene to close the office door. "Guys, I'm sorry for the no-notice departure. This thing came up in a hurry. You're gonna fly a tippy top secret mission, laid on by General Eisenhower...personally."

General Tyler's voice was taut. He had agonized for two days before selecting Ted and Robb for this crucial and dangerous mission. But it was essential that he had someone he could trust, no matter the cost.

RICHARD M BAUGHN

"Security's so tight it squeaks. Only Air Chief Marshal Tedder and I have been read in on it here. Not even our friendly Frenchman, General Pierre Koenig, Ike's chief of clandestine operations has been told," he paused and smiled. "General Spaatz is the only person on the Air Force side who knows. The other people involved are being told just enough to get their part of the job done, but not enough to know what's goin' on.

"I asked your group commander to cut orders sendin' you on R and R, but told him that you'd be workin' on a special project for me here at headquarters. That's all he knows.

"The thing that kicked off this mission was an intel report we got two weeks ago from the French underground. It said the Atlantic wall might soon be defended by 2,000,000 German troops, supported by powerful new tanks and maybe some jet aircraft. The troop count and new tanks don't track with what we know, but the jet threat could be real.

"General Donovan's OSS sources in Switzerland believe the French underground might have been penetrated and the report is part of a Nazi disinformation effort. But the Brit's aren't convinced. They think it may be the real thing.

"General Eisenhower doesn't know what to believe. He knows that if Germany's military forces are properly deployed, they can make the most difficult invasion in the history of warfare a lot tougher...maybe impossible. Ike needs solid intel that's not manipulated by the enemy or filtered, waffled and fluffed through six layers of Allied bureaucracy. It's absolutely crucial that we find out the true situation before the invasion. So we're goin' to insert two top-notch agents, a Brit and an American. Both have been on ice and had a deep cover for several years. They are fluent in French and German and have lived and traveled extensively on the Continent.

"General Donovan suggested a completely new team be used to insert the agents instead of usin' the regular clandestine aerial supply unit. Says it'll attract less attention in spookland and there'll be less chance of compromisin' security. He's assigned one of his hot buns, an Ivy Leaguer fresh from Washington, to run the project.

"General Eisenhower asked me to find two damned good pilots who could keep their mouths shut. I reviewed hundreds of records, but yours kept comin' to the top. Besides, you both were overdue an R and R, which is an excellent cover for your time away from the 345th. So I volunteered the two of you. Can't over emphasize the importance of security. You must promise not to discuss this mission...ever. Not even with one another."

"Understand," Ted said, looking at Robb.

"Yes sir," Robb nodded.

"It's gonna require some tricky flyin' to get in and out of France. You'll take a doctored-up UC-64, land in France and drop off the two agents and their special communications equipment."

Ted and Robb glanced at one another and smiled.

"Somethin' wrong?"

"Nothing, dad. Just a mutual joke about UC-64's."

"You'll have to land because we want to avoid takin' a chance on damaging' the radios with a parachute drop. You'll fly in on the deck on a moonless night. So a radar altimeter has been installed in the UC-64 to give you an accurate readin' of your height above the ground and water. The 64's exhaust has been modified to suppress the flames and noise. Experts say the suppresser has been designed to make it sound a little like a Stuke. A manual direction finding radio has also been installed for the right seater to operate. You'll need it to help locate your destination.

"Mission has to go within the next eight days. So you've gotta hurry and get yourselves proficient in the UC-64. You'll be kept under wraps until the mission is completed. Any questions?"

Ted looked at Robb. Robb shook his head. General Tyler picked up his phone, "Lieutenant Bradford, send in Captain Katterbaum."

"You can go in now, Captain Katterbaum." Darlene said, putting the phone down. She had tried to engage him in conversation twice but he never answered and continued to read the small, red leather-bound book with *Essays of Plato* embossed in gold on the cover.

Captain Ezekiel Katterbaum looked up from the book. He quickly closed the book and put it in his briefcase, then stood and walked toward General Tyler's office. The thick lenses in his black horn-rimmed glasses magnified his cold, blue eyes, which never once looked toward Darlene.

Darlene held the door and looked down at him, as he approached. He was a small man, not more than five foot three, 120 pounds, and looked lost in his uniform. The pads in his green blouse drooped on his narrow shoulders. His khaki shirt was too large for his thin neck, and the large knot in his khaki tie was almost hidden beneath the collar. Both his blouse and baggy trousers still had the wrinkles from the PX shipping carton.

Darlene noticed a white tag on the bottom of his blouse. "Just a minute, Captain," Darlene said. She reached down and removed the tag, as he looked straight ahead. She held the tag. He glanced at it, shrugged and walked through the door.

£££

Minutes later, Robb, Ted and Captain Katterbaum departed General Tyler's office. Robb noticed that tears welled in General Tyler's eyes when he said goodbye to Ted.

Outside they climbed into the waiting jeep. Ted in the front seat and Robb and Ezekiel in the back seat. The young GI driver slammed the gearshift to low, gunned the engine and sped away heading southwest along narrow winding roads. Ezekiel resumed his reading while Robb and Ted looked at the passing countryside

American soldiers were every where—in the villages, camped in fields and in truck convoys on the roads. In one village, troops fresh from the States were off-loading from a train onto trucks that would take them to their pre-invasion campsites. Further down the road, the jeep driver had to work his way past a long line of parked American troop trucks. Some soldiers were eating K-rations while a chaplain held services in an open field. Robb suddenly remembered that it was Sunday.

A heavily wooded area appeared on the left side of the road and the driver turned into a winding lane that resembled a tunnel cut through the thick green trees. Ezekiel closed his book and put it in his briefcase.

A half-mile into the forest, the lane straightened and Robb saw a small grass strip straight ahead. One hundred yards short of the strip, the driver slowed and turned right. Back in the trees stood a large red brick manor house with a gray slate roof.

The jeep sped around the half-moon gravel drive in front of the manor house and stopped at the door. Ezekiel's briefcase banged against Robb's leg. The weight of the briefcase indicated that it contained something a lot heavier than the *Essays of Plato*.

Two men in civilian clothes with Thompson submachine guns and German Shepherd guard dogs watched from the edge of the trees. Another civilian with a Thompson and guard dog appeared at the far corner of the house.

A large man with a shouldered Thompson came out the front door, walked briskly to the jeep, stopped with the British military two-step and clicked his heels together. "Captain Katterbaum, SUH. You 'ave a phone call, SUH," he said with his clipped British accent.

Without speaking or returning the salute, Ezekiel crawled from the jeep, took his briefcase and hurried inside.

"Captain Tyler and Lieutenant Baines, I am Sergeant Major Ian Cooke. I'll be your escort while you're 'ere. Let me 'elp you with your bags." He snatched the two B-4 bags from the jeep like they were boxes of Kleenex.

Inside the door on the right an operator with a holstered pistol sat at an army field telephone switchboard. While Ted and Robb followed Ian upstairs, they heard the hushed voice of Captain Katterbaum talking on a phone in the sitting room.

"You'll share this room, gentlemen," Ian said, opening the bedroom door at the end of the hall. It was a large room whose windows faced lush green trees on three sides.

"Gentlemen, I'm also responsible for the servicing and readiness of the mission aircraft. There are two copies of its flight-operating manual on the table. I'll escort you to the Norseman after you've made a proper examination of the manuals."

"That won't be necessary, we can go by ourselves," Ted replied.

"Sorry suh. Security, you know."

"Okay. We'll go now. We can check the aircraft while we read about it."

"Jolly good, suh. There are two flight suits and jackets in the chest of drawers."

While Robb and Ted changed clothes, the jeep with Captain Katterbaum and the young GI scrunched around the half-moon drive and turned onto the lane leading to the road.

Thirty-foot trees bordered the short, narrow grass landing strip. A black unmarked UC-64 sat back in the woods with a camouflage net stretched above it.

"Flying off this postage stamp's gonna be like flying out of a dead end canyon," Ted said, surveying the strip. "Gonna really be fun at night."

Robb nodded.

Behind the UC-64's tail was a two-wheeled fuel trailer. Further back in the trees, two guards and their dogs stood near a small storage shed.

Stepping up on the left wheel, Ted opened the cockpit door and looked inside. Robb walked around the UC-64's nose, stepped on the right wheel, opened the cockpit door and looked in the right side.

"More like a truck cab than a cockpit," Robb said.

"Yeah. I'd forgotten that the damned thing has only one yoke," Ted said, seeing the control column mounted in the center of floor, just forward of the two seats. The arm that held the yoke ran nearly perpendicular from the control column to the pilot's side. Ted pushed the knob that unlocked the horizontal arm and yoke and swung it to Robb's side, then swung it back to his side. "Weird."

"Yeah."

For the next two hours, they read and discussed the contents of the operating manual, studied switch and instrument locations, then took turns simulating engine starts.

Ted turned to the flight section. "I'll be damned. Ailerons droop when you lower the flaps to provide more lift. Strange old bird. Let's see what the operating manual says about short field landings. Use full flaps...power on approach...minimum speed...control rate of descent with power. That all makes sense. Robb, wanta crank her up and take a little spin around the pattern?"

"Might as well get with it. See how this old goat handles."

Ted motioned to Ian who was talking to one of the guards. "Ian, I think we'll take her up."

"Suh, it's ten minutes till one," he said looking at his watch. "Would you mind waiting until after you eat? Desmond loathes tardiness."

"Fair enough. Ian, think you could find some light colored paint and a small brush. This old girl needs a name.

"Suh, I'll get paint and a brush from Desmond."

When Baron Pitt-Brown loaned his southern estate to the British military for the war, Desmond, the 70-year-old butler became the *de facto* lord of the manor. With most of the servants in His Majesty's Service, Desmond established strict rules for the temporary military visitors so his small staff could manage. At the top of his list was being seated on time for their meals.

Desmond had never served Americans, but had heard the Baron talk about their uncouthness. From his old boy net, he had learned Americans substituted chumminess for their lack of social graces and many had a tendency to overindulge. Desmond decided that no cocktails would be served and he would limit the Americans to one glass of wine during the evening meal.

He looked forward to displaying his talents and teaching the crude Americans the civilized ways of the British. It would provide him with some badly needed therapy. In anticipation of the Americans arrival, he increased his bending and stretching exercises.

With his chin jutted high and his six-foot body straight as a drill sergeant, Desmond strode through the swinging door of his butler's pantry, pushing the serving cart. His long thick white hair was combed straight back and held in place with hair oil. He wore an immaculate white jacket, white shirt with a celluloid collar, black tie and black trousers.

Seeing Robb and Ted at his dining room table in flight suits only served to reinforce his impression of Americans as bloody boors who needed to be sent back their wilderness the minute the war ended.

But Desmond concealed his displeasure. Fifty-five years in the service of the Baron Pitt-Brown family had made him unflappable.

Desmond stopped the serving cart next to the table, stood erect, looked down his long nose through half-closed eyes like a maestro capturing the attention of his audience. He was delighted that neither Ted nor Robb had taken their napkins. It would provide him with a perfect *entrée* for his performance.

Desmond moved to the table, snatched the white napkin from in front of Ted. He yanked the napkin from the silver holder and swung it high like a saber being pulled from its scabbard. He lowered the napkin, snapped it open and placed it on Ted's lap, "Your *serviette*...suhh!"

Desmond repeated the performance for Robb, returned to the cart, stood erect and looked straight ahead.

Robb and Ted glanced at one another, then back at Desmond.

Like a flash, Desmond whisked the ornate silver warmer from the first of the two white porcelain plates. The plate contained a small slice of ham, boiled potato, Brussels sprouts and a slice of tomato. The potato had been garnished with butter and parsley.

Desmond set the silver warmer to one side. Using a folded napkin, he picked up the plate with his left hand. He then placed the bottom of the plate on the fingertips of his right hand and raised the plate above his head. Standing perfectly straight, he did a two step military stomp, clicked his heels and performed an about-face like a sergeant major. He moved to Ted's left side, bent from the waist, swung the plate down and around until it was two inches above the table in front of Ted. With the napkin, he took the plate with his left hand and lowered the plate to the table. He stood erect, looked down his nose and stomped his feet, "Suhh!"

Seeing the Americans' startled expressions Desmond wanted to smile, but he did a quick about-face to look the other way. He repeated his plate performance for Robb, then returned to the cart. "Milk with your tea, suh?"

"I'll take mine plain, thank you," Ted replied.

"Same for me, thank you," Robb added.

Desmond took a deep breath and readied himself for the grand finale. With cat-like deftness, his left hand snatched the cozy from the teapot—whisked it shoulder high, then placed it on the cart. He picked up the teapot in his right hand, did the military stomp, clicked his heels, about-faced and moved to Ted's side. He bent from the waist until his eyes were level with Ted's, filled the cup, stood erect. "Suhh!"

Forcing back another smile, Desmond stomped and clicked, did an about-face and marched to Robb's side, bent and poured. But as he started to straighten up, a knife-like pain sliced through the small of his back.

Unable to straighten up, he winced, gritted his teeth and remained stooped as he shuffled to the cart and set the teapot down. Another shot of pain knifed through the small of his back. He gripped the cart's handle, gritted his teeth harder and held his breath while beads of sweat formed on his forehead. Finally he turned his head. "If I can be…of further service…suhh…use the bell." He glanced at the bell next to Ted.

"Thank you very much, Desmond. We should be fine." Ted wanted to help, but knew it would only embarrass the proud old butler.

Still bent over, he gritted his teeth, raised his head slightly and jutted his chin, before wheeling the serving cart toward the pantry door. The downstairs maid, who had been watching through the peephole, swung the door open. A stooped Desmond marched through and the door closed behind him.

Ted and Robb looked at one another, smiled and shrugged, then ate their lunch.

£££

"Suh, I 'ave the paint and brush you wanted," Ian said on the way to the landing strip.

"What color did you get?" Ted asked.

"Orange."

"Perfect. We'll give her a name after we finish our flight."

"Suh, we 'ave a crude light system for night landings, just like you'll 'ave in France. There's a light mounted on a pole, just above the trees on the approach end. A jeep will be parked at the far end of the landing strip with its headlights on. When properly aligned, the lights will 'elp guide you down the final approach. We'll 'ave them on for this afternoon's flight, so you can develop your techniques for using them at night."

"That's good. We'll begin our landing practice as soon as we complete our air work," Ted answered.

Ted, Robb and Ian preflighted the UC-64, fired up its engine, taxied to the end of the grass strip, completed the engine checks and double-checked the trim tabs. Ted looked back at Ian who was sitting in the second passenger's seat with his Thompson on the floor beside him. He smiled and gave Ted a thumb's up.

Ted eased the throttle forward to full power; the engine roared like thunder. He released the brakes; the UC-64 slowly gained speed and tried to veer to the right. Ted tapped the brake and kept it straight. Its tail rose; Ted eased back on the yoke; the UC-64 came off the ground and climbed, clearing the trees by ten feet.

Ted looked at Robb and smiled. "Made it."

Robb smiled and nodded.

At 5000 feet, Ted and Robb took turns stalling the UC-64, straight ahead and in turns, with and without power and flaps. Then they practiced slow flight using power and full flaps. Having the ailerons droop when the flaps were lowered made the UC-64's sluggish response worse.

"This thing flies like a Mack truck," Robb said, swinging the yoke back to Ted.

"Yeah. Robb, I'm going to fly the pattern at 500 feet and keep it in close," Ted said, descending to the downwind leg. "Give me a call when we're abeam the tree light. I'll wait three seconds then turn to base. You watch the jeep lights through your side window. Make a mental note of their location on the window when I start the turn to final and then note their location on windshield after we're lined up. Call when we get a jump on the radar altimeter indicating we've cleared the trees. Then call our height above ground at ten-foot intervals. Make your last call at five feet. Lowering the flaps now," Ted called turning on a short downwind leg.

Robb watched the light. "We're abeam the light."

Ted started a descending right turn to the base leg and rolled out at 300 feet.

Robb noted where the jeep lights were on the side window. Ted started the descending right turn to final and rolled out of the turn at 100 feet. The lights were centered, two inches from the bottom of the windshield.

Ted held the airspeed at 65 mph and used the power to control the rate of descent. The tree light disappeared under the UC-64's nose; the jeep lights remained in the center, near the bottom of the windshield's frame.

"Got a jump on the radar altimeter," Robb shouted. "Shows 45 feet."

Ted reduced power slightly; the UC-64's rate of sink increased.

"Thirty feet...20...10...5," Robb called.

At five feet, Ted added a slight amount of power to reduce the rate of descent; the UC-64 touched down on all three wheels. Ted snapped the throttle back to idle and pulled back the yoke. The 64 tried to veer to the left; he tapped the right brake, eased in the right rudder pedal and kept the 64's nose pointed down the runway. After rolling several hundred feet, he applied the brakes. "That wasn't too bad."

"Yeah, worked out pretty good," Robb replied, resetting the flaps and trim tabs for take off.

Ted turned the old bird around, taxied back to the end of the strip, pushed the prop pitch full forward, gunned the engine, checked the trim tab settings and released the brakes. The UC-64 roared down the strip.

After Robb and Ted had each shot 15 landings, Ted taxied the UC-64 back to its parking spot and cut the engine. "Boy, oh boy, this old bird takes muscle to fly. UC-64 pilots don't need to lift weights to stay in shape."

"Yeah. Flying her is more like a wrestling match," Robb added.

"Suh, ah've ridden in this old scrubber many times with a number of pilots. You both 'ave done quite well."

The three of them and a guard pushed the 64 back under the camouflage net. Ian handed Ted the paint and brush.

"How about naming this old scrubber, *Double Ugly?*" Ted asked with a smile.

Robb and Ian smiled and nodded.

Ted shook the can of paint, removed the lid and printed *Double Ugly* on each side of her bulbous nose.

Captain Katterbaum was waiting when they returned to the manor house. "Been on the phone all afternoon. There's been a change in plans. Bad weather is coming in the next 36 hours. It'll remain bad for at least three days, maybe longer. So we've got to fly the mission tomorrow night. Can you be ready by then?"

"We can hack it," Ted replied. "Before our next flight, load the 64 with the identical load that we'll carry to France. Need to see how she's going to handle with the extra weight. In addition, make sure it's loaded, so it can be off-loaded fast. I want minimum ground time in France."

"Good suggestions. They'll be done," Ezekiel replied.

The next morning, Ian and a guard sat in the rear with *Double Ugly's* load of cargo while Robb and Ted took turns shooting landings, using the light procedures and techniques they developed the day before.

"Had enough?" Ted asked after Robb completed his tenth landing.

"More than enough. I'm ready," Robb replied. "Besides, it's getting close to lunch time."

"Mustn't keep Desmond waiting," Ted smiled.

After lunch, Captain Katterbaum waited for them in the study. "How'd the flight go?" he asked as they entered.

"With a load, the old bird just takes a lot more muscle and power to move it around the sky," Ted replied. "Do you have a launch time?"

"Takeoff is planned for ten o'clock. Your call sign will be Deep Purple," Ezekiel said. "We have a perfect night, no moon, a thick overcast and the winds are forecast to be light to calm. You'll get a detailed weather briefing before takeoff."

Ezekiel spread the aeronautical chart on the table and used his pencil as a pointer. "You'll fly south from Bournemouth, pass between the tip of Cherbourg and Alderney. If you remain at 100 or less, you'll be below the German radar.

"From Alderney, you'll continue southeast and parallel the coast. Your route will keep you about seven to ten miles from the coast and about seven miles from Jersey.

"A frigate, call sign Web Foot, will track you across the English Channel. They know your route of flight and have been told you'll be maintaining 120 mph. Before you leave their radar coverage, they'll give you your ground speed and a course correction to null any changes in the crosswind. Then they'll send a coded message to the *Marquis* giving them your estimated time of arrival at the landing strip.

"Forty-eight miles south of Alderney, turn due east. Two *Marquis* will also be on the beach, east of your turn point. When they hear your engine, they'll flash a light, which'll mark your course. After crossing the coast, continue due east for 12 miles to the landing strip, which is located five miles southeast of Coutances. The strip runs east and west and is in a forested area very similar to the Baron's strip. You'll land to the east.

"The *Marquis* radio beacon at the strip will transmit on frequency 930, starting four minutes before your ETA. The tree and jeep lights will be turned on when they hear your engine. The radio beacon will play Les Brown's arrangement of "*Sentimental Journey*," if you're clear to land and Glenn Miller's *Chattanooga* "*Choo Choo*," if a landing is not possible. In that case, you'll fly five miles due east, climb to 1500 feet, drop the agents and equipment by parachute, in an area marked by four red lights.

"The *Marquis* has planned a diversionary attack about 15 minutes before your arrival. They'll blow up a German supply train northeast of Coutances.

"On the way back to Britain, check in with Web Foot and give him a report. Either a landing or air drop. Any questions?"

"Not for me," Ted said looking at Robb. Robb shook his head.

Without a word, Ezekiel got up, put on his coat, took his briefcase and walked out the door. Seconds later, Robb and Ted watched the jeep roar down the drive with Ezekiel reading his red book.

"Looks like a spook fade-out," Ted smiled. "We won't see him again."

They finished drawing their course lines, figured their no wind headings, then cut and folded the map for easy reference in flight.

"Robb, thought we might try flying at 50 feet over water and 200 feet over that 12-mile stretch in France. Can pop up to 500 feet two minutes out from the strip."

"Sounds good."

"Let's try to get some rest before dinner."

Robb stared at the ceiling and thought about landing in the pitch-blackness, in enemy territory. Last night he'd dreamed the SS had been waiting and jerked him and Ted from the cockpit. *Think about something else. Try to get some sleep.* He rolled onto his side and stared out the window.

"Robb, I can't sleep either," Ted said. "Wanta take a look at *Double Ugly?*"

"Okay. Glad everything's happening fast. Less time to think."

"Yeah."

Ian and his ground crew were replacing *Double Ugly's* engine cowl. "Suh, she's going to be in tip-top shape. 'We've given 'er new plugs and battery. We'll run the engine as soon as they finish replacing the cowl and check for oil and fuel leaks."

"How about the load?" Ted asked.

"Suh, we've loaded and unloaded your cargo eleven times. The off load can be done in 22 seconds." Ian checked his watch. "Suh, it's nearly time for dinner."

"Thanks, Ian, see you later," Ted said.

Desmond had been pleasantly surprised by the civility of the two young Americans. Knowing they were going on a very dangerous mission, he decided to treat them to his favorite dinner, *Filet de Poisson Poches Au Vin Blanc*. It had been the first recipe taught during his training in France, at the *L'ecole Professionelle de la Boucherie de Paris*.

Desmond slipped the fishmonger an extra ten shillings for three of the monger's best filets of sole. He and the downstairs maid would share one. He poached the filets in white wine, added butter, finely chopped shallots, salt, pepper and two cloves of garlic. He made a cream sauce from the poaching fluid, covered the filets with the hot creamy wine sauce, poured melted butter with finely minced shallots over the boiled potatoes and included a serving of green peas that he had managed to find. For desert, Desmond prepared his best *Mousseline au Chocolat* and brewed his favorite French coffee from his prewar stock.

"Delicious dinner," Ted said, pushing his chair back from the table.

"Perfect," Robb added.

Desmond smiled and nodded. He wanted to bow, but his back still hadn't recovered. He handed Ted two neatly wrapped sandwiches and a thermos of tea. "Suh...I wish you both...the very best."

Ted and Robb preflighted *Double Ugly*, pulled the chocks, climbed inside, set the trim tabs for take off and waited in the pitch-black cockpit for the agents to arrive.

"This overcast has taken blackness to the third power," Ted said. "I've never seen a darker night."

"Yeah, made to order for vertigo," Robb replied.

"Robb, this strip's so damned narrow, I'm going to use the landing lights for takeoff."

"Good idea. Ten minutes to ten," Robb said, shining his flashlight on the clock. "Time to get going."

The rear door opened; the two agents jumped inside and Ian helped them with their parachutes and safety belts. "Suh, passengers are ready. Good luck." Ian closed the door.

"Clear!" Ted yelled out the cockpit window. He pushed on the brake pedals, turned on the mag and battery switches, flipped the starter switch; the prop turned twice; the engine coughed, spit fire, then cracked a steady beat. The modified exhaust hid much of the blue flame. Ted turned on the landing lights, eased the throttle forward and taxied the heavily loaded *Double Ugly* to the end of the strip. He completed the mag and prop checks, reset the directional gyro, and looked at Robb. "Ready?"

Robb double-checked the trim tabs and gave a thumb's up.

Ted eased the throttle forward to full power; the engine roared; *Double Ugly* shook; her fuselage fabric rattled against her spruce ribs. At exactly 10:00 o'clock, he released the brakes.

Double Ugly inched her way down the strip. Ted tapped the brakes to keep her straight. She gradually gained speed. Her tail rose; he eased back on the yoke; she staggered into the black sky. The radar altimeter jumped to five feet, as *Double Ugly* skimmed the treetops.

"Close!" Ted yelled, turning off the landing lights. "Going on the gauges. You look ahead, keep us clear. I'm turning on course and will level at 200 feet."

Four minutes later, the radar altimeter jumped. "Crossing the coast," Robb called. He looked south. There was no sky, no English Channel—nothing but pitch-blackness. Vertigo tweaked his senses and he glanced at the flight instruments, then looked ahead. "Like flying through a tunnel filled with soot."

"Yeah. Starting a very slow descent," Ted said. "Keep your eye on the radar altimeter and give me a call at 50 feet."

Robb watched the radar altimeter needle swing past the 100-foot mark. "Passing 70 feet...60 feet...50 feet."

"Rog, barometric altimeter reads the same." Ted leveled *Double Ugly* at 50 feet. "This is gonna be work. Cantankerous old girl's hard to keep in trim. Feel like you're dragging your butt across the water?"

"Yeah. Do I ever."

"Web Foot, Deep Purple here." Ted transmitted.

"Web Foot reads you five square Deep Purple. Show you bang-on, suh."

"Deep Purple copies."

For the next 16 minutes, Ted had his eyes glued to the flight instruments and Robb glanced back and forth between the black nothingness and radar altimeter. He was impressed by the way Ted never varied more than five feet above or below the altimeter's 50-foot marker while his heading held steady. *He's good... really good.*

"Deep Purple, Web Foot here." The transmission cracked through the silent black night, like a clap of thunder. "Correct two degrees right. Show your ground speed as 119. You're about to fade from my scope. I'll be standing by."

"Deep Purple copied."

Robb computed the time to the turn point and checked the aircraft clock. "Turn point at 11:05. Want me to hold it up for a while, give you a break?"

"No thanks. I'm in the groove, might as well take it all the way." Ted held *Double Ugly's* altitude and heading steady.

"Stand by to turn," Robb said, as the minute and second hands approached 11:05. "Ready...turn now."

Ted started the turn and added power. In one minute, he rolled *Double Ugly* out on a heading of 90 degrees and leveled her off at 200 feet. "This is like high altitude. First time I've been able to relax."

"Yeah," Robb sighed. "Got the flashing light, dead ahead."

One minute later, the radar altimeter dropped to 140 feet, indicating they had crossed the coast. Ted climbed another 60 feet.

"Landing strip, five minutes." Robb called when the clock showed 11:08. He rotated the antenna of the directional finding radio. Les Brown's *"Sentimental" Journey* came in loud and clear. It was one of Robb's favorites, but he barely heard it tonight. "Directional antenna shows the strip three degrees to the right."

At 11:11, Ted added power and climbed to 500 feet.

"Tree and vehicle lights, ten degrees right," Robb called.

"I have them," Ted replied. "I'll turn right onto a base leg, save time. Robb! Got vehicle lights, coming from Coutances!"

Robb's pucker string snapped tight.

"Tell our passengers to get the cargo ready for off-loading," Ted shouted, turning onto the base leg.

Robb turned and yelled, "Untie the cargo and get ready to unload! Gotta hurry! Vehicle lights headed toward the field!"

The agents unbuckled their safety belts and took off their parachutes, then started untying the ropes from the tie-down rings on the floor.

Ted turned *Double Ugly* onto final approach.

After checking that the lights were lined up, Robb looked back. One agent was having a problem. Robb shined his flashlight on the tie-down, saw the hands of a woman. "Can I help?"

She looked up and shook her head no. Her cat-like eyes beamed beneath the bill of her cap. Robb did a double take. *My God. . .it's Joyce!*

"Give me a call at the tree line!" Ted shouted.

Robb looked back at the windshield; the lights were lined up. Ted had slowed *Double Ugly'* and was holding her on the edge of a stall, with power. The radar altimeter jumped.

"Tree line, 60 feet!" Robb shouted. "50, 40, 30, 20, 10, 5."

Double Ugly' shuddered and made a solid three point touch down. Ted cut the power, pulled the yoke back in his gut, stood on the brakes and *Double Ugly* stopped.

Robb unsnapped his safety belt and shoulder harness, took off his chute and hurried back to help with the cargo. The passenger door swung open. Joyce and the other agent pushed the containers out the door to the waiting *Marquis*. Then they both jumped to the ground and ran to the waiting truck. Beyond the truck, back in the woods, Robb saw muzzle flashes.

"*Monsieur,* you are clear for zee takeoff! You must hurree! *Le boche!*" one of the *Marquis* shouted to Robb, before slamming the door.

"Clear to roll! Gunfire to your left!" Robb yelled to Ted.

Ted gunned the engine, kicked the right rudder and held the right brake and *Double Ugly* spun around.

During the turn, Robb braced himself against the side of the fuselage to keep from being slammed to the floor.

Just as the *Double Ugly's* nose pointed west, Ted slammed the throttle full forward, quickly flicked the landing lights on and off to make sure nothing was in front of them. He released the brakes; *Double Ugly* roared down the strip.

Robb scrambled to the cockpi t, pulled himself into his seat, got into his chute, then buckled his safety belt and shoulder harness.

Double Ugly leaped into the black sky, heading west. The clock read II:17. Robb put on his headset. The radio beacon had shut down. *Hope to hell Joyce and the others got away.*

Ted leveled *Double Ugly'* at 200 feet, let her speed increase, then throttled back. "Close."

"Yeah," Robb replied. "Hope they made it okay."

"I'm sure they did. That's probably a normal operation for the *Marquis*. They're damned skilled at their trade."

As they roared west, Robb wanted to tell Ted about Joyce, but remembered what General Tyler had said.

When they crossed the coast, Ted descended to 50 feet. After two minutes, he turned north.

Robb checked the clock; it showed II:27. "Should be abeam Alderney at 5I past the hour."

"Rog."

Droning through the blackness, Robb thought about Joyce. In less than an hour, he and Ted would be safely back in Britain. But she would be facing danger, every minute of every day until the end of the war. *She's a classy lady. . .maybe the classiest lady I'll ever know. How in the hell can her husband let her do this? He's gotta be some kind'a nut. Maybe the snooty old fart's just part of her cover. Dear God. . .please keep her safe.*

"Web Foot, Deep Purple here," Ted transmitted at II:45.

"Ah say, Deep Purple, make your cockerel crow, suh."

"Deep Purple's cockerel is crowing."

"Strangle cockerel and vector 002 degrees, ground speed 121. Report, suh."

"Web Foot. Deep Purple had a three pointer," Ted replied.

"Good show, Deep Purple. Your feet will be dry at 12:20."

"Rog, Web Foot. We're climbing to 200 feet," Ted transmitted. He increased the power and started the climb.

"How about a sandwich and some tea?" Robb asked, as Ted leveled *Double Ugly*.

"Sounds good."

They finished their cheese sandwiches, which had French mustard and sliced tomato. Robb poured Ted a cup of tea and handed it to him. "Should cross the coast any second now."

"That's good. I'll be glad to get on the ground. Been a long day."

WHOOMP! WHOOMP! WHOOMP! Three orange fireballs exploded in the blackness, 100 feet in front of *Double Ugly's* nose.

"Shit! Some trigger happy gunner didn't get the word!" Ted yelled, as he dropped his cup of tea and struggled to turn the yoke to get them out of the line of fire.

WHOOMP! WHOOMP! WHAAAM! *Double Ugly* took a hit in her nose. Robb and Ted slammed against their safety belts and shoulder harnesses.

Double Ugly's engine quit; flames leaped from the right side of her bulbous nose and shot past the door window next to Robb. A hellish orange light filled the cockpit and passenger compartment.

Ted stomped on the right rudder; *Double Ugly's* nose yawed to the right and the flames pulled away from the fuselage before the fabric caught on fire.

"Mayday! Mayday! Deep Purple hit by flak! Engine on fire! No power, goin' down! Near the coast!" Ted shouted over the radio.

"Web Foot copies. Calling rescue."

"Roger," Ted replied, but there was no side tone. "SHIT! Radio's dead! Turn on the landing lights so we can see something."

Robb flipped the landing lights on. They beamed through the pitch-black sky and lit the foaming breakers on the coast. Just beyond the breakers was the anti-invasion barrier of steel beams that had been angled into the sand like cross swords. On the beach beyond the steel beams lay a short strip of open sand.

"Gonna try for that strip of sand!" Ted pushed hard on the right rudder and started a skidding right turn to line up for a landing. "Give me full flaps!"

"Radar altimeter shows 50 feet," Robb called, as he lowered *Double Ugly's* flaps.

"Little high! Gonna slip her!" Ted jammed harder on the right rudder and forced the stick to the left; *Double Ugly* shuddered as she dropped. The skid carried her toward the steel beams.

Robb glanced out the right side. "Getting close to the beams!"

Ted stopped the skid. The engine flames leaped past Robb's cockpit window and blocked his side view. He felt the heat through the window.

"We're five feet above the ground!" Robb shouted, after checking the radar altimeter.

Ted pulled *Double Ugly's* nose higher and she shuddered. THUMP! Her tail wheel hit the sand. WHOOMP! Her main gear hit.

A few hundred feet beyond *Double Ugly's* nose, Robb saw a large mound of sand. He grabbed the armrests and braced himself for the crash.

Ted snatched the yoke all the way back. Fifty feet short of the mound, he kicked full right rudder and locked the right brake. *Double Ugly* swung right.

SCRUNCH! Her left gear dug into the sand and collapsed; her left wing tip hit the mound.

Robb's body slammed hard to the left; the safety belt cut into his gut; the left shoulder harness strap dug into his neck and his head banged his left shoulder. Flames from *Double Ugly* 's bulbous nose shot higher and leaped across the windshield.

"Get your door open! Mine's jammed!" Ted shouted.

Robb turned the latch and kicked the cockpit door open. They scrambled out and ran.

BAA-BOOM! An orange flash lit the sky. The blast sent them sprawling— head first toward the hard wet sand.

Robb closed his eyes; his face hit. He saw a flash as his teeth dug into his lips and his mouth filled with sand.

Stunned, he lay there while his mind played catch up. Finally, he rolled on to his right side. With his left index finger, he gently scooped a big chunk of the sand out of his mouth. The sickening sweetness of warm blood from his lips mixed with the salty-fishy sand. He scooped more sand out of his mouth, then spit several times.

"Robb, you okay?" Ted asked.

"Yeah. Got a cut lip, mouth full of sand and a couple of bruises," he grunted, then spit more sand. "You okay?"

"Yeah. Just skinned the side of my face and have a few bruises."

They both sat up and looked back at *Double Ugly*. Channel winds whipped the flames coming from her wreckage. The black shadows of the rusty steel beams danced along the foaming surf.

"Like losing a friend," Ted sighed. "Never thought I'd feel that way about a UC-64. Makes you want to plant a cross and write an epitaph, Here lies *Double Ugly*...a good old gal...who got blind-sided...by friendly flak."

Robb nodded.

££££

An American beach patrol took Robb and Ted to a dispensary where a doctor treated them. Afterward, they were taken to the manor house in a jeep. Desmond met them at the front door. "May I pour you a Scotch and soda?"

"That would be great," Ted replied.

The next morning, Desmond served them bacon and eggs, with tea, toast and orange marmalade. Despite his back problem, he bowed from the waist as Robb and Ted departed for General Tyler's office.

££££

"That was a great effort, guys," General Tyler said.

"Thanks, dad."

"Hell of a note to get shot down by one of your own. But those things happen in combat. Always have, always will. Lucky you didn't get wounded or seriously injured durin' the crash. Wish we could put you in for an award, but security won't permit it. Maybe sometime after the war is over this story can be told."

"We're not concerned about that. Robb and I just want to get back to the group."

"Guys, I'm sorry to be the one to tell you this. Your boss, Major Brown got shot down on a strafin' mission."

"Shit! Did he get out of the aircraft okay?"

"He crash-landed on an airfield and the krauts captured him. He's a big fish, so the krauts made a lotta noise about it on the radio last night."

"He was a great commander and combat leader," Ted said staring at the floor. "We'll really miss him."

"Ted, you're takin' his place. You'll be promoted to major as soon as you return."

CHAPTER 19

D-Day

"Maximum effort, gentlemen. Briefing in an hour and fifteen minutes," the sergeant said turning on the light bulb.

Robb struggled to open his eyes, then closed them. He had gone to bed at 9:00, but felt tired. *I'll lie here just for a few seconds.* He went back to sleep.

"Sir, maximum effort. Briefing in an hour and fifteen minutes," the sergeant repeated.

Robb squinted at his watch. It read 12:15. *Can't be. . .right.* He squinted again. It still read 12:15. He held it to his ear. *Damned thing's running.* "What the hell's goin' on?"

"It's D-Day, sir. Teletype's have been clacking for the last four hours. When I came to work at ten o'clock, there were hundreds of C-47's and gliders load-ed with paratroopers circling overhead. About an hour ago they set course for France. Now you can hear the RAF Lancasters, B-17's and B-24's forming up. Sir, we let you sleep as long as we could. So there's no time to spare."

Robb leaped out of bed and snatched his clothes off the footlocker.

"Sumbitch." Rocko grunted, sitting up in bed. "Ike never mentioned D-Day during our double-date last night." He grinned and reached for a sock and ran it between his toes. "Oooh, that feels good."

Art Steel from Bellingham, Washington and Jack Morris from Omaha, Nebraska both smiled as they jumped out of bed and dressed. D-Day would be their third combat mission.

Rocko stood, slipped on his pants, buttoned the fly and then rubbed the cheeks of his butt. "Gonna sue that sumbitchin' dinghy company after the war."

"Shake a leg, guys." Robb grabbed his towel, toothbrush and Ipana and headed for the door.

£££

Ted finished his spam and eggs, leaned against the snack bar and sipped his coffee while Harry James's *I had the Craziest Dream* came from the radio. He heard footsteps and looked up. Robb, Rocko, Art and Jack entered the pilot's lounge with four other pilots.

Big John scooped a large chunk of lard onto the hot kerosene grill with his spatula. He spread the melted lard until the grill was covered with a layer of hot grease. From the large steel bowl filled with eggs, he grabbed an egg in each hand and held them a few inches above the grill. He cracked both eggshells with his thumbs and forefingers and gently twisted the two shells open. Two raw eggs slid onto the grill. He tossed the empty shells into the garbage can and quickly repeated the drill until there were sixteen eggs, all with unbroken yokes, sizzling in the hot grease.

He dropped eight thick slices of bread and eight slices of Spam next to the eggs. After basting each egg three times, he turned over the bread and Spam, then basted the eggs again.

Big John tossed the spatula end over end into the air and caught its wooden handle. He scooped the eggs, Spam and bread onto eight plates and banged the grill with the spatula's steel blade.

Corporal Perkins grabbed the plates of Spam and eggs and placed them on the snack bar. Then he sliced more bread and Spam and put the slices next to the egg bowl.

Glenn Miller's "*GI Jive*" started to play as Rocko grabbed the first plate of Spam and eggs and reached for a cup of coffee. "Sumbitch, that little jump tune grabs me up front," he said, wiggling his butt. "Make room for the Hoboken champ." He danced across the room, placed his cup of coffee on the arm of a chair, sat down and hurriedly chopped up the Spam and eggs with his fork.

Holding the handle of the fork in his teeth, he ripped the hot greasy bread into pieces and dropped them onto the Spam and eggs. He took his fork and stirred the pile until everything was covered with egg yoke, then used his index finger to slide a large chunk of the mixture onto the fork and stuffed it into his mouth. He chewed a few times and washed it down with coffee.

When he finished, he ran his index finger around his teeth and scraped the chunks loose. He chewed the chunks, licked his finger clean, smacked his lips and wiped his mouth on the back of his hand.

Instead of returning the dirty plate and cup to the snack bar counter, he placed them on the floor and scootched down in the chair with his legs extended. He pulled a used toothpick from his shirt pocket, picked and sucked more food from his teeth and chewed.

"No shortage of entertainment in this squadron," Ted smiled.

Robb smiled and shook his head.

Ted finished his coffee and glanced at his watch. It was 1:20. He tapped his tin cup with a fork. "We're due to brief in ten minutes. Guys, after the group briefing, let's rendezvous in the lounge."

£££

"HOFFICERS, TEN—SHUN!" The large clock above the map read 1:30.

"Please be seated." The Colonel hurried down the aisle and stopped next to his striped chair in Bugeye's section. He turned and faced the pilots. "D-Day gents. Lotta stuff to talk about and not much time. Let's get started, Stormy."

"Sumbitch, old man's eyes look like two piss holes in the snow," Rocko whispered.

Robb held his index finger to his lips and frowned at Rocko.

"Sir, there'll be a layer of clouds covering Britain and the invasion area for at least the next 18 hours. Cloud bases will vary from 3500 to 5000 feet and the visibility below them will be three to five miles. There will be a few breaks in the clouds inland." Captain Knight covered the synoptic situation and handed the cue to Major Watson.

"The Colonel asked me to prepare a map overlay to give you some idea of the vast air and surface activity today." Major Watson untied a string at the top of the map and the roll of clear acetate dropped across the map. It contained a maze of colored lines that started from the south coast of Britain and extended 50 miles past the Normandy invasion area. "This schematic shows the planned flow of today's air and surface activity."

"Schematic," Rocko snorted. "Another of old Geoffrey's two-bit words."

Major Watson's beady eyes glared at Rocko. "There'll be two to three thousand RAF and American aircraft over the invasion force all day, and night fighters when it gets dark.

"These solid black lines in the channel mark the north-south corridors the surface ships will follow from the British coast to their assembly areas." He tapped them with the cue stick. "The assembled ships will orbit in two race track patterns indicated by the broken black lines north of the beaches." He tapped the cue again. "The south track is the initial invasion force and the second track is the follow-on force.

"The dotted orange lines running perpendicular to the route of the invasion force indicates the patrol area for five groups of P-38's providing close air cover for the entire armada. The P-38's are being used because they are easier for our ground forces to identify and should reduce the possibility of air losses by friendly fire.

"The color codes along the Normandy beaches are the assault areas. The British and Canadians are landing here on the east," he said tapping each of them. "And the Americans are landing further west, here at these two locations called Omaha and Utah.

"Before the American invasion force comes ashore at 0630 hours, their landing areas will be struck by 1400 heavy bombers, 300 medium bombers, 160 fighter/bombers and naval gun fire.

"Solid green lines are the air corridors through which the heavy and medium bombers will fly to reach their targets in France." Major Watson ran the tip of the cue stick from the north end of the corridor to the south. "For separation, the mediums will fly below 10,000 feet and the heavies will remain above them. The parallel dotted green lines are the routes the fighters and fighter/bombers will follow to and from the invasion area. Inbound aircraft will fly at odd thousands and outbound will fly at even thousands.

"The three red race tracks, 50 miles to the east, west and south of the invasion area, are the 8th Air Force air defense zones. Our fighters will start patrolling at dawn and end at dusk tonight.

"These purple lines converging on the Cherbourg peninsula from the west are the C-47 routes leading to the drop zones for the 82nd and 101st Airborne Divisions. First wave of 900 C-47's and 50 gliders dropped their troopers at midnight. The troopers landed here, just northwest of Coutances," he said tapping the cue.

Robb wondered about Joyce. *Dear God...keep her safe.*

"Second wave of troopers will drop before first light this morning. The blue lines bordering the C-47 routes across France and around the drop zones indicate the patrol patterns for the radar jamming aircraft and night fighters covering the airborne operation."

Major Watson pointed to three temporary airfields the *Luftwaffe* had recently constructed. He gave the estimated numbers and types of aircraft at each. "The *Luftwaffe* is in such a sad state they shouldn't present a problem. They have very few aircraft, are short on parts, have very little fuel and their pilots are poorly trained."

He finished with the escape and evasion information for France then handed the cue stick to Major Hunt.

"Guys, when you get to your aircraft this morning, you'll notice that large black and white identification stripes have been painted on the fuselage and wings. They are called invasion stripes and hopefully they'll help keep our ground troops from shooting at us. As Geoffrey mentioned, five groups of P-38's, four from the 8th AF and one from the 9th AF, will provide close cover for the invasion forces. The easy-to-recognize 38's were selected for this job to reduce the possibility of air losses from friendly fire like we had during the Sicilian invasion.

"Our 8th AF fighters will patrol these three defense zones around the invasion force." Major Hunt tapped each zone with the tip of the cue stick. "This is our zone and we've got to start patrolling by first light, which will be about 0330 hours, and we'll finish tonight at 2200 hours after last light. Those of you flying the first mission this morning will fly the last mission tonight. You'll have a night landing after a long day. So as soon as you land after your morning mission, I would suggest that you eat, hit the sack and get as much sleep as you can.

"We'll patrol for at least four hours and there'll be a minimum of 300 fighters in the three zones at all times.

"Our group will start patrolling near Coutances," he said pointing. "Our area of responsibility runs east and passes a few miles south of Saint Lo, then to Villers-Bocage, past Saint Pierre-sur-Divest on to Lisieux. Bugeye will take the eastern section of the zone, Hot Rod'll take the center and Snapper'll patrol in the west.

"We've been tasked to keep the *Luftwaffe* from attacking our forces and *Wehrmacht* from sending in reinforcements. Snapper, you'll have to be careful when you attack ground targets because you're working close to the area where our airborne troops landed. The last thing we want to do is strafe our troops. If in doubt, don't attack.

"During the hours of darkness this morning and tonight, there will be a complete blackout from the coast of Britain through the invasion zone. So before we leave Britain this morning we'll have to turn off our navigation lights and fly night formation using the fire from the engine exhaust stacks as our reference."

"Shithouse mouse! Ain't that nice," Rocko snorted.

"*C'est la guerre*, Rocko," Major Hunt smiled. "We'll take 30-second spacing between flights on takeoff and hold 250 mph indicated en route to our patrol zone. Just as soon as it gets light enough to see something, spread out in combat formation.

"Shipborne radar will be available to the tactical aircraft providing direct support for the ground forces, but we can use it if we need it. They'll be on Charlie channel and their call sign is Frog Leg. Better write it down.

"Although you'll be above the undercast on the way in, you'll probably see bomb flashes when the heavies unload on the beaches. They're dropping 500 pounders with instantaneous fuses to reduce cratering, which will kill Germans but not dig big holes to slow our troops. So the bomb flashes should be a little brighter.

"Any questions?" There were none and Major Hunt looked at the Colonel. "Sir."

The Colonel hopped onto the platform and took the cue stick. "As you've heard, there are *beaucoup* aircraft in the sky and they will be for at least the next 36 hours. Traffic may be our number one hazard.

"I don't think there'll be many kraut fighters flyin' today. Each squadron, make one sweep of your area at altitude. If there are no krauts about, send two flights down to strafe and keep one flight high just in case a kraut fighter strays into the area.

"Some of our new guys have never strafed and it'll be new stuff for them. *Terra incognita*, as my New Jersey Italian friend used to say in Spain. You must always remember that strafin' can be deadly—anytime, anyplace. Unlike air-to-air combat, you gotta use finesse and don't get too aggressive. Remember to vary your attack headings and give the gunners a different sight problem on each firin' pass. If you're outgunned, be smart and don't get into a pissin' contest with a skunk. Make one pass, cut grass and move on to another target. The idea is to kill krauts, not let them kill you. No damned gun position is worth a pilot and a P-51.

"Our 9th AF friends have reported that some trains have flak cars. So flight leads, when you attack trains, split your flights. Two aircraft on one side, two on the other. Send one element down and if a flak car opens fire the second element can attack the guns from the rear. Once we knock out the steam engine, the tank cars should get top priority. General Spaatz's oil attacks have made the krauts critically short of gasoline. If we eliminate their resupply effort near the invasion area, they'll have to park more of their tanks and trucks and we can whip their asses faster.

"The krauts still have some flak towers scattered about. They resemble water towers or aboveground silos that we have back in the Midwest. Be on the lookout for them because they're heavily armed. Okay, let's get strapped up and have at the bastards."

Ted waited at the snack bar until everyone had entered. "I have an announcement. We just got word last night that we have a new captain. Captain Robb Baines. Front and center, Robb."

Ted took the silver bar off the collar of Robb's green uniform shirt and pinned on captain's bars. "Take good care of them, they were mine." He smiled and shook Robb's hand. "Okay guys, time to get strapped up."

As Robb and Rocko walked toward the locker room, Robb finally said, "I wish there was some way we could get you promoted."

"Hey, *Amigo*. Don't sweat it. Ted told me several months ago that I'd probably be stuck with my blue bar for the duration. Bein' a permanent flight officer's okay by me. Pay's good and my blue pickle gets me into most classy bars. As I've said before, all I wanna do is drive a fighter. Not lookin' for a lotta rank, just a lotta flyin' time so I can go to work for the airlines after the war."

Robb put on his flight and G-suit, recalling how nervous he had been before his first combat mission seven months ago. Back then a captain had seemed like a fatherly figure with all the answers. *Now I am one...can't believe it. But there's so much I don't know. Forget that...these new guys are depending on you and you have a job to do. So get your ass in gear.*

£££

In the predawn blackness, Robb leveled his P-51 at 11,000 feet, throttled back and turned south. He glanced at the aircraft clock. *English Channel in three minutes.* He looked ahead for other aircraft and saw nothing but black sky. *There*

are hundreds of aircraft out there and I can't see damned thing. Might as well keep my head in the
cockpit and pray.

Three minutes later Robb turned off his navigation lights. Art, Rocko and
Jack turned off their navigation lights and moved a few feet closer. In the blackness, the engine's blue exhaust flames highlighted the sleek noses of their 51's.

Half way across the Channel, Robb saw orange flashes light the clouds
above the invasion beaches as the first wave of B-17's and B-24's dropped their
bombs. Eventually the 8th Air Force bombers would drop more than 11,000 five
hundred-pound bombs and the RAF and 9th Air Force would drop thousands
more.

WHOOMP! Four blue exhaust flames shot past—less than 50 feet above
Robb's head.   *Shit. . .that was close! Stop watchin' the sights and look for aircraft.*

"Sumbitch! That multi-motored job damned near creamed us, *amigo.*"

God damn it, Rocko I know that! Robb wanted to tell him to shut up but maintained radio silence.

Seven minutes south of the French coast, Robb rechecked the clock. *One*
minute to our turn point. Sixty seconds later, he turned right and rolled out on a
heading of 263 degrees.

After several minutes, Robb noticed the faint rays of the sun in his rearview
mirrors. He searched the sky ahead and finally saw Ted's flight. "Snapper Yellow
here, I have Snapper Red at my 12 o'clock."

"Snapper Red, roger."

"Snapper White has a tally ho on Yellow."

"Snapper Red here, let's go combat spread."

Approaching their patrol area, Robb spotted a section of the Cherbourg
Peninsula's western coastline through a small break in the undercast. He also no-
ticed the railroad and highway that ran from Carentan to the city of Cherbourg.
At Coutances, Ted made a wide left turn and headed south along the coast to
Granville. After turning east, he flew to Fleurs and turned north toward Villers
Bocage. From Villers Bocage, he returned to Coutances.

"Snapper, here. White, remain high. Yellow. go in trail and follow me." Ted
descended through a small break in the clouds. He leveled at 3000 feet southeast
of Granville, then turned north toward the highway and railroad intersection at
Villedieu.

"Snapper Yellow, go line abreast to increase our look area."

Robb moved his flight out a half-mile to Ted's right. About a minute later,
he saw smoke. "Yellow One has a train twelve o'clock, two miles."

"Red here. Take 'em, we'll give you cover," Ted replied.

"Yellow, roger. Let's check switches hot, go 2500 RPM and 42 inches. One
and Two will attack from the south and take out the engine. Three and Four
swing wide to the north and watch for a flak car. If there's no flak car, attack

from the north side as we pull up. Make steep pull ups after each firing pass," Robb added, recalling the P-40 pilot back in the States who had made a shallow recovery from a strafing attack and flown into his ricochets.

Robb rolled his 51 into a dive and placed the gun sight's pipper just below the locomotive's boiler. In the dive, he counted ten freight cars and the third car was a tank car.

Two thousand feet out, he let the pipper drift up to the locomotive's boiler and squeezed the trigger. The four 50-caliber machine guns clacked and his 51 shook; APIs sparkled on the boiler; two huge geysers of steam jetted skyward and the train started to slow down.

Robb yanked back on the stick, zoomed through the steam and started a climbing turn to the left. At 500 feet, he looked back.

"Yellow Three didn't see any flak. I'm startin' down the chute, goin' for the tank car." Rocko opened fire and API's sparkled on the tank car.

WHOOM! The tank car exploded. A huge fireball mushroomed a thousand feet in the sky; jagged pieces of the fuel tank, wheels and sections of track tumbled out of the fireball.

Rocko yanked back on the stick. His 51 shot into the ball of fire.

The freight car in front of the tanker flipped off the track, pulling the other freight car and locomotive with it. Three of the cars behind slammed into the wreckage and folded like an accordion. The last four cars angled off the track and rolled onto their sides.

Robb saw Rocko's 51 zoom out of the flames.

"Sumbitch. Almost got my ass fried." His raspy voice had taken on a higher pitch.

"Check your engine instruments while I move in and check your bird," Robb transmitted.

"Gauges are all green. Sumbitchin' krauts had some kind'a crazy go-juice in that frickin' tank car."

"Yellow Three, you're not spraying coolant or oil, but your bird has some holes and your invasion stripes look singed. Play it safe and head for homeplate. Contact Frog Leg on Charlie channel, request the shortest route back and have him alert air sea rescue."

"Yellow Three, will do," Rocko replied, as he and Jack turned north. "Let's go Charlie channel, Yellow Four."

Robb glanced at the train. A tower of black smoke reached the clouds and 200 foot orange flames had engulfed the locomotive and all the freight cars except the last four.

Two horse-drawn carts were moving across a field toward the four unburned freight cars. More French civilians were running to join in the scavenger hunt.

"Snapper Yellow, Red is passing on your left side. We'll leave the remaining freight cars for the French and look for more targets," Ted transmitted.

"Yellow, roger."

Ted followed the highway that led to Caen. For the next four minutes they saw nothing on the highway and there were no farmers in the fields.

"Red has four trucks at twelve o'clock." Ted turned 20-degrees right to get set for his attack.

Robb saw the trucks speeding toward the bridge that crossed the Vire River.

"Red One and Two will take the first two trucks. There may be flak around the bridge, so keep your eyes peeled."

The first truck started across the bridge. It had eight soldiers and was towing a cannon. Ted rolled his 51 into a dive and opened fire and API's sparkled on the cab. The truck whipped to the left, crashed through the rail and tumbled off the bridge. The cannon broke loose and twisted through the air. The soldiers catapulted from the truck. Their arms and legs flailed as they tried in vain to slow their fall. The truck, men and cannon splashed into the river.

Snapper Red Two opened fire on the second truck as it reached the far end of the bridge. API's sparkled on the engine and cab; the truck whipped to the right, ran off the road, flipped over and slid on its side. Wooden ammunition boxes and cannon shell crates flew out and shattered. Thousands of bullets and shells scattered along the road and hedgerow.

Ted and his wingman pulled up. Red Three raked the third truck with machine gun fire. It ran off the road, hit a tree and started to burn. Red Four opened fire on the last truck. API's sparkled on the truck bed and a ball of fire exploded from beneath the canvas top. The burning truck swerved to the right; the driver leaped out and slammed into the ground.

"Snapper gang, we're finished here. Let's form up." Ted flew north to Saint-Lo and started a shallow turn to the west to follow the railroad. Five miles north of Coutances, Robb saw a group of 24 B-26's that had just attacked a target. Their bombs had set off secondary explosions and columns of black smoke reached the overcast.

Further east, more columns of black smoke lined the highway where twelve P-47's were bombing and strafing a convoy of German vehicles that had been speeding toward the invasion zone.

Five miles south of Coutances, Robb noticed a short grass landing strip that ran east and west through a small forest. *That's gotta be it! Wonder if Ted sees it. . .?* Once again he prayed that she was okay.

Ted led them past the smoking train they had strafed earlier. The Frenchmen had loaded the carts and were pulling away from the damaged freight cars. They waved as the P-51's flew by.

For the next two hours, Snapper crisscrossed the area looking for German fighters, trains and military vehicles, but found none.

"Shotgun here. Tarzan is inbound with 36 chicks. We are clear to depart."

"Hot Rod copies."

"Snapper roger. Snapper going Charlie channel now." Ted changed channels and waited a few seconds. "Snapper Red's on."

"Snapper Yellow."

"White's on and closing at your six o'clock." Snapper White had dived through a hole in the clouds and was closing fast on Red and Yellow.

"Frog Leg, Snapper Red here."

"Snapper, Frog Leg reads you five square. Go."

"Frog Leg, Snapper is approaching from the southwest with ten chicks, at angels three. Request permission to pass through the west side of your area?"

"Snapper, make your parrot crow."

"Snapper's parrot is crowing now." He flicked on the IFF switch.

"Frog Leg has you, Snapper. Strangle your parrot and turn port to 350."

"Snapper's strangling parrot and turning 350." Ted switched off the IFF and turned.

Passing Carentan, Robb saw about 30 B-26's due west of Omaha beach. They were bombing targets near Isigny. About five miles south of Omaha beach, 36 P-47's were dive-bombing and strafing German troop positions.

Ted flew a mile west of the railroad and highway that ran from Carentan northwest to Cherbourg.

North of Carentan, Robb spotted many of the large gliders that had carried airborne troops to France before daylight that morning. Some had landed to the north, some to the south, some to the east and west. A few had struck buildings, trees or hedgerows bordering the small fields. In another field, where two had collided head-on during landing and eight bodies were lined up on the ground. Three more gliders were broken in half by hard landings. The pilots either misjudged their height above the ground in the darkness, or were wounded.

In another field, the wreckage pattern of two gliders indicated they had collided in the air and dropped straight to the ground. Bodies of at least 30 troopers were scattered around the wreckage. A mile west lay two burned out C-47's that had been shot down before they reached the drop zones.

At Omaha beach, mortar shells exploded in the sand. Towers of black smoke marked burning landing craft, vehicles and equipment. A flight of P-38's passed 1000 feet above Snapper to make certain the P-51's weren't German ME-109's.

Flying past Pointe de Barfleur on the northeast tip of the Cherbourg Peninsula, Robb saw the city of Cherbourg to the west. To the east, hundreds of freighters and landing craft orbited in the racetrack pattern, waiting their turn to head for the invasion beach. Destroyer escorts covered their flanks while more P-38's circled above.

"Snapper, Frog Leg here. Steer starboard to 010."

"Snapper turning right to 010."

As Snapper approached the Isle of Wight, Robb saw two formations of B-26's heading south toward France.

"Frog Leg, Snapper Red's departing your area," Ted called.

"Snapper, you're clear."

Ted changed channels and called Sunshine for a steer to Boxted. After landing, the exhausted pilots had a quick debriefing and lunch before going to bed.

£££

"Briefing in an hour and fifteen minutes," the sergeant said.

Robb tried to hold his eyes open, but couldn't and he went back to sleep.

"Sir, briefing in an hour and fifteen minutes," the sergeant repeated. "You don't have much time."

Robb opened his eyes again and struggled to look at his watch; it read 5:00 o'clock. "Is it afternoon or morning?"

"Afternoon, sir. This is the briefing for your second mission today."

"Okay." Robb's mind slowly engaged with his brain.

"Sumbitch, that was a short five hours. My ass is so sore I can't sleep on my back. After the frickin' war I'm gonna get my uncle Benito to sue that frickin' dinghy company." Rocko groped for one of his socks and ran it between his toes.

"Come on Rocko," Robb said after starting toward the door with Art and Jack.

Rocko leaped out of bed, slipped into his pants and only buttoned the waist button. He put on his shirt but left it unbuttoned. He jammed his feet into his GI shoes and never tied them. After rubbing his hand across the bristles of his heavy black beard, he grabbed his Lifebuoy soap and razor. Rocko always bragged about being the only real man in the flight, but this evening he would have traded his heavy beard for their "peach fuzz."

Kicking the door open, he stumbled outside and shuffled along the macadam lane. The breeze parted his unbuttoned shirt and revealed a mat of black hair on his chest and stomach. The unfastened belt let his pants hang low on his hips. His pants legs draped over his untied shoes and his open fly revealed olive drab shorts.

Before entering the latrine, Robb glanced back and what he saw made him smile and shake his head. *If Bill Mauldin could see him now, he'd change his comic strip to Willie, Joe and Rocko.*

£££

RICHARD M BAUGHN

Captain Knight said they would have rain showers when they returned to-night. Major Watson reported that the Americans had secured a foothold on Utah Beach, but there was still fierce fighting at Omaha Beach. He added that the German activity in their patrol areas would probably be less than it was in the morning.

Major Hunt finished the operations portion of the briefing and held out the cue stick, "Sir."

"Don't need it, Bob," the Colonel said standing next to his chair. His eyes were still puffy from his rare five hours of uninterrupted sleep. "Gents, this will probably be a borin' four to five hour mission. But tonight we'll have to return to this soggy island through a crowded sky and make a dicey landin' in the rain. We're all gonna be very tired, but we'll have to save a shot of adrenaline to get us on the ground safely."

£££

Ted took all three flights down through a break in the clouds near the west coast of Cherbourg Peninsula and turned south. During their first sweep around the area, Robb spotted a few more damaged *Wehrmacht* trucks that had attempted to move troops and supplies to the front. But now there were no trains or trucks on the move and very few French civilians were out. In one small village, three Frenchmen waved as the P-51's passed above them.

For the next three hours they criss-crossed the area six times. Although Robb's butt felt like two spikes had been driven through the cheeks into his hip joints, he had to struggle to keep his eyes open. Twice, Ted led them through a five-minute rat race to help ward off drowsiness. But when it ended, Robb contin-ued to struggle to hold his eyes open. *SHIT...we're all exhausted and not accomplishing a damned thing except boring holes in the sky. If we don't get on the ground soon someone's gonna get killed.*

The sun's rays dropped from sight, leaving an orange glow on the horizon. Robb's eyelids felt like they had five-pound weights tied to them. He moved his head and stretched his arms and legs, trying to stay awake. But as soon as he stopped, his eyes closed, his head bobbled and—he dozed off.

A shot of fear bolted through him and his eyes snapped open.

"YOU DUMB ASS!" he shouted at himself, wondering how long he had slept. He whipped his head to the left and right, Art, Rocko and Jack were still there.

Thank God we didn't slam together! Baines, that's the dumbest thing you've ever done in an airplane. You've got less than an hour to go...now keep your damned eyes open.

"Snapper Red here. Yellow and White, close your formations and go flights in trail with 2000 feet spacing."

Robb knew that Ted wanted to get them ready for the flight back to Britain before the sky turned black. *Thank God. . .we're gonna head home.*

"Snapper Red is turning north and I'll hold 250 mph from here on. Let's go Charlie channel and check in." After Yellow and White flights checked in, Ted received permission to pass through the west side of Frog Leg's area.

Darkness settled over France and Robb dimmed his cockpit lights to reduce the reflection on the canopy to help him see outside. He glanced to the east toward Omaha beach. Muzzle flashes and exploding shells glowed through the blackness like fiery eruptions from a volcanic fissure. *Dear God. . .help our guys.*

Further north over the Channel, a few flicks of light came from the hundreds of ships in the invasion fleet. Robb checked his aircraft clock. *Bloke coast in one minute. Hope it's not raining when we get to Boxted.*

"Frog Leg, this Snapper Red. Permission to leave your frequency."

"Frog Leg here. Snapper, you're four miles from the coast and cleared to change frequency."

"Snapper, roger. Snapper gang, let's go tower channel now." Everyone changed channels and checked in with Ted.

"Sunshine, Snapper Red here. A steer for twelve chicks."

"Roger Snapper, give Sunshine a short count, please," the Boxted controller replied.

"Snapper, one, two, three, four, five, five, four, three, two, one. Over to you, Sunshine."

"Snapper, steer 038."

"Snapper Red's turning to 038. Snapper gang, nav lights on...ready... now."

Robb turned on his navigation lights, looked up, saw the four sets of red and green navigation lights in Ted's flight. Glancing in his rearview mirror, he saw the lights of White flight.

"Sunshine, Snapper Red here. How's the weather?"

"Sunshine has 800 feet with two to three miles visibility in light rain and the wind is 10 mph out of the west. Also have scattered showers with heavier rain in the area. A shower passed over the field about 15 minutes ago and the visibility dropped to one mile."

"Snapper Red, roger. Snapper gang, let's reduce speed to 220 and descend to 700 feet. We'll stay under this stuff."

Robb reduced power slightly and started to descend. He leveled off at 700 feet and let his airspeed stabilize at 220 mph. *Flying this low at night without navigational radios or radar is piss poor. . .but I guess it's better than flying blind through the clouds with hundreds of aircraft.*

Robb had heard that future fighters would have navigational radios like the bombers and cargo aircraft. There had even been reports that ground radar units would one day be located at military airfields to guide aircraft in for landings in bad weather. *Wish we had them tonight.*

Light rain started hitting Robb's windshield making it difficult to see Ted's flight. "Snapper Yellow's moving in closer to Red to keep you in sight."

"Snapper Red, roger."

"Snapper White's moving closer to Yellow."

WHOOMP! Four sets of red and green lights popped out the bottom of the clouds and shot past at a right angle less than two hundred feet in front of Robb. Before he could call them out, the four fighters disappeared in the rainy darkness to his left.

WHOOSH! WHUMP! His 51 bounced, bumped and rocked violently through the prop wash of the passing fighters. Every muscle in his body knotted and his heart pounded in his chest. He held a vise like grip on the stick and stood on the rudder pedals trying to hold his 51 straight and level.

An eternal instant passed and the prop wash ended. Robb blinked sweat from his eyes and glanced to his right and left. Art, Rocko and Jack's 51's were bouncing—but they were still there. *Thank God.*

"Shithouse mouse! Those sumbitches damned near creamed us."

"Snapper Red here. Have a problem Yellow?"

"Had a near miss," Robb replied.

"Snapper gang hang in there. We'll be on the ground in a few minutes. Go to your fullest tank and check your switches for landing. Sunshine, Snapper's counting for another steer. One, two, three, four, five, five, four, three, two, one."

"Snapper, steer 041."

"Snapper's steering 041. Yellow and White, once I see the field I'll turn right and fly the downwind leg about a half-mile south of the runway. We'll go right echelon, drop the landing gear and 20 degrees of flaps, and slow to 160 mph. As soon as I pass the approach end of the runway, I'll turn to base and lower full flaps. Each aircraft in Red flight will follow me with one second spacing. Yellow and White do the same.

"Yellow rog."

"White copy."

Robb changed to his fullest fuel tank, checked that the fuel booster pump switch and the mixture were set on normal, then glanced at the oil and coolant shutter switches to make sure they were both on auto.

"Snapper Red here, have the field eleven o'clock, mile-and-a-half, turning to 120." Ted rolled out of the turn. "Red, echelon right." Once his flight moved to his right side, he transmitted, "Red, gear down...ready...now. Flaps 20 degrees...ready now."

Seconds later, Robb saw the runway lights, "Yellow turning downwind...
now." He rolled out of the turn, "Yellow, echelon right...now." He waited for Art
to move to the right side with Rocko and Jack. "Yellow, gear down...ready...now.
Flaps 20 degrees of flap...ready...now."

"Sunshine, Snapper Red's turning base, gear down and locked, flaps going
full and I've got 3000 rpm."

"Red, you're clear to land. There's a rain shower passing from west to east
across the field," Sunshine replied.

"Red Two, base. Gear down and checked."

"Red Three, base. Gear down and checked."

"Red Four, base. Gear down and checked."

Robb saw the landing lights of Ted's 51 as it rolled down the runway.

"Red One. Rain's getting heavy, guys," Ted called. "Turn off your landing
lights or their reflection on the rain will cause you to lose sight of the runway
lights."

"Yellow One's turning base, gear down," Robb called.

"Yellow, you're flight is clear to land," Sunshine replied.

Robb shoved the prop pitch to 3000, lowered the flaps to full, and double-
checked that the green landing gear light was on and the hydraulic pressure was
1000 psi.

"Yellow Two, base, gear down."

"Yellow Three's base, gear down."

"Yellow, Sunshine here. Rain shower is close to approach end of runway."

"Yellow One copies." Robb rolled out on the final approach and turned
on his landing light to check for the rain. A crystal wall of rain hid the runway
lights. He flicked the landing light off. "Yellow, don't use your landing lights. I'm
in heavy rain near the end of the runway."

"Yellow Four, base, gear down," Jack called.

A few seconds later, White One called turning base, followed quickly by
the rest of the flight.

Robb's 51 touched down and he eased it closer to the left side of the runway, leaving the rightside clear in case Yellow Two landed a little fast.

"Yellow Two has slowed down and has One in sight," Art transmitted.

"Three, samo."

"Yellow Four has all three in sight."

Seconds later, Robb turned off the end of the runway onto the taxiway as
White Three landed.

"WHITE FOUR'S LOST SIGHT OF THREE!"

WHOOM! Orange flames shot across the blackness, as White Four and
Three streaked collided. Their flaming wreckage streaked along the runway.

Fire trucks had their engines running and were parked less than 1000 feet from where the wreckage stopped. But when the firemen reached the crash, the fire from the high-octane fuel was too intense for them to extract the pilots, Tom Woodson and Carl Massoni.

It was midnight before the weary pilots finished debriefing and returned to their huts. Exhausted and sad, Robb lay on his back and thought about Tom and Carl. Unlike combat losses over enemy territory where at least there was hope of pilots returning when the war ended, these deaths were final—more painful.

They were right behind us this morning and again tonight when we almost got killed in midair collisions. Probably thought they had it made when they reached the landing pattern. I wondered how many men were lost in operational accidents today and how many more were lost in combat? Maybe thousands?

CHAPTER 20

Rest and Recuperation in the U.S.

Before Robb and Rocko finished their combat tours in July 1944, Ted persuaded them to volunteer for a second tour, which qualified them for 30 days of R and R in the States. On July 29th, two days before they departed Britain, Robb went to London early in the morning to get the last fitting on his handmade flight boots.

It was warm and sunny when Robb departed the Bond Street Bookmaker's shop and he decided to take a stroll around London. But first he wanted to stop at the American Red Cross Hotel, just up the street.

The doors were open and the normally dim lobby was flooded with sunshine. Halfway from the door to the counter, he stopped and stared. Being so close to where Joyce had stood with her yellow rose that night eight months ago triggered his desire to be with her. *Dear God. . .please let me see her just one more time.*

"May I 'elp you, captain?" The middle-aged lady asked as she raised her head and looked through the black horn-rimmed glasses that rested halfway down her hooked nose.

"Uh. . .a. No thank you, mam." Robb's cheeks felt warm and he grinned sheepishly before he turned and walked out the door. *Forget Joyce. She's outta your league. Get on with your life.*

He strolled in the direction of the Grosvenor House. Passing through Berkeley Square, he recalled the night he and Joyce had stopped and kissed wildly under a tree. The words to the song *A Nightingale Sang in Berkeley Square passed through his mind.* "That certain night, the night we met, there was magic abroad in the air. There were angels dining at the Ritz, and a nightingale sang in Berkeley Square." Joyce loved the song and now it was a favorite of his.

At the Grosvenor House, he went to the mezzanine for a beer but the bar was jam-packed, noisy and surrounded by a cloud of cigarette smoke. He walked around the mezzanine to the table for two next to the rail where he and Joyce had sat. He ordered a beer and slowly sipped it as memories of her swirled through his mind. When he finished, he decided to go to Joyce's apartment. *Maybe the old white-haired elevator operator has heard something about her.* Outside the Grosvenor House he turned left onto Park Lane.

BAAROOM—AROOM—AROOM—AROOM—AROOM! The ear-splitting roar of a buzzbomb with its pulsating ram jet engine turned Robb's body to rock.

Tires screeched as buses and taxis slammed on their brakes. Some bus passengers had already dropped to the floor while the remainder scrambled for cover in bomb shelters and doorways.

Robb followed three middle-aged women inside a doorway. An old man marched in wearing a bowler, a black suit coat and gray vest, dark gray pinstriped pants, gray gloves and carrying a neatly folded umbrella. He stood erect and looked straight ahead with a jutted chin as he centered the umbrella's metal tip on the concrete in front of his brightly polished shoes.

Overhead the buzzbomb's uneven roar suddenly stopped. Robb's muscles tightened and he prayed in silence. The three women held hands, closed their eyes and looked skyward while they prayed out loud. The old man tightened his jaw and his steely blue eyes appeared more defiant.

WHOOM! The concrete shook beneath their feet. The women continued to look up and pray.

"Bloody Heinies," the old man snarled. He snatched the umbrella to his right side, did a British military left turn and stomped his feet, swung the umbrella forward to the horizontal and snapped it back to his side. "Bloody Heinies," he repeated and marched away like a regimental adjutant.

Robb smiled. *Wonder if he's a baron or butler?*

Passengers returned to their buses and taxis. The three women grasped hands one last time and walked out of the doorway to join the other stoic pedestrians who had resumed their brisk pace down the sidewalk.

At the Sloane Street apartment, Robb was told the old elevator operator was on holiday and a lady and her three small dogs were living in the apartment.

£££

Ted had been unable to get three seats on the 8th Air Force courier flight, a B-17 that went from RAF Station Honington to Bolling Field, Washington, D.C., twice a month. He did manage to get seats on it for their return on September 1st. He finally got them space on the Queen Mary, which was carrying 3000 seriously wounded back to New York City.

A storm made the Atlantic crossing seem longer. When they docked, they exchanged telephone numbers. Robb gave them the Alamo Hotel's number in Austin. Ted said that he would call a week before their departure date and update them if there were any changes.

Rocko waved down a taxi and turned to Robb. "*Amigo*, if you get enough of that little shit kickin' cowboy town, give me a call. Got plenty of room at my house and I'll check you out on New York City's lights and the cute little broads." Rocko jumped inside the taxi and rolled down the back window. "Get one for me, Yanks," he called, as the driver sped away.

Ted called Mitchell Field on Long Island and learned that a C-54 carrying cargo was departing that night for Kelly Field in San Antonio, Texas, with four open seats. They hailed a taxi and hurried to the field.

"Let's get something to eat," Ted said after they signed up for the last two seats on the plane. "Wanta go to the club and get a meal, or should we have some hamburgers and a Coca-Cola?"

"After nine months without them, I'm for hamburgers and a Coke."

They each ordered two hamburgers with pickles and onions and two bottles of Coca-Cola.

"Never realized how much I missed this bit of Americana," Ted said after washing down his first bite.

"Yeah. It's worth fighting for."

£££

The C-54 passed over Lufkin's navigational radio and turned southwest toward San Antonio. Thirty minutes later Robb saw Austin's "moonlights" looming through the darkness of Central Texas. "Ted, see the lights. That's Austin."

"Never seen anything like it," Ted said, looking out the window.

The large lights were mounted on 31 steel towers that were 165 feet high and strategically placed around the city. Robb recalled the first time he had seen them from the air at night, flying out of Aloe Field in Victoria, Texas during his advanced flight training. From 5000 feet, the lights had a slight bluish hue and were visible for more than 50 miles.

The C-54 landed at Kelly Field an hour before dawn. The warm Texas morning felt good after frigid Britain. Ted got booked on another military flight departing in three hours for Norton Field in San Bernardino, California. He and Robb rode the bus to the BOQ, showered, shaved, changed into their summer khakis, then went to the officer's club for a breakfast of eggs, bacon and grits.

£££

Afterwards they pick up their B-4 bags and went to the bus stop in front of the club. "I'll be staying with my mother," Ted said as the flight line bus approached. "Let me know if you'd like to come out and spend some time."

"Thanks," Robb replied. Although he had no relatives and all his friends were in the service, he longed to see Austin.

In the crowded San Antonio bus depot, Robb's Distinguished Flying Cross, Air Medal and service ribbons caught the eyes of teenage soldiers who had just completed their six weeks of basic training. Four of them going to Dallas on the same bus quizzed him about the war on the way to Austin. The conversation helped pass the time as the slow moving bus made stops at Selma, New Braunfels, San Marcos, Buda and other "wide spots" on the narrow highway.

A few miles south of Austin, Robb saw the state capitol on the horizon. At the bus depot, he took one of Roy's taxis for the short ride to the Alamo Hotel.

After checking in, he walked into the crowded dining room where once again his combat ribbons made heads turn. Unlike British restaurants where people dined on small portions of overcooked potatoes, cabbage and bilious looking sausage filled mostly with breadcrumbs, the plates in the Alamo dinning room were heaped with meat, potatoes and fresh vegetables. The dessert table was crammed with pecan and apple pies, three-layered chocolate cakes and butterscotch puddings with whipped cream.

Robb ordered the roast beef dinner and drank two glasses of milk, his first in over a year. While he ate, a conversation at the next table centered on business, money and the war. One man said, "If the war'll just last 18 months longer, I'll be in tall cotton. Never have to worry about money or work another day in my life."

Finishing his second piece of pecan pie, Robb asked for his check. The waitress told him it had been paid and pointed to a well-dressed civilian across the room. The man smiled and gave a civilian's version of a salute. When Robb thanked him, the man said his son flew B-17's in the South Pacific.

The dinner and excitement of being home had invigorated him and although he hadn't slept in over 30 hours, he decided to walk to his aunt's old house in West Austin. Shade from the green live oak trees and a south breeze provided some relief from the heat of the August sun. From his aunt's house, he strolled past Austin High School toward the University of Texas campus stopping for a large fountain Coke at Renfro's Drug Store on Guadalupe Street. He finished half of his Coke in the first swallow and in the large wall mirror behind the counter he noticed a pretty green-eyed brunette sitting two stools down smiling at him. He picked up his Coke and walked over to introduce himself.

"I'm Robb Baines."

"I'm Ronnie Sue Blackstone." Her green eyes sparkled.

"May I join you?" Robb asked.

"You're more than welcome, Captain, but I'm just leaving for a class," she said getting up. She was tall and well proportioned with a nice tan.

"May I walk you to your class, then?" he persisted.

"That would be nice." While they strolled across the campus, she told him she was a sophomore from Llano, Texas, studying to become a teacher. Other coeds glanced up and smiled at Robb as he and Ronnie Sue walked by. These flirtations reminded him that Joyce had made him realize he had sex appeal and also changed his attitude toward women by whetting his appetite for sex. He thought about taking Ronnie Sue to bed.

"Would you care to have a bite to eat and catch an early movie tonight?" he asked when they reached her classroom door.

"I'd enjoy that very much." She wrote her address and telephone number on a sheet of notebook paper and handed it to him.

"I'll be there at six," he said, looking at the address.

They had huge hamburgers, a basket of French fried onions and large chocolate milk shakes before going to the Paramount to see the movie *Laura*. Later they walked beneath the towering moonlights and past the brightly-lit store windows. After blackouts and buzzbombs, Robb had forgotten how enjoyable an evening walk could be.

Ronnie Sue had a good sense of humor and Robb enjoyed hearing stories about her growing up in Llano and her close-knit family. She had four brothers—two younger ones in high school and two older ones in the Navy. She told Robb how she used to hunt and fish with them, and how she played second base during their pickup ball games. But she also helped her mother with the housework and preparing meals. Her openness disarmed Robb and he told her much more about himself than he had planned. But as they talked he kept thinking how nice it would be to take Ronnie Sue to bed.

The next morning Robb had Roy's taxi wait at the cemetery while he put flowers on his aunt's grave. She had always been proud of him and he knew she would burst with pride if you saw him in his uniform.

Robb left the cemetery and headed out to the Robert Mueller Airport to see Pinkey Hutchins and the red and white Waco. But Pinkey and the Waco were gone. The Waco was in storage at Fort Worth and Pinkey had become the chief civilian flight instructor at one of the Army Air Forces' Primary Flight Schools near Oklahoma City. Robb had wanted Pinkey to see him in uniform and to hear some of his combat stories. He wondered if he would ever see Pinkey again. Riding back to town he thought about how the war had changed Austin and everything in his life.

That afternoon he met Ronnie Sue at Renfro's and they went swimming at Barton Springs. She was stunning in her bathing suit, with a full bosom, narrowed waist, firm curved hips and long tapered legs.

They both enjoyed the swim and agreed to meet there every afternoon for as long as Robb was in town. Ronnie Sue was an excellent swimmer and when their bodies touched in the water, it stoked the fire inside him. Several times he tried to kiss her, but she always laughed and pulled away. After a week, he couldn't stand it any longer, and one night walking Ronnie Sue back to the dorm he pulled her close and tried to kiss her. This time she didn't laugh. She gently, but firmly pushed him away.

"Robb, I know how you feel, but I don't feel the same. I'm flattered that you want me, but that's as far as it goes. This will happen again, so we must stop seeing one another. You shouldn't have a problem finding another girl in Austin."

Robb felt annoyed by the rejection and walking back to the hotel, he wondered why British women had a more casual view of sex. Maybe it was the war and nearness of death that made them that way. One thing he knew for sure: he was too old for another teenage rebuff.

The next few days and nights passed slowly, and on the third day, he thought about calling Ted or Rocko. But he changed his mind during lunch at the Driskill Hotel when he was seated next to an attractive and well-endowed brunette in her mid twenties. She said her name was Jean Glen and her husband was a dentist stationed in the Pacific. She invited him to her home for tea later that afternoon. But when he arrived she served bourbon and water. For the next week he went to see her after dark and left before daylight.

With the days to himself, he would swim in the morning and after lunch he went to the library to read newspapers. One afternoon he glanced out the window and was startled to see his old girl friend and her husband walk past. Beth had a young baby in her arms and was pregnant with another. Waddling down the sidewalk in a baggy maternity dress, she looked much older than her 20 years. Robb recalled the hurt and bitterness he had felt when he first learned about her marriage. But now, he felt sorry for her.

On August 23rd Robb was awakened from his afternoon nap with a phone call from Ted.

"Robb, I wanted to let you know I've confirmed our flight back to Britain," he said. "We depart Bolling Field at noon on September 1st. If you like, we could meet up early in DC and spend a few days there before heading back. Don't know about you, but I'm ready for a change."

"Know what you mean. I'm ready to leave now."

"Okay, let's rendezvous in Washington on the 25th. I'll call Rocko, then reserve three rooms at the Jefferson Hotel

Robb caught a C-47 flight from Bergstrom Field to Langley Field, Virginia, then took a bus up to Washington, DC. He checked into the Jefferson and went to the bar. Rocko was sitting at a table drinking a beer.

"*Amigo.* Glad to see ya. Garcon, bring my friend a blabbermouth!" Rocko shouted to the waiter.

"Good to see you, Rocko. How long have you been here?"

"Got here yesterday. Frickin' city is a happy hunting ground for fighter pilots. Loaded with eager women...even better than London. After beddin' down with those old sumbitchin' politicians and business tycoons that populate this town, women can't keep their hands off me." He took a swig of beer and grinned. "They love my blue bar. None of 'em have seen a blue pickle before. No flight officers in the Puzzle Palace. Nothin' but captains and above. I tell 'em that my blue pickle is a special rank for the hottest of hot rock fighter pilots. Got us fixed up tonight with three of the cutest tooties in town...for a little tension reliever." He winked and took another swig.

£££

THE HELLISH VORTEX

On September 1st Robb, Ted and Rocko departed on the B-17. They spent a night in Goose Bay, Labrador and another night at the Prestwick Airport, near Glasgow, Scotland. They arrived back at RAF Station Boxted on the evening of September 3rd. That night the Colonel announced that Ted and Bob Hunt had been promoted to lieutenant colonel.

But on the heels of that good news came the bad. Art and Jack had been lost while strafing German AAA positions. Fred Barcus from St. Louis, Missouri and Jim Harper from Hollywood, Florida had replaced them.

While they were gone, 30 of the group's war-weary P-51 B's and C's had been replaced by new P-51D's, with the remaining replacements due in within 30 days. The new D's had six machine guns rather than four, carried more ammunition, had a gyro optical computing gun sight and a Plexiglas bubble canopy that gave the pilot much better visibility. But the improvements added weight and the bubble canopy disturbed the fuselage airflow, which caused more drag. As a result, the D was about 15 mph slower than the B's and C's.

Ted, Robb and Rocko flew three the new fighters early the next morning.

"Sumbitch, one hour of solid rat racing," Rocko said. Hanging up his flight gear after the flight. "You really worked us over boss."

"Wanted to make sure you hadn't lost your touch after all that easy living," Ted said with a smile. "Better hurry, we're due for an intelligence update in ten minutes."

Major Watson was waiting at the lectern when they entered the group briefing room.

"Good morning, Geoffrey," Ted said.

"Good morning, sir. Congratulations on your promotion," Major Watson added.

"Thank you, Geoffrey."

"Gentlemen, I would like to give you a very quick situational update on the war," he said, pulling back the curtain that covered the map.

"Ain't no regular update, it's a frickin' situational update. Old Geoffrey and his two bit words," Rocko whispered to Robb.

Major Watson glared as he took the cue stick from the lectern. "Our ground offensive is beginning to slow down, due to our inability to get supplies to the front...especially gasoline. The B-24's have started to haul gasoline and supplies, to help alleviate the situation.

"On the air side, we have solid intelligence that says since last month the *Luftwaffe* has been given priority to rebuilding their fighter force. In addition to training new pilots, they are transferring bomber pilots into fighters. It appears they could increase their strength from 1200 to at least 2000 pilots by December. It's a Herculean effort. In my opinion, they have something big in the wind. It's too soon to tell what, but my guess is that it's going to be bold and audacious."

CHAPTER 21

Battle of the Bulge

Although the Allied ground offensive had to slow down in October and November to replenish supplies, the 8th AF continued to attack Germany's oil refineries, marshalling yards, key rail bridges and choke points, as well as military factories. At the same time, 9th AF and RAF tactical air forces attacked German tanks, trucks, trains, troop concentrations, supply dumps, and railroad and highway bridges near the front.

During this two-month period, most 8th AF attacks went unchallenged until November 26th when 550 German fighters attacked. The *Luftwaffe* managed to shoot down 25 bombers, but lost 100 fighters. The next day the *Luftwaffe* launched 700 fighters, but German radar mistakenly vectored them to eight P-51 groups from the 8th AF. The Germans lost 98 fighters versus eleven US fighters and no bombers. Then, for no apparent reason, the *Luftwaffe* attacks suddenly stopped on December 5th.

"Been ten days since we've seen sumbitchin' kraut fighters," Rocko grunted as he and Robb crunched through the remnants of previous night's snowfall to get from their P-51's to the waiting operations truck. "Wonder what's goin' on?"

"Don't know," Robb replied. "But I'd guess they have something up their sleeves."

"Maybe the sumbitches just too smart to fly in this frickin' weather."

"They've flown in it before."

"True, *amigo*. Maybe it's because there are only ten more shoppin' days til Christmas and they're out blowin' their nazi flight pay.'"

"Speaking of Christmas, it's hard to believe we've been flying combat for a year." A gust added an extra chill to the icy air as Robb recalled his father's suicide.

"Sumbitch, it's cold! Frickin' weather's worse than last year."

"Uh huh."

"*Amigo*, doesn't this frickin' cold weather get to ya?"

"I guess," Robb muttered.

"You can't be a frickin' rebel and not suffer from this shit eatin' bloke weather."

"I hate this weather. I'll take Texas anytime. Don't know why anybody would want to live in this damned country," Robb snapped as he climbed into the back of the truck and sat down on the wooden bench.

"Glad to hear that, *amigo*. I was beginnin' to worry about you," Rocko said as they waited for Fred and Jim. "*Amigo*, one Christmas present for me will be plenty this year." He looked at Robb and grinned.

"Okay. I'll give you one bottle of Mennen's instead of two to hold down your goat-power count."

"*Amigo*, guess I forgot to tell ya. I have two London ho's now and they don't mind a little goat count. In fact they say a low goat count turns 'em on. Since I can't drink that frickin' Mennen's and you never use all of your whiskey ration, thought you might give me some booze."

"I'll check with Santa."

"Somthin' botherin' ya, *Amigo*?"

"I always get a little down around Christmas time." Although Robb had told Ted about his father's suicide, he had never told Rocko.

Fred and Jim climbed in, and the truck's gears growled as the driver jammed the gearshift into low. He pushed too hard on the accelerator; the engine roared; the exhaust popped and cracked in the icy air. He released the clutch and the truck's rear wheels spun on a patch of packed snow. Then they squealed as they hit the bare macadam and the truck lurched forward. Robb and Rocko grabbed the wooden bench.

"Sumbitch! Another frickin' hick who spent his childhood hoppin' clods behind plow horses. Hadn't been for the war, he'd still be hoppin' the frickin' clods."

The driver eased off the accelerator. Afraid to shift, he drove in second gear along the taxiway toward operations.

In November, Snapper squadron's first sergeant was killed in a jeep accident one foggy morning. Knowing there was no better first sergeant in the group than Big John; Ted offered to get his stripes back if he promised to control his drinking and fighting. Big John was quick to promise. He was 40 years old and had 24 years service and knew this would be his last chance to have his master sergeant stripes returned before retirement. But Ted warned him that if he broke his promise, he'd be lucky to retire as a buck private.

"Physical go okay, sir?" Big John asked, placing the two reports on the snack bar counter for Ted to sign. Big John's uniform was meticulous. His shirt was pressed and the six stripes on his tailor made chevrons had a golden hue. His brass belt buckle glistened; his pants were neatly creased and you could see reflections on his shoes from the spit shine.

"Yeah. But I hate to miss a mission, just to take a physical," Ted replied. "You look sharp, Big John."

"Thank you, colonel, sir."

Ted read and signed the reports, then handed them back to Big John as Robb and Rocko approached.

Big John clicked his heels and did an about face. He glanced at Robb and Rocko and nodded. "Gentlemen." Before they could say anything, he walked briskly across the room and out the door.

"How'd it go today?" Ted asked.

"Bad weather, plenty of flak and no kraut fighters again," Robb answered.

"I'm really uneasy about the krauts not showing, because we know the *Luftwaffe* is capable of launching hundreds of fighters," Ted replied.

"Maybe the sumbitches are gonna give us a surprise for Christmas."

"You may be right, Rocko."

"How'd your physical go today?" Robb asked.

"Okay. Doc Herny says I'm good for another year. For what that's worth," Ted added with a smile.

"Comin' from that pecker head Herny, it can't be worth much. Someone should blow in his ear and give him a refill," Rocko grunted. "That bastard needs a frickin' check up...from the neck up."

"Rocko, when your physical comes due, we'll send you to another squadron's flight surgeon so you don't get grounded," Ted said.

"Here you go, Captain Baines, Flight Officer Fazzio," Corporal Perkins squeaked. He placed two Spam sandwiches on the counter and poured two cups of coffee. The shy young private helping Corporal Perkins continued washing the tin plates and cups without looking up.

"Thank you, Corporal Perkins," Robb said.

"Thanks, Perkie," Rocko grunted before taking a giant bite from his sandwich. He finished the sandwich in four bites and downed his coffee.

"Guys, it's debriefing time," Ted said, looking at his watch.

Robb and Rocko hurried out of the room and down the hall.

"Gentlemen, it looks like we're going to be hit by the granddaddy of all winter storm systems," Captain Knight said, taking the cue stick from Major Watson. "It could clobber all of Northern Europe and Great Britain for the next six to seven days. The Continent will get heavy snow for a couple of days, then the clouds will hug the deck for the next four to five days with freezing temperatures. Although we'll get some snow, our main problem in Britain will be thick fog. Starting tonight, our visibility will vary from zero to 75 yards. It may get up to a mile, or maybe two, for a few hours during the day, then sock in before dusk."

"Sumbitch, my achin' ass'll finally get a break for a few days. Maybe I can catch up on my sex life." Everyone went to bed that night thinking they would be able to sleep late due to the bad weather.

£££

"Gentlemen, briefing in one hour for all pilots!" the excited duty sergeant said.

Awakened from deep sleep, Robb rolled onto his back, shielded his eyes with his hands and squinted at his watch. It read 4:30. "What's going on?" The cold condensation from his breath settled onto his face.

"Don't know, sir. But whatever it is, it's big. The entire group is on 15 minute alert," the duty sergeant replied.

"What's the weather like?" Robb grabbed his pants from the end of the bed. "Heavy fog. Can hardly see my hand in front of my face. Got to hurry, sir." The duty sergeant turned and went out the door.

Remaining under the blankets, Robb slipped into his pants, then his shirt and threw the blankets back. *Surely we're not gonna fly in this stuff. Wonder what's going on?* He held his feet above the floor and put on his shoes.

"Sumbitch, so much for my fun trip to Colchester."

£££

"HOFFICERS, TEN--SHUN!"

The Colonel hopped onto the platform and took the cue stick from the lectern. "Gents, the krauts have thrown some shit into the game. They've broken through our lines in the Ardennes and are hammerin' the hell outta our ground forces.

"I got you all up early because things may get worse in a hurry. Until we know how this is gonna play out, I've cancelled all passes and put the entire group on 15-minute alert. That means that if you're not flyin,' you're restricted to your huts, the club or your squadron ops. Stormy, tell us about this lousy weather." The Colonel handed Captain Knight the cue stick, then jumped off the platform and sat in his striped chair.

"Sir, most fields in Britain are covered by dense fog and most 9th AF fields on the Continent are reporting heavy snow. Our visibility may increase to a mile and a half by mid morning, then drop back down to zero later this afternoon. If you have to take off this morning, you can expect less than 75 yards."

"Sumbitch! Takin' off in that'll tighten your fuzzy growler."

Captain Knight smiled. "Over the Continent, it'll be one of those days where you'll be flying in and out of the clouds and contrails and never see the ground or sky...." He finished and handed the cue stick to Major Watson.

"Gentlemen. The Supreme Allied Headquarters reported early this morning that the *Wehrmacht* had launched a surprise attack against American forces in the Ardennes. They are attacking on a 20-mile front with a large combined armor and infantry force. The situation is so confused and fluid, that we have very few details on the extent of the German penetration.

"Since we do not have a takeoff time yet, I would like to give you some information regarding the German offensive that you won't hear any place else. First, I can't understand how our ground forces could have been so surprised by this attack. I say this because since the 17th of November, the two 9th Air Force Reconnaissance Groups have flown 509 missions over German forces east of the Ardennes.

"On almost every mission the reconnaissance pilots reported visual sightings or provided pictures of the extensive truck and train movements of German armor, infantry, artillery, medical forces and vast quantities of supplies. Moreover, infantry patrols also reported that German units were being repositioned in the Ardennes. In addition, fighter-bomber units have reported strafing and bombing many of these *Wehrmacht* units while they were on the move.

"Then a few days ago, both reconnaissance and fighter pilots reported a general westward movement of men and fighting equipment toward the Ardennes front. Why this activity didn't alert our ground commanders is beyond me."

"Frickin' ground pounders can only think one grunt at a time," Rocko whispered to Robb.

Robb looked straight ahead and held his forefinger to his lips without shushing.

Major Watson glared at Rocko, then continued. "Despite all these reports, 18 hours before the Germans launched their attack, General Eisenhower's operations people told the air commanders that there was, 'nothing to report in the Ardennes.'

"After carefully reviewing the extent and sequence of the reconnaissance reports, I'd say the *Wehrmacht* has been ready to launch this attack for at least a week. It now seems quite clear they waited for this bad winter storm, hoping to avoid being mauled by Allied airpower.

"We can expect the headline seeking British and American press to make more out of this German thrust than is warranted. I'm not down playing it because there will be heavy fighting with lots of casualties, and it could end up being one of the bloodiest chapters of the ground war. But it will be no more than a temporary set back. In my opinion, it is a desperate, last gasp effort that defies sound military thinking. The Germans can ill afford to enter a slugfest against the vastly stronger Americans. In the end, the German assault will only hasten the fall of the Nazi regime.

"My thesis is based on the Nazi's military message traffic, which tells us that due to our air strikes, the entire German military has critical shortages of fuel, weapons, ammunition and almost everything else required to fight a war. For example, some *Wehrmacht* commanders have been limited to the number of artillery rounds they can fire, regardless of the intensity of the opposition. We all know that our oil strikes have created a fuel shortage for the *Luftwaffe*. And since

D-Day, we've all read reports about how the fuel shortage has forced the *Wehrmacht* to abandon thousands of their tanks and fighting vehicles during a battle.

"Based on Nazi military message traffic, one can conclude that our strategic and tactical air effort has reduced Germany's war making industry to about 30 percent of its normal capacity. I also believe that their transportation system has been damaged to where it's incapable of moving much of what little they produce. Only by giving the military top priority are they able to sustain a limited fighting capability. I shudder to think what our ground casualties would be without the air effort.

"I would like to make one more observation. Since the German military receives top priority on production and transportation and are still facing severe shortages, their civilian economy must be teetering on the brink. They must be struggling just to find enough food to eat and enough fuel to keep warm. If our high-level intelligence people had time to monitor the thousands of Nazi civil and commerce messages, as well as the military traffic, I think they would find that Germany's economy and way of life has disintegrated. Only a deranged paper hanger would continue to subject the German people to such senseless death, destruction and deprivation in the face of inevitable defeat."

"Sumbitch, old Geoffrey's all fired up," Rocko whispered to Robb.

Robb turned toward Rocko and whispered, "Just be quiet...let him finish."

"Okay, *amigo.*"

Major Watson hesitated long enough to glare at Rocko again. "If the 900 bombers that are scheduled today get off the ground, they will employ radar bombing and strike the railroad marshalling yards at Cologne, Kaiserslautern, Koblenz, Lutzel and Bonn. German troops, tanks and supplies are still being funneled through these marshalling yards on their way to the front. Our attacks should help to reduce or slow their movement...."

Major Watson completed his briefing and handed the cue stick to Lieutenant Colonel Bob Hunt.

"My counterparts at 8th AF tell me that there's a better than even chance we'll launch today due to the seriousness of the German offensive. They know that many groups will not get off the ground because of the fog, but a few will be better than none.

"If at all possible, they want the fighters to do some strafing after they finish escorting the bombers. The call sign for the American ground radar station that covers Belgium, Northern France and Western Germany is Four Eyes. He'll guide you to ground targets and keep you advised on the weather at Boxted and alternate fields in case Boxted socks in.

"Since we don't know where we may spend the night, we'll carry a couple of GI blankets and three boxes of K-rations. The blankets and rations are being delivered to your squadrons now. Pack 'em behind the cockpit armor plate.

"Okay, now for our taxi and takeoff procedures to launch in this fog. The start engine time will be set when we get a go from 8th Air Force. The second squadron will not taxi until the first squadron has reached the end of the runway, and the third squadron will wait until the second is at the runway.

"Two jeeps towing carts with high intensity lights will lead each squadron. One jeep will drive on the extreme left edge of the taxiway and the other jeep will follow the right edge. Don't use your landing lights while taxiing because they'll reflect on this dense fog and eliminate what little forward visibility you have.

"To help you see the aircraft ahead, without making S-turns while taxiing, your crew chief will stand on the left wing next to the cockpit. He'll have a good view of the red and green wingtip and taillights on the aircraft ahead.

"We'll increase our takeoff interval between elements to five seconds. When you're lined up for takeoff, make damned sure you double check that your directional gyro is aligned with the runway heading. Because of the poor vis, let's plan on making a radio call instead of a hand signal to inform your wingman when you're releasing your brakes to roll and retracting your landing gear

"On the takeoff roll, flight and element leaders should be able to see the runway lights in their peripheral vision. But the directional gyro is your number one reference.

"Two trucks will be parked on each side of the far end of the runway, perpendicular to the edge. Their headlights can be used as reference in case you have to abort your takeoff.

"After you're off the ground, it's just plain old instrument flying. The one good thing about fogs—it's smooth, making instrument flying easier. We should be on top of the first layer at eight grand where we can make our join up. Our join up will take a little longer with these procedures, but we have plenty of fuel, so we'll start a little early.

"If Boxted has at least a mile of visibility, we'll land here. We'll take about 2000 foot spacing between flights while were over the North Sea and still above the weather. The Colonel will start down with Snapper, holding 260 mph and 1000 feet per minute. Bug Eye will follow after taking spacing with a 360-degree turn. Hot Rod will take spacing behind Bug Eye.

"Once we get below the clouds and can see the water, we'll get our usual DF steers to Boxted. When you cross the coast, echelon right and get set for a landing. Over the end of the runway, flight leads will make a tight 360 to keep the field in sight. Wingmen will hang in close to their leaders and follow him around. We'll have someone on the end of the runway that will fire a flare or two for each flight, to help you get lined up on the final approach. If the vis drops below a mile, we'll go to Manston and their radar will bring you down.

"Okay, let's hack our watches. In 17 seconds, I'll have ten after. Counting now. Five, four, three, two, one...hack. Any questions?" But there were none.

Before he could pass the cue to the Colonel, an operations sergeant handed him a message from the Teletype.

"Sir," Colonel Hunt said. "Three groups of bombers have started to take off and two more are getting ready. Based on this info our start engine time will be 0730."

"Thanks Bob. Gents, I know many of you are concerned about takin' off in this stuff. But a blind takeoff in real weather is much easier than doin' it under the bag. Okay guys, we've got plenty of time to pack our blankets and rations. If there are any changes we'll let the squadrons know right away." The Colonel hopped off the platform, walked briskly down the aisle and out the door.

Robb knew from what the Colonel had said and the way he had said it, that they were going. *Shit. . .he has ice water in his veins. Taking off in this crap may be easier than taking off under the bag in the back seat of a trainer, but we eventually have to come back and land. And landing with 75 yards of visibility will be like playing Russian roulette with five shells in the cylinder of a six-gun.*

When Robb arrived at his P-51, Sergeant Edgington took the blankets and K-rations, then shined his flashlight on the wing as Robb climbed up. Robb stuffed his blankets and rations behind the armor plate and stepped into the cockpit. After completing the preflight, he hooked the dinghy to his chute, fastened his shoulder harness and safety belt, and connected the oxygen hose and radio cords to his mask and helmet.

Neither Robb nor Sergeant Edgington spoke, while they waited for the start engine time. Robb stared into the foggy blackness that hid the ground and sky and everything in between. *In five days you'll be 21. If you make it. You'll finally be old enough to buy a drink legally in a stateside bar. In four days you'll have been flying combat for one year. It seems like a lifetime. But in combat you're always playing catch-up.*

Robb thought again about his under-the-bag takeoffs back in training. But they were made on a wide concrete runway with "Iron Ass" in the front seat to keep him out of trouble. Today he'd be taking off on a narrow and slippery pierced steel-planking runway with Fred on his wing. The slightest error in directional control could put one or both of them off the runway into the bottomless muck where the 51's would roll up into a ball of fire. And yet he knew the take-off would be nothing compared to a landing in the fog.

He checked the clock. It showed seven seconds to go. He watched the second hand jump five times, turned off his flashlight and shouted, "CLEAR!"

"CLEAR!" the assistant crew chief shouted back.

Robb flicked the starter switch to ON, counted six blades on the prop, then turned the ignition switch to BOTH, flipped the fuel boost pump switch to ON and held the primer switch for one second.

Fire shot from the engine exhaust stacks and the engine cracked a steady beat. He moved the mixture control to NORMAL and checked the oil pressure;

it showed 50 psi. Robb signaled for the assistant crew chief to pull the battery cart before he turned the battery-disconnect switch to ON.

In the dense fog, the reflection of the engine exhaust flames ringed his 51's nose with a blue glow. Robb turned on the navigation lights, then looked to his left and right. The red and green wingtip lights resembled illuminated balls of cotton candy suspended in the fog.

On the opposite side of the revetment, Robb saw the faint glows of the red and green navigation lights on Rocko's 51. They looked like dim Yuletide luminaries. He recalled last year's pseudo Christmas scene when he had flown his first combat mission in weather unfit for flying. *Shit. . .British weather seems to go from bad to worse.*

"Shotgun's taxiin.'"

Here we go. Robb forced himself to remain calm as he signaled the assistant crew chief to pull the chocks. The assistant pulled them and signaled Robb to taxi.

Robb released the brakes and watched Sergeant Edgington who was kneeling next to the cockpit. The 51 rolled slowly from the parking spot and Sergeant Edgington pointed to the left. Robb started to turn and watched Sergeant Edgington. He finally moved his hand up and down and Robb stopped the turn. When they reached the edge of the taxiway, Sergeant Edgington signaled Robb to stop.

The two Jeeps and their trailer lights passed, followed by the Colonel with Snapper Red and Yellow flights.

"I COUNTED EIGHT BIRDS!" Robb yelled.

"GOT THE SAME! LOOKS CLEAR!" Sergeant Edgington shouted back.

Robb released the brakes and let his 51 roll a few feet and Sergeant Edgington signaled Robb to turn. Then he moved his hand up and down and Robb stopped the turn. Several times as they taxied, Sergeant Edgington motioned with a closed fist and extended thumb for Robb to correct a few degrees left or right to keep their 51 centered on the taxiway. Once Sergeant Edgington held his arm up and made a backward motion for Robb to slow down, to maintain the spacing behind Yellow Four.

When they reached the end of the runway, Robb saw the lights of Yellow Three and Four turning onto the runway in front of him. Sergeant Edgington signaled for a right turn. In the turn Yellow Three disappeared behind the long nose of Robb's 51, but Yellow Four remained visible on the right side of the runway.

Sergeant Edgington signaled for Robb to stop. "YOU'RE CLEAR TO RUN UP!"

Robb gave him an okay signal and Sergeant Edgington jumped off the trailing edge of the wing and ran clear.

Robb popped the stick forward to unlock the tail wheel steering and cocked his 51's tail 45 degrees off the side of the runway. To his left, Yellow Three's green wingtip light glistened in the fog and the white taillight sparkled on the wet pierced steel runway. On the opposite side of the runway, Robb saw the faint glows of Fred's wingtip lights. Rocko and Jim pulled into position, followed by the two spares.

"Shotgun, Snapper spares are in position."

"Shotgun, copies. Let's run 'em up."

Feeling like he was neck deep in a barrel of molasses, Robb blinked sweat from his eyes and eased the throttle forward. His 51 roared and tried to leap forward as he completed the engine checks. He recalled how he had skipped most of them on his first combat mission. *You were lucky you didn't bust your ass. Hope Fred and Jim don't skip anything.*

"Shotgun's rollin' in five seconds. Peter heat is on."

Yellow Three turned and pointed the nose of his 51 down the runway.

Robb quickly turned his 51 for takeoff, then glanced at the directional gyro. It was aligned with the runway heading.

"Shotgun's rollin'...now." Hidden by the fog, the Colonel and his wingman roared down the runway.

"Red Three's rolling...now." The two 51's roared through the blackness.

Robb flicked on the pitot heat and glanced at Fred to make sure he was ready.

"Yellow One and Two rolling ...now." The two 51's roared and rolled.

Robb pushed the throttle to takeoff power; the powerful Merlin engine thundered; the 51 danced on its gear. He stood on the brakes and glanced at the engine instruments. They were in the green.

"Yellow Three's rolling...now." The two 51's roared and rolled.

Robb glanced at Fred again, then watched the second hand of the clock. After three clicks, he transmitted, "White One's rolling...now."

With his eyes locked to the directional gyro, he released the brakes; his 51 leaped forward into the black fog. In his peripheral vision he could see the fuzzy runway lights passing slowly on the left.

As he accelerated, the lights shot past faster and faster. His 51's tail rose. The runway lights resembled the burning golf balls of a 20-millimeter cannon.

At 100 mph, he eased the stick back.

His 51 hopped off the ground; the runway lights disappeared. In the corner of his eye, he saw the blue glow from the Fred's engine on the right.

Robb held the nose dot of the attitude indicator just above the artificial horizon bar. He waited until the rate of climb indicator read 300 per minute, then transmitted, "White One, gear up... now." The landing gear thumped into the wells.

The smooth air made it easy to hold his 51 in a steady climb. At 1000 feet, Robb felt that warm tingling sensation from the surge of adrenaline that always followed a deadly encounter.

"Shotgun's levelin' in between layers at 6000. Weather ain't the best. Got some scattered clouds at this level, but it may be worse upstairs. I'll orbit here until we get joined up."

Robb broke out of the clouds at 6000 feet into the gray light of dawn. Four miles south he saw four fighters in formation and four more in trail.

"Snapper White has Red and Yellow at ten o'clock." Robb started a left turn. He glanced in his rearview mirror. Rocko and Jim were closing. Just as Robb looked forward, he entered a thin cloud.

"Big friend, passing right to left!" Rocko shouted.

Robb broke out of the cloud and looked up. A lone B-24 zoomed past— 100 feet below. *Shit...that was close.* He continued to turn and closed on Red and Yellow. "Shotgun, Snapper White is in position."

"Shotgun copy."

After two more orbits, Hot Rod and Bugeye joined up and the Colonel set course and started to climb through the clouds. The 36 P-51's broke out at 24,000 feet and leveled off at 28,000 feet. Above a layer of clouds hid the sky and sun.

"Shotgun has contrails at eleven o'clock. Ringo, Shotgun is five o'clock, five miles. Looks like you have less than two combat wings."

"Ringo here. That's right, Shotgun. Fog either held them on the ground or they couldn't find us in the clouds."

"Shotgun copies." The Colonel started to crisscross above the B-17's.

Ringo and the Colonel amazed Robb. *They're always on the toughest combat missions. Two old war-horses that have flown more combat than anyone in the deadliest air war the world has ever seen. I wonder how they feel about facing the deadliest flying hazard of all—a zero-zero landing?*

For the next 58 minutes, the B-17 pilots struggled to hold their fully loaded bombers in formation as they flew in and out of the clouds through the will-o'-the-wisp arena. With only 105 bombers, Ringo decided to limit their attack to the Stuttgart marshalling yards. At Stuttgart, hundreds of orange explosions and black puffs greeted them and two B-17's took hits and twisted out of control. There were no chutes.

After releasing their bombs, Ringo started a right turn and headed for Britain. Bomber crews tended to their wounded, covered the dead and prayed they wouldn't face a zero-zero landing.

"Ringo, this is Shotgun."

"Ringo here. Go ahead, Shotgun."

"I'll let Bugeye and Hot Rod escort you back. I'm gonna contact Four Eyes to see if he has some strafin' targets near the front for my lead squadron."

"Ringo here. Good hunting, Shotgun."

"Snapper gang, let's go Charlie channel." The Colonel changed channels and waited five seconds. "Shotgun's on."

"Snapper Yellow."

"Snapper White," Robb called. *Shit...I knew he'd do this...we should be heading back to beat the bad weather.*

"Four Eyes, this Shotgun," the Colonel transmitted after Yellow and White had checked in. "How are the oranges at Sunshine?"

"Shotgun, Sunshine has a ragged 900 foot ceiling and a mile and a half visibility. They say that should hold for the next two hours."

"Shotgun roger. I have twelve chicks loaded with 50-caliber ammo. Do you have something for us?"

"Four Eyes here. Give me a squawk, Shotgun."

"Shotgun's squawking," the Colonel turned on his IFF transponder.

"Four Eyes has you, Shotgun. Strangle your parrot. About 20 minutes ago, a squadron of 9th AF P-47's reported German truck and train traffic between Koblenz and Trier. The Jugs attacked a train and destroyed some trucks, but reported there were more. I can vector you to a large valley near the highway and railroad where you can get below the weather."

"Shotgun here. How large is the valley? How high are the rocks around it and what's the ceilin' visibility in it?"

"Four Eyes here. The map shows the valley to be three miles wide and it runs north and south for four miles. Hills around the valley go up to 1500 feet. The Jug pilots reported a ragged 1200-foot ceiling with two to three miles visibility in the valley."

"Shotgun copied. It's on our way home, so we'll drop down and have a look."

"Four Eyes here. Steer 315 degrees for 135 miles. Set your altimeters at 29.90 and descend at 1000 feet per minute. Don't go below 3500 feet without my clearance."

"Shotgun roger. Guys, let's close it up and go flights in trail. I'm gonna hold cruise power in our descent and make a high-speed letdown to save time. Set your altimeters at 29.90 and check that your peter heat is on."

As they started down, Robb moved in 30 feet behind and ten below Yellow One. From this position he could sit up straight while flying formation with Yellow One and still see Yellow Two, Three and Four in his peripheral vision.

They zoomed into the clouds at 300 mph. *Shit...never thought we'd ever be letting down in a strange valley with a low ceiling and poor visibility. Damn it...I love the Colonel but sometimes he pushes too hard. If Four Eyes screws up just a tiny bit we'll bust our asses on some hill. If we make it to the valley, some of us could slam into a hill while strafing in this lousy weather. We should head back to Britain before the bottom drops outta that bloke weather or we ALL will bust our asses trying to make a zero-zero landing.*

"Shotgun's levelin' at 3500 feet."

"Four Eyes has you 16 miles from the valley. Turn to 360 degrees and descend to 2500 feet."

"Shotgun is departin' 3500 feet for 2500, turnin' to 360 and reducin' power to slow down to 240 mph."

Red Two, Three and Four bounced slightly as they adjusted to the change in direction and power reduction. Yellow flight bounced a little higher and lower.

Keeping a sharp eye on Yellow Two and Four, Robb gripped hard on the stick and throttle and struggled to hold formation without overcontrolling. *SHIT…with twelve aircraft, Four Eyes should have given us that turn sooner so we could have settled down before we started to descend.*

"Shotgun's level at 2500 feet and holdin' 360 degrees."

The bouncing finally stopped. Robb eased his grip on the stick and throttle, took a deep breath and blinked the sweat from his eyes.

"Four Eyes has Shotgun nine miles from the valley. Turn right ten degrees, start your descent at 300 feet per minute and hold 240 mph."

SHIT…NOT AGAIN! That dumb son of a bitch's gonna cause a midair collision with all of this last minute maneuvering!

"Shotgun turnin' right ten degrees and departin' 2500 feet."

The bouncing started again. Robb tightened his grip on the stick and throttle, trying not to bounce.

"Four Eyes has Shotgun five miles out."

"Shotgun's passin' 2100 feet."

"Four Eyes has Shotgun one mile out."

"Shotgun's passin' 1700."

Robb's body turned to rock and he blinked sweat from his eyes so he could see. *Shit…we're dragging our asses across the rocks. This is dumber than hell. Damned weather in the valley could've turned sour and we'll never breakout! Just slam into a hill.*

"Four Eyes shows Shotgun on the edge of the valley."

"Shotgun's passin' 1100 feet."

Robb's heart pounded in his chest. *SHIT…I DON'T SEE THE GROUND! "LET'S PULL UP…GET THE HELL OUT OF HERE," he shouted to himself.*

"Shotgun's below the stuff. Gang, spread out and look around."

Robb saw the snow covered ground below. He blinked more sweat from his eyes and slid back about 50 feet so he could look around. *Thank God we made it.* He relaxed his grip on the stick and throttle, opened his mouth to ease the pressure on his aching teeth and the pain in the jaw muscles. *This damned letdown shortened my life by at least five years.*

"Shotgun here. Four Eyes, you did great work. Where've you been all my life?"

"Four Eyes is a new kid on the block, but we're trying to make up for lost time. The highway and railroad, where the traffic was reported, are two miles ahead. They parallel the Mosel River and should be easy to spot. That's about all the help I can give you now. Give me a call when you're ready to head home and we'll get you pointed in the right direction."

"Will do, Four Eyes. Snapper gang, I have the highway, railroad and river, dead ahead. Flights go staggered trail. I'm increasin' my power to 2500 rpm and 38 inches. Double check your gun switches on and dim your sights, so you can see what's in front of you in this murk. Keep your nav lights on bright to help keep one another in sight. I'm turnin' right toward the northeast. Red and Yellow will follow the railroad. White, you work the highway. We'll all depart the area in fifteen minutes and head back to blokeland."

"Yellow, copy."

"White copies." Robb punched his clock to start the timing for their 15-minute departure and scanned the area ahead. A train and four cars were still smoking. *Looks like the Jugs worked it over pretty good.*

Robb crossed the river and railroad, saw the highway a few miles north and turned right to follow it. In the turn, Rocko and Jim crossed from Robb's right side to his left.

"Sumbitch! Gotta bunch of kraut grunts at 12 o'clock low! They're lined up in a field. Gonna get the bastards!" Rocko rolled out of his turn and lined up for a strafing attack.

Robb rolled out of the turn so he could see the Germans and Rocko. In a field next to the highway, he saw approximately 200 soldiers. Most of them were in two lines that ran perpendicular to Rocko's line of flight. Parked on a side road next to the field were 15 trucks.

"White Three, make a sharp pull out to avoid ricochets," Robb transmitted, recalling the P-40 strafing incident back in the States.

"Will do, *amigo*." Rocko and Jim opened fire while they dived and turned. Twelve streams of armor piercing incendiary shells raked the surprised Germans. The API's sparkled as they hit the soldiers and sent them tumbling into the air. Their arms and legs flailed, while their rifles, steel helmets and metal mess kits sailed in all directions.

Rocko flipped his 51 into a vertical bank, so he could continue to turn and shoot. Some of the soldiers near the head of the line started running toward the ditch next to road, but for most, it was too late. They were blasted like their brethren behind them.

At 100 feet, Jim pulled up and swung wide to remain clear of Rocko while he continued to fire.

THE HELLISH VORTEX

At 30 feet, Rocko flipped his 51 level and abruptly pulled up to 300 feet. "White One here. Nice shooting."

"Pay back time for Bill, Pete, Matt, Dan, Bob, Jack and Major Brown," Rocko grunted.

"White One's crossing behind Three. Gonna go after the trucks. Two take spacing, so we both can give 'em a squirt."

Robb rolled his 51 in to a diving turn. When the gunsight's pipper was on the first truck, he squeezed the trigger. The drumbeat of his machine guns vibrated his 51 and API's sparkled on the truck. He continued to fire in the diving turn and the API's passed from truck to truck.

At 30 feet, he flipped the 51's wings level, yanked the stick back and started to turn. At 300 feet, he started to turn and looked over his left shoulder. Four trucks were burning.

Fred rolled into a dive and opened fire. API's moved rapidly from truck to truck, shredding their canvas-covered beds and blasting holes in the cabs and engine hoods. Three more trucks started to burn.

"White One's at eight o'clock to White Two," Robb called

"White Two has a tally." Fred turned sharply and closed on Robb.

"White Three, One here. What's left of this outfit won't make it to Bastogne for a while. I'm turning northeast to look for fresh meat."

"Sounds good, *amigo.*"

Four miles down the highway, the clouds got lower and the visibility dropped to two miles. Robb reduced his airspeed and tighten his S turns to keep the highway in sight.

"White One has more trucks, 12 o'clock low. Three and Four, swing to the south side of the convoy and I'll swing north. We'll attack by elements from opposite directions. In this crappy weather, only One and Three will fire. Two and Four just hang on tight and stay outta the clouds and avoid the rocks."

"Copy, *amigo.*"

Robb swung to the left, then turned back to the right for his attack. As he started to dive, he saw a fuel truck in front of him and another further back. "White Three, there are two fuel trucks in the convoy. Let's go for them first," Robb transmitted.

"Copy, *amigo.*"

In the dive, Robb took aim and opened fire. API's ripped into the truck.

WHOOOM! A huge orange fireball filled the sky in front of Robb.

His body turned to rock. He yanked back the stick and zoomed into the wall of fire, held his breath—and waited to die.

Before he could exhale, Robb shot out of the other side—blinded by the flames.

"WHITE ONE, I CAN'T SEE A DAMNED THING!" His heart pounded in his chest and blooded thundered in his ears.

"Ease off on the backpressure and start a turn, amigo."

Robb released some backpressure and eased the stick to the left.

"Hold that angle of bank, amigo."

Robb held the stick steady and blinked his eyes trying to eliminate the flash blindness.

"You're doin' great, amigo"

Robb kept blinking his eyes. Finally, he saw the dim outline of his windshield and canopy, then the blur of snowflakes racing by. "I can see!"

"Shit house mouse! That's great, amigo."

Robb looked down. The top of a hill shot past 100 feet below his wing tip. *Shit...that was close!* He decreased the angle of bank and climbed. At 400 feet, his legs began to shake. He took a deep breath and gas fumes filled his nostrils. He flipped his oxygen control lever to 100 per cent, inhaled deeply and glanced to the right. Fred had moved in close.

Robb took several more deep breaths, then pressed the mike button. "White Three...thanks for saving my butt."

"My pleasure, amigo. Check your engine gauges. And in case you hadn't noticed, it's snowin' pretty hard."

"Everything is in the green and I see the snow." Rocko had moved in closer, but Jim had fallen behind. "I'll continue to turn so you can join up and we'll head back to blokeland."

"Sounds good, amigo. Close it up, Four."

"Four is moving up," Jim replied.

In the turn, Robb noticed that burning fuel had flowed across the highway and three trucks had driven into the flames.

WHOOOM! An orange fireball appeared in the corner of Robb's left eye. *What the hell was that?*

"SUMBITCH! Jim augured!"

OOOH...SHIT! Robb snapped his head to the left. Burning wreckage from Jim's 51 tumbled along the crest of a hill. *DAMN IT!* That sickening feeling of helplessness that came with each loss gnawed at Robb's gut.

Rocko joined in close formation and Robb turned to fly past the hill where Jim had crashed. Burning wreckage lined its crest. *Shit...the point of impact is only ten feet below the top of the hill. If we could just go back a few lousy seconds and get him ten feet higher. DAMN IT!*

Robb swallowed the lump in his throat. "White, let's go climb power. Four Eyes, this is Snapper White with three chicks, climbing through the soup on a heading of 320. Can you give us the weather at Sunshine and a heading that'll take us about ten miles east of the Thames Estuary?"

"Four Eyes will do. Make your parrot squawk."

"Snapper White's squawking now." Robb turned on his IFF.

"Snapper White, strangle your parrot and steer 322 degrees. Sunshine reported a 700-foot ceiling with two miles visibility. They're expecting the weather to drop to zero-zero in less than two hours."

"White's steering 322. White, let's push it up to 46 inches and 2700 rpm. We'll use max cruise and try to beat the fog. Four Eyes, we'll maintain 10,000 feet and cruise at 325 mph. Can you give us the time en route?"

"Snapper White, Four Eyes here. At that speed and with the reported winds at ten grand, it should take 49 minutes. Could you give me your activity report?"

"Snapper White, roger. I counted 12 trucks either destroyed or heavily damaged, which includes a fuel truck destroyed. Strafed a couple hundred kraut soldiers in a field. I'd guess that about 50 of 'em were killed and a like number were wounded. Probably killed another 15 to 20 troops in a second convoy. White Three, does that sound about right?"

"That's close enough for government work, *amigo.*"

Two minutes later, the Colonel checked in with Four Eyes and reported that his flight had blown up a steam engine and damaged six boxcars. Then Snapper Yellow reported that his flight had strafed a convoy and destroyed a fuel truck, four supply trucks and damaged two more.

The minutes passed slowly as Robb, Rocko and Fred raced through the gray clouds at 325 mph. After 43 minutes, Robb transmitted, "Snapper White, we should be over the water now and I'm starting to descend. Let's go to Sunshine channel."

Rocko and Fred checked in and Robb called for a steer.

"Snapper White, give Sunshine a short count."

"White is counting. One, two, three, four, five, five, four, three, two, one. Over to you Sunshine."

"Sunshine here, steer 305 degrees. Ceiling is a ragged 700 feet and the visibility is a mile and a half. Altimeter is 29.89."

"White steering 305 and setting altimeter at 29.89." Robb turned left and continued to descend.

"Snapper White is level at 600 feet over the water and counting for a steer. One, two, three, four, five, five, four, three, two, one. Over to you, Sunshine."

"White, steer 309."

"White's steering 309 and reducing power to 20 inches. Let's go right echelon and we'll hold 200mph." He kept looking for the coastline. *There it is.*

"Sunshine, White's crossing the coast and my forward visibility is only about three-quarters of a mile. So when you see us, fire a flare. "

"Sunshine, wilco."

Robb saw the Colchester-Ipswich railroad. "Sunshine, White's passing the railroad and looking for highway A-12."

"Sunshine copies."

"White's approaching A-12."

"White, I have you. Sunshine's firing the first flare." The red flare arched through the gray half-light in front of the three 51's.

"Snapper White has the runway. On the break. Stay with me, guys." He yanked his throttle back to idle, put his 51into a vertical bank, tightened the turn, pushed the propeller pitch to full, and double checked that the fuel mixture was set at normal. At 170 mph, he lowered the landing gear. The airspeed quickly dropped below 160 and he lowered full flaps.

"White's turning base to final. Gear down and checked. Fire another flare, please."

"Sunshine's firing a flare."

"White has the runway." Robb rolled out on the final approach and glanced in the rearview mirror. The pointed nose of Fred's 51 was 200 feet behind and Rocko was close to Fred.

"White Two's has gear down and checked."

Robb crossed the airfield fence. The airspeed indicator showed 110 mph; he slowly eased the stick back. Just as his 51 reached the three-point attitude, it touched down at 90 mph. In his review mirror, Robb saw Fred touching down.

"White Three's on final. Gear down and bolted," Rocko transmitted.

As Robb's 51 slowed, he saw Fred and Rocko's 51 about 100 feet behind. At the end of the runway, they turned onto the taxiway and the Colonel told Sunshine that he was crossing the railroad. *Dear God, keep the visibility up until the Colonel and rest of Snapper get on the ground.* In the parking revetment, Robb heard Yellow flight in the landing pattern. *Thank God they're all back.*

Robb, Rocko and Fred walked from their 51's and climbed into the back of the weapons carrier. Robb couldn't forget about Jim. *If I had stopped strafing sooner he would still be alive.*

"That sumbitchin' mission added ten years to my frickin' life," Rocko grunted as the weapons carrier started to move. "A few more like that and I'll die of old age before I'm 30."

After storing their flight gear in the locker room, they went to snack bar for their Spam sandwiches before debriefing. As Robb ate, he thought about what he would say in the letter to Jim's mother and father. *I can't tell his folks that he flew into the top of a hill. Just tell them that he was lost on a strafing mission.*

Robb took his last bite, washed it down with coffee and glanced at his watch. "Time to debrief."

Captain Knight took the cue stick from Major Watson. "Since you landed, the fog has moved in and every airfield in East Anglia is reporting zero-zero.

It's the thickest fog I've ever seen. Real pea soup, as the blokes say, and it could last for a couple of days....." Captain Knight handed the cue stick to Lieutenant Colonel Hunt.

"Guys, the weather's so bad that the Colonel has grounded all vehicle traffic. He has also requested that the memorial service for Second Lieutenant Jim Harper be conducted in the club so we don't have to walk to the chapel. You had better carry your flashlights and you may need your escape and evasion compasses. Getting around tonight will test your navigational skills."

Robb opened the door to operations to leave and the dense fog rolled a few feet inside the hallway. He turned on his flashlight, but the light reflected off the thick fog.

"The flashlight doesn't help," he said turning it off.

"Sumbitch. Can't see squat," Rocko grunted, as they stepped outside.

"Let's follow the edge of the sidewalk to curb. I have no sense of direction. It's like having one dimensional vertigo," Robb said, moving slowly.

"Sumbitch. It's a damned good thing we got back before this crap moved in or we would've had to step over the side of our Mustangos and made nylon landings."

Robb stopped at the curb. "This may be our last known checkpoint." He looked at his escape and evasion compass attached to zipper tab on his flight jacket. "Looks like a heading of southeast should get us there."

"Sounds good, amigo."

"Who goes there?" a voiced asked from out of the fog.

"Three pilots heading for the O club," Robb answered as a figure appeared pushing a bicycle.

"Sir, I'm Master Sergeant McDougal. I left the flight line to go to the mess hall, but I'm not sure which way to go. Can you give me some help?"

"We just came out of group ops. You need to make a 180 and go back two blocks. It'll be on your left. Just follow the curb."

"Thank you, sir. Never seen anything like this."

The normal 15-minute walk from operations to the club took 25 minutes. Robb, Rocko and Fred had a beer before dinner and drank a toast to Jim. After dinner, they attended Jim's memorial service in the lounge.

"Amigo, what's the date?" Rocko asked, looking at the movie schedule.

"December 16," Robb replied.

"The movie is a shit kickin' western with Tex Ritter. Wanta watch it?"

"Not really. But I don't feel like going back to the hut."

£££

Thick fog covered Britain and kept the 8th AF on the ground the next day, but the 9th AF launched more than 1000 fighter-bombers. They attacked tanks, trains, trucks, and bridges, and struck targets requested by the 8th, 28th, 78th, 99th, and 106th Army Divisions.

Despite extremely poor weather on December 18th, the 8th AF attacked three railroad marshalling yards with 350 bombers and 228 escort fighters. Once again, 8th AF units had to race back to Britain before the fog returned. Robb, Patrick O'Leary, a new pilot from Baltimore, Rocko and Fred were the last flight in the group to land and before they reached operations the ceiling and visibility dropped to zero-zero.

"Shit house, mouse, we played that close," Rocko grunted, as he stuffed his flight gear into his locker. "We keep this shit up and we're gonna lose a bunch."

Robb agreed, but didn't comment in front of Patrick. "Patrick, I'm sorry we had to take you on your first mission in such bad weather."

"Sir, you warned me that things would move fast in combat, but I never dreamed it would be this fast."

"You did a great job, Patrick." *He looks so young. No tanned crow's feet around his eyes yet. What a difference a year of combat makes.*

"Hey guys, snap it up. The Colonel has called a short pilots meeting after our debriefing," Ted yelled through the door of the locker room.

Robb watched the Colonel sit down in his striped chair. *Boy. . .he looks madder than hell. Wonder what's wrong?*

"Gentlemen," Major Watson said, walking to the center of the platform. "We just received some very disturbing information from General Eisenhower's headquarters and the Colonel wanted me to bring it to your attention immediately. Today, our ground forces discovered nearly 100 bodies of captured Americans in the Ardennes. They were found at these three locations." He touched each location on the map with the cue stick. "They had been lined up and raked with machine gun fire. They were cold-blooded executions. It appears the Germans don't intend to use any of their manpower to guard prisoners and it's feared there will be many more executions." He finished and looked at the Colonel. "Sir."

"Thank you, Geoffery." The Colonel stood and faced the pilots. His steely blue eyes had a fierceness that Robb had never seen before. "I wanted you to hear this report right away. I've asked a lot from all of you in the past and you've always come through, even when it seemed the deck was stacked hopelessly against us. If ever we had a reason to fight like hell this is it. We're not gonna sit on our duffs and let these murderin' kraut bastards get by with this crap. It's time to cinch up our G-suits, go balls to the wall, and let it all hang out. This meeting is over."

Everyone stood at attention as the Colonel stepped off the platform, walked down the aisle and out the door.

From December 16, 1944 through January 31, 1945, the 8th AF and 9th AF each flew 38 combat missions and attacked German forces in the Battle of the

Bulge. Despite very bad weather, the 345th was the only 8th AF fighter group to fly every mission and the Colonel led them all.

On February 15, 1945, Major General William E. Kepner, the Commander of 8th AF Fighter Command, presented the Presidential Unit Citation to the 345th Fighter Group for their action during the Battle of the Bulge. It read:

£££

Presidential Unit Citation

£££

During the Battle of the Bulge, December 16, 1944 through January 31, 1945, the 345th Fighter Group flew 38 combat missions, many times in treacherous weather, to support the beleaguered US ground forces in the Ardennes. Seven times the group took off in weather that kept many or all of the other fighter units on the ground. Three of the seven missions were flown on the 16th, 18th and 19th of December, a critical period when our ground forces were being overrun and US prisoners were being murdered.

In addition to the 400 German soldiers the 345th Fighter Group either killed or wounded, the group destroyed 24 gun positions, 243 supply/troop trucks, six fuel trucks, 18 locomotives, 47 freight cars and four tank cars loaded with gasoline. Another 42 freight cars and 51 trucks were damaged.

The destruction of critical fuel supplies forced the *Wehrmacht* to delay or slow many of their attacks. When the battle ended, hundreds of abandoned tanks, trucks and military vehicles were found. The 345th's contribution to this effort was greater than any other 8th AF fighter group.

Before most of their ground attacks, the 345th escorted B-17's and B-24's that were attacking transportation targets supporting the German offensive. On one mission, the 345th engaged over 150 German fighters. On five other missions they engaged 25-30 German fighters. Gun camera film and eyewitnesses confirmed 93 aircraft destroyed and 62 damaged.

During the Battle of the Bulge, the 345th lost 16 fighter pilots, 14 per cent of their assigned pilots. Twelve pilots were shot down while attacking *Wehrmacht* ground targets and four were lost in air-to-air combat with the *Luftwaffe*. Despite the high losses, the 345th pilots continued their fierce attacks against the Germans in the air and on the ground.

Special recognition must also be given the 345th Fighter Group's maintenance, armament, communications and other ground personnel, who worked around the clock, in harsh conditions to keep their pilots and aircraft flying. Without their yeoman effort, the group's achievements would not have been possible.

RICHARD M BAUGHN

The performance of the men in the 345th Fighter Group during the Battle of the Bulge reflects great credit on the US Army Air Forces and the United States of America.

£££

"Nice ceremony," Ted said, pouring Scotch into three glasses. He gave each glass a squirt of soda and handed one to Robb and the other to Rocko. "I noticed the Colonel had to fight back tears during the presentation. He's so damned proud of the group."

"He's quite a guy." Robb always enjoyed it when the three of them had a drink in the quiet of Ted's quarters. Although his bedroom and sitting room were austere, they had a homey atmosphere compared to the noisy club and the open bay huts.

"None better," Ted replied. "He's molded the group into a great team. He's one of a kind."

"You know what really chaps my frickin' ass about the sumbitchin' Battle of the Bulge?"

"What's that?" Robb asked.

"The sumbitchin' newspapers hardly mentioned air force activity durin' the frickin' battle, other than to say most of the air force was grounded due to the lousy weather. For six weeks we fought our asses off, flyin' in weather that even kept the frickin' birds on the ground. And we lost 16 of our pilots in the process. The other groups did the same and we didn't read shit about it in the newspapers."

"Yeah," Robb replied. "Remember the P-47 pilot who knocked out a German fuel truck and delayed a kraut armor division's attack on Liege for two days? The ground pounder's public relations types and STARS and STRIPES never mentioned it. We only heard about it in one of Geoffery's intelligence reports."

"Yeah. If some infantryman had knocked it out, the grunts would have gone ape shit and given him at least a Silver Star and a front pa ge story in the STRIPES."

"Just a continuation of the turf battle between army ground and air forces regarding future budgets," Ted said.

"I don't give a shit about those sumbitchin' turf battles and budgets. But the thing that really jerked my chain more than anything was gettin' a frickin' letter from my dad, sayin' how happy he was that I was safe in England and not involved in the Battle of the Bulge. That's enough to piss off a happy Italian."

344

CHAPTER 22

German Jets and Russians

"Sumbitchin' newspaper doesn't know shit!" Rocko wadded the March 17, 1945 issue of STARS AND STRIPES into a ball and threw across the hut. "Five and half hours of freezin' my ass off today, watchin' those frickin' jets flyin' circles around us and shootin' down Patrick O'Leary. Yesterday they shot down that new guy from Hot Rod squadron. Now some asshole reporter says the frickin' war is over. Pinheaded know-it-alls ought'a get outta those Paris bars and London pubs and see what's goin' on."

A saddened Harold "Hal" Lotz, Patrick O'Leary's close friend, stared at the floor as Rocko railed. Hal and Patrick had gone through flight school together before being assigned to Snapper squadron. Robb made certain that he, Rocko, Fred and Hal remained together for dinner and Patrick's memorial service afterwards.

After breakfast the next morning, the four of them entered the group briefing room. As usual, the adjutant stood next to the lectern and fiddled with the cue stick while he glanced at his watch and the wall clock.

"Some things never change," Robb said as they sat in the yellow row of chairs.

"Yeah. Think the shit eatin' mission would get scrubbed if some sumbitch stole that frickin' cue stick?"

"My guess is, like everything else, there's a spare."

One minute before 7:00, the adjutant glanced at the wall clock, then his watch and walked briskly to the rear door.

"HOFFICERS, TEN—SHUN!"

"Please be seated," the Colonel said, walking down the aisle. He stopped next to his striped chair, turned and faced the pilots. "Gents, I know that I'm singin' to the choir when I say that despite all of the scuttlebutt we've read in the STARS AND STRIPES or heard over the Armed Forces Radio, the war ain't over yet. So we can't drop our guard on this mission. Stormy."

"Thick haze will restrict the visibility over Britain, Holland and Western Germany. When looking into the morning sun, you'll have very little forward visibility," Captain Knight said. "Over central Germany the visibility will improve, but you'll encounter high cirrus and more persistent contrails. Winds aloft are...."

RICHARD M BAUGHN

"Gentlemen," Major Watson said, taking the cue stick. "As you know, the Russians have been stalled along the Oder River since February 16th. So today the 8th AF will attack the Berlin rail yards with 1350 bombers and 750 fighters to slow German shipments of men and supplies to the Oder. This will be the largest attack that we have ever made against Berlin.

"Yesterday you encountered a few ME-262's, but today you should see many more. That's because the bomber's route will take you close to Achmer and Hesepe, two jet fields located near Osnabruck. ME-262's are also operating from fields at Brandenburg and Oranienburg near Berlin, and at Parchim, 100 miles northwest of Berlin. It's estimated the *Luftwaffe* has enough trained pilots to man at least 60 to 70 ME-262's for combat. We have solid intelligence that the Germans have several hundred more new jets waiting for pilots and it's estimated that the pilots will be combat ready in less than two weeks.

"Since the 1st US Army took the Remagen Bridge on March 7, American and British forces have consolidated their positions along the Rhine River. So anywhere west of the Rhine is safe territory. If you have an emergency in the target area, the Russian lines are only 60 miles east.

"A word of caution. Russian YAK-9's and LA-5's have been operating around Berlin for the past three weeks, so you can expect to see them. Since Russian air operations and ours have gotten closer, we have had several serious incidents with Russian pilots when they ignored mutually agreed upon recognition procedures. But this is not surprising because our fighters flying out of Italy have had problems with the Russians since November." He handed the cue stick to Colonel Hunt.

"We're escorting the lead combat wing so we'll be first in line for the kraut jets. The jet drivers are finally taking advantage of their superior performance and becoming very aggressive. With the help of radar and their superior speed, they can hit us lightening fast. We've lost two pilots to jets in the past two days and I'm sure you all remember what happened on March 3rd when some of our escort fighters got careless and didn't look around. The krauts nailed six P-51's. We've got to keep our eyes peeled and our heads on a swivel.

"As Geoffery said, Russian YAK-9's and LA-5's are operating around Berlin. So remember to dip your left wing twice if you encounter YAK-9' or LA-5's. They should dip their wings in return. Even if they do, be cautious, because you never know what the bastards are gonna do. The other day near Berlin, one of our fighter units dipped their wings and the YAK-9's dipped theirs, then attacked. The way the damned Russians behave makes you wonder if they're on the same side. Colonel, Sir."

The Colonel hopped onto the platform and took the cue stick. "Gang, there's no doubt about it, we're gonna see kraut jets today. Although the ME-262's have 100-mph speed advantage and their 30-millimeter cannons can reach well beyond our 50's, we can turn inside of them. So when we hit jet country near Osnabruck, keep your heads out. If you see 'em first, you can easily hold your own. And you may find one dumb enough to try and turn with you.

"Let me add a word of caution about those Rooskie fighters. Watch 'em like a hawk. My dealing's with the *Bolsheviks* bastards in Spain taught me that the sonsabitches can never be trusted. Okay, let's get strapped up and go to work."

£££

Over Holland, the sun was on the horizon and the haze was so thick that Robb had to look straight down to see the ground. *Stormy had it right again.*

"Ringo, Shotgun here with 36 chicks. We're comin' in high at your five o'clock," the Colonel called 20 miles west of the German border.

"Ringo here, I copy. Nice hearing your voice, Shotgun." Everyone knew that Ringo had been promoted to brigadier general but continued to fly combat.

The Colonel led Bug Eye's twelve P-51's past Ringo's 63 B-17's to patrol 20 miles in front. Ted began a slow weave above the bombers with Snapper's twelve 51's while Hot Rod covered the bomber's rear.

"Ringo, Shotgun here. I'm near Osnabruck...jet country. I had to drop from 31 grand to 28 to remain under a cirrus layer. Ideal conditions for kraut radar to vector jets in on us."

"Ringo here, I'll alert my crews."

Robb started a right turn to cross to the other side of the bombers. He saw two contrails streak out of the cirrus layer on a westerly heading. Their speed left no doubt that they were jets. "Snapper Yellow has jets, three o'clock, high. They're turning toward the bombers."

"Snapper Red here. Yellow take 'em, you're closest," Ted transmitted.

"Yellow roger. Let's jettison tanks, ready...now. Full power and suck it in guys, they're closing fast!" Robb pulled up in to a steep climbing turn.

Just before the ME-262's passed below him, Robb rolled his 51 upside down and let his 51's nose drop. When he reached a 60-degree dive, he rolled it right side up and went to full power. At 24,000 feet, the rudder pedals started to vibrate; the stick shook in his hands, then the 51's nose tried to pitch down. He glanced at the airspeed indicator. The airspeed and limiting mach needles were nearly overlapped at 370 mph—indicating his 51 had reached its maximum permissible speed for that altitude.

"Snapper Yellow's at max speed. Reducing power and dive angle before we hit compressibility," Robb transmitted.

Until three months ago, very few pilots had paid much attention to the short paragraph entitled COMPRESSIBILITY EFFECTS, on page 68 of the P-51 Flight Handbook. The paragraph read:

"At high diving speeds, there is danger of the airplane being affected by compressibility as it approaches the speed of sound. Instability, uncontrollable rolling or pitching, stiffness of controls or combinations of these effects indicate compressibility. A nose-heaviness will be noticed and will become more severe as speed increases."

But when Robb's friend Don Bloodgood nearly lost his life after his 51 hit compressibility, compressibility became a hot issue. A closer reading of the Flight Handbook revealed another paragraph on page 75 under the section DIVES. In it, the compressibility paragraph was repeated with the addition of:

£££

"The longitudinal characteristics remain normal until the speed of the airplane reaches approximately 72 to 74 percent of the speed of sound. At this speed, the airplane may become slightly nose-heavy because of the compressibility. Inasmuch as further increases in speed may result in more severe nose-heaviness, diving speed should be limited at this point and recovery started immediately after the change in longitudinal trim is evident."

£££

Due to the number of accidents caused by compressibility, aeronautical engineers from the Flight Test Center at Wright Field, Ohio joined with engineers at the National Advisory Committee for Aeronautics (NACA) at Langley Field, Virginia to study the problem. They began analyzing all known and suspected compressibility accidents in the Army Air Force. Since most pilots lost their lives when they encountered compressibility the few surviving pilots were immediately interviewed.

Within four days after Don's accident an aeronautical engineer came to Europe to interview him. Before departing he briefed the pilots on what his investigative group had found. He said the prewar wind tunnels had been incapable of testing the relatively high speeds of WWII fighters and wartime demanded that fighters be sent into combat with incomplete testing.

During a group briefing of the pilots he told them the first flight test data came from interviews of the few pilots who survived a bout with compressibility. Pilot interviews revealed the more radical the entry into compressibility (high-speed dives, combined with high G maneuvering), the more violent compressibility became. They also indicated each fighter had its own peculiarities. Compressibility on some fighters worsened when changes in propeller pitch or power settings were made. On some fighters a few pilots lost control of their aircraft or experienced a catastrophic failure when they attempted to recover from compressibility. He informed them there was much more to learn and the compressibility analysis would not be complete for another six months to a year.

£££

That night Robb and Rocko sat on the empty bed in Don's hospital room. He had a cast covering his left arm, shoulder and upper body and another that covered his foot and entire left leg.

"Amigo, you look like a frickin' mummy," Rocko said with a smile.

"I feel like a frickin' mummy who's been run over by a steamroller," Don replied.

"Don, tell us what happened?" Robb asked.

"I had just completed the required checks on a maintenance test flight and was in a hurry to get back on the ground so the discrepancies could be fixed for the next day's mission. I rolled into a steep dive from 26,000 feet and accelerated rapidly to maximum speed and my bird started to buffet. Then its nose got heavy and pitched down.

"I pulled back on the stick to recover and heard a loud noise, then felt a thump. My bird did a violent snap roll to the right and its nose pitched down abruptly.

The negative G's pinned me against the safety belt and shoulder straps. Despite the negative G's and severe buffeting, I sneaked a peek at the instrument panel. The airspeed indicator showed 440 mph and the altimeter needle swung past the 18,000-foot mark.

"I was going down like a rocket and I knew I had to get out. But the risks of a high-speed bailout scared the hell outta me. So I did a high intensity prayer— not that regular stuff but the heavy duty, eyeball-to-eyeball praying that's known only to those of us who've faced certain death with no more than an instant to spare.

"I grabbed the canopy's emergency release handle, yanked hard and the canopy flew off. Near sonic air thundered in my ears, ripped off my leather helmet, goggles and oxygen mask and slammed my head and shoulders against the back of the seat.

"It all happened lightening fast. The air blasted my eyeballs until they felt like they were being crushed in their sockets while it ripped open my mouth, stretched my lips, filled my cheeks and—shot down my throat. I couldn't breathe and thought I'd choke.

"It would have been easy to give up and ride it out. But something forced me to grab the safety belt buckle and unsnap it. When I did, I shot out of the cockpit, saw a flash and everything went black.

"Sometime later, I felt myself tumbling through the rock hard air like a lop-sided top. Each tumble sent pain shooting through my body like a bolt of lightening. It was so intense that I didn't give a shit if I lived or died. I just wanted it to stop.

"The tumbling finally slowed and the air softened. I opened my eyes but couldn't see anything out of my left eye and the vision out of my right eye was blurred. I had only a murky view of the sky and earth doing a slow motion flip-flop.

"I snatched the 'D' ring with my right hand and yanked it—but nothing happened.

"Fear exploded inside me and my mind tried to spin out of control. But once again something made me fight back. I looked down, saw the 'D' ring in my hand. I could tell from the lanyard that it was only partially pulled.

"I yanked harder and the parachute's white canopy popped out of its pack. The canopy blossomed; the leg straps dug into my groin; my body jerked to the vertical and excruciating pain shot from left foot, up the left side of my body to my left shoulder and out through my arm.

"I looked down and saw the top of a tree rushing at me. My mind went into overdrive and I recalled what I'd been taught about tree landings. Cross your legs...protect your jewels. Cover your eyes and face with your arms.

"I couldn't move my left arm or left leg, so I crossed my right leg over my left and tried to shield my eyes with my right arm. The tree's top branches raked my left ankle; pain bolted up my leg. Before I could moan, the branches banged my left arm and shoulder. I passed out and never felt the jerk of the parachute straps when the canopy and risers caught the branches and stopped my fall.

"When I regained consciousness, I felt weak and nauseous. Somehow I re-called the symptoms of shock that we had been taught in flight school and knew I had to do something before I passed out again.

"With all the strength I could muster, I gritted my teeth, pulled myself to a large branch, swung my right leg over it and straddled it. I grabbed the first aid kit, opened it and took out the morphine syringe. Pulling the needle cover off with my teeth, I jammed the needle through my flight and G-suit into my thigh and squeezed the syringe.

"Within seconds, the pain started to subside, I glanced at my left shoulder and arm. There was no blood, but my arm was dangling like an empty sleeve. For an instant, I thought it was gone. Finally, I touched it and it was still there. Then I looked down and saw my left foot. It was cocked about 20 degrees to the right. My GI shoe had been slit and the shoe was covered with blood.

"When I got the full boot of the morphine, my mind and body felt like they were in zero G flight. I was so damned glad to be alive; I just sat there on the limb and laughed my ass off for a few seconds.

"But not being able to see out of my left eye brought me back to the real world. I wondered if my eyeball had been ripped out of my head. I pulled the right glove off my hand with my teeth and held it. Then I gently touched the area around my eye. There was a lump as large as my fist. It felt soft and puffy like bread dough, but it felt like the eyeball was still there.

"While holding the glove with my teeth and working my hand back inside, I noticed the column of black smoke coming from the crater where my 51 had hit. I don't know what made me think of it, but I wondered where my parachute 'D' ring and lanyard had landed. Someone had once said that if you kept them, you'd have good luck.

"Then I recalled a combat report I had read about a teenage bomber crewman who bailed out. He said he'd been so scared he nearly clawed through the right side of his leather jacket before he remembered the 'D' ring was on the left side. Now I had a better understanding why something like that could happen."

Don finally heard the familiar sound of a Merlin engine and saw a P-51 approaching. He waved as the 51 flew past and the pilot rocked his wings. The pilot circled and guided the ambulance to the crash site. At the dispensary, the doctors determined that Don had a dislocated shoulder and a shattered shoulder blade. His left elbow and left ankle had multiple fractures and his left eye had almost been knocked completely out of its socket. Later, the accident investigation confirmed that he had collided with the aircraft during bailout. After several weeks, Don was sent home in his casts.

£££

Robb kept his 51 at maximum speed, trying to close on the jets below. Puffs of smoke came from the jets' cannons and flames torched from two B-17's. The jets pulled up into a steep climb. Robb tried to cut them off but the jets zoomed into the high cirrus.

"Snapper Yellow, let's throttle back." Robb watched the two burning B-17's twist out of control. There were no chutes. He felt sad and helpless. Only 18 months ago, the P-51 had been the best fighter in the world. But the ME-262's had made it obsolete and incapable of protecting the bombers.

"Frickin' jets suck themselves through sky like greased lightening. Sumbitches make you feel like a frickin' spectator."

"Snapper Red has three jets, two o'clock high. Red, go full power and internal fuel. Let's jettison our bathtubs, ready. . .now!" Ted turned toward another three ME-262's that were about to attack the bombers.

Robb watched the contrails of the four P-51's and three jets. The 51's appeared to be flying in slow motion. Ted pulled up high, rolled and dived at the 262's as they passed below. But the jets pulled away.

The 262's fired their two rockets and all six missed. Then the Germans fired their cannons.

A shell exploded near a B-17's wing root. The wing tore off and flames shot back to the tail; the 17 flipped violently and hit the 17 next to it. The burning wreckage twisted crazily toward the earth with 20 airmen trapped inside.

The 262's pulled up and quickly disappeared into the layer of high cirrus. Robb watched the burning wreckage, hoping to see some white chutes--but there were none. *Poor bastards...didn't have a chance to get out.*

From the west came the clipped radio chatter of P-51 pilots trying to engage more ME-262's that were attacking the second and third combat wings. Before the chatter ended, two B-17's and a P-51 were shot down. The jets streaked away and the eerie silence returned to the sky.

Robb knew that the bomber crews had to be stunned by the ease with which the small force of ME-262's had outperformed the P-51's and shot down the B17's. *This damned war needs to end before the krauts can man more jets. If they ever launch 100 of 'em they'll clobber bunches of bombers and we won't be able to do shit.*

Three minutes later, Ringo's wing of B-17's turned southeast toward Berlin and the three combat boxes took spacing for the bomb run. The crews hurriedly adjusted their steel helmets, tightened their flak jackets and got ready to face the antiaircraft cannons.

Beyond Berlin, Robb saw Bug Eye's twelve contrails circling as the Colonel waited for Ringo to come off the target. Ted turned left to fly five miles east of Berlin. In the turn, Robb could see the Oder River. A few miles back from each side of it, German and Russian cannons flashed. Their shells exploded along the banks, creating walls of black smoke, dirt and debris. *Haven't seen that much artillery fire since D-Day.*

Antiaircraft cannons flashed on the north side of Berlin; 36 orange fireballs exploded around Ringo's 59 B-17's. Before they could cast their hideous black puffs, more cannons flashed, more fireballs exploded and more black puffs appeared.

A fireball engulfed a B-17; the burning giant twisted crazily from the formation. Robb saw one white chute.

Within seconds, every antiaircraft cannon around Berlin flashed. Dirty orange fireballs and black puffs filled the sky around the 58 B-17's. Ringo's bombardiers opened their bomb bay doors and took aim through the flak-filled sky.

Another B-17 exploded. A large chunk of its wing and fuselage slammed into the bomber on the right; the second B-17 twisted out of control. There were no chutes.

Robb had been to Berlin 14 times and each time the flak seemed to get heavier. But today was the worst ever. Ringo's bombardiers pressed their pickle buttons and 448 bombs dropped from the bellies of the 56 B-17's. The 500 pounders streaked through the exploding flak toward the target.

The B-17's turned toward the west. In the turn, six heavily wounded bombers moved away from the formation. Each had gapping holes in the fuselages or chunks missing from the tails and wings. Each had one or more engines out. The pilots throttled back to save their good engines and the six bombers fell behind.

"Snapper, Shotgun here. You stay with the six stragglers. Hot Rod, take top cover for the wing," the Colonel ordered as he pulled ahead of the bombers.

"Snapper, wilco," Ted replied.

"Hot Rod, roger."

Ringo's remaining 50 bombers closed ranks to get ready for more jet attacks. The aircrews hurriedly cared for the wounded, covered the dead and double-checked their 50 calibers.

Robb watched the six battered stragglers struggling to remain in the sky. So far the wing had seven B-17's shot down. Many of the remaining 50 B-17's look like sieves and had wounded and dead on board. *I wonder how many of the stragglers will go down before they reach Britain? Let some newspaper clown covering the war from Paris or London try telling Ringo's wing that the war's all but over.*

"Snapper Yellow Three has bogies low at two o'clock headin' this way," Rocko transmitted.

"Snapper Red here. Check 'em out, Yellow," Ted replied.

"Yellow, roger." Robb pulled up and waited until the 9 aircraft passed beneath him then dived toward them. "Snapper Yellow One here. They're Yak-9's." He turned right 20 degrees to let the Russians know they weren't being attacked. As he passed the Yak's, he dipped his left wing. The Russian pilots looked but never dipped theirs. Robb remembered what the Colonel had said and used his excess speed to zoom 5000 feet above the Yaks and turned to rejoin with Snapper.

"Yellow Three here. Sumbitchin' Rooskies are turnin' in behind us!"

"Yellow One roger. Let's dip our wings again."

"Sumbitchin' Rooskies are still comin' after us. Bastards either blind, stupid or tryin' to start World War III."

The first three Yaks turned toward Robb and Hal. Robb pulled his 51 straight up, did a reverse vertical roll and sliced down behind them.

"Yellow Three has four Yaks comin' in on us. You're on your own, *Amigo*," Rocko called as he and Fred racked their 51's into a tight climbing turn.

"Rog," Robb grunted as he lowered his head and he took aim through the gunsight. He opened fire on the last Yak, API's sparkled on its nose, the propeller stopped turning and the engine poured black smoke. The Russian pilot rolled upside down and bailed out.

With his excess speed, Robb pulled high to remain behind the Yaks. He spotted Rocko and Fred off to the right. Rocko had maneuvered in behind one of the Yaks, but more Yaks were turning in behind him.

"Yellow Three, Snapper Red's coming in at your six o'clock. We'll lend a hand," Ted called.

"Yellow Four has you, Red," Fred replied as Rocko opened fire on the Yak in front of him. API's sparkled near the cockpit then sparkled back to the tail. The tail broke off and the Yak snapped out of control.

Ted and his element leader sliced in behind the four Yaks that were attacking Rocko and Fred. Ted opened fire on the leader and Red Three fired at the third Yak. API's sparkled on both Yaks. The one in front of Ted caught fire and the pilot bailed out. A fireball shot from the Yak in front of Red Three. A trail of black smoke followed it as it snapped violently out of control.

The remaining Yaks rocked their wings, and broke off the attack and headed east.

"Snapper Red here. Looks like they've had enough. Let's form up." Ted started to turn. "Snapper Red here. Shotgun, Red and Yellow clobbered four Yaks."

"Shotgun roger. Snapper Red and Yellow get back to home plate *muy pronto* and send a flash report. Let's get our version out before the Rooskies snow our State Department wienies in Moscow. Snapper White, you can join with me."

"Snapper Red, wilco."

"Snapper White, roger."

£££

Ted taxied into the parking revetment, swung the tail of his 51 around and cut the engine. Before landing he had ask the controller to call group operations and have Colonel Hunt meet him with transportation. Bob Hunt eased his jeep closer and got out. "Let me take your chute, Ted."

"Thanks, Bob. Let's pick up Robb and Rocko. The rest of the guys can ride in the weapons carrier."

"What's goin' on?" Bob Hunt asked as Robb and Rocko climbed in the back seat.

"We got into a tussle with some Yak-9's. Shot four of them down. Need to send a Flash Report right away."

"Holy Cow!" Colonel Hunt floor-boarded the jeep and raced to operations.

Major Watson and two of his intelligence officers debriefed all eight pilots, then prepared a Flash Report. Colonel Hunt, Ted, Robb and Rocko reviewed the draft and made a few changes before it was typed in final.

Colonel Hunt signed the report and sent it to the headquarters of Generals Marshal, Arnold, Eisenhower, Spaatz, Eaker, Doolittle, and Twining. "Now we can standby and wait for the shit to hit the fan."

Ted nodded.

£££

The Colonel finished his tour of the flight line and hurried to his office to see if the group had received a response to the Flash Report. He wondered how it would play out. He was certain that the closer they got to the end of the war, the closer they got to scapegoat time. Politicians would want to make some political hay, have a hearing and hang someone. "Charlie, anything on the Flash Report?"

"Sir, the only thing I've seen is a mention of it in the mission summary," Charlie said, handing the Colonel a cup of coffee and the 8th AF Mission Summary."

"Strange we haven't heard somethin' about that damned report. Seems like someone should be askin' questions. Maybe it's so big, they're all choked up." He smiled and poured three fingers of Scotch into the glass, handed it to Charlie, then poured a like amount into his cup of coffee.

Charlie quickly downed his Scotch. "I'll go to ops, see if they have received anything on it."

"Thanks, Charlie."

Charlie closed the office door. The Colonel leaned back in his swivel chair, put his feet up on his desk, took another big swig of his Scotch-coffee and started to read the mission summary.

8th Air Force
Preliminary Mission Summary
March 18, 1945

£££

I. Today, the 8th AF launched 1329 bombers and 733 escort fighters and attacked railroad targets in Berlin to help the Russians. It was the largest 8th AF raid against the Nazi capital. The bombers used both visual aiming and radar for bombing. Accuracy ranged from good to poor.

2. An estimated force of 36 ME-262's attacked our bombers and fighters. It was the largest, best-coordinated and most aggressive jet attack to date. The *Luftwaffe* pilots utilized their jets' superior performance and completely outclassed our P-51's....

3. Thirteen bombers and six fighters were lost. Another 15 bombers and one fighter were damaged beyond repair, bringing the total loss to 35 aircraft....

4. Aircrews reported the flak over Berlin to be the most intense seen at the German capital and more than 300 of the returning aircraft suffered moderate to severe battle damage....

5.　　Several fighter groups encountered Russian Yak-9's in the target area. One group was attacked by the Yaks and shot down four of the Russians. (See Top Secret Flash Report Number 364 for details)....

£££

Charlie tapped on the door before entering. "Sir, there's nothing so far on the Russian incident."

"Thanks, Charlie. How about another drink?"

"That'd be great, sir." He could always tell when the Colonel wanted to get something off his chest.

"Krauts flew circles around us in those damned jets today," the Colonel said as he poured Charlie's Scotch. "That's the second time I've been outclassed by German aircraft."

"The second time? When was the first?" Charlie asked taking his drink.

"In July 1937 during the Spanish Civil War. I was on patrol when a ME-109 streaked out of the sun with his guns blazing and nearly shot my ass down. It looked like something from another planet and going so damned fast that all I could do was to keep in a tight turn and watch. Just like today." The Colonel paused and took another sip of his Scotch-coffee.

"Harry Matthews, the New York Times correspondent, had told me about Willy Messerschmitt's radically new monoplane a few weeks earlier. Harry and I were sharing a bottle of 1918 *Tondonia* at one of Madrid's small cafes on the *Gran Via*. He had seen the new German fighter during the 1936 Olympic Games in Berlin. His informants had also told him the ME-109 would soon be deployed to Spain for combat testing."

"How much faster were the 109's?" Charlie asked.

"They were easily 100 mph faster than anything we had and the Germans immediately improved its performance and killing power. They replaced its wooden propeller with the American Hamilton-Standard variable pitch propeller, installed British wing slats and added more guns to improve its firepower. In November 1937, the ME-109 set a world's speed record of 379.39 mph—an unheard of feat for a production line military fighter."

"With all that performance, how did you survive?"

"Many didn't. Our only salvation was to see them in time to take evasive action. But later that became more difficult because the Germans developed new formations and tactics. Charlie, I don't want to bore you with a long story," the Colonel said before taking a sip.

"Sir, I love this stuff. I can include it in one of my history courses when I go home after the war," Charlie replied.

"In the 1930's most of the world's air forces used the three ship V. The V formation was easy to fly, looked nice and permitted hand signals between aircraft before radios were available or reliable. But it was less than ideal for air to air combat.

"With the ME-I09's enclosed cockpit and reliable radio the *Luftwaffe* began to fly a two ship spread formation which they called a *rotte*. It permitted each pilot to look around while allowing maximum maneuvering. In a fight the leader became the shooter and the wingman became the looker. The Germans then developed the *schwarme*, a formation with two *rottes*. Later the RAF and Americans adopted it and called it the finger four or finger tip formation, because the four aircraft formation resembled the plan view of the four fingertips on a person's hand. Each pilot is assigned a search area and the areas overlap guarding every axis of attack open to enemy aircraft.

"Sir, the Germans are really an ingenious bunch, aren't they?"

"Yeah. Our military was on a starvation diet before the war and we've been playin' catch-up since. It took almost two years to get the P-5I so we could take the fight to the ME-I09's and FW-I90's anywhere in Germany. Now it'll take at least six months before we have enough P-80's to take on the ME-262's." He paused to take a sip.

"When the war's over...I hope the congress won't let our military sink to its prewar depths. It's damned obvious the Rooskies are lookin' for trouble and we had better be ready."

CHAPTER 23

Der Nazis Kaputt

Heavy ground fighting and a second accidental bombing of Switzerland made Snapper's shoot down of the Russian Yak-9's a minor ripple in the political waters. General Spaatz's headquarters did send a message to all fighter units summarizing the Yak-9 incident and cautioning units "to avoid aerial maneuvers that the Russians might misconstrue as hostile." But it also said, "Keep your guard up and don't hesitate to protect yourselves when it's necessary."

By the end of March 1945, Allied ground forces had broken out of their Rhine River bridgeheads. On April 1, American and British ground forces linked up at Lippstadt after capturing the heavily defended Ruhr valley with its 300,000 plus German soldiers. In the north, British forces slowly reached and crossed the Ems River. Further south, the Americans swept more than a 100 miles east into central Germany.

As the German ground forces were driven back, they took many of their AAA weapons with them. The number of guns protecting aerial targets increased and 8th AF losses remained high. They lost 997 heavy bombers and 270 fighters to AAA during January, February, March and April 1945.

£££

On April 5, General Spaatz declared that all worthwhile strategic targets had been destroyed. From then on his strategic bombers struck every rail line and highway to stop the north-to-south and west-to-east movement of Nazi troops and supplies. A small part of Spaatz's forces continued to strike what was left of the battered *Luftwaffe*.

President Franklin Delano Roosevelt died on April 12. Morning services were held in every 8th AF chapel and on every flight line. Roosevelt had led the country since 1933 and he had been the only president that many of the young men in the Army Air Forces could remember.

The 8th AF flew its last combat mission April 25, 1945 and a few days later they began dropping food supplies to starving people in Holland. On May 7, the German High Command formally surrendered and the victory in Europe became known as V-E Day.

The night before V-E Day, General Doolittle declared a two-day holiday for the 8th AF. Within hours of his announcement, nearly every town and village in East Anglia was inundated with American airmen carrying musette bags filled with cigarettes and Hershey bars.

Ted made his rounds of Snapper squadron to thank everyone and inform them of the German surrender and the two-day holiday. Later, he invited Robb and Rocko to join him in his hut for a drink before going to the victory party at the club.

"Come on in," Ted shouted, hearing Robb's knock on the door. "Grab a seat." Ted poured two fingers of Scotch into each of three glasses, added a squirt of soda and handed Robb and Rocko their drinks. "Just wanted the three of us to have a quiet drink together." He raised his glass. "Here's to all of our buddies who didn't make it and to the ones who completed their tours and returned to the States, and to the three of us. The combat was the toughest, the weather was the lousiest, but we managed to survive. May our deep bonds last forever." They touched their glasses and took big swigs.

"I'm having difficulty believing the war in Europe is over," Robb mused as he rotated the glass in his right hand.

"Yeah. Seems like we've been fighting for a long time," Ted added.

"The frickin' Russians act like they wanta fight some more. Maybe we should kick the shit outta the sumbitches before we go home so we don't have to come back and do it later."

"You can damned well bet they'll continue to cause problems. But right now we've got to concentrate on the Japs," Ted said before taking another sip of his drink.

"Speaking of the Japs, wonder what will happen to us?" Robb asked.

"Those of us with a lot of combat time will probably go back to the States, get some time off before going to the Pacific. Some of us could stay in Germany for occupational duty. By the way, I'm flying to Paris tomorrow to spend the day with my dad. Would you guys like to go?"

"That'd be great," Robb answered.

"If you were spendin' a couple of nights so I could get my hands on one or two of those French broadies, I'd tag along," Rocko said with a grin. "But I've already booked my London hos and they can hardly wait to get their hands on me."

Ted and Robb leveled their P-51's at 5,000 feet and raced through the clear morning sky at 300 mph toward Dover. Not having to face enemy fighters or flak made flying a joy again and reminded Robb of his flights in the red and white Waco and PT-19.

Even the English Channel looked less foreboding. Yet he couldn't forget that its icy waters had taken Captain Draper and many others. He recalled the deaths of Bill, Pete, Matt, Bob, Art, Jack, Jim and Patrick. Deep down, their losses had seemed like a game, like they'd return when the war ended. But when they didn't appear with the 345th Group's POW's that passed through Boxted on their way to the States, their deaths became real. Robb recalled how angry he, Ted and Rocko had been when they learned that Major Brown had died in solitary confinement after he tried to escape. He wondered if he'd ever understand why some of them lived and others died.

"Snapper One has Calais, nine o'clock. Let's descend for a closer look at the countryside," Ted called.

"Two, roger." Robb saw Calais three miles ahead.

Ted turned 20 degrees to the right and followed the coastline south toward Abbeville, the former home of the feared "Abbeville Kids" and their yellow nosed ME-109's.

Spring's lush green growth had softened Mother Nature's D-Day battle scars, while the damage to man-made objects looked worse. France always appeared sun drenched after waterlogged Britain. Farmers and their families were working in the vineyards and sugar beet fields and a light breeze created gentle sways in the fields of small grain.

Two dairymen moved along a road, in small horse drawn milk carts on their way to village markets. North of Abbeville, smoke poured from the steam engine that was pulling a passenger train toward Rue. Instinctively, Robb looked for yellow nosed 109's, then remembered the war had ended.

Speeding through the clear blue sky, above a few puffy white clouds, reminded him of how much the war had changed his life. Growing up without parents had made him an oddity. Not until he became an aviation cadet, where the camaraderie of flying was all that mattered, did he feel like everyone else.

Now he was a captain in the United States Army Air Forces, flying to Paris in a P-51. Shortly, he would land at *Le Bourget* Airport where Charles A. Lindbergh had landed on his 1927 solo flight across the Atlantic. *Unbelievable. . .unbelievable.*

Ted had suggested many times that Robb apply for a regular commission and go for 30 years. But he had been afraid that he might not be accepted and didn't want to chance failure. *You love flying fighters and won't be happy doing anything else. Better try for it. . .may not be another opportunity.*

"Snapper One has Paris twelve o'clock," Ted transmitted. "Descending to 1000 feet."

Robb saw *Le Bourget* Airport on the north edge of the city. *I can't believe it! I wonder if it's changed much since Lindberg landed in 1927. . .?*

"Snapper, I'm going to continue south and circle the city before landing. We own the sky today and may never have another opportunity for a private aerial viewing of Paris."

"Snapper Two, roger."

In the bright sunlight, the Seine River glistened between its banks as it snaked its way through the center of Paris and joined the Marne. Passenger boats and barges slid beneath the many bridges that crossed the two rivers. Parks with trees and brightly colored flower gardens enhanced the beauty of the old ornate buildings. Boulevards bustled with pedestrians, taxis and buses, while morning diners crowded the sidewalk tables for their *café complet.*

Near the south side of the city, Ted turned west, flew over *Orly* Field, then headed north. They passed the *Eiffel* Tower, crossed the *Champs-Elysees* with its flowered gardens and chestnut trees, then zoomed by the *Arc d' Triomphe.* Further north, the sun's rays illuminated the snow white *Basillice* of the *Sacre Coeur.* It stood above the surrounding buildings like a heavenly castle, towering against the blue horizon.

"Snapper One here. Paris looks alive and well. Let's go tower frequency… now."

Robb changed channels. "Snapper Two's on."

"Roger Two. *Le Bourget* tower, this is Snapper One. Landing instructions for two P-51's," Ted transmitted.

Robb felt the excitement building inside him.

"*Le Bourget* tower, Snapper One, landing instructions for two 51's," Ted repeated when they didn't answer.

"Snapper One, Le Bourget tower. Sorree Snapper One. We have no flight plan for you and you cannot be cleared for zee landing," the tower operator said with his thick French accent.

"Le Bourget tower, Snapper One's flight plan was sent from RAF Station Boxted and approved more than two hours ago," Ted transmitted as he and Robb continued to circle.

"Sorree Snapper, we have no flight plan and you cannot be cleared for zee landing."

After two orbits and more discussion, an American tower operator got on the radio. "Snapper One, *Le Bourget* tower here, wind is ten mph, from 320. You are cleared to land."

Turning off the end of the runway, Robb tried to recall some of the pictures he'd seen in books and magazines about Lindbergh and 'The Spirit of St. Louis' at *Le Bourget,* but nothing looked familiar. The American tower operator guided them to their parking spots. They cut their 51's engines and climbed out.

A young American lieutenant pulled up in a jeep, stopped in front of Ted, got out and saluted. "Colonel sir, I'm Lieutenant Whitehead. General Tyler sent me to bring you to General Spaatz's headquarters at *Saint Germain.*"

"Appreciate the lift, lieutenant," Ted replied, climbing into the jeep.

"Sir, I saw you circling. Did you have a problem?" the lieutenant asked.

"French tower operator said we hadn't filed a flight plan and wouldn't clear us to land," Ted said with a smile.

"French traffic controllers and tower operators are giving many of our aircraft a rough time all over France. It's gotten so bad here that we had to put Americans in the tower since 98 percent of Paris air traffic is U.S. or British."

"Why are they being that way?" Robb asked.

"I'm not sure. Some of the old timers say that's just the French way. We saved their butts from the Nazis, now the bastards can dust off their superiority complexes and look down their French noses again," the lieutenant said, as the jeep accelerated along the taxiway.

Ted smiled and looked at Robb. Robb leaned closer to Ted. "Ted, on the way over, I decided to apply for a regular commission. I wouldn't be happy being a civilian and flying something other than fighters."

"That's great, Robb! You made the right decision."

Speeding along the road to *Saint Germain* in the topless jeep, Robb couldn't help but notice the clearness of the blue sky and the brightness of the sun. Even on clear days in Britain, the sky and sun were normally dulled by haze.

£££

"Good morning, Colonel Tyler and Captain Baines." Darlene smiled broadly as Ted and Robb entered her office.

"So nice to see you, Darlene," Ted said. He didn't ask about her brother because his dad had told him that her brother and his crew had been shot down and killed by a ME-262 in March.

"Hi, Darlene," Robb added. Her tan made her even more beautiful. A month ago, General Tyler had told Ted that he and Darlene were planning to get married. *I can't help but wonder how Ted feels about Darlene becoming his stepmother.*

"So nice to see you both." Darlene noticed how 18 months of squinting into the sun had deepened the crow's feet in the tanned area around their eyes. "It's only been nine months, but it seems ages since we last saw one another back in Britain."

"Are Ted and Robb here?" General Tyler shouted from his office.

"You'd better go in. He's been on pins and needles waiting for the two of you to arrive."

General Tyler hung up the phone and came from behind his desk. He had a few more flecks of gray, but the French sun had tanned his face and made him look younger and more handsome. He hugged Ted and reached for Robb's hand, pulled him closer, then hugged them both. "I've missed seein' you guys."

Darlene carried a tray with a thermos of coffee, three cups, a plate of warm *croissants* and a small plate heaped with butter. She placed the tray on a table and poured three cups of coffee before departing as quietly as she had entered.

RICHARD M BAUGHN

"Help yourselves while the *croissants* are still warm. I just finished coffee before you arrived. That's real butter, churned by hand on a nearby farm," General Tyler winked. "First butter I've had since the war started."

"Can't believe it. *Croissants* and real butter." Ted took a croissant and spread a thick layer of butter on top of it. "Come on Robb, dig in."

Robb took one. He had never had a croissant. He heaped a thick layer of butter on it, trying to remember the last time he had butter. He took big and the *croissant* seemed to melt in his mouth. He took another bite and melted butter ran down his fingers onto the back of his hand. He hurriedly licked it off. "This is great. Never had these in Texas."

General Tyler smiled. "Heard the French tower operator gave you a rough time."

"Yeah, that's right." Ted answered. He swallowed, then continued. "An American operator finally took over and cleared us to land. Wonder if the French treated the *Luftwaffe* the same way?" Ted took another big bite.

"If they thought they could get by with it, they would," General Tyler replied. "It's amazin' how fast they're sheddin' their guilt for collaboratin' with the krauts. They've nearly regained all of their mulish ways. Julius Caesar once described Parisians as clever, inventive, and given to quarreling among themselves. However, Caesar's description left out a few other traits. Like their haughtiness and self-indulgence. They enjoy wallowin' in their creature comforts and can easily become annoyed by outsiders, all of whom they believe to be inferior.

"But since they have dropped several rungs as a world power, I suspect they may also be sufferin' with an inferiority complex. Like the Italians, the French are excellent cooks and these croissants are an indicator. But they always seem to have their noses bent outta joint. Before the war, a friend of mine referred to the French as pissed off Italians."

Ted and Robb smiled as they each grabbed a second *croissant* and covered the top with a thick layer of butter.

"Dad, have some good news. Robb's going to apply for a regular commission." Ted took another big bite.

"Robb, that's great. Good time to do it before Tooey Spaatz leaves Europe. I've kept him posted on you and Ted. You'll have to meet a board, but with Tooey's four star endorsement, it'll be wired. I'll have Darlene run down an application form. You can fill it out today while you're here."

"Dad, when did you leave General Eisenhower's headquarters?" Ted asked, before taking another bite.

"Been back with Tooey for ten days. Workin' on plans to move some of our European strategic air forces to the Pacific. What we'd like to do is leave much of our 9th AF tactical units in Europe as part of the occupation force to keep the Russians from getting' ideas about gobblin' up Europe. We want to phase

364

our heavy bomber units through the States, train some of 'em in the new B-29's, then send 'em to the Pacific. But we can't firm up a plan because the politicians are screamin' to discharge everyone comin' home from Europe. As always, the politico's are more concerned about votes than fightin' the war.

"To get around the discharge crowd in Congress, we're gonna fly a few P-51 groups directly to the Pacific. Plan to send the first squadron, all volunteers, within the next few weeks. Bulk of support personnel and some key equipment will go by C-54's. Unit should be ready to escort the B-29's within days after their arrival."

"When's the word coming out on that?" Ted asked after washing down his last bite with coffee.

"Any day now. Just waitin' for General Spaatz to approve it. Today he's in Rhiems. He and Bedell Smith are signin' the German surrender agreement in a few hours. Tomorrow Tooey'll go to Berlin for the signing of the German surrender to the Russians. Once he gets back, the staff will brief him on the proposed fighter move. Robb, could you close the door, please? I've got some info for both of you."

"Yes, sir." Robb stuffed the last bite of the croissant into his mouth, got up and quietly shut the door.

"Although it's still tippy top secret, I wanted to tell you about that mission you flew into France before D-Day. The OSS reported that the British and American agents you dropped off made it to their destination, which was near *Saint-Lo*. They obtained a great deal of information on German troop deployments and coastal defenses. Unfortunately, the American agent was killed and the British agent was wounded durin' one of our pre-invasion bombin' missions.

"That special radio you carried over was also damaged. So the second part of their mission, to use their radio to guide the troop carrier aircraft in for the airborne drop on D-Day failed.

"After General Bradley's breakout at *Saint-Lo*, the British agent was recovered and put under deep cover somewhere in the British Empire. That's all I know. But I felt you should have the information. The same rules apply. Neither of you are to discuss this with one another or anyone else."

Robb took a sip of his coffee, feeling relieved that Joyce was still alive. He wondered where in the British Empire she might be, but knew better than to ask.

"Dad, what are your personal plans?"

"Don't know right now. I think Hap Arnold's gonna send Tooey Spaatz to the Pacific to command the B-29 forces. Arnold's not gonna let the Army ground pounders or admirals divide up the B-29 forces and use 'em solely for plowin' up beaches in front of the Army and Marines. The only person Arnold trusts to hold the B-29 forces together and make sure they are properly used is Tooey. If this turns out to be the case, I wanta stick with Tooey, see this damned war to the end even if it delays my weddin.'

"Also gonna do my bit in our effort to create an independent Air Force. Some of the ground pounders and sailors are already workin' like hell to undermine our efforts for independence. You wouldn't believe the back bitin' that's goin' on. It's worse than it's ever been. Thank God for Eisenhower and Marshall. They're not buyin' all of the crap put out by the grunts and sailors.

"But we're at a disadvantage with the press and historians, too. They like to write about the land war because the battles are slow movin,' easy to follow, leave *beaucoup* remnants to help 'em reconstruct the fighting. Aerial combat's a different ball of wax. In a few minutes of aerial combat, hundreds of men are killed, maimed or shot down, with aircraft wreckage scattered for hundreds of miles. Before the day ends, the sky cleanses itself with a heavenly blue like nothin' happened. On many missions we lost twice as many men as General Custer lost at his last stand and the press never created a sensation about any of 'em. To write about aerial combat, you got to have been there...seen it...felt it...and survived its hellish vortex."

The words hellish vortex had been edged in Robb's mind ever since the first time Ted's father had used them. No two words better described what Robb had felt during more than a year and a half of aerial combat.

"The fact that 60,000 American and British airmen were lost while softening up the Nazis to make the D-Day invasion possible has been all but forgotten," General Tyler continued. "It would have been nice if we could have taken newsmen and historians on most missions. Show 'em the air war where there ain't no high ground, nor trenches, nor foxholes to hide in. If things turn sour, there's no callin' for reserves. You fight with what ya brung...bare assed...in the wild blue yonder."

General Tyler smiled. "You probably have heard me say something like that before, but it's good stuff. Gonna repeat it anytime it's appropriate and try to keep the air war from endin' up as a historical footnote on WWII.

"We've got a high powered team evaluatin' our war performance. They're spendin' a lot of time countin' our bomb misses and hits. If the Army and Navy had to be evaluated on their hits and misses, the number of their misses would shock the American public. Tax payers would probably demand that some of their money be returned."

"Dad, I'd like to volunteer to command one of the P-51 squadrons going to the Pacific."

"I'll mention that to Tooey. Good idea to keep your fightin' skills honed because we'll soon be at it with the Rooskies. Bastards have been givin' us a bad time ever since they became one of our so-called allies. They've been pushy and refuse to cooperate on most things. It has become obvious that they want to expand their borders. As soon as Congress lets everyone out of the service, the Rooskies will really put it to us, probably make a grab for the control of Europe, Middle East, Asia, Africa and other parts of the world. But I don't have to tell you guys about the ways of Rooskies. You both know better than most because you've had a taste of the bastards over Berlin…."

£££

While Ted and Robb were flying to Paris, a young staff sergeant waited in the corner office of Base Operations at RAF Station Honington. He checked the 8th AF courier orders again, wondering how a master sergeant had managed to get the coveted courier duty to Washington DC, normally reserved for well connected senior officers.

Through the window, he noticed a jeep speeding across the aircraft-parking ramp. It turned into the driveway leading to Base Operations. A tall, gray haired master sergeant, wearing a garrison cap with 50-mission crush and pilot's sunglasses, sat ramrod straight in the right front seat. The driver, a small corporal, was humped over the steering wheel like a racecar driver. The jeep skidded to a stop in front of Base Operations.

The big sergeant stepped out of the jeep, holding the courier's brief case that had been chained to his left wrist. He wore a Bronze Star, Soldier's Medal and Purple Heart above two rows of brightly colored service ribbons. He re-adjusted his 50-mission garrison cap, then double-checked that the bill of the cap was two fingers above his nose. After straightening his tailor made uniform blouse, he repositioned the shiny holster that held the pearl handled 45 and barked something to the corporal. The corporal hurried to the rear of the jeep and struggled to pull the bulging B-4 bag from the back seat while the sergeant swaggered up the sidewalk to Base Operations.

"Master Sergeant John Burnham, 8th Air Force Courier," Big John barked as he strode through the door.

"Yes, sir," the young sergeant snapped, jumping to his feet. "Please sit down, sir." To him the guy was acting more like a general than a sergeant, and the young sergeant's guard was up. "May I get you a cup of coffee?"

"Okay. I'll have it straight," Big John replied.

Corporal Perkins opened the door, shuffled through, carrying the heavy B-4 bag with both hands in front of him and let it drop to the floor.

"Here you go, sir." The young sergeant handed Big John the cup of coffee. "I'll call 8th AF Headquarters to let them know you have arrived, sir."

Two months earlier, Big John and Veronica had parted ways when her husband returned from Italy seriously wounded. Big John knew he had to get the money he had made on black market eggs and moonshine sales back to the States before the inevitable peacetime restrictions were instituted. He contacted an old sergeant friend who worked in the 8th AF Protocol Office and promised his friend $1500 if he persuaded the powers that be to use a few senior noncommissioned officers as couriers to enhance the NCO corps. His friend sold the idea and recommended that Big John be first, due to his length of service.

Once back in the States, Big John's second cousin, a gofer for a small time bookie, would help exchange the $23,000 from pounds to greenbacks. Big John would then put his greenbacks in a safe deposit box. He planned to invest his money in the stock market.

The young sergeant hung up the phone. "Your flight will depart in 35 minutes. I have your in-flight lunch, sir."

"Thank you very much, sergeant," Big John smiled.

"My pleasure, sir."

"Corporal Perkins, you're excused. Report back to your duty station, post haste," Big John winked.

"Yes sir," Perkie squeaked, fighting back a smile. He saluted, did an about face and marched out the door.

£££

Three days after Robb and Ted returned from Paris, orders arrived assigning Ted as commander of the 66th Fighter Squadron. The squadron would be formed at Boxted and Ted had the authority to select volunteers from any 8th AF fighter group. He was directed to have the squadron ready to depart Britain for the Pacific on May 28, 1945. An hour later, General Tyler called Ted to make sure he had received his orders. He told Ted that the Colonel had volunteered to go to the Pacific, but General Spaatz had turned him down. Spaatz wanted the Colonel to return to the States to go on tour selling War Bonds and to lobby for an independent Air Force.

After talking to his dad, Ted called Robb and Rocko to his office. "You're my first two contacts. Would you like to join me and do battle with the Japs?"

"I'll go," Robb answered.

"Not me," Rocko grunted. "After my fabulous rise in the 8th AF, I'm gonna take my permanent blue bar, go back to the States and ride out the rest of the war as an instructor. That'll give me plenty of time to look for one of those cushy airline jobs. Then I can make that easy dough, flyin' from A to B with a cute little stew sittin' on lap servin' me hot coffee." He paused and grinned. "Don't even have to raise and lower the frickin' gear or flaps because ya got somethin' called a copilot to do all that heavy liftin.' With all that help, one of the first thing I intend to do is join the mile high club."

Working 16-hour days, seven days a week, Ted got the squadron manned, equipped and the aircraft ready within two weeks. On the afternoon of May 26th, he invited Robb and Rocko to his hut for drinks. "I wanted the three of us to get together before Robb and I depart," Ted said, handing them a Scotch and soda. "The three of us have been through a lot. We're going to miss you, Rocko. It's still not too late to volunteer."

"You're two of my favorites and I enjoy the hell out of flyin' fighters. But my mind's made up."

"I understand. I thought I'd try one last time," Ted smiled and took a sip of his drink. "Change of subject. Just got a phone call from dad. He wanted to tell me that Robb got his regular commission. Robb, you're now a regular second lieutenant with the temporary grade of captain. Paper work will catch up with you after we get to the Pacific. Congratulations," Ted said, shaking Robb's hand.

"Can't believe it. Never dreamed I'd get a regular commission. Thought you had to be a West Pointer or have a college degree. I owe so much to you and your dad."

"Sumbitch, that's great news, *amigo*. Now that you're a hired killer, hope you don't mind shakin' hands with a Christmas helper. Congrats," he said as they shook hands.

On the evening of May 27th, five C-54's took off for Athens, Greece carrying one third of the squadron maintenance and support personnel. They would service the P-51's on the first stop. Another five C-54's departed for Tehran, Persia, to await the arrival of the squadron on their second stop. The two sections of C-54's would continue leapfrogging at stops along the route to the Pacific to receive and launch the P-51's. The last third of the squadron would follow behind in five more C-54's to repair 51's that required maintenance before continuing on.

The next morning, Rocko waited outside the briefing room door. When Ted and Robb came out, the three of them walked to the operations truck.

"Sumbitch, I should've gone ahead with the maintenance team and checked out the bimbos in Athens and Tehran," Rocko said with a grin.

"Too bad we didn't think of that sooner. Well, I guess this is it, Rocko," Ted said. "Our flight gear's in our birds and we're ready to go. Due to take off in about 30 minutes." Ted and Rocko shook hands, then hugged. "Let's stay in touch."

Rocko nodded and turned to Robb. "*Amigo*, I'm gonna miss you." Tears welled in Rocko's eyes. "If I had another year, could've made you into a real Yankee."

"I'll miss you too, Rocko." They hugged one another. "Gotta go." Robb blnked tears as he climbed in to the truck next to Ted.

"Cheerio *amigos*. One day, you patriots can visit me on my estate. I plan to have hot and cold runnin' blondes and brunettes. Mostly hot." He paused and grinned. "*Amigo*s, don't let one of those frickin' Japs shoot your asses down."

£££

The Colonel was sitting in his staff car off the side of the runway. Just before Ted released his brakes to roll, he and the Colonel exchanged salutes.

Robb pushed his throttle forward for takeoff and glanced to his left. The Colonel was saluting him. Robb saluted and released his brakes.

As his P-51 accelerated down the runway, he saw Rocko waving from the control tower's walkway. Robb swallowed the lump in his throat and waved back.

£££

The End